THE GOLDSMITH'S WIFE

The Goldsmith's Wife is Jane Shore, favourite mistress of the greatest lover in English history, King Edward IV.

Wayward, passionate, goodhearted and loved by many men, Jane passes from a background of trade in Cheapside and Lombard Street, to rule the brilliant, profligate court, the morals of which are set by its amorous King. Her attempted abduction by Lord Hastings, her seduction by the merchant who is really the King in disguise, her flight from the goldsmith's house to the King's court— all this is but the prelude to her colourful and exciting story.

And although Jane is the central figure, her life is necessarily closely interwoven with those of many fascinating personalities of the court.

All these famous characters from a background for the goldsmith's wife, and among these people moves Jane—a dainty, golden-haired figure, the loveliest and the merriest lady of the court. She is seen gracing royal banquets, laden with jewels; and doing penance through the streets of London, with only a kirtle and her golden hair to cover her. She is seen begging favours for others from the King, and begging alms for herself in the streets.

Humble mercer's daughter, goldsmith's wife, King's favourite, publicly proclaimed harlot, prisoner and beggerwoman, hers is a story of amazing contrasts set against the colourful, dangerous background of 15th century London.

The Goldsmith's Wife

JEAN PLAIDY

© Jean Plaidy 1950

First published 1950
Reprinted 1962
Reprinted 1966
Reprinted 1969
Reprinted 1972
New edition 1978

ISBN-330-37423-0

Robert Hale Limited
Clerkenwell House
Clerkenwell Green
London EC1R oHT

This edition published 1998 by Pan Books
an imprint of Macmillan Publishers Ltd
25 Eccleston Place, London SW1W 9NF
and Basingstoke

Associated companies throughout the world

1 2 3 4 5 6 7 8 9

Printed in Great Britain by
Mackays of Chatham plc, Chatham Kent

CONTENTS

AUTHOR'S NOTE

It is unfortunate that Shakespeare's play, *Richard III*, with its misstatements and distortions and exaggerated character-drawing- of the central figure, should be generally accepted as history. But such is the case, so that if Richard is written about from any other angle an explanation seems advisable.

Handicapped as he was by living under Tudor rule, Shakespeare naturally dared not contradict the historians of his day, whose concern it was to vilify Richard in order to applaud the Tudor usurpation, and in so doing lay the blame for the foulest crimes of the period upon Richard.

Since the Tudors guiltily destroyed any state papers which might confound their falsehoods, it is not easy to discover the truth of what happened during Richard's brief reign. The evidence obtainable has been sifted and analysed, and I am sure that the fair-minded will agree that the picture of Richard as presented in The Goldsmith's Wife is a balanced one.

As for Jane's discovery of Anne Neville, that is entirely fictional. How Richard discovered his future wife is a mystery; but, taking into consideration Jane's adventurous and warm-hearted nature, together with the fact that, owing to her upbringing in Cheapside, it is more likely that she, rather than any other at court, would have been in touch with the humbler citizens of London, my theory of Anne's rescue seems plausible.

The books to which I am indebted are too numerous to set out here in detail, but the chief of them are:

History of England, by William Hickman Smith Aubrey.
The Lives of the Queens of England, by Agnes Strickland.
Life of Richard III, by Sir Thomas More.
Richard III, by Caroline Halsted.
History of the Life and Reign of Richard the Third, by James Gairdner.
Life and Papers of Richard III, edited by James Gairdner.
Prejudice and Promise in the Fifteenth Century, by C. L. Kingsford.
Historic Doubts on the Life of Richard III, by Horace Walpole.

J. P.

CHEAPSIDE

Down in the cellars under his house in Cheapside, Thomas Wainstead was instructing his servant, Jeffers, on the drawing of good Malmsey which would be needed for supper. Thomas, a round and plump man, his face rosy with good living, his clothes plain but of the very best material to be bought, looked what he was—a successful mercer of Cheapside. He was God-fearing, zealous in the carrying out of his duties, an honest tradesman, a good citizen, a man of substance. Yet, as he talked to Jeffers, there were signs of uneasiness upon his face; and Jeffers, twenty-eight, and good-looking enough to make many a housemaid, serving wench, or even a citizen's wife turn to take a second look at him, knew full well the cause of his master's uneasiness; for Jeffers also felt this apprehensive elation which, since yesterday, had filled the house.

The reason was tangible enough. Upstairs in her room, with the help of her maid Kate, Thomas Wainstead's daughter Jane was preparing herself for this evening's company. When Thomas and his servant came up from the cellars to the ground floor it would doubtless be possible to hear the young voice of Mistress Jane singing as she made her toilet. She was a gay young girl, and her speech was ever interrupted with laughter that set even her father's lips twitching, in spite of his determination to be stern and suppress those lively spirits, which, together with the most uncommon beauty of the child, were driving him, so he told himself, to an early grave.

Jane, but yesterday returned from Northamptonshire, had, in twelve hours, made a different place of this house; and, in spite of his pride in the girl, Thomas was far from pleased. He had hoped that a year or so in Northamptonshire might change her, for the country should have a quietening effect. Thomas mourned afresh his gay and pretty wife, who had died when Jane was but a child. Perhaps she would have known the right way in which to treat their daughter. Yesterday, when the girl had returned home, he had known immediately that he would have to find a husband for her, and that speedily. Jane was irrepressible. She was sixteen now, and lovelier than she had been at fifteen when he had sent her into Northamptonshire; and at fifteen he had seen troubles ahead.

She was very beautiful, with her sparkling blue-grey eyes, her abundant yellow hair and her delicate colouring. People spoilt her. The servants and apprentices—even when she was a child —had risked scoldings and whippings for the sake of young Jane. For she, though so beautiful and in full knowledge of her grace and charm, was warm of heart and easily moved to compassion. Quick of wit, she was no respecter of persons. Once he had found her helping an old woman with the water she was carrying from the conduit—a lousy, dirty old woman with whom she should have known it was not meet for a mercer's daughter to converse. He remembered that day well—a hot day, and the stench from the Fleet, into which the tanners and butchers flung their refuse, had come drifting down Cheapside. He had demanded an explanation of her conduct. "She was so old," said Jane. "And it was little to me." "And did you not know that had you asked my permission to do such a thing it would have been refused?" Her laughter had rung out, clear and sweet, like the bells of St. Mildred's. "But how could I have asked the old woman to wait while I ran home and asked your permission, Father?" Yes, she had always been ready with her answers, and Thomas had known only one way of dealing with undutiful daughters. He had given her such a blow that she was sent from one side of the room to the other. And what had she done? Shrugged her pretty shoulders and tossed her pert head, and given him to understand that she would do the same again should the occasion arise.

Thomas, by no means a calm man, grew hot at the memory. The girl had the power to infuriate him, yet fill him with pride. Not that he had ever let her know by word or gesture that he was proud of her; there had been more blows than smiles, more whippings that soft words.

Thus had she been a constant anxiety to him. He had hoped to beat the boldness out of her, but she was not the sort to lie passive under punishment, and he had often found it necessary to tie her to the whipping post he used for his servants. She hardly ever wept, but at times she looked at him with hard hatred in her eyes. But her hatred passed speedily for she was incapable of bearing resentment for long. And what happened after these beatings? The entire household lined up against him. Not that any of them would dare utter an audible protest; that would have been to ask for the whip to be laid about their shoulders, and they had wisdom enough not to risk that, for when Tom Wainstead laid it on he laid it on sharp. All the same, when he sent Jane to her room, and gave instructions that she was to stay there on bread and water, he knew full well that, between them, the cook and Kate would see that all the daintiest titbits were smuggled up to her. As for Kate, she adored the girl. Kate was a fool, and he should never have taken her into his house. And, by the Holy Virgin, he thought, the first sign of any mischief from her, and out she'll go.

But it was a vain threat. He knew he would not turn the woman out. Ravaged by time and adventure Kate certainly was, but she had been a little beauty once. And well, a man is but a man, even though he be a respected mercer; and a widower of some years' standing may be allowed a lapse or two.

"Hold the candle higher, you fool!" he shouted at Jeffers. "And don't drop tallow all over me."

Jeffers looked hurt, but he was not really alarmed. The whole household knew that the master's sudden outbursts of seeming anger were due to his own thoughts rather than the faults of those he scolded.

Wainstead's eyes beneath his bushy brows looked into

Jeffers's mild ones. "And when we are at table see that Mistress Blague's glass is kept well filled. She's one to like her liquor as well as a little pressing to take it."

"Yes, master," said Jeffers; and the two men enjoyed a smile at the expense of Mistress Blague.

"As for my friend William Shore," said Thomas, "we must give him of our best. I believe him to be a man who will know the quality of good wine, though it may well be that he'll not take over much."

"Yes, master."

The mention of William Shore's name had brought a return of good humour to the mercer's face. His reason for cultivating the goldsmith's friendship had not been an idle one; and a good deal depended on to-night's supper party. Thomas had given much thought to it. There would be just four of them—Shore and Mistress Blague, himself and his daughter. And during the meal, and after, Thomas would keep his ears and eyes open.

He wanted a good marriage for Jane; and he wanted to hand her over, a virgin, to her future husband. He wanted to say, "The responsibility of Thomas Wainstead is done with. Now, Will Shore, it belongs to you."

Shore would be, without doubt, a perfect son-in-law. Had the mercer looked a little high? Perhaps. But then he had good merchandise to offer. Goldsmiths, like Shore, were important men in the City; they were the richest and most respected of the tradesmen; they came into contact with the nobility, and now and then with royalty. Shore, with his fine house in Lombard Street, with his flourishing business, was a man of means and standing. He was also a pious man, and though he had passed marriageable age, being every bit of twenty-eight years, he was not a man to indulge in light living; therefore it was time he took a wife.

If Shore was willing, Jane should marry him, even if she had to be beaten or starved into submission. For her beauty and her wit, Shore must immediately desire her; but her saucy, merry ways, and her rebellious thoughts, which she did not hesitate to translate into conversation, might not please him so well.

"Get along up," he roared at Jeffers. "What are you standing gaping at, man?"

His thoughts, returning to the waywardness of his daughter, had brought the anger back to his mind. He was remembering now what had happened when he had taken her to see the coronation of Queen Elizabeth Woodville. As they had stood on the edge of the crowd, a man who was obviously of the quality had sidled up to them in order to stare at Jane. Then had come to the mercer some glimmer of the fears which would later be his. In this wicked City there abounded unscrupulous men ever ready to seduce innocent girls. The King himself set an example of immorality. "Citizens," was the cry of the townsfolk, "hide your wives and daughters, for the King comes this way!"

There had been yet another occasion, and this more alarming than the first. It was another of those processions in which the Queen, lifted from comparatively humble status to the throne of England, liked to indulge. Through the streets of London had come the knights and squires in cloth of gold and crimson velvet, riding on their stately horses; and one of them, a handsome man of obvious nobility, had let his eyes rest on Jane; the man had smiled, and Jane had returned the smile, with all the freedom, gaiety and charm she would have bestowed with equal generosity upon the lowliest stall-holder in Candlewick Street.

"Who is that man?" he had whispered to his neighbour in the crowd, taking good care that his daughter should not hear the reply, and at the same time assuring himself that she should be whipped soundly for throwing her wanton smiles at the nobility.

"Know you not?" was the whispered answer. "It is Lord William Hastings, favourite of the King, and married to the sister of the Earl of Warwick."

Married! Then he should not be casting his eyes on the

daughters of good citizens. But marriage, by all accounts, did not stop these court gentlemen from seeking amusements other than in their legitimate beds.

Jane had had her beating; and as he had turned from her and gone to the window, he had seen, standing in the very courtyard of his own house, a person who walked off hastily as the mercer appeared at the window; and this person was of the same handsome proportions as Lord Hastings.

The next day Jane had left for his relatives in Northamptonshire; and while she was in the country her father had made his arrangements for her future.

He and Jeffers had reached the big dining hall, and Jeffers carried the wine into a little parlour which led out of it. Thomas's mood had changed again. He had made his plans well. To-night was the sequel to the smiles Jane had bestowed upon my Lord Hastings. To-night Jane should smile at a man of her own class, and he at her; and their smiles should give Jane's father no cause for apprehension, but good reason for delight.

     *   *   *   *   *

The house of Thomas Wainstead was one of the grandest in Cheapside. It was built, as were most of its neighbours, round a courtyard; on either side of its gates, and overlooking the street were the quarters of his servants and apprentices; looking out on the courtyard were his own and his daughter's chambers. The great hall dominated the house, and most of the main windows looked out on to it. It was the custom for all to take their meals in this great hall. Thomas would sit at the head of the table, his daughter on his right hand; and farther down the table sat the apprentices and servants in order of seniority. Opposite the great hall, on the other side of the courtyard, were those premises in which Thomas pursued the business of a very successful mercer, and the apprentices lived over these offices. Below the house were vaults where Thomas kept his merchandise, well locked up against robbery; and the keys of those vaults never left him. There were also his wine cellars, for he loved a good wine, and liked to keep a generous table. He was a benevolent master to those who served him well.

But this evening five o'clock supper was not to be served in the great hall, but in the more intimate parlour at a table set for four only. He did not wish Will Shore and Mistress Blague to sit down with his rough serving people, for Mistress Blague was very genteel, and Will Shore, being a goldsmith, doubtless lived in grander style in Lombard Street than Thomas Wainstead could afford in Cheapside.

He saw that the table had been well prepared, and that the floor of the parlour had been strewn with fresh rushes. The appetising smell of flesh roasting on spits in the kitchen could be detected; and there was a hush throughout the house, as though everyone in it was aware that this was an important occasion.

It was half-past four and his guests should be here at any moment. Ah! He could hear a disturbance in the courtyard now, and looking through the window, saw Mistress Blague arriving. He went out to meet her, frowning because Jane should have been at his side; she would have to learn better manners if she were to grace a goldsmith's house.

Then he smiled, for Mistress Blague amused him somewhat. She was, he guessed, every day of thirty, but she liked to be thought younger. Her small sly eyes and pinched mouth may have been acquired through over-much gentility. She was greatly respected in Cheapside as the King's lace-woman, and she was certainly to be admired for her craft. No one in London could make better lace than Mistress Blague; but the silly woman liked it to be thought that the King honoured her with his patronage because of a certain tender interlude which once passed between them. She would make a pretence of keeping secret about her past, but was always hinting that the King had played a part in it. Of course the King had so many love affairs that Mistress Blague might easily have been the heroine of one of them.

He kissed her on the mouth after the fashion of the day.

"How well you look, Mistress Blague," he said, and she smiled, well pleased.

And indeed she did look well in her stiff dress, the skirt of which would have swept the courtyard had she not held it up daintily at one side, court-fashion; and her steeple hat was inches taller than most of those one saw, and the soft cascade that over-flowed from it reached almost to the hem of her gown.

"You also, Mr. Wainstead. And where is this pretty daughter of yours of whom we have heard so much?"

"The girl's in her room, dressing. She should be here to greet you. But, believe me, Mistress Blague, it is solely on account of her desire to look well in your eyes that she spends so much time on her toilet. I had taken the liberty of telling her that a lady of fashion was coming to supper."

He had well repaid any slight which Jane's lack of courtesy might have brought about. Mistress Blague was all smiles and simpers.

"I fear she will be greatly disappointed when she sees me."

"Doubtless she will be smitten with envy. *She* will want such a gown. *She* will want such a hat."

This pleasant conversation was interrupted by the arrival of Will Shore, who came riding into the courtyard, and Thomas was gratified to see how his head groom sprang forward to take the goldsmith's horse and lead it away while Will came towards his host.

"This is indeed a pleasure," said Thomas warmly.

"The pleasure is with me," said the goldsmith in his quiet voice.

"You know Mistress Blague, of course."

"Indeed I do. And right glad I am to meet her once more."

Mistress Blague smiled and the goldsmith murmured that rarely had he seen her look so well. Thomas was faintly alarmed. What if Will Shore liked the woman so well that he decided she would make a better wife than Jane Wainstead! Thomas studied Will afresh. The man's clothes were more sombre than one would have expected a wealthy goldsmith to wear. Will was a quiet man, a cautious man, devout and far-seeing. Would such a man wish to take to wife a flighty creature like young Jane? And how would Jane feel about him?

Be still, he admonished himself. If Will wants Jane he has her, even if I have to whip her insensible and carry her to the altar.

He was all impatience now to get inside, to call Jane and see the effect she would have on the party.

Will Shore was saying: "So your daughter is back, Thomas?"

"Aye. Back, and as lovely as ever she was when she went away."

Mistress Blague's eyes narrowed. "We are all eagerness to see so much beauty."

There again he had been wrong. He should have let Jane's beauty burst upon them. That was always more effective than preparing people for some dazzling spectacle.

They went into the house, and as they entered Jane came down the staircase. They all stood looking at her. Even her father was taken aback by her beauty. She herself was smiling, seeming unconscious of it. Her dress, like Mistress Blague's, was blue, but blue seemed a different colour on Jane from what it did on Mistress Blague. The blue of the dress was reflected in Jane's eyes so that to-day they seemed more blue than grey, and more beautiful than the colour of the dress; they seemed longer, merrier than Thomas remembered them; her lips were parted to show her even teeth; she was a little flushed with excitement, for she loved gaiety, and the prospect of a party always set a greater sparkle on her. The bodice of her dress was low-cut, and trimmed with white; it was laced across her breasts; she wore a simple lace headdress, and her bright hair streamed over her shoulders. She was a small and dainty creature, and when she lifted her skirt and showed her fashionably pointed shoes as she came downstairs, Mistress Blague suddenly seemed clumsy and crude.

"So you are come," said Thomas. "Methinks it would have been more seemly had you been down to receive your guests."

She bowed low. "I am sure, Father, that you are more able than I to greet them with that courtesy which is their due."

Neither Mistress Blague nor Will Shore could take their eyes from her.

"You have recently come from the country, Mistress Jane?" said Mary Blague.

"But yesterday."

"And doubtless," said the goldsmith, "you find Cheapside a little strange after the country?"

"Not strange," answered Jane, "but delightful. I have longed to see Cheapside again."

"You should not get too attached to it, my dear," said Mary. "Methinks you will not spend many days in the street, unless you marry a neighbour."

"I see," said Jane smiling, "that you think I shall soon marry and go away from all this. That may be so. But I should miss it sadly."

"Come," said her father. "Let us go to the parlour where I will have supper served at once."

It was certainly a good idea to have supper served in the parlour, thought Thomas, as he watched his daughter and his guests. Will was obviously taken with Jane; but being taken with a girl did not necessarily mean marriage. That sad fact was at the very root of all his fears for Jane. He listened to their talk.

"So you are a goldsmith, sir?" said Jane. "That must be interesting."

"I am, Mistress Jane, and it is not without interest. You must call on me in Lombard Street . . . you and your father."

"I shall like that and look forward to meeting your wife."

"I have no wife—yet."

The blue-grey eyes were mischievous. "You speak as though you intend to remedy that lack, sir."

Thomas all but choked with anger. That was no way for a modest girl to speak to a man.

"Holy Mother of God!" he cried. "Where are your manners, girl? An you show sauciness to my guests you'll smart for it."

Will Shore wriggled uncomfortably, but Jane merely smiled reproachfully at her father.

"But was I saucy?" she asked.

"I fear," Will put in hastily, "that the fault may have lain with me. It did seem to me but a natural reply."

"It was," said Jane.

"Be silent, girl," retorted her father, but without much ire, for Jeffers was bringing in roasted peacocks, their bodies decorated with their own feathers. The cook had done well, Shore was taken with Jane; so how could Thomas feel anything but mellow? He turned his attention on Jeffers. Was the man filling Mary Blague's glass? He was. Was he looking after Shore? Shore did not appear to care what he ate; he had no eyes for roast peacocks, ox nor lamb; nor had he taste for Muscatel and Malmsey while he could feast his eyes on Jane and drink in her silly chatter. To-morrow Thomas would talk to Jane and let her know his will.

Kate came in, her fat face beaming and the sweat of exertion running down her cheeks. Her bodice, thought Thomas, was too low cut; it was laced across the bosom as was Jane's, but Kate's great bosom seemed to threaten to break the lace in its eagerness to be free of such restriction. Kate was a temptation and a menace in the house. Thomas knew that she had been a light woman, a camp follower with the Lancastrian army when it came south. She had come to him and told her story and he had taken pity on her. That had happened nearly ten years ago. She grew older, but he fancied not less wanton. And he . . .?

Well, there had been just one small lapse in ten years. No, be honest, Thomas Wainstead . . . more than one. The woman was a constant reminder as well as a constant temptation. Still, being a man of high morals, he could not turn her out simply because she reminded him of his own sin; and he must keep her there that he might be constantly tempted and resist. He believed that she crept into Jeffers' bed now and then; and that Jeffers, an upright man like his master, suffered the same torment of perpetual reminder and temptation.

Jane was smiling at Kate, and Kate returned the smile. He would talk to Jane. There, he would say, is a result of immorality. Had Kate been a good woman, she might have been a wife and mother now. But no. For if he said that, Jane would doubtless remind him of the good women who starved in the streets in winter and begged for alms at the City's gates, while over the river, in the narrow streets of Southwark, there were women whom her father would not call good, yet they could be sure of their food, aye, and fine clothes to put on their backs.

He frowned across the table at Jane. She had ever known too much, and she had ever retorted too sharply. She was far too attractive for the peace of mind of a man so preoccupied with his virtue that immorality, by its very contrast, must be continually in his thoughts.

The conversation had now been led by Mistress Blague to court matters. Jane leaned her elbows on the table and her eyes sparkled as she listened.

"And, Mistress Blague, do you really believe that the Queen's mother is a sorceress?"

"A sorceress she undoubtedly is. Why, my dear, at Grafton Castle she had her own room with its crucible and charts, mixtures and potions, and in it she practised black magic . . . *black* magic, I tell you. If ever a man was led into a trap that man was Edward the King."

"How *I* should love to be able to weave spells," cried Jane.

"Tush, daughter," admonished Thomas. "You know not what you say."

"But think, Father, if one were such a spell-binder, there is nothing—nothing one could not achieve. Do tell us, Mistress

Blague, how His Grace the King was caught. Was it a love potion?"

"A love potion! That came after." Mary Blague's eyes were narrower than ever. There was a flush under her skin. She was very angry. Did she believe, wondered Jane, that, had she possessed a mother who could weave spells, she herself might be the King's wife at this moment and not merely his lace-woman?

Mary Blague had started on her favourite subject of conversation. "He was riding up north to quell a rebellion. Oh, the sight of him! The handsomest man in all England. He stands well over six feet, and his lovely face is irresistible to all. And there, hunting in the forest of Whittlebury, he found standing beneath an oak the widow and her two fatherless sons. It was——"

"Elizabeth Woodville," cried Jane.

"It was," said Mary Blague. "And what did she do but throw herself upon her knees and plead with him to restore her lost inheritance!"

"And he," said Jane with mock-wisdom, "finding all women as irresistible as he is to them—at least, for the first week of acquaintance——"

"You presume too much, girl," interrupted her father. He didn't entirely trust Mary Blague. What if she should pass on what she heard to some person at Court? Many a man's ears had been struck off for saying less than Jane had said just now.

"The King is a gentleman," said Mary reprovingly. "It is true that he has a fondness for our sex. It is part of his manhood. He was touched, and promised to do what he could for the widow. And so was he lured to Grafton Castle where Elizabeth lived with her mother.

"The sorceress," said Jane.

Thomas noticed that Will Shore was looking at Jane and laughing, as though he thought everything the girl said was sheer wit.

"The sorceress indeed," said Mary, thrusting her head forward. "His Grace the King must be entertained at Grafton

How simple, while he was at table, to slip a potion into his wine. He had not been there an hour or two when he fully believed that he desired Elizabeth Woodville more than any woman he had ever met. And she a widow, admitting to seven years of life more than his. 'Tis nearer twelve, I'll swear. 'Oh,' says she, 'I am not worthy to be your wife, but I am too good to be your mistress.' And so, refusing him her bed and aided by her sorceress mother, she at long last made him agree to a secret wedding."

"It's a charming story," said Jane.

"And a romantic one," agreed Shore. "Why should not the King marry to please himself and not the lords about him?"

Jane leaned forward, smiling. "Why, sir, are you also enamoured of His Grace the King? I knew the women were. I had yet to learn he could draw such devotion from the men."

"Be silent, girl," growled Thomas. "How dare you, at my table, speak disrespectfully of your King?"

"But, Father, it is well known that His Grace incurred the displeasure of many noble lords by his marriage. It is only women who sigh and smile and say he is so handsome and charming, and curse the ill fate which did not give them sorceresses for mothers."

Will Shore laughed outright at this, and Thomas allowed his lips to turn up at the corners.

"I ask you, Will," asked Thomas, "what would you do with such a one as this beneath your care?"

"I should be very proud," said Will; and his pale eyes seemed to take on a warmer glow.

So, thought Thomas, for all the girl's forwardness, the evening is taking a good turn.

"I should like to see the King," said Jane.

"You shall when he next rides through the City," promised Mary.

That she shall not, thought Thomas, if she still be under my care. What if my Lord Hastings should be in the throng?

"There is grave news in the City," said Will, sobering.

"Warwick never took kindly to this marriage of the King's. He was all for marriage with a French princess and alliance with the French."

"And not a bad thing either," said Thomas. "Wars, wars, wars! Let's have peace for a change."

The two merchants frowned as they talked of past events and looked gloomily into the future. The threat of war hung over the country still; and surely no war was so terrible as civil war. Looking back over the last ten years there had been nothing but battles—and battles wherein Englishmen fought Englishmen. Now, with Edward on the throne, while they feared war they could hope for peace. Edward was the most magnificent soldier of the day, but by reason of his pleasure-loving nature was not wedded to war. Edward believed in trade and the good things that peaceful trading brought; therefore London merchants supported Edward and had no love for fiery Margaret of Anjou who stormed about the country trying to persuade Englishmen to put her husband, poor, mad Henry the Sixth, back on the throne.

Jane, leaning her elbows on the table, was not listening to them. She knew, of course, why Will Shore had been invited to-night. She had for years been able to read what her father considered his most subtle thoughts. She was being shown off to the wealthy merchant as though she were a bale of fine linen or a roll of silk. Jane studied the goldsmith and shuddered.

Never, she thought, could I find it in my heart to love him.

She was only momentarily depressed by this project of her father's, for it was not in Jane's nature to suffer depression for long. She would find some way of escaping from the goldsmith when the time came, and the time had not yet come.

She was fascinated by Mary's gossip. All the woman's talk of court life was doubtless hearsay, but it made enlivening conversation.

"They say," said Jane provocatively, "that the Queen still rules the King. He has many mistresses, but there is not one of them that can wean him from her for more than a week or two."

"Huh!" Mary's eyes flashed. "What chance have ordinary decent women against a witch?"

"How does one become a witch?" wondered Jane.

Mary was shocked. "To say such things! Wickedness is born in a woman. There is plenty of wickedness and to spare at the court. It makes me shudder to contemplate it."

"Yet also does it delight you to contemplate it," pointed out Jane; and she added quickly: "And so does it me. I would I were there to see it."

"It is not the lot of the merchant class to go to court, my dear."

"Nay, but I would it were."

Mary tittered. "Now and then, of a certainty, a humble girl finds means of spending a week or two in court circles."

"You mean she attracts the attention of . . . shall we say some personage of high eminence. She becomes his mistress and——"

Mary was coy. "It has happened, you know."

"But I hear the King has acquired a most distressing habit," said Jane. "He goes among the common people disguised as one of themselves. He has his love affairs and departs. I call that unfair. How wretched to lose the glory of royal favour as well as one's virtue!"

Jane's voice broke on a laugh and Mary frowned. Thomas looked up from his conversation with Will Shore. Jane was irrepressible. Heaven knew what he was going to do with her.

Mary said: "Methinks they taught you much in Northamptonshire."

"One does not need to go to Northamptonshire to learn that the sunshine or the rain falls. And the King's love affairs are accepted as is the weather."

Thomas banged the table, for really the girl had gone too far. "You will leave us, Jane. I will talk to you later."

Jane rose while Shore intervened. "The evening will be dark without your daughter's bright beauty and sparkling wit."

Jane gave him a grateful smile which made him flush a little.

Thomas noted it, but all the same Jane had to go. She needed a good talking-to before she was allowed to mix in company.

"Nay," insisted Thomas, "I have been over-lenient already. Up to your room, girl."

Jane said a decorous good-night to the guests and went.

Her room overlooked the courtyard. It was by no means an up-to-date room, for Thomas did not believe in pampering his household. The hall was pleasantly furnished, so were the offices where he received his customers, but the bedrooms were simple. There were rushes on the floor, and he had not introduced the new fashionable beds. Jane slept on a kind of mattress on the floor. She had a mirror on a table and a rough stool on which to sit at it. There was a cupboard in which hung her clothes, yet the table was untidy with ribbons, a strip of lace and a horned hat.

She came in and shut the door, went to the glass and looked at herself, grimaced at what she saw, and sitting down began removing her headdress.

There was a faint tap on her door, and Jane swung round on her stool, smiling, for she knew who this was. She was right. Kate came in, her eyes wide, her lips parted. She stood leaning against the door in an expectant attitude. She wanted to know why Jane was in her room and not downstairs with the guests.

"I was sent up," explained Jane, "for talking too much and without respect for the King."

Kate was shocked, for, like Mary Blague, she was devoted to the King. "That was wrong of you, Mistress Jane."

Jane laughed. "Oh, I know he is the most handsome man on earth, but all the same his love affairs are numerous. My father knows it, and as for Mary Blague, she would have us believe that she has the most intimate knowledge in that direction. And yet am I sent to my room for stating a simple fact."

"You'll have no sympathy from me," said Kate. "He is a man, and a man will be a man."

"Even though he be a King. Tell me, Kate, is manhood measured by mistresses then?"

"I'll not hear a word against him. And could you but see His Grace I'll warrant you'd change your tune."

"Indeed I'd not."

"If he turned his bonny smile upon you, you would."

"I'd not be proud to walk in such a crowd, Kate."

"Shall I comb your hair, my love?"

"Yes, Kate. Please do."

They were silent for a second or two and silence was something which rarely existed between them. Kate was thinking of the past in which, strangely enough, the King himself had played a small part. She saw Ludlow Castle, rising gracious and pleasant above green Shropshire fields. She had lived in the castle, for her father had been head groom to the Duke of York, father to King Edward, and now and then she had caught glimpses of His Grace the King—only then he had yet to win his crown—and in those days he had been known as the most handsome and irresistible man in all England. Kind he had been to his serving men and women—particularly to the women —and also to his brothers, George and Richard and his little sister Margaret. Kate was thinking now of a certain October day ten years ago, when she had been a young and innocent girl engaged to marry Walter who had worked at the castle under her father. But on that October day soldiers, led by the enemies of the Duke of York, had ransacked the castle, stealing its beautiful furnishings and ornaments, raping its women, killing its men. Kate had seen Walter lying battered and bloody in the castle grounds. She herself had fallen to the lot of an uncouth Scotsman. She saw herself afterwards tramping behind the Lancastrian army on its way to London, a dirty, wheedling camp woman, eager to please this man and that.

Jane was thinking of the smile about her father's mouth and the glint of something of which she was not quite certain in the eyes of William Shore.

Seeking to escape from unpleasant memories, Kate spoke first. "So you were sent up. This will mean a whipping, as sure as I stand here."

"I hope not, Kate."

"Mind you," went on Kate soothingly, "your father's not so strong in the arm as he was." She stroked Jane's shoulder. "It's a shame to bruise your lovely skin."

Jane burst into the sudden laughter which was characteristic of her. "Perhaps he won't. I've a notion that I'm something more than a daughter now, Kate. I'm a piece of merchandise, and it may well be that I shall never be whipped again. For I am to be offered to a customer, Kate. The company downstairs has been gathered here for a very special reason. Can you not guess?"

Kate blew a shrill little blast between her lips. "Goldsmith Shore!" she cried. She smiled. "He is a very rich gentleman, I have heard."

"He has cold hands. They are like the skin of a fish."

"Holy Virgin! You can get him to warm his hands before he touches you."

"I don't want to marry Will Shore, Kate."

"Why, he is one of the richest men in the City. It does not surprise me that your father has chosen him. You would be wise to listen to your father, that you would. There are not many Will Shores in London to be had for the asking, I do assure you."

"I'm rather frightened, Kate. I seem to have grown up so suddenly. I've got to marry. I've got to let him take me to Lombard Street—and I don't want to go, Kate."

"It's the strangeness of it, lovey."

"But, Kate, I want to wait a while."

"You are too fair for waiting."

"You understand though. You've told me how you loved Walter all those years ago in Ludlow. You wanted to marry him. You loved him."

"Yes, and much good did it do me."

"It would have done much good if you had married Walter." She was silent for a second or two; then she said : "Kate, when you were a serving maid at Ludlow, you saw the King. What manner of man is he, I wonder, that can make Mary Blague's eyes sparkle when she speaks of him? And you are the same, Kate."

"As you would be—should you see him. Heads turned to watch him; eyes followed him. The whole household doted on him—even the cold and haughty lady Duchess, his mother."

"He must have been very conceited."

"Not he. It was all so natural that he should be admired. Wasn't he the strongest, the gayest and most handsome wherever he went!"

"Oh, Kate, what grand circles you have moved in! You have served the King; you have lived under the same roof as his brothers the Dukes of Clarence and Gloucester. Kate, how can you bear a mercer's household after that?"

"You mock me."

"I did not mean to mock. I just long to see the sparkle in your eyes which the memory of the most charming, the most beautiful and the most amorous man in all England can put there."

"I'm not sure that isn't treason," said Kate primly.

"Alas, treason and truth may often go hand in hand."

"It does not surprise me that your father would hand you to another. Come, let me comb your hair and get you to bed, for mayhap if you are sleeping when your father's guests are gone, the whipping will be put off until to-morrow."

Kate combed the lovely golden hair.

The saints preserve this lovely child, she thought. Let her never know the like of what happened to me.

* * * * *

Dusk was falling over the City as Kate hurried back to Cheapside. Kate was anxious not to be out after dark; there were too many ruffians abroad who would be ready to slit the throat of a defenceless woman for the sake of the few coins she might possess. Kate understood the needs of these poor men, old soldiers most of them, who had drifted to London with the

Yorkist or Lancastrian armies. Kate had not followed the camp without learning something of the hardships which befell soldiers in time of peace.

Thomas had sent her out with a piece of silk to one of the great houses beyond Ludgate and towards Temple Bar. It should have fallen to the lot of one of the apprentices to deliver the silk, but Thomas had come upon Kate, idling, as he said, in the kitchen, and as the order was urgent he had despatched her at once.

Kate was worried, for a gloom had settled on the Wainstead household during the last few weeks. Thomas had declared that his daughter should marry Will Shore, since the goldsmith was more than willing; but his daughter had refused; and although Thomas might stamp and rage and swear his daughter should give him obedience, although he might force her to go to church, he could not say the words which would make her the goldsmith's wife. In the meantime, there was Jane, confined to her room and kept there for nigh on three weeks with nothing, so the mercer thought, to nourish her but bread and water. And what objection, Kate asked herself in exasperation, had Jane to the goldsmith? He was rich and he loved her truly. Shore's servants had whispered to Kate that the goldsmith kept good house in Lombard Street; and there was, Kate had ascertained, a most personable gentleman who reigned in the kitchens there. Many scullions worked for him; he was a mighty man in height and girth; he had the merriest of twinkles in his eyes which had not grown less merry when they rested on Kate.

She had come through Ludgate and was hurrying into St. Paul's Churchyard when a horrible fear came to her that the footsteps which she had heard behind her for some minutes must have been following her. Kate started to run, and whoever it was behind her started to run also. There was no doubt about it : Kate was being followed.

She began to sweat with fear. With dusk, lawlessness came to the City. Thieves and ravishers lurked in dark alleys. How many bodies were found in narrow byways! How many were flung into the cold waters of the Thames! Kate ran through the churchyard. She dared not look round. He who followed uttered a curse and she could hear his heavy breathing. The houses rose darkly beside her, for she had reached Cheapside. She saw the Cross loom up before her. Very shortly she would be past Friday Street and have reached her master's house. But even as she turned into its gates a hand shot out and caught her arm. Kate screamed as she was pulled round to face a cloaked figure.

"Be silent," said the man. His was a cultured voice and in it was a hint of laughter; but Kate was not to be fooled by that. She stared up into the face which was peering down into hers. She could not see it clearly, but she did see the jewels at his throat; and life with the family of York, and later in the mercer's household, had taught her to recognise a nobleman's style of dress when she saw it.

"Greetings, sweetheart," said the man; and he kissed her full on the lips. He was no sweating old soldier, and Kate waited breathlessly for what should happen next.

"What do you want of me?" gasped Kate.

"Do not speak so loud, girl. Is it *your* master who has a daughter—the most beautiful girl in London?"

Kate told herself she ought to have known it was Jane whom he was after. "The mercer has a daughter who is beautiful," she said.

"And she is your mistress?"

"Yes."

"Then you shall help me to have a word with her."

"I could not. Why, my master——"

"Your master pays you well to keep a strict eye on his daughter, I doubt not. What if I pay you better?"

"Think you I would betray my mistress for money?"

"If you would not you would be the first maid in London to refuse such easy earnings."

"Pray release me."

"Not yet. Tell me your mistress's name."

"You hurt my arm."

"Her name, woman?"

"It is Jane."

"Which is her room?"

"The third from the gate on the left side. It looks out on the courtyard."

"So. Now listen to me. You are to go to your mistress now. Beg her to bring a lighted candle to the window. I would look on her face, for it is long since I saw it."

"I dare not."

He brought a coin from his pocket, but Kate turned away.

"You are a foolish wench."

"I am true to my master and my mistress."

"How do you know that it would not please her to come to the window?"

"She does not know you, sir."

"She would be very happy if she did."

"She would not." Kate never could stop her tongue running on. "She is to be married to a goldsmith—when her father can force her to it."

"Force her, eh? So would her father force her? I'd have his head off his shoulders."

"There's no law that I know to take a man's head off his shoulders for arranging his daughter's marriage." Kate had lost her fright now and was enjoying the adventure.

"You're too saucy, girl. You must do as I say and you'll not be sorry. What's your name?"

"Kate."

"Kate, to-morrow at this hour you will come to Paul's Churchyard and there I will give you a message for your mistress."

"I do not promise."

"It will be the worse for you if you do not. Help me and all will go well with you. Betray me to that old scoundrel and one dark night when you come home from meeting your lover . . ."

"I do not go out at night to meet my lover."

"Do not tell me the old rascal allows you to have him in the house! Now listen. You will come to St. Paul's Churchyard to-morrow night or . . ."

"I—I will come. There can be no harm in it, for she will not listen to you."

Kate was released. "Go now," he said. "I will wait here. Tell her I wait. And to-morrow, Kate, at this hour, we meet. Remember now. Do not betray me. I am a person of some import in this City. I could have you put in the pillory or taken as a harlot. My servants shall waylay you."

"No!" cried Kate.

"No," he said soothingly, "it shall not be, for you are a wise wench. Go now, and remember what I have said."

Kate ran into the house and went up to Jane's room.

Jane was lying on the bed, disconsolate and defiant. She raised herself and leaned on her elbow to look at Kate, for it was obvious that Kate was agitated.

"What has happened, Kate?"

"I cannot tell you yet." She went to the table and with trembling hands took up the lighted candle which stood there.

"Kate!" Jane leaped up and stood beside her. "You look so strange. What is it that has frightened you? Tell me quickly."

"Come with me," said Kate; and she took Jane's hand and led her to the window.

"What are you looking for?" demanded Jane. "Why—there is someone down there. Kate!"

Jane turned from the window, dragging Kate with her. "What does this mean, Kate? You were showing me to someone down there. Oh, Kate, how dare you! It was a man—was it not?"

"It *was* a man, mistress."

"How dare you! How dare you! First my father will show me off as though I am a roll of silk; and now you will show me off as though I am a harlot and you a procuress."

"That," said Kate with dignity, "is no talk for a young girl."

"Talk is not important. It is action that matters. And you have acted most unwisely. You had better tell me all about it."

"He followed me. It was in Paul's Churchyard that I heard his footsteps behind me. I have not been so frightened since Ludlow. And then—as I turned in at the gates—he caught me and held me, so that I could not escape an I would."

"An you would!" cried Jane scornfully. "You know full well you had no wish to escape."

"Well, I will admit to a little curiosity as to what he wanted. There were jewels at his throat and the cloth of his garments would have made your father's eyes glisten."

"It made yours glisten too, Kate, I'll warrant." Now they were laughing together like two schoolgirls. "What said he, Kate?"

"He asked about you. He is very handsome. His voice is beautiful and he said things that frightened me. I have to be in the churchyard to-morrow for a message he has for you. Then we shall know who he is."

"Quiet, Kate! You're shouting."

"Oh, mistress, suppose he be a noble lord, and suppose he is so smitten in love for you that he will marry you!"

"The love that smites these noble lords for merchants' daughters does not carry them as far as marriage, Kate."

"There are many wonders in the world."

"But nothing so wonderful as that. If my father gets to know of this . . ."

"He shall not."

"If you continue to shout to the housetops he will."

"But it is so beautiful."

"What is beautiful? The man? His clothes? His brutal way of frightening you?"

"I was not really frightened. I have prayed the Virgin to show us a way out. I have prayed that you might have your will and not fall to the goldsmith. This is an answer to my prayers."

"Wait a while before you see too much in this. To me it would appear just another gentleman in search of adventure. Rest assured he will not find it here."

"You would shut yourself away from the world," grumbled Kate. "You wait for someone you can love. One does not *wait* for love, but goes out to meet it."

"I shall not go out to meet it in the form of this swaggering fellow who dares accost you in the street. I hope he did not think I went freely to the window. But he will, of course. These creatures are puffed out with conceit. Oh, Kate, Kate, you have a lot to answer for."

They looked at each other solemnly for a moment, and then fell to laughing; they laughed so much that they feared the mercer would hear; then they were quieter, whispering in the darkness.

*   *   *   *   *

In the great dining hall Thomas Wainstead nodded over the table. In a moment or two he would snore. The apprentices dozed; even the chatter of some of the servants sounded sleepy. Among the rushes the dogs were still gnawing the bones which had been thrown to them, and giving little grunts of satisfaction as they came upon gobbets of fat and gristle which had been spat out by the diners.

Jane looked along the table. She was no longer on bread and water diet. Her father had become frightened by her pallor, and had said she was to come down to eat good flesh and drink some wine. He would rather have a disobedient daughter, thought Jane affectionately, than a dead one. He worried too much about her and she did wish that she could please him. She was ready to admit that she was wayward and daring, but at the same time she would insist she knew how to take care of herself. For instance, in exactly five minutes' time she was going to slip out into the courtyard and there by the stables meet the mysterious nobleman who was infatuated with her. Kate had brought her several messages in which he had declared that he was deep in love with her, and that he could not sleep nor eat until she consented to listen to his pleading. It was all very exciting and exhilarating after her imprisonment, and as there was a spice of danger in the adventure it was irresistible to Jane. Her father had said that she might take a turn in the courtyard, although she was not to go into the streets unaccompanied by himself. There, again, Jane must smile for him. Poor dear foolish man, did he not know that it could be equally daring to venture into the courtyard as the street?

Kate came in, her lips pursed, her eyes betraying that something was afoot. Jane put her fingers to her lips and looked cautiously along the table. Thomas was snoring, and Jane rose and tiptoed lightly out of the room.

Kate whispered: "He is come. Outside, he awaits you."

Jane drew round her the cape which Kate had brought with her and went speedily out. A dark figure came swiftly towards her.

William, Lord Hastings was dressed in the most exaggerated fashion, for although he wished to keep his identity a secret, he wanted Jane to know that he was of the nobility. He would have told her that he was Hastings, friend of the King, but since he was well known all over the country, that would not do, for Jane would surely know—or soon discover—that he had a wife, no less a person than the sister of the great Earl of Warwick. He must content himself therefore with wearing such clothes as could only be worn by the highest in the country. His shoes were long and very pointed. His short jacket exposed the shape of handsome legs and thighs, and this jacket was trimmed with rich fur, while its wide hanging sleeves were so exaggerated as to be ridiculous. His hat was feathered and there were jewels at his throat.

"Jane!" He put his hands on her shoulders, kissed her, and would not release her.

"Enough," she said. "What is it you wish to say to me?"

"Say to you! That which I have said a thousand times already. Leave this squalor and come with me."

"My father would not be pleased to hear you speak thus of his house, my lord."

"Nevertheless, Jane, if you could but see the house I would give you, you would be unable to resist it."

"My lord, if you would keep your hands from touching me, I should enjoy your company the better."

"You are cruel, Jane."

"Nay, only curious."

"So you keep me dancing to your tune in this manner simply because—you are curious?"

"I am too curious. You are too amorous. Now, if I weren't curious and you weren't amorous, all this would never have arisen."

"Mean you that there is naught in it but curiosity for you?"

"How could there be aught else when I scarce know you?"

"Jane, you are amused to tease me. Come here and kiss me. Let me show you what life with me would be like."

She laughed. "That I know full well. Life with you would doubtless be lived in an apartment in one of those grey houses on the other side of the river, whither you would take me; and there, after a week or so, leave me."

"Leave you!"

"Aye, leave me. I might ask, 'And where are you going now, kind sir?' And you would say, 'To find another simple maiden like yourself.' That is, if you were truthful. Dost think I was born yesterday? No. Do not come near me. If you do I shall scream. My father is in the dining hall. He will loosen the dogs. . . ."

"Why do you wish to humiliate me? By God's Holy Virgin, I have never been made to suffer such indignity. Doth that not show how I love thee?"

"It does but show what a mighty conceit of yourself you have."

"Listen to me, Jane. . . ."

"Listen to you when you will not even tell me your name!"

"You shall learn that ere long. Then you will be sorry that you have treated me with such indignity."

"Tell me," she mocked, "you are not his Grace the King?" He hesitated, for the desire to have her believe this was so great that he was reluctant to deny it. "I hear," she went on, "that he doth love to go among his female subjects. Here in the City they say, 'Hide your wives and daughters, for the King comes this way.' But you are not the King."

"You are sure of that?"

"I am indeed. For it is said that there is not a woman in the world who could say no to him. Well, am I not a woman, and so easily do I say No to you. Therefore must it seem that you are not His Grace."

"It pleases you to tease me."

"Just as it pleases you to pursue me."

"Jane, could you not love me a little? I would give you everything you desire. Jane, think of it . . . beautiful jewels . . . a life at court . . . everything."

"Everything but marriage."

"I did not say I would not marry you."

"Nor did you say you would."

"Why, look you, Jane, should you insist . . ."

"I insist! But it is you who are insistent."

"Have done with this banter. I adore you, Jane."

"The truth would be more pleasing than your adoration. If you are ready to make honourable proposals, why do you not go to my father's house, and not to his stables? The answer is easy. You wish to seduce me and then desert me. Mayhap you have already a wife."

"I swear . . ."

"That you have not? Then I have solved one mystery. You are not the King. And methinks I have had enough, for there is a chill in the air, and my father will beat me if he finds me here talking to an amorous gentleman, whatever his rank at court. Good-night to you, sir."

"Jane!" He caught her hand.

"Let me go."

"I will not. Do you think you may come out here and tease *me* thus? I will have your lips. By Christ's Holy Mother, you are fairer than I ever dreamed. Why, Jane, come with me and you will never regret it."

She was frightened now, realising her folly in giving way to her love of excitement. He held her fast while she banged her fists ineffectually against his chest, making him laugh.

"And what shall you do now, think you? See! I could sling you across my shoulder thus. I would make off with you."

"Put me down."

"What? Now I have you in my power? I shall not put you down until I have had my will of you, and after that mayhap you'll not be so eager to be put aside."

"I hate you," she cried; and she kicked him as he held her.

He gave a sudden cry of anger, and, seizing her opportunity, she pulled his feathered hat over his eyes while she gave him yet another kick which made him release her as he doubled up with pain. She ran towards the house.

Panting, laughing, she fell against Kate, who was standing at the door in case it should be necessary to warn her that her father was coming.

"Shut the door, Kate. Bolt it. Holy Virgin, that was a near thing! He had me slung across his shoulder. Why, he might have run off with me there and then. I was a fool, Kate. It was my own fault." She was half laughing, half serious. "Oh, Kate, he was comic. I asked him if he were the King, and he tried to make me believe he was."

"'Sh. Your father is stirring. Better slip upstairs, dearie, or my back'll be sore, and so will yours if he gets wind of what we're at."

"Do not ever allow me to go out and meet him again!" said Jane. "He's dangerous."

"I ever liked a man to be bold," said Kate wistfully, "and 'tis my belief he loves you true."

*   *   *   *   *

William Lord Hastings was far from pleased with the progress he was making with the mercer's daughter. The whole affair was maddeningly undignified. He was no adventurous young boy to indulge in the romp that this was turning out to be. The girl was unusual; she could make a fool of him; and it was a preposterous situation wherein the Chamberlain of the Royal Household and Master of the Mint, a baron and associate of the King, a man of sober years—for he was approaching forty—should have to hang about in a mercer's courtyard at dusk, there to be trounced by that mercer's daughter.

He was weary of the chase. He had decided more than once that he had had enough of it, but he found it impossible to forget the girl. He was a rake, a profligate; he obeyed the fashion of the day, and promiscuity was the fashion. He was not the man, however, to admit himself beaten, but he was determined to subject himself to no more indignity. He had hoped for help from the woman Kate. He had threatened to have her whipped through the streets for harlotry or put in the pillory for thieving. "Or," he had said, "I'll set my men upon you . . . lusty fellows and a whole dozen of them." That had terrified her more than anything, so that he felt he could be sure of the help he would need from her.

His plan was simple and he was going to set about it immediately. He wrapped a long gown about himself—for he had clad himself in his plainest garments for this purpose—and setting out from his apartments in Westminster Palace, he went swiftly to the river where he hailed a waterman to row him to Southwark.

He sat in the boat, listening to the splash of the oars, glancing along the river towards the bridge and beyond where the great stone walls of the Tower of London reached up to the sky. Along the north bank he saw the lovely old houses with their gardens and orchards running down to the river's edge; but it was not with the gracious north bank he was concerned; his business lay with the squalid south, and as soon as the boat touched land he had leaped out, tossed a coin to the man, and was hurrying up the steps towards the streets of Southwark. He lifted the side of his mouth as he walked along. In a very short time Mistress Jane would be not quite so haughty. In Southwark she would learn docility as many a woman had learned it before her.

As he walked through the narrow streets he knew that eyes watched him through the discreetly curtained windows. A woman with lewd eyes and naked, he saw, beneath her cloak, for she allowed the cloak to fall open as she came towards him, smiled invitingly. He waved her aside with nonchalance, for he was no newcomer to Southwark.

He stopped before a tall house about which there was a cleanliness lacking in its neighbours. He mounted the steps and knocked at the door which was opened almost immediately by a fat girl in her twenties. She wore a cap with ribands and a low-cut gown. She curtseyed, knowing him for a nobleman and patron of the house; she expected at least a kiss, but his preoccupation with Jane Wainstead made him ignore her.

He said curtly : "Conduct me to your mistress."

The girl, pouting, bid him enter.

He was taken to a small room which might have belonged to a well-to-do middle-class home. There were clean rushes on the floor, and the hangings were not of common worsted, but of tapestry woven to represent scenes from the French wars which Henry the Fifth had conducted to the satisfaction of his countrymen. Harfleur was represented, together with Agincourt. Hastings did not spare them a glance. He had seen them before.

A woman came into the room. She was middle-aged and very neatly and simply dressed; hanging on a chain about her neck was a silver cross. There was about her a puritanical look which her surroundings seemed to stress. She was called Madam by all who had dealings with her; and it was known that, under the mysterious Mistress Bee who owned this place and had never been seen here even by its most honoured patrons, she was the head of this establishment.

Now she smiled ingratiatingly. She was eager, she said, to

know the requirements of the noble lord. But first she would tell him that there was a very charming acquisition to the house. A girl not more than fourteen—a Venus and almost a virgin.

"Nay," said Hastings. "I have come to ask you to reserve an apartment for me."

"An apartment, my lord?"

"Come, come," said Hastings impatiently. "It will cost much, I know. I am ready to pay. The apartment is to be of your best. It is to be in readiness for me and a lady."

"You are bringing the lady, my lord?"

"I am. It may be to-night. It may be to-morrow. But you must be ready for me. It is understood?"

"It is, my lord, but . . ."

"Bother not your head about money, good woman. I will pay now."

"Ah," said Madam, "you shall have the very best apartment in the house. It shall be made clean and sweet. And how long shall you be needing the apartment, my lord?"

"That, I do not yet know."

"Until further orders shall we say, my lord?"

"It is enough," said Hastings. "And another matter . . . The lady may be . . ."

"A little indisposed when she arrives?" Madame patted her prim collar. Madam had genius. She made the most lecherous adventure sound puritanical; abductions, left to her, seemed as dignified as the ceremonies of the Church.

"I see you are going to help me," said Hastings; and he laid his money on the table.

"My lord," said Madam, "it is the custom of this house to satisfy our gentlemen."

He came out humming. It was very simple. He hailed a boat and in a very short time was across the river; he hurried northwards and did not pause until he reached Bucklersbury. He stopped now before a shop whose window was full of brightly coloured bottles. He stepped down three stone stairs, pushed open a door, and went into the dark little shop which smelt of musk and herbs.

Leppus, the dried-up little apothecary, hearing the door open, emerged from the darkness behind the shop. He took one swift look at Lord Hastings and bowed obsequiously. He had served many gentlemen of the court and recognised one when he saw him. Leppus's skin was brown as walnut and his teeth were yellow; his nose was long and artfully hooked; his eyes were black and bright; and his eyebrows hung over them half-concealing the cunning that lay in them. It was said at the court that he was more than an apothecary. His love potions were true love potions inasmuch as they could be relied upon to rouse the most sluggish to amorous revelry. He could supply poisons, and it was said of him that he never asked questions, merely high prices. The King himself was reputed to patronise Leppus; and Leppus was suspected of being very rich. He was, it seemed, a master of magic. He could produce herbal drinks to make women fruitful; and if they were unwillingly with child, potions to terminate their pregnancies. He had sleeping draughts which, he would remind his patron with a leer, if taken in double doses would produce death. He had herbs to make the complexion good, lotions to make the eyes bright; he had aphrodisiacs to rejuvenate flagging desires; he could make wax images to resemble the enemies of his patrons and supply pins with which to pierce the waxen bodies; he had the tears and sweat of martyrs which he sold in costly containers, and which were holy charms against plague and disaster. Now Leppus recognised my Lord Hastings and muttered that he was eager to know how he could serve such a noble lord.

Hastings followed the old man into an inner chamber and sat down. Leppus stood with his back to the light watching the nobleman's face. Was it a strong sleeping dose for a rival? Leppus would know. An aphrodisiac for a reluctant maid? He was amused by these matters which occupied these men of the gay court, and pleased to wield the power he did over them.

What mattered it to Leppus who sat on the throne? Edward or Henry, he would still have customers glad to use his brains and buy his goods.

"Leppus, I want a sleeping draught."

Leppus nodded. "A not too strong sleeping draught, my lord?"

"A sleeping draught that could be slipped into a glass of wine and none be the wiser."

"I know. I know. I have the very thing." Leppus went to a bench at one end of the room, drew up a stool, took from a shelf a bottle containing white powder, and spread on the bench before him a piece of paper on to which he ladled out a small quantity of the powder.

"How long will the effect of this last, Leppus?"

"For two or three hours, my lord."

"That is what I need. She—the one who takes it—cannot possibly wake, even though . . ."

"Even though she"—Leppus corrected himself with some elaboration—"even though this person were, shall we say, carried on horseback across the City; even then this—er—person would not wake until the draught had had its way."

It was uncanny, thought Hastings, frowning at the old man's back, how much Leppus knew. One would feel like murdering him if one did not know that he held similar secrets regarding half the men and women of the court.

"And have you some little potion—a love potion—something that would change the——"

"Something that would change the heart of an icy maiden? Oh, I have that also, my lord. Now, here is your sleeping draught. Slip it in the wine. It will only take a few minutes to work its effect."

"You are sure that——"

"It is absolutely safe, my lord. And now for the love potion." He had turned his back to Hastings, who knew that his ugly old face was creased in smiles and that the seduction of Jane Wainstead in Mistress Bee's Southwark rooms was being enacted before his eyes. Others had said old Leppus made them feel like that. How gratifying it would be to take the old man by his shabby coat and cut out his tongue so that he might never make his sneering remarks again, to put out his eyes so that one need not feel he saw things not intended for him. But if old Leppus was hated, he was certainly respected. He was too wise, too useful to be treated badly.

"Now," said Leppus, "a little charm, I think, to bring you luck with the lady."

"I think the draught and the potion will be sufficient."

"You must have a charm for luck, my lord. Now look. Here is a little figure. It is an ancient god of some foreign land. Set it on a table where it can see you and smile on you and bring you luck."

He wanted five shillings for the charm; the potion and draught were another five. The figure had a look of old Leppus about it, and Hastings imagined it propped up in some conspicuous spot in the apartment Madam had reserved for him. It would seem as if that repulsive old man was looking through the ugly eyes of the god. Hastings believed that was possible. He would have liked to destroy the thing but he dared not. If he did, Leppus, with his obscene magic, might destroy the potency of both those small neat packages.

Hastings paid the apothecary what he asked, and Leppus leered after him as he left the shop and hurried away.

*   *   *   *   *

Jane lay back in bed watching Kate fidgeting at the table. Kate seemed strange to-night. She was flushed and nervous.

"Kate," said Jane, "you seem ill at ease to-night. Have you been to St. Paul's Churchyard this day?"

"Yes, I have then." Kate spoke defiantly.

"And did you see him?"

"I saw him."

"And what said he?"

"He said that you were cold and cruel and would doubtless

dally until it was too late to find a man to marry you. You knew not, he said, when life was offering you something good."

"So *he* is something good? I doubt it, Kate. I doubt very much that he is something good. And, Kate, you had better be careful, for I have a fancy that my father has grown suspicious of late."

"No!" cried Kate, shivering suddenly.

"Indeed, yes. He looked at me most oddly. I believe he has seen your gallant gentleman lurking about the house."

"*My* gallant gentleman!" cried Kate.

"Well, 'tis you who have so many dealings with him. Have I not told you that I will have none of him?"

Kate leaned against the table and spread her trembling hands over her skirt until her fingers touched the pocket. In that pocket was a neat little package. She looked wistfully at Jane. Kate had assured herself that the noble lord had spoken the truth when he said he meant to marry the girl and make a great lady of her. Jane was too young as yet to know what was good for her; and once the dangerous business was done with, how grateful would Jane be—and so would he—to clever Kate who had made it all possible!

What she had to do was perfectly simple. There was nothing evil in the little package which she carried in her pocket. It would merely produce a pleasant sleep. She was to give it to Jane last thing to-night, just before the girl was ready to sleep. That would be in a few minutes' time; and then, when the household was asleep, all Kate had to do was tiptoe downstairs, let in the man who loved Jane so romantically, conduct him up to this chamber, and let him carry out the sleeping girl. As for Kate, she was to be in Paul's Churchyard at midday on the morrow and there she would be told where Jane was and when she might see her; and then as soon as Jane was in her new grand home—at court most likely—Kate would be sent for to act as maid to her newly elevated mistress. It seemed like a dream coming true; but, of course, the dangerous part had to be lived through first, and if she and the gentleman were caught, she knew she would be thrust out into the streets; but this she would risk for the sake of what would come after. No wonder she was trembling now.

She said: "You do not want to marry Will Shore, so why are you so cold to this noble lord? You will not even stand at the window that he may see you."

"Assuredly I will not. And at least Will Shore is an honest man."

"You think the noble lord is not?"

"I think, Kate, that he is not."

"He is very fascinating."

"Doubtless he is, Kate. I will take your word for that."

"Have you no desire to see him again?"

"I have no desire to be his mistress for a week."

"The jewels in his clothes . . ."

"I do not care so much for jewels. Nor do they mean an assurance of honesty."

Kate thought, This is driving me mad. How do I know what I ought to do? Sooner or later her father will force her to marry Will Shore, and then she will be unhappy.

"Enough of this noble lord," said Jane. "Give me a cup of wine and I will settle down to sleep."

There were shadows in the room. The single candle cast a flickering light upon the table.

It is now I must do this, thought Kate. He said she would not taste it. He said it would do no harm. It will be a sweet peaceful sleep and she will wake up in his arms. Well, I promised and I will do it.

Kate shot the powder into the wine and took it to Jane, almost spilling it, so much did she tremble. Cold sweat ran down her back. What should she do? Snatch the cup from Jane and confess what she had done? But it was for Jane's sake that she did it.

It was too late now, for Jane had drunk the wine. She had noticed nothing. She lay back; her face had grown pale and her eyelids drooped already. Kate sat, watching her.

The minutes passed and Kate did not move; she listened to those sounds which meant that the household was retiring for the night. She heard Thomas go to his room; she heard the servants first making their beds in the great hall and then settling down to sleep. They would not remark on her absence, for they would think she was sleeping in Jane's room. Moreover, they were usually so fatigued that they fell into their beds as soon as they were ready and were quickly asleep. Later she must creep down to the hall, and in the morning she must pretend that she had spent the whole night there. Time enough for that. Kate rarely thought of more than one thing at a time.

She waited until she could hear no sound but the creaking of the oldest boards in the staircase before she crept to the window and stood there waiting. She did not wait long. From below came a long low whistle. That was the signal. All she had to do was creep downstairs and let him into the house. He would do the rest.

But now that the moment had come Kate was filled with a great doubt. She was about to give this helpless girl into the hands of a man of whom she knew very little. Quite suddenly Kate knew she dared not do it.

She could never recall what happened during the next few seconds. She did know that she ran screaming along the corridor and started to hammer on the door of her master's room. It seemed that she stood there for a long time before he flung open the door and stood before her in a coat he had picked up in a hurry; his face was purple, his lips sagging.

"What means this, woman?" he demanded; and Kate fell sobbing against him.

"He is there, master. He is there. He is coming to take Mistress Jane away. He gave me stuff to put in her wine."

"What's this? *What's* this? Who is where?" The mention of his daughter's name had set fear stirring in Thomas. He knew enough of the nature of those adventures indulged in by promiscuous young men to get, even from Kate's incoherent words, some idea of what was afoot. He seized Kate by the arm and dragged her along to Jane's room. He stared in horror at his daughter's face; it was so unnaturally pale and still.

"Jane!" He dropped Kate's arm to lean over his daughter. "My little Jane." He felt her heart and an immense relief showed in his face. He understood. Jane was not the first to be drugged before an abduction. He turned to Kate, gripped her shoulder, shook her violently, and then flung her on to the floor, where she lay staring up at him with terror in her eyes. He leaned over her, took her by the throat and shook her afresh.

"You had better tell me everything, before I kill you," he said.

It came out in jerks, the whole story—Kate's meeting with the man in St. Paul's Churchyard, the messages, Jane's indifference, and finally the plot. As Kate talked she was shaken and beaten, but there was on her face a vacant smile of relief. She would be beaten as she had never before been beaten, but she did not care. She had saved Jane.

Thomas left her lying exhausted on the floor. He went downstairs and unlocked the front door. For one wrathful second he stood face to face with Lord Hastings. Hastings recovered himself first. He turned and walked rapidly away. Thomas followed him, calling him scoundrel, commanding him to stop; but Hastings had leaped on to his horse and was away, leaving the furious mercer, barelegged and barefooted, to shake a trembling fist at the fleeing figure.

Now the whole household was astir. Apprentices had gathered on the stairs; they whispered with the serving men and women. A robbery? Someone trying to break into the vaults?

"Back to your beds, all of you!" Thomas shouted; and they slunk away, while their master stamped barefooted back to his daughter's room. Kate was on her knees by the bed, sobbing, while Jane still slept her deep unnatural sleep.

Thomas leaned over Kate, gripped her by the ear, and pulled her up.

"Go to my room and get me a wrap. Bring it back here at once."

Kate went and was back in a few seconds. He snatched the robe from her and wrapped it round himself while Kate stood trembling before him.

"How long will my daughter remain like that?"

"I—do not know."

"You do not know, you wicked, wanton woman! And *you* gave her the drug, did you not?"

Kate nodded. "I wish I were dead, master."

"Wish you were dead! You're going to wish you'd never been born before I've done with you. Stop snivelling, I tell you. By God's Holy Mother, you shall pay for this."

"I would wish that," cried Kate. "I will welcome every stroke, for now I see how richly I deserve it."

"Stroke! Think not that a mere beating will be your reward for this night's work. You'll be out on the street this time to-morrow."

Kate was shocked into silence. Out on the street, no home, nothing to eat but what she could beg. Who would take her in after the way she had repaid Thomas Wainstead for his goodness?

He made her tell the story over and over again. What had the man said? What had Jane said? He was satisfied that his daughter had not had a hand in this sordid intrigue and he was inclined to be more lenient with Kate on that account.

There they sat through the long night, Thomas occasionally roaring out a question; Kate moaning softly, contemplating a dreary and most wretched future.

Not until dawn came did Jane begin to stir. Thomas leaned over the bed. "Jane," he whispered. "Daughter." His voice was tender.

Jane opened her eyes and looked at him.

"All is well, daughter. Your father is here with you."

"Father . . . I feel . . . so strange. I . . ."

Thomas put an arm about her. "Bring a cup of wine," he

shouted to Kate. "Quick, woman." And Kate ran, eager to obey, to make up in every small way for the great harm she had done.

Thomas snatched the wine from her and held it to Jane's lips. Jane sipped and a little colour came into her face.

"That's better," said Thomas with relief.

"Father . . . what happened . . . to me?"

Thomas said viciously: "You were drugged by that drab."

"Drugged?"

"Aye. Drugged by that slut, that sloven, that harlot there. Working for a scoundrel she was. Eating my meat, drinking my wine and working for a scoundrel. By God, by Christ, she'll wish she'd never been born!"

"Kate!" cried Jane.

"Oh, mistress," sobbed Kate. "I never thought . . . I never meant to. . . ."

"Kate," said Jane; and she held out her hand. But Thomas struck Kate as she would approach the bed, so that she staggered across the room and fell, cutting her head against the table. This violence seemed to lift Jane out of her drugged stupor.

"Father . . . no . . . no."

"But yes," cried Thomas. "Get up, you harlot," he shouted at Kate; and Kate got up.

"Come here, you strumpet," he said; and Kate came. "Nearer," he roared at her, and pulled her by her hair, which was hanging loose about her shoulders.

"Now, daughter," he said. "Understand this: This woman, whom you trusted, sought to betray you. She drugged your wine and she had schemed to hand you over to a scoundrel."

"Kate!" said Jane in shocked horror.

"Nay," screamed Kate. "I did not do it. It is true I put the powder in your wine, and when I saw you sleeping . . . I knew it was wrong. Believe me, mistress. At first I thought it would be right for you. I thought he would marry you, make a grand lady of you and save you from the goldsmith. But then . . . suddenly I knew it was wrong, and, instead of letting him in, I called your father."

Thomas eyed her narrowly. It was true. At least she had had the sense to do that. He felt the rising of uncontrollable anger. Everything he had done to shield his daughter was of no avail. This brought home to him how easy it was for her to deceive him. If he had lacked peace before, how much more would he lack that happy state now. He thought longingly of what his daughter's marriage to the goldsmith would mean.

Jane was making a great effort to rouse herself from the stupefying effects of the drug. She herself was safe, so all her thoughts were for Kate. She saw the blood on Kate's face and the terrible fear in her eyes as she visualised her future. She understood Kate well enough to know what had gone on in her mind. Kate was a simple woman, for all she believed herself to be so wise. She had genuinely believed that she was helping her mistress to a happier life. Poor Kate!

"Father," she said weakly, "Kate meant no harm."

"Meant no harm!" cried Thomas. "No, she only meant to pass you over to a rascally fellow."

"But she repented in time, you see, Father, for here I am in my own room, and all through Kate."

Kate had brightened, and Jane was deeply moved to see the hope which came into the woman's face.

"Father," persisted Jane, "you will not be hard on her . . . for my sake."

"For your sake! What have I had but disobedience from you? Let me tell you this, daughter, to-morrow I go to William Shore and tell him you have come to your senses."

"No," said Jane, "you will not do that."

"Oh, yes I will. To-morrow you will be betrothed to Shore. Aye, and married to him as soon as I can manage it. And that slut"—he pointed at Kate with a trembling finger—"gets out of my house, and I never wish to look into her wicked face again."

"But, Father, where will she go?"

"She'll go over to Southwark most like. That's where her bawdy friends live and where she belongs. The harlot! I knew from the moment I took the drab into my house that I was making a mistake. 'I was turned out of Ludlow Castle when the soldiers came,' she said. 'There was naught I could do but follow the camp to London.' Followed the camp of her free will, I'll swear. Well, back she goes to where she belongs —and that's not in the house of an honest merchant."

"But, Father, what will become of her if you turn her out?" asked Jane. "She has nowhere to go."

"Mayhap the scoundrel she was about to let into my house will do something for her."

"She did not let him into your house."

"I'll hear no more now. Get you to sleep." He turned to Kate. "As for you . . . you'll go straight out of this house . . . now. And don't let me see you whining at the back door or I'll have you flung into Ludgate."

"Father!" cried Jane.

"I said I would hear no more."

Jane roused herself from the effect of the drug which seemed to chain her to the bed. "You shall hear me," she said.

Relieved by her improved appearance, Thomas shouted at her: "Think you it is your lot to command me, girl? You have been pampered enough already. Another word from you and I'll put a whip about your shoulders."

"Do so," said Jane, "but still I shall speak."

He advanced towards the bed. Jane smiled at him. She felt light-headed and very weary, but she could not rest while Kate had that look in her face, for Kate was obviously more frightened than any living creature should be.

"Father," she said, "you want me to marry Will Shore, don t you?"

"A foolish question. You know well my wishes."

"Then, Father, I will marry him."

Thomas smiled. "So you have come to your senses at last.

Right glad I am, girl, for it gave me no pleasure to shut you up and starve you."

"There is a condition, Father."

"A condition?"

"Yes. I marry Will and Kate stays with me."

Thomas narrowed his eyes and looked from Kate to Jane; then slowly his mouth began to turn up at the corners.

*   *   *   *   *

There was something gloomy about the house in Cheapside after that night, although the mercer went about whistling gaily.

Kate's part in that night's abortive abduction had not gone unpunished, although the mercer kept his promise to his daughter, and Kate stayed on in his house. Thomas had lashed her to the whipping post and given her a beating she would never forget. She had screamed, then groaned and become unconscious, sagging there at the post before the mercer had done. She had to keep to her bed for three days after the beating, while a pale-faced Jane—grown quieter and more serious—fiercely condemned her father for what he had done.

Thomas smarted under his daughter's tongue, and wondered why he allowed her to call him a savage. But at the same time he could congratulate himself that it would not be long before Will Shore must be the one to deal with her waywardness.

Jane rubbed ointments into Kate's wounds, and herself waited on her maid during those three days; and both maid and mistress were more subdued than any had ever seen them before.

Kate would bear the marks of that beating on her body for as long as she lived. But it seemed that Jane suffered more than Kate from that night's adventure, for she had become betrothed to Will Shore, the goldsmith.

*   *   *   *   *

LOMBARD STREET

THE goldsmith was bewildered. For nearly two years Jane had been his wife, and yet that complete satisfaction, that fulfilment, which he had thought must be the natural outcome of his marriage, was denied him. He loved her with all the passion of which he was capable. He loved too his fine house, his business, all the beautifully wrought and valuable articles which made up his stock; he was proud of his standing in the City; but the pride and love he felt for Jane were greater than he felt for any other of his possessions. The love of the goldsmith for all his treasures was bound up in the esteem in which he wished all men to hold him. He longed to be a strutting giant, feared for his strength, a wit admired for his ready tongue. Instead, he was a man of small stature, of gentle almost timid manners. He had grown rich, though, through saving the groat here, the shilling there. But for all that he was a small man, and he knew it.

Being unable therefore to attract attention to himself through his own personality, he sought to do it through his possessions; and thus had he become an acquisitive man. He liked to go into his vaults and to handle the precious metals there; he liked to stroke Jane's golden hair, caress her lovely limbs. "The gold is mine," he could gloat, and know that men envied him. "Jane is mine," he could tell himself; and for Jane he was also envied.

He should have been satisfied, but he was not, for he did not understand the lovely high-spirited girl whom he had bought with his own treasured gold and his years of hard work and shrewd dealing. He had heard her laughing with the woman, Kate, whom she had insisted on bringing with her. It worried him that when she was alone with him she rarely laughed. He disliked Kate. She was not the sort of woman he would have had in his house but for Jane. She was, he suspected, lazy. He suspected certain revelries in his kitchens. Belper, his fat and clever cook, loved women almost as much as he loved food. Belper had been a disturbing element in his house even before Kate had come into it; but Belper was worth a little inconvenience. He was one of the best cooks in London, and a goldsmith often found it necessary to entertain those of the quality who were his customers; therefore it had been necessary to forget Belper's second love, since he had such a way with his first. Kate was of no such value.

On this particular day he was going the round of his house, locking up all doors, except the front one, for they would have to go out by that and lock it afterwards. All the servants had already gone, except Kate, who was helping Jane to dress. They were late already and should have been in Cheapside by now. He shook his head. He should scold Jane for her lack of punctuality; he would prepare to scold and because she was so beautiful he would forget his impatience and know only pride.

He wished they could have a child. He saw in a child a new treasure; he would like a child that looked exactly like Jane but had his shrewd ways—a child that laughed and was witty and yet had a head for business. So far, there was no sign of a child. It was a continual irritation. He wondered if men and women whispered behind their hands as he passed: "The goldsmith cannot have a child." It was a slight on his manhood.

He went to the front door and opened it. A roar of voices that shrieked and laughed seemed to fill the house. The crowd was already gathering, and he and Jane would not find it easy to get to her father's house in Cheapside, from where they intended to view the procession. Jane took too long in decking herself out in her finery. The goldsmith shook his head uneasily. He doubted not that Jane would attract as much attention as any riding in the King's procession.

It was comforting, though, to contemplate that for a time at least there would be an end to war. As a serious-minded merchant, Will knew that only out of peace could prosperity grow. He rejoiced that King Edward had prevailed, and that the trouble-making Earl of Warwick was dead. Pray the saints, thought Will, that this is an end to civil war. Let Edward reign in peace from now on, and good times will lie ahead. There would be pageantry and revelry in place of discomfort and death. Small wonder that the citizens of London were gathering in their thousands to welcome the return to his capital of victorious Edward.

But he and Jane must be gone or they would not get a glimpse of the pageant, thought the goldsmith, as he made his way upstairs. The women were laughing, and Kate was saying: "We are frail creatures indeed, but if we do aught wrong, is it not because some evil spirit leads us to it? Can we be blamed? Mayhap when we think we sin most it is but the will of God that we should do so."

"Why, Kate," said Jane, "that is a comforting creed. You should preach it at Paul's Cross. I'll swear you'd have half London following you."

Will opened the door and their frivolity was curbed. Kate started to straighten the things on the table busily, as though she was the sort who could not let her hands remain idle for a moment. Did she think to deceive him? Jane gave him what he knew to be a false smile of welcome.

"We are very late," he said harshly. "I doubt if we shall get a view of the King."

He laid a hand on her arm and he looked at her in that appealing way which never failed to move her or fill her with self-reproach. "Tell me where I fail, Jane," said the meekness of his eyes. "Mayhap I could change." But how could she tell him? How could she say, "I do not love you, nor can I ever love you. I like not the heavy way you breathe; the way you pick a bone as though you will get every scrap of meat off it— not in hunger but in fear of waste. I like not the way your hands pat and caress me as though you feel there is something shameful in this, and yet, having bought me in marriage, you have paid for the privilege of being shameful. There are thousands of things about you that I do not like, and though I have tried to like them, though I have prayed that I might like them, I never can."

She got up, trying to smile affectionately at Will; and in a short time they were walking briskly out of Lombard Street past the Stocks Market into the Poultry. Here the crowd was thicker than ever. Men had climbed posts to see over the heads of others. They were shouting and whistling to one another. Some of the traders from the cookshops were pushing their way through the crowds. Trays hung from their necks by means of straps, and the trays were loaded with pieces of meat, bread and cakes, mead and wine. People were eating, laughing and shouting; and every now and then there would break out the cry of "King Edward!"

Too many people cast their eyes on the goldsmith's radiant wife. It disturbed his peace of mind, for much as he liked to see her admired, he did not care that it should be by the rabble of the Poultry.

He scolded her. "You see, you have made us late. How shall we now reach your father's house? We must watch the procession from the streets here . . . among this mob of people. I declare the stench of them is past bearing. And all because you would not be ready in good time."

"But is it not good to see so many people enjoying this day?" said Jane. She was laughing now at a tumbler who was performing for the benefit of the crowd.

"And what your father will say when we do not arrive, I cannot imagine," went on Will.

"I can," said Jane. "He will fall into a rage."

"And that amuses you? I declare I like it not that your father should think me so inconsiderate. . . ."

"Never fear, Will! the entire blame for this will be laid where it belongs . . . on my shoulders."

There was a sudden shout from the crowd. The shouting grew louder, and in the distance the sound of trumpets could be heard.

And now, thought Jane, I shall see the King himself. I shall see this man who is supposed to be so irresistible that virtuous maidens discard their virtue at his command. I shall see the Queen who so enchanted him that, profligate though he was, he could not resist her. Small wonder, that wherever they went people turned out in their thousands to see this romantic King and his Queen.

Now came the first of the brilliant cavalcade—men bejewelled and dazzling in their gorgeously coloured clothes. Then came a chariot surrounded by guards, and a sudden hush fell on the crowd, for the two women in this chariot were enemies of the King and not to be cheered. One was the hated Margaret of Anjou, who had been captured at Tewkesbury where her son Edward had met his death. The other occupant of the chariot could not but excite the pity of all who saw her; and it was her presence which prevented the crowd from actively displaying its hatred. She was a very pale, sad-faced girl of about sixteen, and her name was Anne Neville. She was the younger daughter of the Earl of Warwick, and had been betrothed to Margaret's son who had recently been killed at Tewkesbury. She had spent most of her childhood with the King's youngest brother, Richard of Gloucester, and it was said that, although she had been forced into betrothal with Margaret's son, it was Richard whom she loved. Therefore did it seem sad to these Londoners that this girl, pale as a primrose, must ride as a prisoner, while that very Richard whom she was reputed to love rode in a place of honour near his brother the King.

The chariot rolled on, and as Jane gazed at those gloriously apparelled knights, at the brilliant trappings of the stately horses, she saw among them a face she knew; and as she looked, the handsome head was turned towards her. It was the man who was responsible for that terrifying night when she had been nearly abducted, the man who was responsible for her marriage to Will Shore. The glance he now gave her conveyed his pleasure at seeing her again. There was in it, too, a look of confidence, of arrogance, which seemed to say, "Do I seem the man to accept failure?"

Was it fear or the crowd pressing round her that made her sway towards Will? She felt as though she were about to faint.

"What is wrong?" asked Will anxiously.

"I feel . . . too hot."

"It's the crowd. We should have viewed this from your father's windows. Come. We'll get home before the crowd begins to move."

She felt better as soon as she entered the house, but she let Will take her up to bed. He left her while he went to get some wine. When he brought it back he watched her closely for a few seconds, and then he said with a great hope in his eyes : "Jane, could it be . . . You were so suddenly faint that . . ."

"No," she said quickly. "No."

He smiled in an embarrassed fashion. "I was hoping that you would tell me you were with child."

"I am sorry, Will. But it is not so."

They were both sorry about that, she thought, after he had gone. A child would have made such a difference to them. If only it had been a child, and not that man on horseback. He had brought trouble before; she felt certain he would do so again.

The wine had made Jane drowsy. Through her window she could hear the shouting of the people. The procession was ended, but the crowd was still bent on pleasure. She had, from her father's house in Cheapside, often watched the people after pageants. She had seen their wild dances, their frantic merry-making. Often she had looked from a window on to strange scenes, fantastic, lurid in the glow from lighted torches. She had heard screaming laughter that seemed scarcely human; she had seen men and women fighting together, making love; she had seen them stretched out drunk on the cobbles below the house. Her father had had to bolt his doors and barricade his windows on such nights as these; he must have the apprentices ready with staves in case it should be necessary to protect the house against rioters, for thieves were abroad, and all that was evil in the hysterical drunken crowds was let loose on such nights.

This was another such night, a night for rejoicing, since King Edward, after a few months' exile, was back on the throne; and it seemed that there were many of his subjects who wished to emulate that beautiful profligate, their handsome, popular, lecherous King.

Jane dozed and dreamed she was back in the crowd. She saw again the man on horseback; but in her dream, instead of riding on, he came swiftly towards her, picked her up from beside Will, and slung her across his horse. Jane screamed, and the scream awakened her.

Kate was standing by the bed staring down at her.

"Mercy on us! That was a bad dream, mistress."

"I'm glad I awoke," said Jane.

"So you all but fainted in the street, lovey?"

"It was the heat and crowds, Kate." And when Kate's eyes narrowed knowledgeably, Jane burst out: "Pray do not look sly and secret because you think I ought to be with child. I am not, I tell you." Kate pursed her lips and Jane went on: "Did you see the King?"

"I did; and the Queen was with him. She is very beautiful. I saw her in her litter, that was carried on poles. The horses were splendid creatures."

"Were the horses as beautiful as the Queen?"

"They were not. The Queen has the most lovely yellow hair I ever saw . . . next to yours. She wore it loose and flowing: and they say the King is much in love with her after their long separation. And all the Princesses were lovely, and as for the little Prince . . . he is just a baby. You should have heard the people cheer when they saw *him*."

"Kate, you've something on your mind."

"On my mind, mistress?"

"You know that it is useless to deceive me. You know something and you are waiting to tell me."

"I saw *him* in the procession, mistress," said Kate. "I learned his name. He is Lord Hastings."

Jane caught her breath. She had heard of Hastings. He had distinguished himself at Barnet and Tewkesbury, and he was a close friend of the King's.

"Then," said Jane sharply, to hide her fear, "it is a pity, methinks, that my Lord Hastings does not behave in a more seemly fashion."

"Indeed it is," said Kate, but she could not hide the sparkle in her eyes. She was convinced that life was meant to be a gay affair, and nothing would have pleased her more than to see her beautiful mistress deep in a secret love affair.

"How did you learn who he was?" demanded Jane.

"I asked a man who stood beside me in the crowd."

"He may have been mistaken."

"Nay. There were many who said it. Think of it, mistress. He loves you, and he is the King's closest friend and favourite."

"He would never be friend and favourite of mine."

"That is what you say now."

Jane jumped off the bed and caught Kate by the wrist. "Kate, you have not been . . ."

"No, mistress. No. I have done nothing."

"Because if you ever betrayed me as you promised him to do that night, I should not save you again."

"I would do nothing—nothing without your consent."

There was a sudden knocking at the door. "Who is there?" asked Jane, while Kate hastily began tidying the things on the table for fear it should be the goldsmith.

But it was not the goldsmith, and Kate stopped working at once. It was merely Bess, one of the kitchen girls.

"Yes, Bessy?" asked Jane kindly, while Kate glared at the girl, for they were rivals for the attentions of the fat and affectionate Belper.

"If you please, mistress, there is a gentleman below who says he must have speech with you. It is a matter of some importance."

"A gentleman? Did you not ask his name?"

"Yes, mistress, but he did not give it. He said to ask you to come at once; and he spoke most pressingly."

Jane stood up. "Very well, Bessy. Where is he?"

"I left him in the parlour. He had stepped into the house before I had time to ask him."

"I will go at once and see who it is," said Jane.

She went down, and, opening the parlour door, saw, looking jaunty and very sure of himself, Lord Hastings. He came towards her and would have laid his hands on her shoulders while he kissed her mouth in greeting, had she not held him off.

"Sir," she said haughtily, "I know not why you have come here."

"You know well," he said gravely.

"I must ask you to go at once."

"Has not the goldsmith's lady better hospitality to offer me than this?"

"There is no hospitality for you in this house."

"I am sorry for that, Jane," he said sadly, "for, by my faith, you are more fair than I had thought you."

"How dare you come here! You should be shut in the Tower for what you tried to do to me."

"Speak not of that, Jane. It grieves me."

"I am glad of that. Mayhap there is some decency in you then."

He smiled whimsically. "You do not understand me. It grieves me that I did not succeed in carrying you off."

There was something overpowering about the man that robbed her of her calm. He was very handsome in his fine garments, and though his mouth was firm, his eyes twinkled. He stepped towards her. She was terrified that his intention was to pick her up and walk out of the house with her.

"Will!" she screamed. "Will!"

Hastings was taken aback. His face flushed angrily. "Are you mad? You would call your husband?"

"Will!" called Jane. "Oh—quickly—quickly!"

There followed the sound of running footsteps. Will had heard her cries.

"Jane, where are you? Where are you, Jane?"

"Here," called Jane wildly. "Here in the parlour."

She tried to run past Hastings but he caught her and held her fast. She tried to kick herself free.

"You foolish girl," muttered Hastings. "Be still."

"Foolish!" panted Jane. "Is it foolish to despise you? *I* call it wisdom."

Hastings was furious. He had expected that such daring he had displayed in calling on the woman in her husband's house would be applauded and win her admiration immediately. He had believed that Jane was like other women of his acquaintance who would wish the wooing to be arduous, but who would be ready enough to fall to him after a while. Being absent with the King, he had been unable to continue his pursuit of her since his attempt to abduct her from Cheapside had been foiled, but now he was ready, and the waiting had been long enough. He felt foolish. He had suffered sufficient indignity for her already. He was determined to endure no more.

"This is the last time I'll come courting you," he said.

"That is the best news I've heard for a long time," she flashed back.

Then the door opened and Will, followed by his steward, came in. "Jane!" cried Will.

"Oh, Will, praise the saints you've come. This—man—has dared to come into your house. He is the man who tried to abduct me."

Hastings, having released Jane on the entrance of the goldsmith, stood, his arms folded, looking scornfully down on Will Shore.

"You knave!" shrieked Will. "I'll have you tried for trespass. How dare you force an entry into my house!"

Hastings laughed. "Be silent," he said shortly. "It is clear you do not know whom you address."

"He knows he addresses a knave and a liar," said Jane hotly.

Hastings continued to look at Will. "I would have you know, fellow, that I am Lord Hastings."

"I care not if you are the King himself," said the goldsmith recklessly.

"Bravo!" cried Jane.

Hastings flashed an arrogant glance in her direction. "You speak rashly," he said. "Now stand aside, goldsmith, unless you care to feel the point of my sword through that brave heart of yours."

He pushed past Will, and, reaching the door, turned to look at him and Jane.

"Think not," he said, "that I shall forget this day." His eyes went to Jane. "Methinks, madam, that this husband of yours will, ere long, regret that he dared to insult Lord Hastings."

He went out. They were silent in the parlour as they listened to his footsteps on the cobbles in the courtyard.

Then Will turned to Jane and put an arm about her.

"Have no fear, sweetheart," he said. "I will protect you."

Jane smiled at him. She wished she could believe that he had the power to do so.

    *   *   *   *   *

For the next few days Jane was afraid to go out for fear she should meet Lord Hastings. When dusk fell she did not care to stray far from the side of Will or Kate. She could not forget how vindictive Hastings had looked when he had said they would regret their treatment of him. She wished she could believe that his talk of revenge had been an idle threat, but she knew that terrible things could happen to those who opposed powerful men such as he was. But two days after the incident the King and his court left London abruptly, and Jane's peace of mind returned.

There was a hush over London during those days. King Henry the Sixth, whom the conquering Edward had made a prisoner in the Tower, died mysteriously. He had been murdered, some said, by order of the King. People remembered that, ineffectual as he was, mad as he was, he had been a pious man who had never cared to wrong any, and they began to look upon him as a martyr. His dead body was paraded through the streets, so that all might see it was really the deposed King Henry who was dead; and in view of the attitude of his people, even popular King Edward had thought fit to leave the capital for a little while. It seemed to Jane then that there was some good in all evil, since when the court removed from London, Lord Hastings must go with it.

The goldsmith was almost as relieved as his wife, and when in a few weeks the court returned to Westminster Palace, both Jane and her husband were thinking a good deal less about the threats of Hastings.

Business was good, and rich men came to the premises in Lombard Street; the apprentices were kept running up and down to the vaults to bring up the most precious of their master's goods for the inspection of customers. And Will was almost content, seeing trade flourishing and his wife quieter than he had ever known her.

Then one day there came to the house a handsome merchant who told Will that he wished to buy much gold and plate and would see of his best. He was a tall and well proportioned man, and he had a charming and confiding manner which immediately won the goldsmith's heart.

"I have heard," said this man, "that, an I wish to buy the best gold plate in London, then to William Shore of Lombard Street must I come."

It was not only the words, it was the charming smile that accompanied them that made the goldsmith almost over-eager to please. He could not help feeling oddly flustered as the big man sprawled on a tapestry-covered stool, his long, well-shaped legs thrust out before him. Will sent two apprentices down to the vaults to bring up the very best of his stock that it might be displayed for the rich merchant's approval.

"My name," said the merchant, "is Long. Edward Long."

"At your service, sir," said the goldsmith, "and I trust you will find here that which pleases you."

The merchant selected several pieces. "I will send my servant to collect them," he said. "I verily believe I have found some of the really finest pieces in the town."

"I think so too," said the goldsmith. "Your friends will envy you, good sir."

"I was indeed right to come to William Shore, I see. Odd how men will talk. They said to me, 'William Shore has the finest plate and the handsomest wife in London.' Men talk, sir."

The goldsmith was so pleased that he was filled with a desire that the rich merchant should admire not only the plate but his wife.

"My wife, sir, is considered more beautiful than my plate."

The merchant looked disbelievingly at the plate and gave no indication that he wished to see the woman whose beauty had given rise to such discussion.

"I will call her that you may see her for yourself," said Will.

The merchant lifted his shoulders. "I shall, of course, be delighted to meet the lady, but, alas, I have little time. . . ."

His reluctance made the goldsmith more eager. He sent one of the apprentices up to tell his mistress she was wanted below. Jane came down at her husband's bidding. Her morning gown was of her favourite and most becoming blue, and embroidered on it were flowers which had been worked in gold thread. Spangles glittered as she walked; and her long yellow hair hung over her shoulders.

The merchant looked at her, and Jane looked at the merchant. He was very good to look at, she decided; and she liked the steady gaze of his eyes, liked his admiration the more because he attempted to conceal it.

"Wife," said Will, "this is Merchant Edward Long who has bought some of my finest plate this morning."

"I am glad to hear it and to meet you, sir," said Jane.

Edward Long put his hands on her shoulders and kissed her
on the mouth. It was a strange and startling kiss; yet a kiss was
the habitual greeting between men and women, and since she
was a child Jane had been kissed thus in greeting.

"Tell me," said Edward Long, "what think you of the choice
I have made?"

"I think you have chosen of my husband's best. That is so,
is it not, Will?"

"It is, wife. Pray order one of the servants to bring refreshment to our friend. You can stay a short while, sir?"

The merchant hesitated. "I do confess to being somewhat
fatigued. I should like the opportunity of judging whether
your wine is as good as your plate."

The goldsmith rubbed his hands with pleasure, and Jane
hastily sent the apprentice who was hovering at the door to
the kitchen to have refreshment brought. She felt the colour
heighten in her cheeks. This merchant had aroused her
curiosity. There was about him an air of great dignity, and he
was an exceptionally handsome man; she found it pleasant not
to be stared at in a crude fashion, and at the same time stimulating.

When the wine arrived she poured it out and took it to him.
Over the goblet their eyes met and his were inscrutable.

"I thank you, good mistress." He lifted his goblet. "To good
business."

"To trade," echoed Will. "May it continue as it is going on."

"There is an improvement these last weeks, good Shore?
Trade has been more brisk since . . ."

"Since the King came back and put his enemies to flight."

"To the King," said Edward Long.

"To the King," said Will Shore.

The merchant leaned towards Jane. "Tell me, Madam," he
said. "I have heard that the merchants' wives in this City are
devoted to the King. Is it true?"

"They say he is very handsome," said Jane.

"What? Have you never seen him?"

"Nay."

"Were you not in the City when he rode through?"

"Yes," said Jane.

"And you would not walk a yard or so to see his handsome face?"

"We joined the crowds," explained Will, "but my wife was overcome by the heat."

"But," said Jane, "we saw the first part."

"Mayhap you do not care for these processions?"

"I did not care to see the King's enemies, those two women, in their shame."

"Love you the King's enemies, mistress?" asked the merchant.

"Indeed she does not, sir. Jane talks over-wild and always did. She is a woman to speak before she has thought." Will frowned at Jane. "It makes foolish talk often enough."

"But interesting talk," said the merchant. "I would hear more of it, for pleasant it is to find someone who does not say exactly what everyone else is saying." He and Jane exchanged smiles. "Tell me," he went on, "have you some affection for Margaret of Anjou?"

"I like not her methods," said Jane, "but methinks that once having been in possession of a throne, it is but natural to make some effort to regain it. Moreover, I felt it was unnecessarily cruel to make her humiliation public."

"Kings are often cruel," he said.

"I fear so. Glad I am to be but the wife of a humble citizen."

"*Are* goldsmiths so humble?"

"They are tradesmen, I thank God; not courtiers."

"You like not courtiers, Madam?"

"I cannot say. I know none. But it seems to me that a man whose opinions must be adjusted to keep his head balanced on his shoulders lacks the dignity of . . . shall we say, a goldsmith?"

"You think then that those about the King adjust their opinions to keep their heads on their shoulders?"

"Assuredly," said Jane. "Whereas with us merchants it is just a matter of 'The old King is gone; long live the new one.' As the distance from the throne grows greater, so diminishes the danger. I had rather keep my head in its rightful place than live too near kings."

"Nor does that surprise me; if you will forgive my forwardness, Madam, I would say it is a most beautiful head."

"Thank you," said Jane, and found herself flushing.

Shore said : "So, sir, you think my wife is to be admired as much as my plate?"

"More so. Much more so. I take away my morning's purchases with an easy conscience, knowing I leave behind the greatest of your treasures."

"You are most gracious, sir," said Will.

"I am most interested," said the merchant. He smiled quizzically at Jane. "In her views about Queen Margaret I am very interested. I believe the lady thinks the King something of a monster to imprison the woman."

"Nay, she does not," said Will quickly. "Jane knows, as we do all, that Queen Margaret was a menace to the safety of our country. There is not a citizen in London who does not sleep. more peacefully at nights knowing King Henry and his son are dead and Margaret a prisoner."

"But your lady wife is kind of heart, I see. She regrets the King's conduct in exposing Margaret to public shame. *I* forget not the death of the King's father. It is not so long ago that he was killed near Wakefield. Mayhap it is forgotten that Margaret's men cut off his head and set upon it a paper crown before it was placed in mockery over the gates of York. I am inclined to think a public ride was little to ask in exchange for that."

"That was a terrible thing," said Jane, "but I do not think that one act of cruelty needs another to balance it. Revenge is not only evil; it is stupid. There is no good to grow out of it. To forgive one's enemies is not a good thing only, but a wise one also."

"Methinks, sir," said the merchant, draining his glass, "that your wife should be first adviser to the King."

They all laughed.

"It pleases you to mock me," said Jane. "I care not. I know I am right."

The merchant laughed afresh, and he had infectious and delightful laugher. "Forgive me," he said, "if I say that from what I have heard of the King he would lend a willing ear to a lady as charming as yourself should she deign to advise him."

"They say," said Jane, "that for all his grandeur he is very easily led."

"By women," said Shore.

"Ah, yes," said the merchant, "I hear his Grace is most susceptible to the ladies."

"Which shows," put in Jane, "that he is not strong."

"Think you then that he is a weakling? They tell me that he stands well over six feet and that without his boots."

"Giants may be weak," said Jane, "and dwarfs be strong men."

"He was certainly said to be weak over that marriage of his," said Will.

"I liked him for it," declared Jane.

"Did you indeed, Madam?"

"I did. And how I should love to see the Queen!"

"And the King?"

"Yes. But more the Queen. I think she must be truly wonderful to have tamed such a . . ."

"Notorious lover of women?" said the merchant.

"Such a rake," said Jane.

"Hush, Jane. You talk too wildly."

"Why must the truth always be wild?"

"Doubtless," suggested the merchant, "because the truth is often dangerous. Lies are so comforting, so easy. Therefore are lies safe."

"I scorn such safety."

"I see you do, Madam. Never fear, sir, I shall whisper nothing of this to the King."

They laughed afresh, and after a short while the merchant said he must go. "I will send my servant to collect my purchases. He will bring the money. Meantime, I thank you for a most enlivening morning. Such pleasant wine . . . and company."

"Good day, sir," said Will. And, "Good day, sir," said Jane. Will added: "I trust we shall have the pleasure of seeing you again, sir."

"That may well be."

"A most profitable morning," said Will, when he and Jane were alone. "Was he not a charming man?"

"He was indeed," said Jane; and she went upstairs smiling; it was not easy to get the handsome merchant out of her thoughts.

＊　　　＊　　　＊　　　＊　　　＊

"My dear Will," said Mary Blague, the satin of her gown crackling, her narrow eyes smiling, "I would you could lend me our dear Jane for this afternoon. I know you are busy with your accounts. Therefore, thought I, it would be a small favour to ask you to give up your wife's company. I am doing a new pattern—a beautiful lace it is. I swear the King will like it when he sees it. I want to show it to Jane."

"My dear Mary," said Will, "you must ask Jane herself." He went to the door and called Jane who soon came running in.

"I want you to spend the afternoon with me, dear," said Mary. "Now you must come. I'll have no refusal. Please, Will, plead for me."

"There is no need to plead," said Jane, who enjoyed any outing. "I will gladly come."

"Mary wishes to show you a new pattern," said Will.

Jane was surprised at that, and wondered why Mary Blague should want to show *her* a new pattern. Jane herself had never excelled in such womanly arts as lace-making and embroidery; it seemed strange that Mary should be so excited and seem to dread a refusal. But perhaps she was a lonely woman.

"You'll come after dinner?" said Mary.

"After dinner," agreed Jane.

Mary left them then and Will, seeing Jane thoughtful, said: "Did you not wish to go, my dear?"

Jane shrugged her shoulders. "I find her amusing, though I cannot like her very much. But I do like her gossip about the court, and I must confess I delight in her sly suggestions of that remote and most romantic friendship with the King."

"There is a streak of mischief in your nature, Jane. I should pray for strength to resist that."

"But I enjoy my streak of mischief, Will. I should miss it sorely."

"You should also pray that your frivolity might be subdued."

"And pray too that God will strengthen my desire for you," she retorted.

"Wife! What sort of talk is this!"

She was immediately repentant. "I am sorry, Will, but you angered me. You have said that I am over-cold and you wished me warmer, and as I have so many sins, I thought that was very likely one of them." She put her arm through his. "Forgive me, Will. I am unkind to you who are so good to me."

He patted her arm. "Now, Jane, no tears."

She put her hand to her eyes; there were tears there. Why am I so unhappy? she asked herself. What have I to be un-happy about?

"I think a little prayer . . ." said Will; and she wanted to scream at him, though she managed to smile and quickly left him.

After dinner Jane set out to see Mary Blague. Quickly she left Lombard Street and came past the Stocks Market into the Poultry and on to Cheapside where, close to the corner of Bucklersbury, stood Mary's house. That house was like Mary herself; its windows were heavily curtained as though it was necessary to keep from the prying eye what went on behind them.

Mary was in the courtyard waiting for Jane, and she greeted her guest not only with affection but with something like relief. She took Jane into the shop, and when they were there she opened a drawer in which she kept her laces.

"Which is the one you wished to show me?" asked Jane.

Mary held up a piece of beautifully made lace. "It is for the King's exclusive use," she said.

"It must be gratifying," said Jane slyly, "to continue to please the King."

"I can think of no greater pleasure than to serve His Grace," answered Mary primly. "But come, let us to my sitting-room, where we may talk in peace." She took Jane's arm and led her from the shop into a dark passage behind it. "Ah—Danok," said Mary, as a huge man appeared suddenly in the darkness of the passage.

Jane started. She had seen Danok before, but the sight of him never failed to make her shudder. Jane's father had once said that the creature was not in full possession of his wits, but Jane did not believe this; the eyes beneath the shaggy brows were sane enough, though they seemed to look back at experiences which, the saints be praised, were not known to all men. He had been a prisoner in the Tower years ago, and there he had engaged the attention of the torturers. He was without a tongue, and Mary had hinted that other parts of his body had been mutilated. She called him rather coyly her Eunuch. Danok was a strong man for all his disabilities. He worshipped her, Mary said, because when he had been released from prison she had found him wandering along the river bank, bewildered and starving; she had taken pity on him, brought him to her house and made him her servant. Now, she said, he would protect her with his life's blood if need be.

"Danok," said Mary, "go and bring Doll to me."

Danok inclined his head and went off silently; and as Jane mounted the stairs with Mary, an elderly woman of neat ap-

pearance, but who was grotesquely disfigured by the King's
evil, came into the passage and looked up the stairs towards
her mistress and the guest.

"Doll, guard the shop. Let me know if anyone of importance
needs me. I shall be in my sitting-room with Mistress Shore."

"Yes, madam," said Doll; and she went hurriedly to do her
mistress's bidding.

"Now," said Mary, "we shall be comfortable. How nice it is
to see you, dear. There—sit there where I can see your pretty
face. Every time I see you I declare you grow bonnier. I will
show you how I draw my patterns. Mind you, there is not
another soul in London I'd show these to. What if my patterns
were copied, eh? And taken to the King's Master of the Wardrobe! Ah, you think the King would be sure to take mine.
Mayhap. There are some who remember old friends and some
who forget them; but methinks His Grace is of the first kind.
My dear, would you like to try a little of my special wine?"

"Thank you, no. It is too soon after dinner."

Mary went to the window, drew aside the heavy curtain and
looked down into the courtyard. "I do hope none will come to
demand my attention this afternoon. But if that should happen
—you will understand, dearest Jane?"

"Assuredly I will."

"Why—bless my soul." Mary looked over her shoulder and
frowned. "Why—yes. He *is* coming here."

"Who is it?" asked Jane.

"No one you would know, dear. A friend—a rather special
friend. Now had I known he was going to call this afternoon . . ."

"I'll go," said Jane. "You know I can come any afternoon,
and as he is a special friend . . ."

"Indeed you will *not* go, my dear. He is going to the side
door. If you will excuse me just a moment, I will go down and
let him in myself. It is rather an important merchant friend
whom I supply."

"Then if it is business . . ."

"No matter. No matter. We will see what it is he wants. I will bring him up. I am sure you will like to meet him. He is a very charming and amusing man." She went out murmuring apologies and in a few minutes returned, accompanied by a tall richly dressed merchant. Jane and the merchant looked at each other in astonishment.

He spoke first. "By God's blessed Virgin, it is Mistress Shore."

"And you—are the merchant . . ."

"Who came to your husband to buy plate."

"So you know each other already," said Mary. "Well, that is a surprise. A pleasant one, I can see, for you both."

"For me most certainly," he said; and now he was different, bolder than he had been that morning in Lombard Street. Jane felt an exhilaration which manifested itself in the hot blood in her cheeks and the thumping of her heart.

"It is a pleasure," she said, and he kissed her lingeringly in greeting.

He settled himself on the couch very near to Jane. His personality filled the room, which seemed suddenly tawdry and unworthy of him. He crossed his well-shaped legs and let his eyes rest for a second or two on his pointed shoes, but only for a second or two; then they were back on Jane's face. "Indeed," he went on, "I remember well our last meeting. It was our first, too. Pray God there will be many more. I remember well the views you expressed, madam. I remember your criticism of the King."

Mary gasped. "My dear Jane, you could not have been guilty . . ."

"Most guilty," he said, laughing, "but, I suspect, most just. And I told her, Mistress Blague, that she ought to be chief adviser to His Grace."

Mary went off into laughter which seemed exaggerated to Jane.

"I am sure," said Jane coolly, "I should be most unfitted for the post."

"Doubtless," said Mary, "His Grace would take upon himself the task of schooling you."

The merchant leaned forward in his chair; he took Jane's hand and stared down at her palm. "I see great things for you in life. Riches, fame and happiness."

"Do you jest?" asked Jane. "Or do you know of such matters?"

"One does not need to look into your hand to see that joy awaits you. It is writ in your face."

"Jane receives so many compliments," said Mary, "that they mean little to her. She accepts them and forgets them, and remains, withal, the most virtuous lady in the town."

"I read that also," he said.

"In my hands or my face?" asked Jane.

"In both," he told her.

"I will bring refreshment," said Mary; and she went out, leaving them together.

"Did you ever think to see me again?" he asked.

"I did not think I ever should."

"I trust you were saddened at the thought?"

"Mayhap I was. It is often sad to meet someone, to laugh awhile and then never to see that person again as long as one lives."

"But you would have to have some esteem for the person, would you not, to feel so sad?"

"Esteem?" She shrugged her shoulders, no longer embarrassed now that the shock of meeting him was over, but only stimulated. "Scarcely. One might have been amused merely."

"Surely people esteem those who amuse them?"

"It depends, I dare say, on what they set a value."

"How glad I am I came to Mary Blague's this day."

"I could see that you were as surprised as I. But I shall leave you soon as I understand you have come to discuss business."

"I shall be desolate if you do. Jane . . ."

"I think we have known each other scarcely long enough to indulge in the familiarity of Christian names."

"We know much about each other. What matters it if it has taken us a short time to learn it?"

"I know little of you, sir."

"You know you like me. Therefore must you know a good deal."

"You assume a good deal."

"Come, Jane, I am sure you do not smile so sweetly on those you hate. If you do I must think you a hypocrite; and that I could never do."

"Did I then smile so sweetly?"

"Delightfully and in most friendly fashion. I'll warrant you were not displeased to see me. I'll swear you thought when I entered the room, 'God be praised, here is someone to enliven the gloomy hour I must spend with Mary Blague.' "

"Did I show that?"

"You did."

"It was wrong of me."

"It was, and for penance you shall call me Edward and I will call you Jane."

Mary returned, carrying a flagon of wine. Jane noticed that her face was flushed patchily. Mary was behaving oddly this afternoon. Jane saw that she was serving her very best wine. She seemed to have great esteem for Mr. Edward Long, and at the same time be a little afraid of him. As for the man himself, he was perfectly at ease, charming to both of them, but showing most decidedly that it was Jane who interested him.

Mary turned the conversation to court matters and asked Edward Long what was the latest dance.

He explained to Jane: "I serve the court, and therefore know much of what goes on."

Jane laughed, for the wine and the man's company were making her feel very gay. "Then must you have been vastly amused when I told you what I thought of the court and courtiers."

"No. I would not say that you were wrong. As for the

dance . . . Well, I discover a little of these matters. Let us try a step or two." He stood up, towering over Jane.

"In the room adjoining this one I have a lute," said Mary. "Shall I play for you? I am sure that Jane would learn the steps more quickly than I."

Dancing with him, laughing when she made a false step, Jane thought, After this afternoon I shall not see him again. I must not see him again.

There was a sudden knock on the door, and when Mary laid aside her lute and went to it, Jane heard her say : "A customer? I will come down at once." Mary turned to the dancers with a "Pray forgive me. I must go down to the shop. I trust I shall not be kept long."

"We understand perfectly," said Edward, "and we will entertain ourselves until your return." When the door shut on Mary, he went on : "I trust she will be long, though however long she may be, I fear that it will seem to me but a short time." He took Jane's hand. "Jane! Dost know that ever since I set eyes on thee I have thought of little else?"

Jane withdrew her hand. "That will not do, sir. Why, when you left my husband's house you thought nothing of me until you came into this room this afternoon."

"Why do you think thus, Jane?"

"Had you been so eager, would you not have come back to admire the goldsmith's plate—and his wife—and not waited until by chance you were confronted with her?"

"Ah! I did remember that you were the goldsmith's wife, and, thought I, 'If only it were as easy to possess his wife as his plate!' "

"You are over-forward, sir, and I like it not." Jane's manner was very cool now.

"Then pray forgive me, for, believe me, I am not myself this afternoon."

"I trust you are not. I do not like these professions of affection on such short acquaintance. But mayhap you go to court and there learn your manners."

"Yet would you like court ways, did you know them."

"I shall never like the light and easy way in which court manners assume it is possible, nay simple, to seduce the honest wives of honest citizens."

"I am heartily in agreement with you, Jane."

"Then shall we talk of other matters?"

"Pray let us. What shall it be? The recent wars? The weather? Will the plague return to London this summer, think you?"

Jane laughed. "Can you not think of more pleasant subjects?"

"The only subject I can entertain, with you before me, is such that, while wholly pleasant to me, may offend your pretty ears."

She regarded him shrewdly. "When you were in my husband's house you played the merchant to perfection. Your eyes said you were a thousandfold more interested in his goods than in his wife. But now, in another house you play the . . ."

"What would I play?"

"Am I being presumptuous when I say you would play the lover?"

"It is a matter of simple logic, I fear, Jane. Why, even the most hard-headed merchant must long to do that when he is face to face with Jane Shore."

"And it would seem to me that it is a part familiar to you."

"What gave you such impression, Jane?"

"I cannot but believe that the merchant who, before he met me, had never had the time nor inclination to play lover, would stammer a little, would not express himself in such a practised way."

"But you must see that I am no ordinary man. Look at me and tell me that you do."

"I see a man with merry eyes which like to laugh. I see a man who loves good wine—and Mary Blague's best is hardly good enough for you. You love gaiety and pleasure."

"Ah, I see I must tread warily with you."

"You must tread as you please."

"Then I will, Jane." He was laughing as he seized her and bent his face down to hers. She was angry—not, she realised, because he wished to make love to her, but that he should do it casually on this their second meeting.

"I beg of you to release me at once," she said with dignity.

He was quick to see that her anger was real. "I pray you will forgive me," he said meekly.

"And I pray that you will tell Mary I had to leave at once."

"Allow me a few words of explanation."

"There can be no explanation." She went into the next room where she had laid her cape. He followed her and stood watching her almost humbly.

"I never wish to see you again," she told him. She was trembling, for decidedly this was not true. He had changed her from the moment she had first seen him. She felt that if she had never known him she might eventually have learned contentment; now she never would. She would remember him all her life—his handsome face, his great figure and his merry laughter. She knew she was in great danger. She knew her own weakness; he had made her aware of that in the last half-hour. She must run quickly, while she had the power to run. His virility, his overwhelming manliness, could not belong to one indifferent to women; such grace and charm, such an easy way of saying the things one wanted to hear, could only grow out of long practice. He was as profligate as Hastings. But he was more dangerous, for already, after a small taste of his company, she was finding her will to resist him growing very weak indeed.

He had laid a hand on her shoulder and was saying: "I have been over-forward. Believe me when I tell you I had no intention of being so. You must forgive me if the sight of you threw me momentarily off my balance. Say you'll be friends or I shall die of melancholy. Put aside your cape and give me one more chance."

"Chance for what?"

"That we may know each other better. That we may be friends."

"What good could it do us to be friends?"

"Think you then that you could quickly feel something stronger than friendship for me?"

"If that were so, what good could it do?" She turned to him suddenly, searching his face for some hint of laughter; there was none, only a deadly seriousness.

He said: "Jane, I would be honest with you. Had I only but seen you before you met the goldsmith! But what is to be, will be. Yet cannot a poor man take the crumbs which fall from the rich man's table?"

"I understand you not."

"Lovers we cannot be, for I see you are a virtuous woman. I also would be virtuous, but alas! my flesh is weak. Jane, give me your friendship. That I will cherish."

Jane let her hood fall on to the stool where she had laid it when she came in. She said: "Let us return to the other room, or Mary will wonder why we left it."

"I am forgiven then?"

"You are. But pray remember that I will not have a repetition of such conduct."

"I will remember it, Jane."

They looked at each other suddenly and burst into laughter. Jane did not know why she laughed, except that being with him had such an effect upon her that she wanted to laugh for sheer happiness.

"This is no matter for laughter," she said, with an attempt at severity.

"Of a certainty it is," he assured her. "For it was the laughter of happiness, Jane. I am happy because I am forgiven."

"Doubtless you think me a prudish woman?"

"I could never look into your eyes and think that. There is great warmth in you, Jane, for the lucky man who could kindle the fire."

"Once, before my marriage, I had a most unhappy experience," she said. "It might well have proved disastrous. I was all but abducted; and ever since that day I have felt the need to tread cautiously."

"You poor child! The blackguard should have been shut up in the Tower."

"That is what I think. But it seems he is a gentleman of the court."

"Would I knew his name!"

"It would avail you little if you did. He was of high rank."

"Pray tell me, Jane."

"I believe him to be Lord Hastings."

"The knave!"

"So say I, and still tremble to think of what might have been my lot had his plans succeeded."

" 'Tis the penalty of so much beauty." He went on gently: "Have no such fear of me. I would not undertake such knavery. Were I so blessed that you should come to me, it should be willingly or not at all."

"There is no question of what you suggest. You forget I am already a wife."

"I would I could forget it."

"So now you understand my recent anger. That experience has put me on my guard against all seducers."

"There is a world of difference between lust and love."

"One can be born in a moment," she said slowly. "The other needs longer and more arduous labour."

"There you are wrong, Jane. There are times when love is born more swift than lust."

"They are twins, then, and mayhap it is difficult to tell the two apart. Mary Blague returns, methinks. Now I shall go."

"Then I shall escort you back to Lombard Street."

"Pray do not."

"I would obey your wishes in all things, Jane."

"Then I will go alone. It is only after dark I fear the streets."

"Jane, we shall meet again."

"I think this should be our last meeting."

Mary was hesitating at the door; she coughed, waited a while and then came in.

"Mary," said Jane, "it grows late and I must go home."

Mary looked from one to the other.

"She would go alone," said Edward.

"And leave you two to discuss your business together," said Jane.

Hurrying through the streets, she felt bewildered; and when she was back in Lombard Street, Kate's inquisitive glances irritated her; and when the goldsmith laid his hands upon her she found it difficult not to implore him to leave her alone.

*   *   *   *   *

Mary Blague came hurrying out of the house near the waterfront. A cape, with an all-concealing hood, covered her from head to foot. She must quickly find a waterman to row her across, for she was always relieved when she reached the other side of the water. Time after time she had asked herself why she did not go out of business and live the life of a lady, perhaps in some village well out of London, such as Bethnal Green or Brentford—or mayhap farther out still, into Sussex or Surrey. But she knew that, had this really been her wish, she could have set about doing it to-morrow. She could not, however, bring herself to give up her profitable business. Lace-woman to the King? Well, yes; and there was money to be made in lace if you had the patronage of those of high rank. But there were other and more easy ways of earning money; and Mary Blague was first a business woman whatever else she might be.

In Cheapside she was the respected lace-woman, almost as highly placed as the mercers and the grocers, though, of course, not as the goldsmiths. But Will Shore himself could scarcely be more wealthy than she was. In Cheapside, then, Mary Blague dined out and entertained all the most respected of her neighbours. But it was in Southwark, as Mistress Bee, that she wielded a greater power. To her belonged the roomy house, the girls who worked for her. There was not one of them who, on the orders of Mistress Bee, could not be turned out on the streets to starve. She liked to reflect on that, for, almost more than money, she loved power.

At fifteen Mary had come to London from the country home where she was the twelfth child of needy parents. She was to be the companion of an aunt who had a little money laid by, and Mary had hoped that one day the money would come to her. But when her eyes had been opened to City ways, she had learned that there were more speedy methods of acquiring wealth than awaiting the death of an old lady whose capital was only large in the eyes of Mary's needy parents.

Matters had not gone well at first. There had been a love affair, a lover who fled, a child born in a house very like the one she now owned in Southwark, a spell of working for a while in that house; and then had followed a clever stroke of business involving a little blackmail. Mary did not like blackmail, for she knew it to be dangerous; but this was so simple. It was the case of a rich young merchant with a newly married wife. "Give me the money to set myself up in a little lace-shop, and you shall never hear from me again." This was done and the lace-shop prospered, and then the Southwark house had come into being; and the latter gave her greater pleasure than the former. It brought greater sums of money and greater power. She derived much pleasure from shaping the lives of those about her. Many a young girl came to her house in Cheapside to learn lace-making; some came as servants. How simple to put temptation in their way! And how quickly they responded to her sympathetic advice! "I know of a way to help you. There is a house in Southwark . . ." And what life had done to Mary Blague all those years ago, Mary would let it do to these girls. She was for ever on the lookout for victims. And now—Jane Shore.

It was an interesting life Mary led. Cleverly she kept her two existences apart; it was amusing to be two different people. There was only one person in Cheapside who knew the connection between the lace-woman and the brothel-keeper. This was Danok, and he could never speak of it to any.

A waterman came towards her; he brought his boat to the stairs and she got hurriedly into it; very soon she was on the north side of the river. She loosened her cloak. She had left Mistress Bee on the south side of the Thames.

She was smiling, for she was thinking now of the attractive man who had asked her to help him with Jane. For none other, she thought, would I have allowed my house in Cheapside to be used to such purpose.

Her eyes were wistful; she was wishing she had Jane's youth and beauty, just as though she were a foolish sentimental girl. Well, he would soon tire of Jane, and then when the goldsmith learned of his wife's frailty and mayhap turned from her, that good business woman, Mary Blague, would be waiting to help her.

She turned into Bucklersbury and drawing her cloak round her, as though by so doing she could transform herself once more from Mary Blague to Mistress Bee, she went quickly down the stone stairs and into a shop.

She and Leppus knew each other. Perhaps he wondered why she should make so many strange purchases in his shop. It did not matter. Let Leppus look to his own affairs. There was doubtless much he might wish to hide.

He came forward as she entered. A hideous little black beetle, she thought him. His hook nose twitched.

"Good-day to you, lady. What can I do for you this day?"

She followed him through to the room behind the shop. He sat on his high stool and peered at her.

"I want some of your elixir of life," she said.

"The rejuvenating mixture! My elixir of life! For life is love and love is life, lady. My elixir costs good money, and it is of greater worth than money, is it not? It makes the aged young."

"Yes, yes. Let me have it, please."

"I will. But first tell me, is it for a lady or a gentleman?"

"Does that make any difference?"

"But how can I whisper the magic into it if I do not know? It is different for a man and a woman."

"It is for a woman, then."

"Is she young or old—or is she getting to that state when we may not ask her age?"

Was he insolent or was it necessary that he should know?

"She is young," she snapped.

"Is it not sad that we should force in the young that which should come naturally?"

"Give me the powder, please. I am busy and must hurry. Here is the money."

But it was useless to try to hurry him. She sensed in him that love of power that she understood so well because she shared it.

"Money!" he said, flashing his beady eyes upon her so that they peered between the drooping eyebrows which hung over them like a creeping plant over the windows of a deserted house. "What is money to an artist such as I am!"

He was powerful, she knew. He was the possessor of many strange secrets. She wished him to know that she understood his power and respected it; but at the same time she wished him to respect hers.

"This is for a person of some importance."

"Ah, good lady, to the starving dog the beggar with a crust of bread is of importance. To the apprentice, so is the humble tradesman. Importance is relative, and you must know that I have served His Grace the King."

Mary's cheeks flushed suddenly. A retort came to her lips, but she repressed it.

"Come," said Leppus slyly, "you are angry with me. Have I said aught to distress you? Why, from the look of you one would think the little love drink was for another who charms your lover."

Was it true that he saw with the eyes of a wizard? She liked the uncanny atmosphere of his shop even less to-day than usual.

"I will pay you and take up no more of your time," she said.

"As you will." He stretched out his hollow palm.

She felt hot and flustered as she turned into the Poultry and hurried towards Lombard Street; though it was not with

Leppus she was angry, but with Jane Shore. The sly creature, she thought, I hate her. All the same, she is the fairest female I ever clapped eyes on, and one day she is going to be very useful to me.

Will was just riding out when she reached his house. He dismounted to greet her. "This is unfortunate," he said courteously. "I have to ride out to a customer. You will find Jane in." When Mary said she would go in to see her, Will hesitated for a while and then added: "She seems listless of late. I wonder if aught ails her. Mayhap you could do something to cheer her."

"Be assured that I will do my best," she told him.

Jane received her in the parlour. The girl was pale. No wonder! Doubtless she had suffered many a sleepless night. Well, well, my chuck, thought Mary, you cannot have your pleasure and keep your virtue, though doubtless a little beauty such as you thinks there may be some way of doing it.

"It is long since I saw you," said Mary. "Why did you not come yester eve? I was expecting you."

"Mary—I cannot come."

Mary sat on a stool and arranged her cape about her. "I would not wish to ask what you might not wish to tell," she said. "But is it because of a certain person that you stay away?"

Jane burst out: "Every day I come he is there."

"He is there every day in the hope of seeing you. I am sorry —sorry that mine should have been the house where you should meet. It places me most awkwardly."

"Oh, Mary, it was no fault of yours. It was the purest accident. Tell me—how is he?"

"Sad of heart because you do not come to meet him."

"I cannot meet him, Mary. I dare not. You are my friend, Mary, and glad I am that none but you knows—nor ever shall."

"Your secret is safe with me. You love him, do you not?"

"I do, Mary. If I had never gone to your home that day . . ."

"It is sad, when love comes, to say it nay. But you are right, my dear. You are a wife. There is naught to be said. You will not see him again."

"I must not. The other day I took up my cloak and all but ran to your house. Oh, Mary, I am a wicked woman. I think of him continually. I see his face. I hear his laughter. Oh, Mary, what am I to do?"

"My dear child, you are overwrought."

"There is so much wickedness in me, I fear. This day I all but confessed this wild and unreasoning thing. . . . I almost confessed it to Will."

"What good would that do you or Will? Now listen. Come to me to-morrow. Come early. If he comes also we will not let him in. There you can unburden your heart to me and I will give you my advice for what it is worth."

"Mary, you would promise not to let him in?"

"For shame! You look at me as though you are begging me to let him in."

"I dare not see him. I dare not listen to him. Mary, try to understand what has happened to me. It is true I have met him but three times at your house . . . and once here, and yet . . ."

"Hush! Come to-morrow and we will talk."

"You are a good friend to me, Mary."

Aye, thought Mary; and to him also. She touched the little packet in her pocket, and a deep frustrated rage swept over her. Why should Mary Blague have to accept the insults of old Leppus for the sake of this girl? She was in no need of the old magician's elixir. Never mind. Mary Blague could wait, and one day there would be no need for her to accept insults on account of Jane Shore.

*   *   *   *   *

In Mary's parlour she and Jane sat looking at one another. Each was tense and waiting. Jane was thinking, Will he come? If he does, I shall not see him. Mary thought, There she sits feigning primness. She will say Nay with her lips and Yes with her eyes. I know her sort. And doubtless he doth too.

"You will take a little wine, my dear?"

"No, thank you. Listen! Mary! Someone is in the court-yard." Jane jumped up and went to the window. She stood there looking down on him. How unfair that she had been married so early to the goldsmith!

Mary said in an exasperated voice: "I will go and send him away. I told him not to come."

"Yes," said Jane, "send him away."

Jane turned from the window. She thought wretchedly over the past. She hated afresh the man Hastings who was respon-sible for her marriage, for never would she have married Will but for that planned abduction. More than anyone on earth she hated Hastings. But for him she would be free now. It would not be necessary to send her lover away. Surely it would do no harm to see him once more.

"Mary," she called; but Mary had already gone.

She thought of him, how he had looked the last time they had met here in this very room; he had talked to her very earnestly then; that was after he had dismissed Mary with such gay assurance, such charming arrogance, that it might have been his house they were in instead of Mary's. And Mary had gone meekly, though she had been perplexed and doubtful. Then he had pleaded with her; he had wished her to leave Will, to go away with him. She had wavered and all but agreed, so was she bewitched by him; and then, wrenching herself free, she made a vow that she would not see him again. He was below now, and so weak was she that in spite of that vow she was saying to herself, Just once more!

The door opened and he came into the room.

"So you would conspire with Mary Blague to keep us apart?" he demanded reproachfully. He lifted her in his arms.

"Put me down," she begged. But he did not, and she was still in his arms when Mary came in.

"Jane, you must not blame me," said Mary.

"I do not, Mary."

He smiled, first at Jane, then at Mary. "Blame? Who is to be blamed for love such as this? And listen. I'll not be kept away again, I swear it."

"Let us have some wine," said Mary faintly.

"Yes, good friend," said Edward, "let us have some wine." Mary poured it out, watching them.

"Drink this," she said. " 'Twill help you to discuss your troubles."

"Since when was love a trouble?" asked Edward.

"You are right," said Mary quickly. "Love is no trouble . . . only a joy. . . ."

While it lasts, she thought. Let him tire of her quickly. Then, Jane Shore, it will be my turn.

"A joy indeed," he said. "What folly it is to love and not to love!"

"Please do not speak of it now," pleaded Jane.

"Mary knows, does she not? You know, Mary, of this that has happened to us."

"I do. I reproach myself that it is in my house that you have met."

"You may cease to reproach yourself," he told her. "Rather rejoice with us."

"I cannot forget what I have done in allowing . . ."

"Depend upon it, we shall not forget you." He went to the table and poured more wine. He said: "You may go now."

Mary went. Jane hardly noticed her going, for a strange light-headedness was stealing over her. Her eyes were dilated, her body tingled.

He sat close to her and took her hands. "Jane, you know I'll not let you go from me."

"But you must," she said weakly.

"Why? Can you say you do not love me?"

"No, but . . ."

"Then that is enough."

"You forget I have a husband. He is a good man and kind to me."

"I will be kind to you."

"I could not hurt him."

"Then will you hurt me? You cannot, I tell you. When my arms are about you, you'll not be able to."

"You frighten me. You look so strange."

"It is my love for you that you see in my face."

"It is great, is it not?"

"So great that there is no denying it. Listen to me, Jane. We will go from here together. . . . You need never go back to his house. I will give you such a house that . . ."

"Say no more. I must go now, Edward. I begin to feel so strange. . . ."

"Strange, dearest?"

"So light-headed, so gay . . . and very happy. I must go. I know I must. This must be the end of our friendship. I will say good-bye now. Do not look at me. Do not touch me."

She heard his laughter close to her ear as he lifted her up.

"Look at me," he commanded. "Look at me, sweet Jane, and then tell me that I must never see your face again."

"Oh, Edward, I cannot. You should have let me go."

"And now that I have not done so?" He laid his lips against her cheek. "What now, Jane?"

She thought wildly, This is what I always wanted. This is why I fought as hard as I could against marriage with Will. If only I had waited!

But this was no time for regretting the past, for the present was filled with joy and pleasure waiting to be explored. She knew now that she had gone too far to turn back. She had not the will to turn back.

"Jane," he said, "you must not be afraid. You would not wish to escape now!"

She shook her head; his voice, low with passion, seemed to fill the room. "No, you must not be afraid, Jane. There is nothing but this, our world inside the four walls of this house, which has become more beautiful than any palace because it holds us two."

He kissed her, and his kiss was slow and gentle; it warmed

swiftly, and then it was as though she were scorched with the white-hot passion that was in him.

"You cannot say No to this, Jane," he said. "You cannot say No to me."

*   *   *   *   *

Will Shore knocked at the door of Mary Blague's house. Danok let him in and conducted him to the parlour beyond the shop. Will waited there nervously until Mary appeared.

"My good friend," cried Mary, "how pleasant to see you! But you look worried. What ails you?"

"I am going out on business," explained Will, "so I looked in on my way. It is about Jane. You are her friend. I thought that you might help me."

"I will tell my servant to bring us wine. Then we will talk in peace."

When the wine was brought, Will said: "Methinks Jane is ill. Of late she has behaved with such oddness that is beyond my understanding."

"Since when was this?"

"For some weeks. But of late her malady seems to have taken a different turn. It seemed to start a few days ago, after she had returned from your hospitality. She came into the house, and I thought at once that she was sickening for something. She went straight to her bed. She seemed so wild, and when I asked her if aught ailed her she said she felt very sick indeed. I wanted to send for a physician, to which she said she thought there was little a physician could do for her. I tried to soothe her but my caresses seemed but to aggravate the malady. She has grown melancholy. I swear it is a fever that besets her. What can I do?"

"Does she weep much?"

"She does. Then I have heard her laughing with that maid of hers. It is a wild sort of laughter. I seem to upset her. She trembles beside me when abed at night, and if I would as much as touch her, she bursts into tears."

"And it has gone on for a week. It is indeed too long."

Indeed it was too long, she thought, for Jane's lover was an impatient man, apt to be angry with those to whom no blame should be attached; and Mary was fearful of his anger.

"It seems to me that Jane needs a little gaiety to forget her melancholy. Will you forgive my forwardness if I say what is in my mind?"

"*Your* forwardness, Mary! You are the most reserved of ladies."

"Then you will know that what I say now is but to help you. What Jane needs is a child. It is a strange need that comes to women. Give her a child and she will forget her melancholy. But first we must try to cheer her. Now, you know that I have friends at court. There is to be a ball, and I—as the King's lace-woman—have an invitation to go. I may take one friend, and I suggest it shall be Jane. You will see that the thought of a grand occasion will cheer her. And then when you have her gay and happy . . . forgive my lack of discretion, dear friend . . . well, what I mean is this : I have heard it said that a contented woman is more likely to conceive. . . ."

The goldsmith was grateful. "You are indeed a friend, Mary," he said fervently.

"Let us hope that I may be fortunate enough to help my friends when they need me. Now if you will excuse me, I will go to your house and see Jane at once. I will tell her of the ball, and doubtless you will see a change in her when you return."

The goldsmith left, and Mary, slipping on her cloak, thought, I should have been a diplomat so cleverly do I manage the affairs of others. I had to get Jane to the ball, and now I have without the least difficulty obtained her husband's consent.

She found Jane in her bedroom with Kate, who was at once dismissed.

Jane wept when Kate had gone. "It is such a relief," she said, "to be with someone who knows me for what I am. You have seen him?"

"He comes every day and asks for you. He regrets that he ever let you go."

Jane smiled wanly. "He would have had me leave there and then with him. Oh, Mary, I must talk of it to someone, or I shall go mad. I cannot think what happened to me. I love . . . Of course I love him, but I believed myself capable of remembering my duty to Will and my marriage vows. And then . . . I was so strangely without resistance. I never thought of the wrong I was doing Will . . . until afterwards."

"I believe," said Mary wryly, "it is often thus. It *is* afterwards that realisation comes. But," she added maliciously, "you will never see him again, will you? You betrayed your husband once and are determined not to do so again."

"Oh, I am," said Jane sadly.

"That is very commendable. Now you cannot live all your life in melancholy. How would you like to go to a court ball?"

"A court ball? But how could I?"

Momentarily, thought Mary, she has forgotten her lover.

"You know, my dear, that I have connections at court. I have been invited and may take a friend."

"It . . . it would be interesting, but I have no heart for it."

"Then you shall come with me."

Jane's eyes had begun to sparkle. Had he not said that he had business at the court? "Mary . . . what could I wear . . . if I went?"

"You have many beautiful dresses in your cupboards."

"But for the court!"

"We will see what can be done. A stitch or two here, a touch there . . . and one of your gowns will pass at court."

"Mary, you are a good friend to me."

When Mary left she met Will coming in.

"How did you leave her?" he asked eagerly.

"Excited at the prospect of a ball. Depend upon it, all will go as it should."

"May the Virgin bless you, Mary," said Will.

And Mary went on her way, smiling.

*　　　*　　　*　　　*　　　*

In Mary's bedroom Jane was dressing for the ball. During the last few days she had been constantly in Mary's company. They had taken the grandest of her dresses and with some of Mary's fine lace had renovated it into something worthy of the court. Mary had been filled with an inner excitement which bubbled over now and then into bursts of laughter which she did not seem to be able to control. Jane thought she knew the reason. It was because Edward would be at the ball. He would have received an invitation just as Mary had.

A chariot, Mary had explained, would call at the house and take them to Westminster Palace.

"A chariot!" Jane had cried when she first heard of this. "Mary, you must have great influence at court."

Now here they were, Jane magnificent and beautiful in her gown, and Mary slightly more magnificent but much less beautiful in hers. When the chariot arrived, the driver and footman treated them with great respect, and Jane had never felt such a grand lady in all her life.

As they drove into the Palace yard, men in royal livery ran to their assistance. What would they say, wondered Jane, if they knew that these seemingly great ladies were but the King's lace-woman and her friend the goldsmith's wife?

It mattered not, for now they were in the great hall, and never in all her life had Jane seen such magnificence. The hangings were of richest velvet and cloth of gold. Jewels sparkled on the clothes of brilliantly clad men and women. Ah, thought Jane, overawed and feeling very insignificant now, they could not have mistaken us for anything but the lace-woman and goldsmith's wife.

But people looked at Jane, for her beauty was remarkable.

"When shall we see the King and Queen?" she whispered.

"Ere long, I think," whispered Mary in her turn. "Look

about you at the great. See you the fair frail lady yonder? That is the Duchess of Clarence and with her her husband the Duke."

"She is very lovely," said Jane.

"She looks not long for this world. She is pale as a lily."

"And he is red as a peony."

"He is overfond of the wine. But do not talk so loudly, Jane."

"I had forgotten. We are at court, and must keep our eyes open, our ears alert and voices unheard. Tell me, who is the pale slender young man?"

"Where?"

"There, next the Duke."

"That is Richard Duke of Gloucester, brother to Clarence and the King."

"I wish the Queen would come. I long to see her."

"You will. Ah—they are coming now."

The rumble of voices had been replaced by silence, startling in its suddenness. It was broken sharply when the heralds at the door blew three blasts on their trumpets.

"Bow your head," whispered Mary. "They are coming now."

Jane bowed, but could not resist peering upwards to see them. The Queen was tall, and her classical features were perfectly moulded; she had a cold face and her yellow hair was her greatest beauty.

And with her—the King. Jane stared at the great figure which dominated the hall. She swayed a little towards Mary, but Mary was waiting for her, and caught her arm to steady her. The hall seemed to swing round Jane, and she was but vaguely aware of the blur of faces and the brilliant colours. It could not be, she told herself again and again. It was just a startling resemblance.

"Mary," she stammered. "I—I——"

Mary hastily put a finger to her lips. "Hush!" warned Mary.

Jane turned her eyes once more upon that magnificent figure that was sparkling with the costliest jewels. Every eye in the hall was upon him. There were diamonds in his coat and rubies

at his throat. Jane, bewildered, had turned to Mary. She looked into the woman's face and understood. Mary knew. Mary had known all the time. Jane remembered how he had said to Mary in her own house, "You may go now." She remembered Mary's sycophantic laughter. Jane was dizzy with this sudden, frightening realisation.

A moment ago she had felt she would faint; now she was angry. The deception he had practised on her was cruel and humiliating. She wanted to run out of the palace and hide herself. She felt now that she would never be able to escape the shame which enveloped her. Her lover had turned out to be the notorious rake, the man who had but to beckon to the women of London—or York or Leicester for that matter—to have them run to him willingly. How she had despised those women—and now she had discovered that she was one of them. The King had come disguised to Jane Shore as he had to dozens before her; he had beckoned and willingly had she gone to him.

Her cheeks flaming, she remembered their conversations. What had she said of the King? Enough to send her to prison doubtless. She was glad. She had meant every word of it. She hated him now as fiercely as she had loved him. He was not only a rake but a liar; and she had allowed him to amuse himself as lightly with her as he had done with so many others.

She turned to Mary angrily. "You knew all the time. You lied to me."

"Lower your voice, Jane. People look your way."

"I wish to go home," said Jane. "I wish to go home at once. How do you think I can endure to stay here when . . ."

"Dear Jane, be sensible, you cannot go now."

"I must and I will. I wish never to see him again."

"There is no shame in being loved by the King. There is scarce a woman here who would not give all she possesses to change places with you."

"He ordered you to bring me here to-night, did he not?"
Mary nodded.

"He commanded you to lure me to your house?"

"He thought it would make a good meeting place."

"What a King is this," cried Jane bitterly, "who spends his time planning the seduction of his subjects!"

"Hush! Hush! You attract attention with this wild talk."

"Oh, Mary, I know you are not to blame. You were helpless. He just used you. I hate him."

"To hate the King is treason. You must be silent, Jane."

"I wish to go home."

"Wait! The King will start the dance. None can leave now. We should be noticed. Besides—he comes this way."

It was true. People drew back as he passed. He was going to choose a partner with whom to start the dance—and he was coming towards the spot where Jane and Mary stood.

"Bow," whispered Mary. She herself curtseyed low. Jane bent her head.

He laughed his easy pleasant laugh that Jane knew so well.

"Well, Jane," he said, "there was no other way, you know. It had to be."

Jane was too hurt and bewildered by her discovery, too humiliated, too wretched in her newly found knowledge of his real character to be overawed by him. She did not think of him as the King, but simply as the man who had deceived and betrayed her.

She looked at him coldly. "I am about to leave," she said.

"No. You will stay. I command you to stay."

He was the same man who had made love to her in Mary Blague's house, yet there was a difference. He had put on a new arrogance; his eyes were tender but there was a ruthlessness about his mouth even while he smiled at her. Her mood had softened, for he had taken her hand, and at his touch she realised afresh that it mattered not who he was—King or commoner—she loved him, and to be with him brought her such happiness as she could never know away from him. He saw her hesitation and smiled, certain of his power over her.

"Come," he said, "we will start the dance, you and I."

"I—to dance with you—with the King?"

"Do not think of me as your King, Jane, but as the man who most humbly loves you."

She allowed him to lead her to the centre of the hall. The whole court knew what this scene meant, for Edward had never been reticent about his love affairs. Obviously this lovely girl had been brought to court because the King had found her somewhere and she had caught his fancy. It had happened before; it would happen again. No one was very surprised, only amused and interested. This time though, it was whispered, she was indeed a beauty. They made bets as to how long she would hold the King's favour. Three months, some suggested, for she was indeed a charming creature. *Three* months? To whom had Edward the Fourth ever remained constant for more than one?

Edward was whispering passionately as they danced: "Jane, why did you stay away so long? Why do you turn your face from me?"

"I never meant to see you again," she answered. "I never shall—after to-night. I wish to go as soon as I can. Mary was wrong to bring me here. Perhaps you will be so good as to release me after this dance."

"You are very angry, are you not?" he said sadly. "It is the first time I have ever seen you angry."

Her voice trembled. "I would not have believed you could have so deceived me."

"It was necessary, Jane."

"Necessary? To come to my husband's house disguised as a merchant, to—trap me as you did?"

"But, Jane, I am your lover. I will be your lover for ever. And you were willing, were you not?"

"To my shame, yes."

"Nay, to your delight and mine. Know this: I have scarce slept at all since that day when you and I were truly lovers. You shall not leave my side again."

"You could not make me stay. You could not do that."

He laughed. "What if I command it? I remember well, Mistress Shore, you have said some treasonable things of me."

"And right glad I am of it," she flashed at him. "I declared my abhorrence of the King's light manner of living, and I do so again."

"It would not have been light had he met you years ago. He was seeking you, Jane. Do you not understand that?"

Jane laughed, for that stimulating excitement was creeping over her. She must face the truth. She cared for nothing except that she might stay beside him.

"You do not expect me to believe that—Your Grace. I suppose I must remember to call you that now, must I not?"

"If you should forget the respect due to us," he said in a tone of affected dignity, "rest assured we should not find it in our hearts to send you to the dungeons. The rats would make indifferent bed-fellows, and, by the Virgin, I know of a better one for you."

"You are different," she said sadly. "You now speak lightly of what was once a sacred matter."

"If I seem light," he answered soberly, "it is but because I fear to have lost your esteem, and I joke to hide my fears. Jane, you loved a merchant. Cannot you love a King?"

"You seemed so sincere," she said, "and it is alarming to discover you but played a part."

"I but put on airs with garments of state. Divest me of these and beneath them you will find the same man who loved you so completely. But we cannot talk here. We will slip away together where we may be quiet."

"I do not wish to go," cried Jane in alarm. "I will stay here, and when this dance is done——"

His grip on her fingers tightened. "Nevertheless, Jane, you *shall* come. I shall not let you go until you have listened to me. Come this way."

His eyes glittered as they met hers. She was afraid of him, yet the fascination of him was as strong as ever. He held her fingers firmly and drew her towards a door which led out of the hall. She was hot with shame, for she knew that everyone in the hall was watching their withdrawal. What thought the Queen?

The beautiful Queen whom he had met so romantically in Whittlebury Forest, whom he had loved so blindly that, against the wishes of his counsellors, he had married her—what did she think of this unconventional behaviour with the wife of a goldsmith?

He drew her into a small room hung with rich tapestry. On the floor was a carpet of deep blue embroidered with golden thread. Even in her present state of mind Jane was not insensible to the extreme luxury of this room. On the deep window seats were exquisitely embroidered cushions; and the tapestry-covered seat with its ornate canopy led her to believe that this was one of the King's less formal presence chambers. The room was perfumed with musk and sweet herbs.

The King shut the door and leaned against it, watching her closely. "Here," he said, "we may have peace for a while, but first I will kiss you." This he did with great warmth. "Now you must tell me that you love me," he added.

She shook her head in distress. "I cannot say. I have just discovered that you have deceived me."

"You shall forget that discovery in another. You shall learn, my sweet Jane, that no matter who I am, you love me."

"You have been led by many to believe yourself irresistible, I know," she told him coolly.

"You were one of them," he retorted. He ran his hands caressingly over her. "Do not blame me for my birth, Jane."

"It was a cruel thing to do and I cannot forget it. To you it seemed amusing. It has not been so to me. How can you ask me to love you—*you* of whom they say, 'Citizens, hide your wives and daughters, for the King comes this way'? That is you —the King. The seducer of women. And I despised them for falling so readily to your will. Do you not understand? I am so shamed—so humiliated. I want to go away—and die."

He said gently: "They fell in love with my rank, dearest Jane. There is no shame in what you did, sweetheart. I beg of you to forget my past sins, for I love you truly. It will be different now. What need of other women? Dost not know that while I flitted hither and thither like a butterfly testing the flowers, 'twas for Jane I searched?" He kissed her bare shoulders. "Forget all that has gone before. 'Tis over and done. I have found you, Jane."

How she longed to believe him! How plausible he was! Common sense whispered, "To how many has he said those words before?" But the passion which the touch of his hands could arouse in her answered, "What matters that? What matters anything as long as you can be with him even for an hour?"

She drew away from him. "It must not be."

"Nevertheless it shall be."

"You mean—you would force me?"

"Never have I forced a woman yet. Should I begin with her I love best of all?"

"Then I shall never see you again after this night."

"Believe it not, Jane. To-morrow morning, the first face you shall see will be mine beside you on the pillow. Thus shall it be throughout our lives. Apartments have been prepared for you here in the palace, for in truth I cannot live without you."

"I will not stay."

He smiled at her. "You cannot still doubt that you and I were meant for one another." He laid his hands on her shoulders. "See how you tremble at my touch. Your lips say, 'I must go home.' But what say your eyes? What says your trembling body? 'Take me, Edward. Take me.' That is what *you* say, Jane. No matter what those sweet lips falsely utter. And so shall it be. I will kiss the Nay from your lips, until they cry Yea. Then wilt thou be all mine."

"You will release me at once," she said with dignity.

His dignity matched hers. "Never fear that I shall do aught but at your will."

"Then I shall go home this night."

"It shall be as you say. But you shall wait until the ball is over. Then a chariot shall take you back with Mary Blague. You may stay the night in her house instead of in your lover's arms. It is for you to say."

"I could never be happy with you now, my lord."

"Call me Edward as you did when you lay in my arms. Say that again, only call me Edward."

"I could never be happy with you now, Edward."

"You will never be happy without me. So you will go back to your husband. It is not for virtue's sake. For what virtue is there in giving him your favours as the price he asked for marriage? You sell yourself to him, Jane; to me you would give. Let not your eyes be blinded. Love is not for sale. Think on that, Jane."

"He tries so hard to please and I have made my vows."

"And did you make them willingly? I swear you never loved him."

"None but thee have I ever loved."

"Why, bless you, Jane. That's true, I know. Cast away your doubts. Come to me and be my love for ever. What joy we will know! There is nothing in this kingdom you could ask and I would not give it. Deny me not, Jane, for if you do, a most melancholy man must sit upon the throne of England."

"You charm me with your words, your looks, your smiles. But I cannot. I *will* go to-night."

"I have said a chariot shall take you back as it brought you. But listen, Jane. To-morrow—just before the hour of five, another chariot will wait outside a certain house in Lombard Street, and in it will wait a very anxious lover. An you come not to him to-morrow, then on the next day will he wait—and the next and the next—so humble is he, so longing for you. Can you disappoint him, sweetheart? Can you stay in the dull house and sell yourself to one so unworthy? Jane, it is immoral."

They laughed together. "You make me forget you are the King," she said.

"I make you remember that I am your lover?"

She nodded. "I would I knew what I should do. But you bewilder me. You make me wretched and happy in turns. I shall never know true peace again."

"I promise you shall find it in my arms."

"I must go to-night."

"It is for you to decide. Come, we must return to the hall. You may forget I am your King; others will not."

Every eye was on her. Smiles came her way. She was at first embarrassed, but Edward's ease of manner brushed embarrassment aside. He took her first to the Queen, who was graciousness itself. It was difficult to believe she knew that she was being introduced to her husband's mistress.

"Mistress Shore, Your Grace," said Edward with nonchalance. "Methinks you will like each other well."

The Queen smiled a cold smile and begged Jane to rise. She said she hoped Jane was enjoying the ball.

Jane looked into the face of the woman who seven years before had enchanted Edward. There was no sign of jealousy in the cold blue-grey eyes; there was only appraisal. Elizabeth Woodville was accustomed to her husband's mistresses; their presence at court did not worry her, for she had kept her own influence over him since their first romantic meeting. She had bent him to her will then, and she continued to do so. It was of no lasting importance that she shared her influence with the various women of his fancy from time to time.

She liked the look of Jane. It was more gratifying to be supplanted by a real beauty than by a woman whose attractions she could not understand; and Elizabeth liked to understand the King. Besides, it was obvious from the sweet expression on the lovely face of Edward's latest mistress that she was no scheming woman and obviously not of the nobility. No serious rival here. Let others enjoy Edward's body as long as Elizabeth kept her sway over his political acts.

The Queen was therefore charming to Jane.

"Now, sweetheart," said Edward, "I'd have you meet some members of my family. My favourite brother first, for he will be your friend as he is my friend." He called : "Richard! Come hither. I would speak with you."

Richard, Duke of Gloucester, came to his brother. He was a pale-faced young man of about nineteen, short and slender; and

it was only when his rather cold eyes smiled at her that Jane saw the resemblance between him and his brother. One of his shoulders was slightly higher than the other, but this was scarcely perceptible.

"This is Mistress Shore, Dickon. And, sweetheart, my brother Richard, the best friend I ever had. Love each other well, you two."

The Duke bowed low and Jane returned the bow.

"We have not met before, I think," said he gravely.

The King laughed. "Assuredly you have not. Think you, young Dickon, that you could have met my Jane and not remembered her?"

"I could not, for never saw I face so fair."

"Now that is good, Jane, coming from Richard. For, let me tell you, he is not over-fond of complimenting the ladies."

Jane was warmed by the sight of these two together, for the looks they gave each other told her clearly that there was deep love between them.

"Bring George and Isabel," said the King.

How different was George from his brothers! He was fattish of body, purple-red of face, and he had the blood-shot eyes of a man who is overfond of wine. He looked at Jane with some slyness. She did not like George; nor, she sensed, did Edward; and she marvelled greatly, remembering the talk she had heard between Will and her father, of how this man had played traitor to his brother the King. There must be much kindliness and family feeling in Edward. Isabel, George's wife, was a fragile girl of some beauty; and to her Edward spoke very kindly.

He would introduce Jane to others of his court. And now, listening to these people, finding herself answering them, even allowing a little of her natural gaiety to seep through her shyness, she was suddenly appalled to realise that she, Jane Shore, was no longer a humble person; she was here at court; and the King was commanding these important people to like her and to be her friend.

"And here," said Edward, "is my good friend Hastings. Come hither, man, and pay your respects to Mistress Shore."

Hastings bowed low. Jane inclined her head. Not a sign,
beyond an almost imperceptible lifting of his lips, did Hastings
give that they had met before. Jane was trembling. She moved
closer to Edward, who took her hand and pressed it. "A good
friend of ours," he said, smiling. "A very good friend indeed is
Hastings."

At the banquet which followed, Jane must sit on the left side
of the King, the Queen being on his right. He would talk to
Jane, pat her hand, declaring by every look and gesture that he
loved her. Everyone present was now eager to please her. It was,
"What is your opinion, Mistress Shore?" And, "What do *you*
say to that?"

As for Jane, she could not help being exhilarated; she could
not help being happy. And if the wine was a little intoxicating,
the close presence and the soft looks of the handsomest man in
England was more so. She would not have been Jane if she had
not thrown aside all thought of what must follow. Let the future
take care of itself. She forgot her shyness. Edward had made
her forget that this was the court and he was the King. He was
her lover, and because she was his mistress she was the most
important lady of the court, next to the Queen. She sparkled;
she did not attempt to curb her merry tongue. It was pleasant
to receive applause instead of scolding. Laughter echoed round
the table.

"Holy Mother!" it was whispered. "Did we give her three
months? I'll give her ten. And look you. My Lord Hastings has
his eyes upon her. The King—then Hastings. This Jane Shore
has a future."

There had never for Jane been such a night of triumph.

"Never have I loved as I love thee," whispered Edward.

Jane thought, I'll remember this day all my life. For never
shall I look upon his face again.

And when the ball was over she stepped into the chariot and
rode away with Mary Blague to Mary's house, where it had
been arranged that she should spend the night.

*   *   *   *   *

It was almost noon before Jane returned to Lombard Street next day. She had not slept until dawn and then had fallen into a deep sleep which was troubled with a jumble of dreams. Mary Blague, her eyes veiled, her lips drawn tightly together as though to hold in her smiles, awakened her. It was eleven o'clock.

As though she still dreamed, Jane dressed and made her way back to her husband's house. She hurried in and went upstairs, hoping she would not see Will. She felt that last night's burning experience must be written on her face.

Kate heard her come in. The inquisitive creature quickly found some pretext for coming to her mistress's room.

"Did you see the King, mistress?" A court ball would seem bliss to Kate.

Jane nodded.

"Tell me true, did you not think he was the handsomest man on earth?"

"He is very attractive," said Jane blankly.

"And saw you the Queen?"

Jane nodded. "She is also very attractive."

Kate watched her mistress slyly. Something had happened; and Kate guessed what. It was certain to happen sooner or later. A noble lord? Could it be Hastings?

"Tell me what you did eat, mistress? And what were the dresses like? And did you dance then? A thousand pities it was old Mistress Blague you went with. You should have had a handsome gentleman to take you."

"Oh, Kate, be silent," said Jane. And then: "I'm so tired. We were late and I scarce slept."

"Too much good food and wine, I'll warrant."

Then Kate was really silent, for the goldsmith had come into the room. She picked up Jane's cloak and put it into the cupboard. The goldsmith looked at her impatiently, and she, interpreting his look, made off as quickly as she could.

Will sat on a stool and watched his wife.

"And how liked you the ball, Jane?"

"It was wonderful."

"And how was the dress?"

"Very simple compared with the others. It looked splendid enough at home, but you should have seen it at court!"

"I'll warrant your face made up for the plainness of your gown, Jane." She shrugged her shoulders and he stood up, and, coming to her, laid a hand on her shoulder. "What ails you, wife?"

"What should ail me?"

"You have changed. Yet you enjoyed the ball—I see that. Tell me, there was none who made too free?" She shook her head swiftly. "Jane, it seems long since I kissed you." He laid his lips against her hair. She could not endure it.

"Will—please."

"What's wrong with you?" He spoke irritably. "One would think you were not my wife. Come, enough of this folly. Have you not had a comfortable home? Am I not good to you? Why, when you were in your father's house he did not hesitate to whip you. Have I ever raised my hands against you?" He went to the door and turned the key in the lock. She felt herself go cold with horror. He went on with a burst of nervous laughter: "That girl of yours comes bursting in. Why, Jane, I love you. You grow lovelier than ever. I swear I never saw you look as beautiful as you do to-day. Court balls suit you, wife. You would have made a lovely court lady, but don't forget you are my wife—*my* wife."

She saw a pulse beating in his throat; she saw his hands reaching out to her; and she could not bear it. She seemed to hear Edward's voice. "A chariot will wait outside a certain house in Lombard Street . . ." She must hold Will off. She could not bear to feel his hands upon her. It was only until five that she must hold him off. She found her voice. It sounded shrill. "No, Will. *No!* Not now."

He smiled; there was a glazed look in his eyes which she had never seen before. Was it because he had always waited to douse the light before making love to her? Had he always looked like that? She could not bear him. There was only one man in the world who must love her.

"Nay, sweetheart," Will was saying. "What matters the hour? We are man and wife—we have God's blessing."

"Kate will come. I know she will."

"Then she will find the door locked on her."

"She will wonder, and spread a tale abroad."

That made him hesitate, for he was always susceptible to people's opinions of him.

"The servants would whisper together. Wait—Will."

His hands dropped to his sides. "You are right, wife." He hastened to unlock the door.

She was still shivering long after he left her. Five o'clock! And it was not yet past midday. She put a few garments together, and then laid them back in the cupboard. I dare not go, she thought. I cannot stay.

She threw herself on to her bed and tried to pray. Kate came in and found her thus.

"Kate, shut the door. I must talk to someone or I shall go mad."

Kate was only too willing. She shut the door and set a stool against it and sat on it, eagerly awaiting confidences.

"Kate, I am in love. Oh—so much in love. You cannot know."

"That I can," said Kate.

"I cannot stay in this house. I am leaving this afternoon. You betrayed me once, Kate. Yet I trust you. I know you will not breathe a word of this to any."

"I'd let them cut my tongue from out my mouth before I would utter a word. Oh, mistress"—Kate's face puckered suddenly—"what will become of me? The goldsmith will not keep me, and your father will not have me back."

"I hadn't thought of that. Mayhap I could take you with me." Kate looked radiantly happy. "Kate, at five of the clock a chariot will be in this street. It will be waiting for me. Let me know when it comes. Let me know the minute it comes. Oh,

Kate, I am very wicked, but I cannot stay longer in this house. I must go to him I love. I believe I was born wicked, because now I am overcome so easily, so naturally. . . ."

"Love's not wicked," declared Kate. "No amount of sermons at Paul's Cross would make me believe that."

"I think you're right, Kate."

"You're sure he'll not send me away, mistress?"

"I am sure of that, Kate."

"Shall I put our things together?"

"No. We take nothing of mine. When the chariot comes we slip our cloaks about us and walk out . . . just as though we are going to the market."

"No clothes?"

"Nothing from this house, Kate."

"Not your jewels?"

"Nothing . . . nothing at all."

" 'Tis a mistake, mistress."

"I do not care." Jane threw herself into Kate's arms and began to sob.

"There, my pretty," soothed Kate. "Stop crying. Stop grieving. Love's to make you happy, not to make you cry . . . just at first in any case."

"Oh, Kate, I could not help but love him. He is so different from all others. Kate, you will love a court life, and so shall I."

"A court life, mistress! I know. It is . . . my Lord Hastings."

"No, Kate. It is . . . the King."

Kate's mouth fell open. She stood up and laid her hands across her breasts and tears ran down her cheeks. She was back in Ludlow Castle, watching from a window while the handsomest man in England rode into the courtyard.

Five o'clock. It would never come. The weary afternoon wore on. Could she trust Kate? Would Kate go to the kitchen for a last farewell with Belper?

She could smell the roasting meat from the kitchens. She heard Will below with a customer. Five o'clock was the supper hour. A difficult time, and there must be no false steps. They must be ready to slip out unnoticed.

At a quarter to five Kate was panting up the stairs.

"Mistress, mistress, a chariot has just drawn up."

"Oh, Kate, are you sure?"

"I have been watching this last hour."

"Have you your cloak?"

"Yes, mistress."

"Then now . . . *now*."

Down the familiar staircase—she would never see it again—past the parlour where Hastings had dared wait for her on the evening of Edward's ceremonial ride through the City . . . out through the porch.

"Run, Kate! Hurry!"

The door of the chariot was flung open. Jane stepped in, Kate at her heels. Jane was drawn into Edward's arms; she heard his quiet laughter.

"I knew you'd come, sweetheart. I knew you'd come."

She said breathlessly : "I have brought Kate. I had to bring Kate. She is my maid, and I could not leave her or he would turn her out. Say I may bring Kate. . . ."

His laughing eyes went beyond Jane to the plump figure that crouched there in the chariot eyeing him with wonder and reverence.

"Greeting, Kate," he said. Then he shouted to the driver : "Whip up and be gone." He turned to Jane and kissed her loudly on the lips. "May you bring Kate? Why, my beloved, bring all the wenches of Lombard Street—what matters it, an Jane Shore comes with them!"

The chariot rattled over the cobbles of Lombard Street, on to Westminster.

WESTMINSTER PALACE

JANE, lying awake in the big bed with its magnificently carved legs and cornices, watched, through an opening in the curtains, the first streaks of red in the early morning sky. She had awakened suddenly after a restless night, and for a moment had thought she was in the room she shared with Will Shore in Lombard Street. But how different was this room in her apartments in Westminster Palace! How different from Will was the man who lay beside her! It was barely a month since Jane had taken up residence at the palace, but what a lot she had learned in that month!

Her eyes travelled across the familiar splendour of the room. There were no common rushes on the floor, for it was tiled, and here and there covered by brightly coloured carpets. There was one chair only in the room—an elaborate affair of velvet and tapestry which was reserved for the use of the King. There were several stools with tapestry-covered seats and beautifully carved legs; and in one corner was a small wooden structure which was curtained off from the rest of the room and which was shaped like an altar. Above this was a crucifix, and before it a velvet rug on which to kneel and say prayers. The bed itself was luxurious. It was set in a square compartment separated from the room by gorgeous curtains suspended from the ceiling. Peacocks in red and blue and gold were embroidered on these curtains and the cushions on the bed were coloured to match.

Jane turned to look at the handsome face of the man who lay beside her on the feather bed; his fair hair was disarrayed, and his face half buried in the fine linen of the sheets. Gently, she removed the sheet and looked at him with uneasy tenderness.

Her eyes went to the full lips which betrayed their owner's love of sensuous pleasure; and she wondered how many women had, waking as she had this morning and looking upon his sleeping face, asked themselves, "How long shall I keep him? How long before some other takes my place?"

Her thoughts went back over the four gay and wildly exciting weeks. Balls, masques and banquets; she had enjoyed them to the full for Edward was beside her. Merry Jane Shore she was called, and the King was proud of her wit. But in this dawn light she must face the truth. Basking in the King's pleasure was like dancing in the summer sunshine, and the summer did not last throughout the year. But I love him so much, thought Jane illogically. That must make a difference. None of the others loved him as I do.

He stirred and murmured something in his sleep. Did he dream of her? She was no fool; and a month at court had taught her that she was a small part of his life. Jane pressed her face into the pillow and tried to forget the faces of some of those who were now sleeping in this great palace; she tried not to think of their moving lips as they asked each other, "How long? A month is a long time with the same woman."

She could not stop thinking of Hastings. Whenever he was present his eyes seemed to watch her unceasingly, as though he waited for some sign that the King was tired of her. She could not forget the waiting sultry desire in the man's eyes.

The Queen troubled her also. What was the meaning of the cold calm smiles bestowed on her by the Queen?

Jane shuddered, for everything at court was gayer, fiercer, more cruel than in the simple homes of Lombard Street and Cheapside. The lavish banquets, the entertainments, the dazzling garments, might have belonged to an eastern court. Here was licentiousness that appalled; lovers were taken in an afternoon and discarded by evening, exchanged, discussed. Amorous adventuring was the main business of the court; and how could she shut her eyes to the fact that the King set the fashion! Just now he was deeply in love with herself. Now she was back at the question which had begun to dominate her life. How long?

There was another side to court life—grim instead of gay, filled with horror instead of colour, hate instead of love. A carelessly spoken word and men and women were despatched to the Tower, their lands confiscated, and perhaps they would never be heard of again. This was a strange life, a life of pleasure and fear. And in the centre of it all was Edward, the most brilliant member of the brilliant court, the most loved and the most feared. For this man, who, it was said, changed his loves as he changed his garments, had Jane left the peaceful security of her husband's house.

Each day she learned more about him, and learning found a different man from the handsome merchant to whom she had given her love. His vanity was extreme enough to be naïve. He would strut in front of the mirror, admiring his person; he would bid her stand beside him, and while he feigned to admire her would in truth be studying himself. His rages were what she feared most. They did not occur often for he was by nature easy-going; but when they did come they could be terrible. She had seen him angry with a tailor who had spoilt the coat he was making; she had heard him threaten to have the tailor flogged. It was she who had saved the tailor. He liked women to plead with him; she was beginning to understand that he wished to see himself as the strong man, weak only where his love was concerned. There was little he enjoyed as much as granting favours to women.

The story of the tailor spread. People in trouble were for ever seeking her out, begging her to intercede for them. Only yesterday a woman had come begging an audience. It was a Mistress Banster of East Cheap who kept a pie shop there. Her son Charlie was in trouble. He had spoken against the King and had been taken to the Tower. She feared they would cut off his ears. He was but fourteen.

She seemed to hear the woman's voice now. "For pity's sake, lady . . . For pity's sake. . . ." The boy had but said what many said before him: Edward had had King Henry murdered, and King Henry was a saint.

Last night Jane had tried to tell Edward that she wanted him to save the boy's ears, and she had chosen a moment when he lay temporarily satisfied beside her.

"Edward," she had said, "there is something I would ask of you."

"Yes?" His voice had been slurred and sleepy.

She had told of the woman, and the boy who was to have his ears cut off. She waited for an outburst of horror. None came. Edward had survived too many bloody battlefields to be disturbed by the cutting off of an unknown boy's ears. He had drawn her towards him and sleepily bitten her ear. "You have pretty ears, Jane. What if I bite them off? You should not tempt me with your talk of ears."

She had been deeply shocked, and rashly had not attempted to hide her feelings. "How can you, when that poor boy—he is but a child—lies in the Tower? Edward, you must listen to me. I cannot sleep for thinking of him."

"That's treason. You must think of none but me."

"Edward, would you not do something for me?"

"Anything for you, sweet Jane."

"Then let this boy go free."

"What did he then?"

"He but repeated some idle gossip."

"Concerning me? Well, then, when he has no ears to hear idle gossip, 'twill be the better for me, will it not?"

He had rolled over and she saw then the cruelty of his mouth.

"But, Edward, if I asked you . . ."

"What said he?"

"It was something about King Henry's death."

That had been a mistake. She had seen the change in his face. She had recognised the look of guilt. He wanted to be good; he wanted to be benign; he wanted laughter all around him and people to adore him; he did not care to see himself as a brutal murderer. A murderer? she had thought. Is my Edward then a murderer?

"My dear Jane!" His voice had been ice-cold. "You must not meddle in such matters. The boy deserves his fate. We cannot allow our enemies to speak thus against us. Rebellions grow out of such talk. You must not ask us to forgive our enemies."

They had lain, a small but hostile space between them. Was this the end then? Jane asked herself. If not, how long?

The discovery of cruelty in him could not kill her love. She was completely fascinated, unable to resist him. She longed now to creep up to him and beg his forgiveness, to tell him that she would never interfere again; she loved him unconditionally.

He awakened suddenly and reached for her. "Jane!" His voice was sleepy, yet it held desire. He drew her to him. "Why, your cheeks are wet! What ails thee, Jane?" The old tenderness was in his voice, melting her fears, wiping away all emotions but this rising, thrilling joy.

"I feared I had offended you."

He laughed. "Nay, you could not do that. You are soft and small and sweet and I love you."

"Then . . . all is as it was before?"

"Give me your lips, my little love," he said, "and I'll give you that boy's ears. How's that for a bargain?"

But afterwards she lay awake, and fear returned. She had saved the boy, but she had had a terrifying glimpse of kingly power and kingly cruelty.

Yet, there could be no happiness for her without this man. She must continue to please him. She would wrap her love so closely about him that he could not escape it; it should be a net to hold him, yet so fine and flexible that he should not be irked by the sight and the feel of it.

She heard the first stirrings of morning in the palace before she fell asleep.

*   *   *   *   *

In the corridor leading from her apartments Jane came face to face with Hastings. It was the first time since she had come to the palace that they had been alone. She would have hurried past him, but he barred her way.

"Please allow me to pass."

He did not move. "How long now, Jane?" he asked.

"I understand you not, my lord."

"I think you do."

"If I do understand you, Lord Hastings, I can only consider you a fool."

"Any man is a fool who allows himself to get caught in love as I have."

"Were I you, I should talk of such matters to those who are interested to hear them."

"You are not interested in my love affairs because you are deep in one with the King, but when that is done with . . ."

"I find your manners as objectionable in Westminster as they were in Lombard Street."

"And I find you a thousand times more desirable in Westminster than I did in Lombard Street. More's the pity."

"It surprises me that the Lord Chancellor should so demean himself."

"There is much that I do that surprises me, Jane," he said sombrely.

In spite of her hatred, her interest was aroused. What a strange man he was! Edward had said he was one of his cleverest ministers, and yet he conducted himself like a schoolboy. She asked him if he did not realise that were she to tell Edward he had accosted her thus he might find himself in a dangerous position.

"I know it." He came closer, and his eyes were earnest. "But I cannot help myself. You say I am a fool. You speak truth. I know now that I should have approached you in a different manner. And now . . . but for me you would never have come here."

"But for *you*?"

"Who do you think told Edward of the goldsmith's lovely wife? Revenge it was to be, revenge on the goldsmith who dared insult me."

"So *you* sent Edward to Lombard Street?"

"One does not send Edward. I merely whispered that I had seen the loveliest girl in London. That was enough. Ah—but perhaps I was not foolish. In a little while, in a month—or perhaps a week . . ."

"Have you not yet learned that I hate you?"

"You shall learn to love me. A Chancellor is not such a bad exchange for a King. Many of Edward's mistresses have had to be content with less." She turned abruptly from him, but he caught her wrist. His eyes glittered. "My lovely Jane, I will make you happy. It will be you first, not for a week, nor a month—but always. That is how I love you, Jane."

"You mock me."

"Nay, I speak the truth."

"I shall tell the King of this."

"Yes, do. It may put the idea of a change into his head. It cannot be too soon for me."

She ran from him, and Hastings, shrugging his shoulders, made his way back to his apartment. He was wondering how Edward had succeeded with her. When Edward was in the midst of a love affair he always deluded himself, as well as his partner in the adventure, that it was the most important in his life. Therein doubtless lay his success.

He found his wife, Catharine, stitching at a piece of embroidery. She looked at him coldly. There was no love between them, and never had been, though both had desired the marriage. He was the great Hastings, and she was the sister of the Earl of Warwick; they came from two of the richest families in the country; they were two aristocrats, each gaining wealth and power from the other.

She looked at him coldly now because she considered him a fool to cast longing eyes upon the King's newest mistress while the King was yet enamoured of her.

There was one thing they shared in common, though—and

that was hatred of the Queen. The Hastings-Warwick alliance was meant to unite two great families and so add to their power. But now, through the Queen's habit of marrying her upstart relations into the richest and oldest families in the land, the Woodvilles were fast becoming very powerful and dangerous. It was therefore the duty of every noble house to stand against them.

Hastings sat on a stool and smiled at his wife. "I am thinking of bringing my cousin to court," he said. "I have spoken to the King of her already."

Catharine thought of the girl of whom he spoke. Fifteen, a charming age. Primed by Hastings she might easily please the King. It was well for a house when the King was amused by one of its women. But did he think to deceive her? Was he bringing the girl to court that she might influence the King for the good of their family? No. He was bringing the girl to court that she might lure the King from Jane Shore!

And he thought to deceive her. Queer, thought the countess, that one so skilled in war and politics as her husband could scheme so clumsily for his women.

*   *   *   *   *

Edward was walking in the gardens of the Palace of Westminster with his brothers when he looked up and saw the Queen at her window. Her maid was combing her hair and it shone like gold coins.

Across the King, his brothers argued. He was weary of the continual strife between these two. He hated displays of temper; if any was to lose a temper, that should be himself.

They were quarrelling about Anne Neville, who had a short while before been a prisoner of state and had now mysteriously disappeared. Edward guessed George was responsible for the girl's disappearance. With Isabel, George's wife, she was co-heiress to the Warwick fortune; and George had no intention of sharing that fortune with Anne Neville. To complicate matters, Richard wanted the girl, wanted to marry her.

"Enough! Enough!" cried Edward. "Take your quarrels

elsewhere. By God, if I wanted the girl I'd find her! Go, Dickon, be a man. Find the girl and marry her, if that's what you want."

"You would give your consent to such a marriage?" demanded George.

"I did not give my consent to your marriage with her sister, but you married her all the same. By God's Holy Virgin, George, I wonder at my clemency towards you!"

That silenced him. Watching him, Edward grew hot at the thought of George's treachery. With Richard it was different. Dear Richard, but a boy for all his cleverness. He was romantically in love with this Anne Neville. Let him enjoy the girl—if he could find her. Richard had been put under her father's care when they were children and they had grown up together. Let Richard find where George had hidden her and then he could marry her, for with her sister she was the biggest heiress in the country. Pray the Virgin there had been no foul play. He wanted no more trouble between his brothers.

But the glint of the Queen's hair in the sunlight was pleasant. He left his brothers and went up to her apartment. The tiring maid curtseyed as he entered. He signed for her to leave him with the Queen. When they were alone he went to Elizabeth and kissed her. "Well, my Lady Bessy, I swear you grow more beautiful every day."

"I saw Your Grace walking with your brothers. I trust nothing is wrong."

"There will always be wrong between those two."

"And how fares Mistress Shore? I declare I have not seen her these last few days."

With some women the question might have been the beginning of reproach and recrimination. But he knew that Elizabeth had no desire to quarrel with him. He told her Jane was well.

"A pleasant and a lovely girl," said Elizabeth.

Now he was momentarily angry with her. She had always had the power to anger him, and how furious she had made him during their courtship! "Your mistress I cannot be." The tight red lips had meant that. Her acceptance of Jane and his other mistresses, while it pleased him, irritated him. It was so unnatural. But then, his Elizabeth, as he had always known, was an exceptional woman; and he did not regret his romantic marriage. He remembered afresh the excitement of the first weeks with Elizabeth. Strange that she should have attracted him so strongly. She was different from all other women, so perhaps that was the reason; though he had never before liked cold women, in her case the attempt to arouse passion in her had the charm of the unattainable. Elizabeth had a love, however. It was love of the power the King brought her, not of the King himself.

"You're thoughtful," she said.

"My thoughts were of you, Bessy."

"I trust they were pleasant, my lord."

"Very pleasant." He sat on the table and, leaning forward, kissed her lips. They were cold against his own. He thought of Jane's soft warm ones. Jane was a loving little thing, but so many had been loving.

"I was recalling that day at Grafton," he said. "Seven years ago, and here I am as deep in love with you as ever. There have been others, 'tis true, but back I come to my lovely Bessy." He laid a hand on her breast; she did not draw back, nor did she respond. "And she," he went on, "is like one made of marble. But no matter. . . . Do you remember that day? Your mother, a priest, and a gentlewoman or two. What secrecy! Oh, Bessy, what were your thoughts when I rode away and left behind me the Queen of England?"

She smiled slowly. "I was very happy, Edward."

"You were indeed, for were you not the Queen? Remember how I would come to stay at your mother's house—a guest for a night or two—and after the retiring hour you would slip along to my apartments?"

Elizabeth nodded. She was not likely to forget the days which had carried her to the summit of her desires. She had become Queen, and after years of widowhood and being forced to live on her mother's bounty, that was pleasant. Now, this talk of their secret marriage could be leading up to one thing only. Could he never be satisfied? God knew he had mistresses enough. He had the virility of ten men. That she discovered in that brief period when she had been the only one to occupy his thoughts. The Virgin be praised that he loves variety, she thought, for did his fancy rest long on one he would kill her. Well, she had children enough now, but perhaps there should be a second boy. It had taken them long enough to get young Edward. Three daughters and then a son. There should be more sons. The times were perilous, and it was dangerous for a woman who set such store upon a throne to have only one son.

She sought now to make what she could out of the situation. Edward was the sort of man who liked to give. She knew him better than did anyone else; she could always choose the most proper moment to press for a favour. Edward would have been kindhearted if he were not utterly selfish. He would have been benevolent if he were not so quick to anger. He would have been great if he had not loved pleasure so completely. He would have been a great lover of his country if he had not loved women so much. That was how she saw Edward—near-great, a man of contrasts, so that every good quality was balanced by its exact opposite. Even his good looks were beginning to be impaired by a life of excesses. Elizabeth guessed that in time his beauty and grace would be lost in grossness of body and manners.

"Edward," she said, for seeing his brothers with him in the grounds had set an idea working in her mind, "have you any knowledge of what happened to the Neville girl?"

He was tired of the Neville girl. She had disappeared, he said testily. That was all he knew.

"One of the richest girls in the country and she disappears! Where to? Someone must know."

"Then that someone is assuredly not I. All I know is that George, as her brother-in-law, would take charge of her, and one day she disappeared from his house."

"George has had something to do with that disappearance.

He has hidden her, because he fears Richard will marry her and take her share of the Warwick fortune."

"And you have other plans for the Warwick fortune, eh? You want Anne for one of your many uncles and cousins."

"I should feel it my duty to find a husband for the girl," said Elizabeth primly. "She is not to be blamed for her father's treachery. The sooner she is married the better."

The King laughed. "Oh, Bessy, Bessy, you'll be the death of me with your marriages. What a woman! What a maker of marriages! Can you not be content with marrying yourself to the King? Surely you have no more penniless brothers and cousins. I thought you had found monied marriages for the lot by now. I don't forget your brother, Bess. How old was he when you married him to the old Dowager of Norfolk? Eighteen was it, Bessy? And the old lady turned eighty! Bessy, is there no end to your matchmaking?"

"Edward," she said, laying her hand on his coat and smiling at him, "you will do what you can to find her, and when she is found you will let me arrange a marriage for her?"

"Why, Bessy, have I ever refused you anything yet?" He laughed, and grasping her golden hair in either hand pulled her gently towards him. Seven years of marriage, and she could still attract him! There was not a woman like her in the king-dom—with the exception of Jane. He would throw Anne Neville to her as, a short while ago, he had thrown her to Richard. She should at least have the pleasure of thinking the Neville fortune was all but in the hands of her greedy family.

She was smiling, but she was as cold as ice. That was what he wanted, for it reminded him most pleasantly of his wedding night.

      *   *   *   *   *

Jane was heartbroken, for the King no longer loved her. It was three days and nights since he had been to her apartments. Kate, busying herself with the wardrobe, kept her frightened eyes downcast. Where would this end? Was the brief period of glory over?

It was due to a tall, slender, black-haired girl—a protégée of my Lord and Lady Hastings. She was the exact opposite of Jane, being tall where Jane was short, dark where Jane was fair. The King, it was said, was very gracious and very merry with everyone who came his way, which was a sure sign that he was preparing to embark on one of his major love affairs.

Jane knew that Hastings had done this, for the man was an evil shadow hanging over her life.

"I hate you! I hate you!" she told him fiercely when he way-laid her.

"I have heard that hate and love are very close, sweet Jane. To-day you hate; to-morrow you will love." There was a sudden tenderness in his voice. "Jane, how can you be such a little fool! Have you not learned yet what folly it is to love the King? His affections are here to-day and gone to-morrow. Come with me. I have plans for us."

"I remember other plans of yours!"

"I have changed. You have changed me. We will leave the court if you wish it. If you will only trust me."

"As well trust a serpent!"

"I would do anything in the world to make you happy."

"So you plotted against me?"

"It is for your good. I am not a careless boy who knows not what he wants."

"You are an evil man, and I hate you. I hate you."

"But, Jane, what is to happen to you? Where will you go? You must come to me then, for I shall be waiting for you."

"I would rather starve."

"You say so because you have never starved. You know not what you say."

"I know well enough that I hate you."

She ran from him into her apartment. She threw herself on to the bed, drew the curtains and gave herself up to bitter weeping. Life was so cruel. The man she had idealised was a philanderer—and worse, yet he had the power to break her heart. She herself had changed from that innocent girl of Cheapside, that young woman of Lombard Street. She had become capable of fierce love for the King, fierce hate for Hastings.

Oh, God, she thought, if only I had a child, then I could bear this. Edward had numerous sons, some in high, some in obscure places—why could she not have one? She had made the acquaintance of the royal children. They were charming, and all with a look of Edward. Elizabeth, the eldest, was proud, but Cecily and Mary were sweet, though Jane's favourite was the baby, who was just a year old and named after his father. But what was the use of thinking of the child! Perhaps she would never see him again. Perhaps she would have to leave the court, and there would be nothing left but memories.

Kate drew aside the curtains of the bed, her eyes wide with excitement. The Queen's woman had brought a message. The Queen would speak with Jane at once.

When Jane reached the Queen's apartment Elizabeth dismissed her women and told Jane she might sit. That in itself was significant, for it was rarely that Elizabeth allowed any to sit in her presence. She could never forget the years of indignity, and they had made her ever conscious of her present power. Often she kept her ladies on their knees for as much as three hours at a stretch; even her own mother, who had been largely responsible for Elizabeth's present glory, must kneel in her daughter's presence and wait until permission was given her to rise. But Jane might sit and listen to what the Queen had to say. Elizabeth came quickly to the point.

"Mistress Shore, you are unhappy, thinking to have lost the King's favour?" In spite of her misery Jane found it difficult to suppress a smile, for it seemed so odd for the King's mistress and the King's wife to be discussing such a matter together. "She who has temporarily supplanted you," went on Elizabeth, "and, mind you, I say temporarily, has not a tenth of your beauty, nor, I understand, your wit. But His Grace the King is susceptible to youth and beauty . . . and above all to variety."

"Your Grace is kind to me," murmured Jane.

Elizabeth inclined her head. "I like you, Jane Shore. And may I say that most of the women with whom the King amuses himself are not to my liking. What I would say to you is that if you lose the King's affection you will have none but yourself to blame."

"I . . . do not understand, Your Grace."

"That, methinks, is because you have been but a short time at court. The King has been mightily taken with you. Indeed, I would go so far as to say that none but myself has ever taken his fancy as you have. I have kept his affection for seven years. I shall continue to do so until one of us shall die. And because I love the King and because you also love him, I know that it is better that he should betray me with you than with the many wanton creatures who would seek to attract him. I will now tell you how you may keep his affection." Elizabeth laughed and her laughter was icy. "Come, my child. You look bewildered. It is simple enough. You have more beauty than any other at court. You can make the King laugh. There is no need for you to throw these gifts into Hastings' waiting arms. The King loves me; he loves you also; he is capable of loving many. But because a man likes roast peacock it does not mean he does not also like a good slice of homely bread. Never fear. He will come back and back again if you are clever enough to let him. Go back to your apartment, and when the King comes to you, as assuredly he will, smile at him, behave as though this interlude had never been; if refer to it you must, refer to it as some trifling incident, too small to be regrettable. What the King hates more than anything is a weeping and reproachful woman. He will run from your tears and run towards your smiles. If you follow my advice, I venture to say that this is not the end of the pleasant attachment between Jane Shore and His Grace the King."

"You are too kind to me, Your Grace. I cannot understand . . ."

Elizabeth smiled at her. If she did not understand then

she was indeed a little fool and doubtless she would lose Edward sooner or later. But perhaps she had not yet learned that the Queen must keep the King from indulging in more than the lightest affairs with the female relatives of her enemies.

"Do not forget what I have said," she commanded, and dismissing Jane, congratulated herself on this day's work.

The Queen was right. The King soon came back to Jane. He felt ashamed and was prepared to be critical of Jane therefore. But she was waiting for him, dressed in the same shade of blue, her yellow hair rioting over her shoulders. He noticed at once that she wore a jewelled ornament which he had given her on an occasion when he had sworn eternal fidelity. Her smile was warm and she seemed merrier than ever.

She ran to him. "Edward, how wonderful to see you!"

He held her at arm's length and looked at her shrewdly. No reproaches. Just a welcome. And she was more beautiful than ever. Why had he ever thought that other one more attractive? He kissed her and his relief changed to passion. He did not know that Jane was fighting to keep back her tears, that her laughter was forced, that she was facing the sad fact that if she could learn to share him he was hers perhaps for always. She felt unclean, humiliated, yet her need of him was as urgent as ever.

"My little one," he said, "there is none on earth to stand against thee."

There was now no need for him to play the faithful lover as he had been doing for so long. It was a great relief. He could be natural with Jane, for in spite of her sweetness and loving ways she had learned the reasonable manners of the court.

He did try to explain at first though. "I think I must have been bewitched. But here I am, back again, and eager to make up for every minute spent away from you."

"Remember it not. 'Twas but the habit of a lifetime doubtless."

Merrily he laughed, and Jane laughed with him, though never had she felt less like laughter.

The story spread through the court. The King is back with Jane Shore. Hastings heard it. He was frustrated and sick at heart.

Lady Hastings laughed at her husband. "Your little plan has failed, my lord," she taunted him. "It would seem your cousin's brief moments with the King did naught but rob the girl of her virginity."

Hastings hated his wife and his cousin; he hated the King. He knew that everyone was laughing at him, and he could not bear to be laughed at. Yet even more than the loss of dignity did he feel the loss of Jane. He could not forget her. She had changed his life. For the first time was he truly in love, and finding it a wretched state to be in. He endeavoured to forget Jane. He left the palace, and, going down to the river, hailed a boat and savagely told the boatman to row him over to Southwark. There, he thought, in those dark rooms where every vice that the devil had put into the minds of men could be practised, there would he forget Jane Shore.

But he found it was impossible to forget her.

*   *   *   *   *

After the King's brief love affair with Hastings' protégée, Jane's position changed subtly. Next to the King and the Queen, she had become the most important person at court. Nobody now speculated as to whether she would retain her position as the King's favourite mistress; it was taken for granted that she would.

Jane was deeply conscious of a change in herself. She was worldly; it was no use denying that she loved the gay court, the good living, the erotic excitements to which Edward introduced her. She knew now why she had longed to escape from the sober life of Cheapside and Lombard Street. She was kind of heart, and it was the easiest thing possible to arouse her pity, but she knew herself to be a courtesan, and she could not forget it. She was treated with great respect, and even the King's brothers, Clarence and Gloucester, cultivated her acquaintance. She was ready to plead with the King for any cause she considered just, and it was rarely that she asked for anything for herself. But always she must scheme to please the King; she had learned even that to plead another's cause she must use wit and laughter, never tears. She must act a part continually.

Outside the court the Town talked of her. The woman Banster and her boy Charlie could not praise the King's favourite too much; there were many like them. Jane knew this and it pleased her.

Always she tried to face the truth; she must hold her place, and she did not see how she could do this unless she saw life as it really was. She was disillusioned. She had learned that Mary Blague, the respected lace-woman of Cheapside, had connections with a house of ill-fame across the river. Kate, who was enjoying court life and all its intrigues and adventures, had on one occasion followed Danok from Cheapside to the house in Southwark, and on another she had followed Mary Blague. Jane was aware, through court gossip, that the house in Southwark was a brothel and that there was a mysterious woman who owned the place. She believed that woman to be Mary Blague. And had not Mary arranged for her seduction in the lace-making establishment? Whom could one trust?"

And I, thought Jane, am as wicked as any, for I am one of those harlots they speak of at Paul's Cross; and were I not the King's harlot I should be forced most likely to do a penance in the streets. Yet, how could she wish that she were back in Lombard Street? How could she wish she were anywhere but where she was? She had the love of the King, and if it was born of the senses—she must be truthful—so was hers for him.

Yet, in their new relationship there was a difference. They were companions, and he enjoyed talking to her. He told her of those desperate days when he had been almost constantly at

war, of the terrible weeks of exile which he had endured more
than once in his stormy journey towards the throne. She understood then his urgent desire to live life fully, to plunder from
it every conceivable pleasure. The times were perilous. He
must enjoy everything that his power could bring him, while
that was possible. They were of a kind, he and Jane.

He told her of his brothers. Clarence, he confessed, was at
the root of his biggest worry. "I must keep him close to me,
Jane, for I swear that when he is out of my sight I tremble to
think what he may be plotting."

"Think you not that he has learned his lesson?"

"George will never learn his lessons. That is his great
failing."

Jane thought constantly of the girl Anne Neville, for her
strange disappearance was discussed often. She tried to talk to
Edward of her, but Edward was weary of the subject.

"The girl's a tiresome creature, Jane. By the Virgin, I fear
murder between those two brothers of mine, one day."

"If only she could be found!"

Edward turned on her, frowning. "If she is found there will
be trouble." He shrugged his shoulders. "Let her stay in
hiding. She is safer there. Picture the strife, Jane, if she were
found. Richard wants to marry her, and the Queen has already
marked her for one of her relations. There'd be trouble between
Richard and Bess. And what of George? By my faith, methinks
there'll be trouble saved if the girl stays in hiding."

"But have you thought what she may be suffering, Edward?"

"Enough!" He was lazy; he liked life to run smoothly.
Anne Neville was unimportant while she remained hidden.
She would be a nuisance if she were found. It did not matter
to him that a gently nurtured girl might be suffering hard-
ship.

Indeed, he was a different man from the merchant who had
seemed perfect to Jane. But I am different too, Jane reminded
herself.

"Let us talk of other matters," said Edward, and kissed her.

It was easy for Jane also to forget Anne Neville . . . for the time being.

But Jane remembered Anne again when Kate brought news to her. Kate had witnessed something very strange and had hastened to tell her mistress. Waiting for a lover, in a secluded part of the gardens, she had witnessed a meeting between . . . whom did Jane think? She would surely never guess, so Kate would tell quickly. None other than the Duke of Clarence and Mary Blague! Surely if the Duke was indulging in a love affair it could not be with Mary Blague!

"No," said Jane, "it could not have been a love affair." She warned Kate to say nothing of this meeting, but she herself could not forget it, and because she thought of Mary Blague as an evil woman, a procuress, a woman who had strange connections with an evil house in Southwark, she began to see a reason why this woman should secretly meet such a person as the Duke of Clarence. Might it not concern the missing girl?

She would go to Edward. But what was the use? Edward would shrug his shoulders. Let the girl remain hidden, he would say. That was the more peaceful way.

Yes, let the girl remain hidden, for on no account must Jane Shore anger the King. But Jane found she had not changed so much as she had thought. A pale, frightened face came between her and whatever she was doing, and there was no peace for Jane. She could not forget the girl she had seen riding in the chariot with Margaret of Anjou. The daughter of a man who had been one of the highest in the land, might now be a prisoner in a brothel.

She would have to risk Edward's displeasure; and so the day after she had the news from Kate, she was making her way to the apartment of the Duke of Gloucester.

Richard was working, and before him on the table lay a pile of documents. He was conscientious, and matters of state interested him far more than the pleasures in which his brothers indulged. There were times when he would have liked to take over the burden of kingship in name as well as in deed. There were so many schemes in his head; had he been the King he would have spent less time feasting and would have enjoyed making laws rather than love. Everything in life would be subordinated to the good of his country; and now, as the King's chief adviser, matters of state occupied a large part of his thoughts.

He looked up as Jane entered, and flicked a speck of dust off his elaborate sleeve. Like his brothers, he loved fine clothes, and he was always careful to wear something about his neck that might hide the fact that one shoulder was higher than the other. He smiled, for he did not dislike Jane Shore. He thought her a graceful lovely creature, but he deplored Edward's lack of wisdom in doting on her so utterly. Still, he guessed that had she not genuinely loved his brother she would have remained a virtuous wife.

"Richard," said Jane haltingly, for they had been commanded by Edward to dispense with ceremony and call each other by their Christian names. They did this, but never without a certain embarrassment on both sides. "Richard, I have some news which I feel may be of interest to you. I hesitate to tell you because there may be nothing in it; yet, on the other hand, there may. It is about Anne Neville."

He laid aside his pen. Only the pulse beating furiously at his temple showed her that he was moved. She looked over her shoulder. He rose swiftly, went to the door and looked out. "We are quite alone. Pray speak."

Jane was afraid now of the wildness of her suspicions, for she saw that this pale, cold-seeming young man was truly in love with the missing girl. She was glad she had come to him. No matter what was to follow, she was glad. Weeks at court had made her conscious of danger, but had done nothing to curb her reckless generosity.

"I fear I may be wrong," she said, "but mayhap it is worth while following this up, and I thought I should come to you." "Yes, yes."

"My maid was in a secluded part of the gardens when she witnessed a meeting between your brother the Duke and a woman—who has connections with a house in Southwark."

"I have heard of that house."

"I wondered if their meeting had anything to do with——"

"Holy Mother! Anne in such a house!"

"The woman lends herself to any dark and evil business and——"

"I shall go at once. I shall take some men with me. I shall search the place. By the Virgin, I'll kill George for this!"

She had never thought to see him so moved. She tried to restrain him, to explain that it was but an idea that occurred to her, but he would not listen. He had gathered up his papers and locked them in a box. It was characteristic of Richard that he could at such a moment think of doing that.

Jane silently prayed that he might find Anne Neville in that house in Southwark, and find her unharmed. Richard would make a good quiet husband, she thought; and thinking of her own exciting and unaccountable lover, she was both sorry for and envious of Anne Neville.

* * * * *

Jane was terrified. She who had merely thought to reunite a pair of lovers had stumbled into danger. She had dared interfere in a desperate game which was being played by ruthless princes.

She had heard from Richard what had happened at the Southwark house. He had knocked at the door, and when Madam opened it, he, with seven well-chosen men, had stepped into the hall. "I believe," he had said, "that you harbour here a certain lady. If that should be so, I ask you to deliver her up to me at once."

The woman had shown surprise and indignation until she discovered Richard's identity. Richard had then been allowed to search the house, but he had not found Anne.

"How sorry I am!" cried Jane. "I fear I but raised your

hopes pointlessly and so made you more unhappy than ever."

"It was no fault of yours," answered Richard. "And I thank you for telling me. If you should discover anything further . . ."

"Depend upon it," Jane warmly assured him, "I shall come straight to you."

The matter might have rested there but for Kate, but Kate could never resist gossiping. She whispered to her lover that the Duke of Clarence and the King's lace-woman had been meeting secretly. The story was whispered round the court, with the result that it reached the Duke's ears. He lost no time in tracking it to its source, and Kate was summoned to the presence of the Duke.

When the Duke's anger was roused he lost all sense of dignity. He was angry now. Kate stood before him, shivering with terror. She was the sort who would not need the rack nor the thumbscrews to make her talk; nevertheless he threatened her with them. And out came the whole story. She had seen him with Mistress Blague and she had told her mistress. So it was Jane Shore who had taken the tale to the Duke of Gloucester. The friends of Gloucester were the natural enemies of Clarence.

"Throw the woman into the Tower," cried George; and the weeping, terrified Kate was led away.

George sought out Jane, and such was his anger that he threw all caution from him.

"Mistress Blague, the brothel-keeper, is a friend of yours, madam?" His insolence was intolerable, and Jane understood at once that the Duke was her open enemy. She was in a dangerous position, but when she was actually face to face with danger she was always stimulated by it.

"How dare you speak to me thus!" she cried. "I do not wish to see you again until you have learned your manners."

George laughed in her face. "Sluts give themselves airs, do they not? Come, tell me, did the brothel-woman procure you for my brother? 'Tis what I had from that slut of yours who spies into the affairs of your betters for you."

"You will allow me to pass."

"Not before I have said my say. And I advise you, madam, to show more respect to me. Think not that I shall disregard such conduct. A day will come when I shall sit upon the throne."

Jane quickly saw her advantage. "You speak treason, sir," she said.

George's face was purple, his bloodshot eyes rolled. "By Christ!" he cried. "I'll not be treated thus by harlots such as you—even if they be the King's harlots."

"Then it was true that she was hidden in that house," said Jane. "It is true that you took that poor girl and subjected her to such horrors . . ."

"Hold your strumpet's tongue!" he cried.

"Your anger leads me to believe my suspicions are correct."

"Be silent, or I'll have you thrown into the Tower along with your maid. I'll set the guards on you. I'll have you racked."

Jane was pale and sick suddenly. "My maid—in the Tower?"

" 'Tis where she should be. God's Holy Virgin, I, the son of my father, to be treated thus by my brother's harlots!"

"You will release my maid at once."

"Release her? Not before we have racked the whole treasonable truth out of her. You too, madam, if needs be."

He laughed in her face and left her. Thus was she terrified of what she had set in motion. Kate in the Tower. Anne Neville undiscovered. And, if Kate were to be rescued, it would be necessary to tell Edward the entire story. Had he not told her she must not meddle in such matters? She held him to her by such flimsy threads. She must set Kate free though, even at the risk of incurring Edward's anger. Experience had taught her to wait until he was in an acquiescent mood before asking favours, yet how could she wait—while Kate was in the Tower? What a fool I am! she thought. Why do I rush in and act before I think? As well ask herself why she had left the security of life with Will for the thousand risks and dangers of life with Edward. She had done these things because she was herself.

There was no help for it. She must confess what she had done, and she must beg Edward for Kate's release; she must beg with more courage and more tact than she had ever used before.

She went to her apartment and put on her most becoming gown; she set her hair in loose curls about her shoulders. She must chaffer with her beauty, for that was all she had to offer. She thought of a proud young girl who had lived with her father in Cheapside. How low have I fallen! she thought. But I am what I am, and my kind must beg for favours thus.

Edward was occupied with matters of state. He was sitting alone in his privy chamber when she sought him. Busy as he was, he looked up and smiled.

"I have something to say to you," she burst out. "Something that will not wait."

"Say on." His eyes grew warm at the sight of her.

"Edward, did you know that Richard has been to Southwark in search of Anne Neville?"

The warmth died out of Edward's eyes, and he brought his fist down sharply on the table. "And brought her back?" he demanded.

"Nay. But he had word that Anne was in Southwark and went there in all haste."

"Had word? What meddlers there are to disturb our peace! Who brought word to Richard that the girl was in Southwark? That is what I would like to know."

"Edward, I fear . . ." She moved nearer to him and laid a trembling hand on his shoulder. "I fear you are going to be angry, for it was I who told Richard that I thought Anne might be there."

He stood up. He towered over her, scowling. "*You!*"

"I discovered that George and Mary Blague had been meeting, and I connected this fact with the disappearance of Anne Neville. I told Richard of it."

His eyes narrowed. "Did I not beg of you to leave this matter alone?"

She nodded. "You did." She was sickened now, not by her

fear but by the thought of herself currying favours with her charms. She saw herself in her apartment, slipping into her most becoming gown, arranging her hair over her bare shoulders. Her eyes blazed suddenly. "You did," she cried, "and I cared not!"

"You cared not!" His voice was dangerously cold.

"No. Because, no matter what you say, it is wrong to leave that girl alone and friendless. It is wrong—wrong, I tell you. I care not what you do."

He said: "You disregard my order. You are a meddlesome woman. Know you not what happens to those who disobey me? You try me too far. You bring your woman's sentiment into those matters which you understand not. You are a fool, Jane; and I suffer not fools about me. It is better for a girl to die a thousand deaths than that civil war should break out in this country. Richard and George will be at each other's throats over this Neville girl. If you were not such a fool you would know how quickly trouble starts. A quarrel is picked, sides are taken and there is the beginning of endless trouble. My brothers have their followers. Know you not . . . But of course you know nothing of these things. My brother George plans for one thing, and that is to throw me from my place and take it himself. And you, because I have shown you favour, will meddle. Go from me now, and if you would please me, listen to what I say. Meddle no more."

"I will go, Edward. But first I must tell you why I came. Kate, my woman, is in the Tower."

"Kate in the Tower? By whose orders?"

"George sent her there."

His anger was more violent; his eyes bulged with fury and the veins were like blue cords upon his temples. He said through half-closed lips: "So George has sent the woman to the Tower!"

"He threatens her with torture. Edward, oh, please—punish me for what I have done, for it is true I did meddle—but please release Kate."

Edward was not listening. He was at the door shouting for an attendant. When the man came he roared at him: "Send the Duke of Clarence here to me instantly."

Even George dared not disobey such a command. He came in, nodded with some insolence to his brother, and scowled at Jane.

"Carrying tales already, I see," he muttered.

Jane looked in terror from one angry brother to the other. The resemblance between them was now very marked. Both faces were distorted with rage, both purple with fury.

"Since when has it been your habit to issue orders as to who shall be sent to the Tower?" demanded Edward.

"The Tower is the place for traitors, brother."

"A traitor to me might well be a friend to you."

"This wanton wretch has carried tales about me," screamed George. "I said, 'To the Tower with her,' and I meant it."

"I would have you know that you have no power to issue such commands." Edward raised his clenched fist as though he would strike his brother. "Would you take the crown from me and wear it yourself?"

"You surround yourself with these insolent wretches," said George. "You surround yourself with those who would spy on my privacy. I will not have it, I say."

"You will regret this day's work while there is blood in your veins. Brother, learn your lesson. Much have I endured at your hands, but my patience is wellnigh at an end. If you have aught of which to complain, bring your complaints to me. If any has sinned, let him be tried first and then imprisoned."

"Is it Your Grace's custom then to try all those he sends to prison?" sneered George.

Edward's hand went to the hilt of his sword. He said slowly: "Have a care, George. I am your King, remember." His rage suddenly burst out into a string of oaths. "By God, if you wish to keep your head on your shoulders, have a care!"

Jane cowered against the hangings, subdued and frightened. Never had she seen such hatred in any face as she now saw in that of Clarence. She knew that if Clarence could have safely murdered the King there and then he would have done so.

"Get you gone!" cried Edward. "Before I do you some injury, get you gone!"

"Right willingly," said Clarence. "And though you are my elder brother and the King, and therefore must be obeyed, think not that I will brook such insolence from your whores and their serving wenches."

"Be silent! You will now give an order for the woman to be released. Do it quickly or, by Christ's blood, I'll have you sent to the Tower in her stead."

George threw a look of hate at his brother, in which Jane was included; then he bowed sardonically and went out. Edward looked after him for a second or so before turning to Jane. She saw the anger fade from his face, and she knew that he had been badly upset by the scene.

"Jane," he said quietly, and when she went to him he put an arm about her. There was something protective in the gesture. "Why," he went on, "you love me, Jane, do you not?" She nodded, and he laid his hand on her hair. "That is well. You have just witnessed an ugly scene. My brother lusts to kill me. Such is the curse of kingship. But when a man has one to love him as you love me, then it seems he should be grateful."

"Edward, I fear it is my meddling which has caused you this pain."

"Nay, suppress your sorrow on that count. His hatred was smouldering in him before this happened. This but brought it out. 'Tis better to know what malice one may have to face than to come upon it in an emergency unaware. There are times when I despair of George. He was ever a difficult boy—vain, strutting, bombastic. Sometimes I can say, 'Poor George!' For poor he is who grasps at the unattainable. Jane, there are times when you have thought me cruel. Nay, deny it not. Let there be truth between us two. Have I not seen a shuddering discomfort in your eyes at times? Know this, Jane: I live on the edge of a volcano. I am most unsafe. And you, living near me, are in danger also. There is room in my life for little softness. He is my brother, yet I should hate him. But hate him I cannot. Jane, do you know what I should do, were I a wise man?"

She shook her head and he put his mouth to her ear that he might whisper. "I should hire some men . . . men who are ready to do aught they are bid for a price. To-morrow my brother should be found dead in the waters of the Thames."

"Oh, no, Edward. No. That cannot be the way."

"I all but lost my crown for softness once. You would not wish me to do so again? Months of exile! You cannot guess what such a man as I would suffer at such a time. A King . . . and not a King. My Queen in sanctuary. My son, the heir of England, born in that place without the comforts a mere tradesman's son would enjoy. The bitter, bitter experience! He was my enemy then . . . that wicked brother of mine. But because he is my brother I forgive him. I remember him as a bright-eyed boy, a boy without those drink-sodden dreams that make him see himself the King of England."

"Edward," said Jane solemnly, "I trust you will do nothing that will haunt you with remorse."

He kissed her tenderly. "Remember, I live in constant danger, and that danger must be shared by those whom I love." His face hardened. "Meddle not in matters that concern you not, Jane. Keep from them, that I may come to you for rest and peace. Now I will send a messenger to the Tower to discover whether good Kate has been released. And if she has not . . ."

"Oh, if she has not, Edward . . .?"

"George shall feel my strength. My brother must tread warily in future."

*   *   *   *   *

Edward had a new mistress with whom he was delighted. All his light loves would be cast off now. Not Jane Shore though; she was as permanent as the Queen herself. It was not surprising. She was the gayest, the wittiest, the most good-natured creature at court. She could, it was true, fly into a temper, but her indignation was more often than not in some-one's cause other than her own.

Behind the curtains of her bed Jane wept bitterly. He will come back, she told herself. He had come back before and he would do so again. Now that she was alone at night her dreams were troubled. Hastings figured largely in them. She had Kate make herself a bed on the floor because she was afraid to be alone.

They were sad days, and at night she would lie awake listen-ing to Kate's deep breathing, while she was filled with re-morse, remembering old days in Lombard Street; then she would pray for forgiveness, until she laughed at herself. It was only the deserted woman who had time to repent. When Edward returned she would be as lighthearted as ever.

Time hung heavily. Often she and Kate donned the sober garments of some of the serving maids, and with their hoods well over their faces went into the streets. On such expeditions they would laugh and giggle together, and Jane would forget her jealousy of the King's new mistress.

Once they wandered into East Cheap and there came face to face with a woman who recognised Jane in spite of her concealing hood.

"I should know your sweet face anywhere," said Mistress Banster. "Dost think I should ever forget what you did for my Charlie? You must come to my back parlour for a cup of wine."

Jane saw that the woman would have been hurt had she refused, so she allowed Mistress Banster to conduct them into the parlour by means of a side door. "For, good gracious me," said the woman, "if I took you through the shop they'd stare you out of countenance. I swear they've never seen such loveli-ness."

It was a fusty little room to which she took them; the smell of greasy cooking hung about it and the flies kept up a con-tinual buzzing. Through the narrow smudgy window it was

possible to see a small square of backyard in which the rats
foraged over refuse heaps.

Charlie came in; he kept touching his ears in such a way
that moved Jane deeply. "You must always count me your
friend," she told them impulsively.

It was a great day for them, Mistress Banster told her; she
and Charlie had never thought to entertain Jane Shore in their
back parlour. If ever Jane and Kate were in East Cheap and in
need of refreshment, the Bansters would deem it a great honour
if they came to this shop parlour to take it.

After that Jane often slipped on the sombre cloak, and she
never passed the cookshop without going in. Sitting in that
frowsty parlour she felt she could regain her self-esteem. It
was so pleasant to slip a little money into the hands of poor
people; and their adoration of her was gratifying, smarting as
she was under Edward's neglect. When she passed the house
in Lombard Street she would suffer deep depression, and feel
heavy with the weight of her sins. She would face the truth
then. She had deserted her duty that her wild passion for a
man might be gratified. She had grown to love the brilliance
and excitement of court life. When Edward's eyes were on
her, admiring, desiring, she felt as though she were engaged
in some mad dance which she could not stop, though she felt
it might be leading her to destruction. Sometimes, wrapped in
her concealing cloak, she would stop to listen to a preacher at
Paul's Cross. "The wages of sin is death," said the preacher,
and although he dared not talk openly of the licentious court,
she knew he preached against it. And was she not one of the
brightest lights of that court—the chief courtesan—passionate,
sensuous, as eager for love as Edward himself! Though she
was faithful to him and he was unfaithful to her, she believed
she sinned as deeply as he did. But when she went to the
humble cookshop in East Cheap, her mood was lightened. To
these people she had done good service. And not only to them.
How many people had been made happier because Jane Shore
was the King's mistress! How many had escaped torture and

death! Watching the stern-faced preacher, she could reason, "I may have lost my own soul, but I have saved the bodies of others."

And these visits to East Cheap had their sequel. Mistress Banster, sipping her wine one day, talked of her neighbour, a certain Mistress Clack, a rival of hers and a woman for whom she had no great liking.

"A hard creature and barely feeds them that work for her. Some of the scum of London she keeps in her kitchens. Poor starving things, they come and look into my rubbish heaps for what they can find. And, my word, I heard a story the other day . . ."

Jane was alert, listening to the story Mistress Banster had to tell. It seemed that a certain Lottie, who had at one time worked at Mistress Clack's, now pursued a different trade in Southwark, and came along now and then to visit Mistress Banster.

"Lottie has changed. A poor shivering thing she used to be. I caught her once picking over my refuse. I brought her in and gave her a crust. We were friends after that. Well, Lottie ran away. I know where she went and I didn't blame her. A girl can't live on Clack's food. She's in a house now . . . over at Southwark. Well, that's another story; and what she told me is past believing. Mind you, I've seen this poor thing in their back yard . . . a little wisp of a thing. 'Tis hard to believe she might be a lady of high rank, and Lottie swears she's mad. But, says Lottie, there was such a to-do when she got away that Lottie can't but think she is this Lady Anne Neville she thinks herself to be."

"Lady Anne Neville!" cried Jane.

"So Lottie says. She was kept in that house, you see . . . and Lottie talked to her, and she talked to Lottie. Stark, raving mad, Lottie thought she were. Lottie told her a girl could get her food and a bed at Clack's place, and to Clack's place the poor thing came when she ran away from Southwark. She's begged and prayed of Lottie not to tell a soul who she is.

Lottie, you see, was in my back when out comes the poor thing to Clack's back . . . and they just stared at one another, and this poor thing goes white as a ghost. She's not in her right senses, she ain't."

Jane gripped her stool. Could it be that unwittingly she had found Anne Neville, and that it was within her power to end the poor girl's suffering? She thought of Edward, eyes narrowed, while the purple blood flooded his face. Edward would be terribly angry if she meddled again. She dared not. She had to think continually of pleasing Edward, and now that he desired someone else more than he desired her, her position was precarious. She would go away and forget this story. That was the wise thing to do.

But one thing Jane had never learned was wisdom. How could she ever be happy again if she did not do all she could for Anne and Richard? She could not shut out of her mind the picture of a poor starving girl, escaped from a brothel, picking over refuse in the backyard of an East Cheap cookshop.

"I must see this girl," she said. "Would it be possible for you to bring her to me?"

Mistress Banster said she could but try. But the girl was timid, for she had already been frightened out of her wits. If she knew someone wanted to see her she would probably fly out of Clack's and never be heard of again. It might be possible to lure her in with the promise of a crust or a little soup.

Jane sat in the Banster parlour while Mistress Banster went into her backyard and waited for someone to come out, whom she might ask to bring the girl to her.

It was a wretchedly miserable hour for Jane. She kept reminding herself how easy it would be to call Mistress Banster in; to go from the shop and forget all about Anne Neville. But that was something she could not bring herself to do.

It seemed a long time before Mistress Banster brought the girl in. Anne's eyes were sunken and there was an unhealthy flush on her cheeks! her hair, which should have been lovely, hung lank and greasy round her gaunt face; she was dressed in

dirty rags that scarcely covered her thin body; but Jane recog
nised her as the girl who had ridden captive in the chariot with
Margaret of Anjou.

Anne was terrified at the sight of Jane and turned to run,
but very gently Jane took her hand, and in Jane's face was all the
kindness of her heart, so that it was impossible even for one as
fear-haunted as Anne Neville to doubt her good intentions.

"I am your friend," said Jane. "I want to help you. Will
you sit here beside me?"

Anne looked down at her dirty garments and shuddered; but
Jane put an arm about her and drew her down beside her. "I
am Jane Shore," said Jane.

"I have heard of you," said Anne. "You are good, the poor
people say."

"Let us talk of you. There is one who loves you dearly and
who has sought you long. He still seeks you."

Anne's face was illumined suddenly: "Richard?" she said.

"He came to search for you in Southwark."

"Then it was he who came." She began to cry weakly. "How
can I tell who is my friend when my own sister's husband . . ."

"George is wicked and cruel," said Jane vehemently. "But
you love Richard and Richard loves you. I will bring him here
to you. And then you will know you are safe."

Anne collapsed into hysterical weeping. She reiterated that
she did not know whom she might trust. Her brother-in-law
had taken her into his house; and from there he had had her
despatched to an evil house in Southwark.

The thin claw-like fingers clutched at Jane's cloak.

"I was a prisoner there. I discovered what sort of house it
was. The girls told me. They told me that when I was well
enough, what had happened to them . . . would happen to
me. It is a terrible house. I heard horrible laughing . . . and
sobbing. Babies are born there . . . but those babies never live.
They throw their bodies in the river. I thought they were
bringing someone to me . . . and I ran away. The women
who looked after me told me I must run away, or what had

happened to them would happen to me. And it was Richard
who came; Richard . . . who came to find me! I ran away
though . . . and so I came to Mistress Clack's. You are good.
I know you are good. You would not betray me. I think George
meant to kill me. But you would not lie to me, Jane Shore.
You have a kind and lovely face and you would not lie to
me. . . ."

Jane wept with her. What terrible things can happen to
women! thought Jane. And she did not care that she had
jeopardised her position with Edward; she did not care that she
had placed herself in greater danger than before.

*   *   *   *   *

Dazed, Anne went back to the kitchen behind Mistress
Clack's cook-shop. Mistress Clack, puffing as she walked
about because she was so fat, cursed her as she came in. Mistress Clack was eating—she ate all the time—and grease ran
down her chin. She picked continuously at the food with her
dirty, greasy, food-stained fingers as she cooked it.

"And where have you been? Missing nigh on an hour.
There'll be no dinner for you. Them that don't work gets no
food, I say."

Food! Who wanted her greasy food? Richard was coming.
Jane Shore was bringing him. Richard would protect her from
George, and Jane Shore would protect her from Edward.

Now she must wash the floor. Usually the task sickened her,
but to-day it mattered not at all. She must go down on her
hands and knees and pick up the greasy bits of chewed gristle
spat out by Mistress Clack. Some cleanliness there had to be or
the rats would have become unmanageable. This she had
endured for weeks—the hot, fetid atmosphere of the kitchen,
the cuffs that had come her way; for there was none, declared
Mistress Clack, as incompetent to work in her kitchen as
Anne, and Anne knew there was justice in the remark. Still,
she preferred this to that frightening Southwark house. This
was hard labour in exchange for scraps of food which were

flung to her as though she were a dog. Indeed, the dogs under her father's tables had fared far better than she did in the Clack kitchen. But this she had to endure if she were to eat and be able to throw herself down on to her straw every night, her limbs aching with the day's fatigue. Nights held their terrors as well as the days; she was worried by lice, and rats that pulled at the coverlet; and those poor miserable half-starved people who worked with her laughed at the way she spoke and her dainty manner of eating; they cursed her and threw things at her when she coughed at night. Then she was glad of the hard work that tired her so completely and gave her some nightly hours of oblivion.

And now . . . it might well be ended. There was about that courtesan, the King's favourite, such an air of kindliness as Anne had never come across in the whole of her life. She had even feared Richard a little, and, although she admired him, was never completely at ease in his company. Yet Jane had been different, gentle and yet hot in her indignation at the suffering of others. She had heard Jane Shore's name mentioned often in the Clack cook-shop, sometimes accompanied by obscenities, but often spoken of with something like reverence. Anne cared not what Jane had done, for Jane was good. Jane had given her new hope and faith. She would trust Jane; and in spite of everything that had happened, she believed only good could come through Jane.

"Mistress Banster's asking for yer," whispered one of her fellow-workers who was more kindly than the others. "Run orf now. P'raps it's a plate of soup she's got for you."

Anne took one last look round the kitchen. She knew she would never see it again; she wanted to remember it in every detail; she would never forget the stale, greasy smell of cheap roasting flesh, the smell of dirt and decay.

She ran out of the room and to the street. Outside the Bansters' was a chariot. Jane was at the side entrance. She had been crying and her smile was very tender; and the way in which she looked at Anne made the girl forget her terrors.

"He is here," whispered Jane.

And there he was, coming towards her, hardly changed at all. His features twisted oddly when he saw her. "Anne!" he cried. "Anne!"

Then he held out his arms and she ran into them. They embraced—the man elegant in his fur-embroidered garments, the girl in her filthy rags.

Jane watched them, silently weeping.

*   *   *   *   *

The King stormed up and down the Queen's apartment.

"A pretty kettle of fish, I'll swear. Warwick's girl found in a cook-shop and brought to Sanctuary! Now we shall have trouble. George is swearing she is his ward and none shall marry her without his consent. Richard was the one to find her —and how, I should like to know. Hath my noble brother formed a habit of visiting the cook-shops of East Cheap? Richard swears he will marry her whether I give my consent or not. Would to God the girl had been left to rot in her cook-shop!"

"My lord," said Elizabeth, "there is one way out of this. Give her to Richard, and George's anger might lead to—anything. Let her stay in Sanctuary until something can be done."

The King's anger faded; he went to the Queen and put his hands on her shoulders, laughing down at her. "Clever Bessy will look after the girl, eh? Bessy will find her a pleasant husband."

"You mock me. I think it our duty . . ."

"That's the trouble, Bess. Your sense of duty towards your family is a little too strong at times."

"I want Anne's happiness and security."

"Together with half the Warwick fortune for the Woodvilles. I am weary of the girl. How *did* Richard find her? He must have had help in this matter. I wish I could find his helpers. They should repent through every vein in their hearts."

The King's anger frightened Jane. She knew he was most

disturbed by the importunings of his brothers. The court kept out of the way of all three as much as possible. An ominous quiet hung over the court. This affair, it was whispered, might well lead to more serious trouble. Grave events had started from less inflammable matter. Next to the King these two men were the most powerful in the country, and here they were, ready to fly at each other's throats.

Edward must give a bold and prompt decision without delay, but Edward was undecided. Clarence was on one side of him, Gloucester on the other, pulling him this way and that; and in the background was the Queen, who said, "Give the girl to neither; give her to the Woodvilles."

Edward did what he always did in times of stress: he went to Jane. There was none, he knew, who loved him as disinterestedly as she did.

"My head feels fit to burst," he told her. "By the Virgin, Jane, there's trouble brewing."

She would have him lie back on her couch while she applied sweet-scented unguents to his temples. Her fingers were cool and soothing.

"There are times," he said, "when I think there is none in this kingdom I can trust save you." He put an arm about her and drew her down beside him. "There is no peace for me. Richard wants the girl; George wants her. What can I do?"

"Give your consent to her marriage with Richard. Let her be brought from Sanctuary, let the wedding be celebrated—and there is an end to the matter."

"An end, Jane? That would be but a beginning. Then would start the real fight between my brothers."

"How so, if she be Richard's wife?"

"It is not the girl they fight for; it is her fortune."

"That may be so with George, but not with Richard."

"Still, Richard was ever one to demand his rights."

"Edward, think not of Anne's fortune, but of herself. She loves Richard and Richard loves her. Let them marry. Do not we ourselves know what it is to love?"

He laughed. "Assuredly we do. And so well that methinks we but waste time in discussing the affairs of others."

"Give your consent to her marriage with Richard."

"You are a fervent advocate."

"Is it such a big thing to ask?"

"It is indeed. Why do you not ask for the things it is easy to give—as do some? Your pleas are all for others. Do this for them, you say, when what I wish is to do some good to you."

"Richard has been true to you always and George has been your enemy. Why should you now seek to please George at Richard's expense?"

"There is no need to placate one's friends, only one's enemies."

"That is cowardly, surely."

"When there is trouble for this land in sight, verily I am a coward. I would to God the girl had never been found!"

"You cannot say that," she cried passionately. "A cook-shop! A foul, stinking place—and she Warwick's daughter! What she must have suffered we cannot know. Edward, you must let her be happy now."

There were tears in her eyes, not only for Anne, but for herself and perhaps for him. She sensed that there was no pity in him. Anne was nothing to him but a nuisance; and Jane trembled to contemplate the blindness of that love she had given to such a man. She had been bewitched by too much beauty, too much charm of manner. She had seen the brilliant shell, not the man he was, until too late. She was frightened, too, because it was not the real Jane whom he loved; it was *her* brilliant shell—the lovely oval face, the soft white skin, the merry laughter.

"By the Virgin," he was saying, "I would I knew how Richard discovered her. *That* he refuses to tell. But this I know —someone found her and carried the tale to him. If I could lay hands on that man I would make him repent it."

She buried her face against the jewelled surface of his coat.

"What would you do to him, Edward?"

"He should die a traitor's death."

Jane closed her eyes, saw the yelling mob, herself dragged to Tyburn all through the streets of London. She imagined rough hands laid upon her, the coarse shouts of the crowd—and the horrible death.

" 'Twould not be just," she said, "for such a little thing."

"A little thing!" How quickly his anger came. She did not look into his face, but she knew the colour would have flamed up under his skin and behind his eyes, and that his mouth would be ugly. There would be little left of that gay and charming merchant who had captured her heart and even now refused to let it go. "A little thing to cause me such uneasiness? You understand not such matters. I have enough of trouble. Is not George waiting—seeking an opportunity to rise against me? In such breeding ground are wars spawned."

When he was calmer she said: "Yet, 'twas wrong that that gentle girl should suffer so. And Richard, who has ever served you well, should be well served by you."

"You are over-soft to lovers, Jane."

"Might that not be because I am one myself?"

"Ah," he said. "I also. And you are the one I love, Jane."

Her heart was beating fast with fear. How much did he love her? How deep did his love go below the senses? That recklessness of hers, which she had never been able to curb, swept over her. She was in a mood now to throw away everything in order to learn the truth.

She knelt up on the couch. Her eyes looked dark and big.

"What ails thee, Jane?"

"I have something to say to you, Edward."

"Say it quickly and come down to me again."

"It was I who found Anne Neville—I who found her for Richard."

"*You* found Anne Neville! *You*—again?"

She bowed her head and closed her eyes, an awful numbing fear taking hold of her. He struggled up; he had her by the shoulders and his grip was fierce. What a fool I was! she thought. Why did I do it? Why did I give Anne to Richard and lose Edward for myself? Or, having done it, why did I tell?

"I would know more of this," said Edward.

She flung up her head, her cheeks flaming and her eyes flashing. "I care not what you say!" she cried. "He loved her. He was unhappy. She was unhappy too. I found her—and I sent him to her. What is it to be—the traitor's death?"

He looked at her flushed and lovely face. "Holy Mother of God!" he exclaimed, and, bursting into sudden laughter, he pulled her down to him and kissed her fiercely. His loud booming laughter shook them both. She laughed with him.

"What is this?" she said at length. "Is it the last rites before the traitor's death?"

"So—it was you, Jane. My sweet and lovely meddling Jane. You shall tell me all about it. But not now."

There was relief in her laughter now. While she had beauty, while she could arouse his desires she had nothing to fear, for his amours were more important to Edward than anything else.

"My loving Jane," he said, "who was so kind to those who loved!"

"Edward!" She caught his face and held him from her for a breathless second. "Edward, promise me—your consent to their marriage."

"What?" he cried. "You would bargain?"

"Yes, I will bargain."

"And you so kind to those who love?"

"I could never resist you, as you well know. Thus it was in the beginning; thus will it always be. Whatever you refuse me, whatever you give me, I can but love you."

"My dearest Jane," he said, "there is nothing I could deny you." His face was close to hers; his voice grew faint and blurred. "Richard shall have his Anne. Let them enjoy each other—as we do. As we shall. . . ."

THE TOWER OF LONDON (PART I)

FROM Fickets Fields to London Bridge the people were assembling. From the Abbey at Westminster to St. Giles's in the midst of green fields, from St. Clement Danes without Temple Bar to St. Peter ad Vincula within the precincts of the Tower of London, the bells rang out.

In the gardens of the Palace of the Tower Jane sat with Anne, Duchess of Gloucester; and with them were the two little Princes, the King's sons, young Edward who was now five years old and his brother Richard who was two years younger. Jane had been reading aloud to the children from Malory's *Morte D'Arthur*, which William Caxton had recently printed and presented to the royal household; but now the book had been laid aside and the children played on the grass while the two women talked desultorily; and there was about women and children an air of expectancy.

It was three years since Anne Neville had married Richard, and she had now a son—another Edward—who was just two years old. She was, Jane knew, calmly happy, but her terrible experiences had left their mark upon her. She was nervous and timid; and she did not like staying in this palace; but that was an aversion she shared with Jane, who could not forget, as she walked in the shelter of the ballium wall or rested in the gardens and saw the weather-washed walls of the White Tower and the solid strength of the Beauchamp, that this was a prison, and behind those great white walls men suffered torment too terrible to be thought of.

Young Edward looked up from his play. "I wonder what time my father will come."

"We cannot be sure," answered Jane, "but we shall hear the shouting and the trumpets long before they reach the Tower."

"One day," said Edward, "I shall ride at the head of the cavalcade as does my father. One day the people will shout for me."

"One day!" echoed Richard, who adored his brother and repeated everything he said, for he had been taught that young Edward was to be King of England.

"Do you think my father has conquered all France?" asked Edward.

"I doubt whether the conquest was as complete as that," Jane told him. "We must wait to hear what he has to tell."

"Four months since they went away," said Anne. "It might have been years."

"Jane," said young Edward, "when the feasting is ended, how long before we return to Westminster or Windsor?"

"You do not like this old palace?" said Jane.

"I like Windsor," said Edward.

"I like Windsor," echoed Richard. "And I like Baynard's Castle with grandmamma."

"This is beautiful," said Jane quickly. "Why, the gardens are lovely. I thought you loved the paintings in the great hall. Did you not tell me the story of Antiochus pictured on the walls there?"

"I like the paintings," said Edward. "But this is a prison—more than a palace. If you walk along by the Beauchamp you see faces at the windows."

"You should not wander about alone."

"I am not afraid to wander alone," said Edward with dignity. "But I like not prisons. I have heard people say that when this place was built years and years ago they buried people alive in these walls—built them in—to bring good fortune to the place. Oh, Jane—Aunt Anne—it was children they built in—like myself and Richard and Elizabeth and Cecily . . ."

"You must not listen to such tales," said Jane quickly. "Shall I read to you?"

Jane read, but the boys were too excited to listen; they wandered off.

"I thank the Virgin," said Anne, "that my little Edward will never wear the crown."

"There are some," said Jane, "who reach up greedily for it, and others who turn away from it."

"King Henry was one to turn away."

Jane found she was shivering. Just beyond this garden in which they sat was that very Wakefield Tower in which, long ago, King Henry the Sixth had been stabbed to death.

Jane hastily changed the subject, and after a while she stood up, declaring it was time they prepared themselves to receive the men.

"Where are the boys?" asked Anne.

"They should not wander off alone. They see sights not meant for their young eyes. Their nurses will be looking for them."

But Jane was not thinking much of the children; she was contemplating the return of Edward with apprehension as well as excitement. It was four months since he had left England to wage war on France; she wondered what those four months had done to change him, for even before he left Edward was rapidly changing from a young and handsome man into a corpulent old one. But his charm had not abated. She remembered how, to raise money to take the war into France, he had gone about the country demanding what he called Benevolences. He had visited even the outlying villages, wheedling money from the pockets of the people, and it was astonishing to see them come to him, reluctant, even sullen, and go away smiling. The sight of him and the words he had spoken were worth every coin the people had pledged themselves to pay him. The women longed to be called before him, to be kissed and complimented and smiled upon; the men talked in the inns, for long after, of what the King had said and how he had shaken them by the hand. The country adored him; he could carry it into war and his people might grumble, but when he appeared with a smile or a kiss they were ready to worship him.

He had sailed with his brothers George and Richard;

Hastings was with them too. Jane had wondered if she would ever see any of them again.

And as she was about to make her way to her apartments, Kate came running out of the palace and with her was one of the nurses of the young Princes. Both women looked distraught.

"Mistress," said the nurse, "I cannot find the young Princes anywhere. They will not be ready to greet their father."

"I have searched the palace," cried Kate. "They are nowhere to be found."

"But they were here a short time ago," said Anne.

"Let us all go and look for them," said Jane. "It will not be long then, I swear, before we find them."

They left the palace gardens and wandered off in different directions—Kate went one way, Jane and Anne another; and the nurse in yet another.

Kate, rather more plump than she had been a few years ago, as gay as ever, called to a warden whom she saw making his way towards one of the towers. He had seen the little boys, he said; they had wandered towards the cook's place. If Kate went through the postern gate, she would see a flight of stairs. That was where the warden had last seen the little boys.

Kate lost no time in hurrying through the postern and down the flight of stairs. She came to a heavy door which was ajar, and, pushing it open, heard someone singing a jolly roystering song. She paused to listen to it, and smelt the appetising smell of roasting flesh.

She was standing on the threshold of a big kitchen with a low ceiling and a floor of stone. In one of the biggest fireplaces she had ever seen a great log fire was burning, sending up cloud after cloud of smoke through the great chimney. Before the fire a huge carcase was roasting, and a poor little scullion, who looked as though he had been scorched and shrivelled by the intense heat, was seated on a stool watching it. At the end of the room was a huge table laden with great pies, cold meat, and fish as yet uncooked. There were several people in the kitchen —warders, jailors, scullions and lower servants of the royal

household; but Kate scarcely paused to look at them, for sitting
on the table, where the food had been pushed aside to make
room for them, their faces flushed with excitement, their legs
dangling, sat the two little Princes. Kate dashed at them.

"My lords! My lords!" she cried. "What do you here? Your
nurse is looking for you. Your noble father will be waiting."

"Look about you," said Edward. "Is this not a wonderful
place?"

Now Kate was aware of a man who was standing beside
her, a mighty man who towered above her so that she had to
lift her head high to see his jolly face that was topped by his
white cook's cap, and as she looked Kate's astonishment was
replaced by a great bounding joy. "Belper!" she cried shrilly.

Belper dropped the ladle he was holding on to a pie of
savoury meats with such force that it broke the top crust of
pastry. He took a pace towards her and let out a mighty roar
of recognition. "Kate! Merry hell! And looking as bonny as a
fresh roast peacock."

Then was Kate held fast against the great white-clad body
that smelt of good wine and delicious food, while she received
a great smacking kiss on the mouth. "Now, Kate, what do
you here?" he demanded when he released her. And what joy
it was for Kate to see his face, fat, red and shining, and his eyes
creased up with delight!

"My fortune changed," she told him. "I followed Mistress
Shore to court."

"Fortune changed for me also," he told her. "I have been
here ever since I left Goldsmith Shore. It suits me. Every soul
in this place depends on me for what he eats. What a life it is!
I eat till I can eat no more. Most work to fill their own bellies,
but I work to fill those of others as well as mine own." Belper
had always roared with laughter at the lightest joke, but when
the joke was his own he was particularly pleased with it. He
nudged Kate in case she had missed the point; but Kate was in
no need of nudges. Now everyone in the kitchen was laughing,
and Kate was remembering Belper's infectious enjoyment.

"Sit down, Kate!" roared Belper. "What'll you have? A

slice of peacock or a wedge of wild boar? I have a fine roasted ox. . . ."

Weak from so much laughter, Kate shook her head. She had been sent in search of the Princes that they might be ready in time to greet their father. "I dare not stay . . . much as you tempt. Another time . . . mayhap."

"Another time it shall be, good Kate. Another time! *Any* time. Ask for me. Belper. Here you shall feast, sweetheart, and if you should at any time of the day feel the need of a mouthful and a tankard to wash it down . . . then come to Belper. Belper has just what you need." He nudged her, his twinkling eyes showing that he was about to go off into another bout of choking laughter. Kate would have been glad to have stayed, but she turned away from the fascinating cook to the two little boys.

Belper paused in his laughter. "Now after the banquet to-night there'll be a feast in these kitchens. . . ."

"After the banquet," said Kate, her eyes glistening.

"To-night," said Belper in a whisper which could be heard throughout the kitchen.

"To-night," whispered Kate, and hurried the Princes out of the kitchen, feeling that if she did not go quickly she would never be able to tear herself away.

"I like Cook Belper," said Edward.

"I like Cook Belper," said Richard.

"Ah," put in Kate fervently, "and well I like him also, my little lordships."

*   *   *   *   *

At the head of the table in the great hall sat Edward the King. He was in a deeply contented mood as he looked along the laden table at the brilliantly-clad people assembled there. The stained glass windows threw a warm and cheerful glow on the table and the velvet hangings and those wonderful pictures which had been painted on the walls added comfort and bright beauty to the ancient and noble room.

Many oxen, sheep and pigs had been roasted to provide this

banquet, together with swans, pike, porpoises, pheasants, peacocks, calves and boars. Edward had given orders that this banquet was to be more lavish than any other, for he was anxious that his people might know that it was given to celebrate a most successful campaign. He would have them know that the French business had been satisfactorily concluded.

Edward frowned as his gaze fell on Richard. Richard looked grim, for he was not pleased with the way things had gone in France; he had gone so far as to dissociate himself from those dealings between Edward and the crafty old French King. Richard, thought Edward impatiently, had too many scruples. Why be ashamed that there had been no real war? Why be ashamed to take French bribes? Better to spend wealth in good living than to squander it on fruitless wars. Naturally Louis was ready to pay so that English soldiers might be removed from French soil. Richard had painstakingly pointed out that the people of England had paid the King their "benevolences" that lost territory in France might be regained. Richard could be a young fool at times with his talk of honour. The King and his nobles were richer by many thousands of French crowns, and Edward's eldest daughter Elizabeth was betrothed to the Dauphin. If Richard refused his share of the French bribe, that was his folly.

The minstrels were coming into the gallery. A year ago Edward would have been the first to dance, either with the Queen or with Jane. He smiled affectionately from one to the other. They had scarcely changed at all, and one of his greatest pleasures in coming home had been to see them again. How lovely Jane was! Louis had insisted that he should make the acquaintance of the most attractive women in France, and this he had quickly set about doing with his habitual skill and conquering charm; yet he had not found one to equal Jane. She had grown plumper, but he liked plump women.

Jane returned his smile. She was fighting hard not to show that the King's appearance shocked her. The purple in his face had deepened, and there were heavy bags under his eyes. He had left his radiant youth behind him in France. He had caught a fever there, an unpleasant ailment that shook him every now and then with returning fits of ague. He was no longer the beautiful Edward.

"Dance!" he cried and sat back watching. Elizabeth the Queen sat with him, for she did not care to dance, fearing it impaired her dignity. But Jane danced. How Jane danced! Jane looked but a girl still; the years had done little to change her. She was now dancing with the elder of his two stepsons, Thomas, Marquis of Dorset. A handsome man, young Thomas, and even the most casual observer could see that Thomas was Elizabeth's boy. Edward wondered idly about Elizabeth's first husband and the marriage which had produced Thomas and his younger brother. Had Elizabeth been warmer to her first husband than she was to her second?

But his attention was back with the dancers. He was not sure that he liked to see Jane and Dorset together. They were much of an age, and the young man had already the reputation of being one of the most profligate at court. He was as haughty as his mother, and doubtless as ambitious, but he certainly had not inherited Elizabeth's cold blood.

Dorset was saying to Jane: "It is a great pleasure to be home again. Give me good English fare and English women. The French! Bah! Their cooking is over-greasy, and their women over-warm."

"It surprises me," said Jane, "not that you find cause for complaint in the former, but that you do also in the latter."

"There you are mistaken, Madam. Warmth should be kindled by the one who desires it."

"You mean it is more pleasant to hunt the wild boar than the tame peacock?"

His beautiful eyes lingered on her. "Indeed, yes. And how exciting it can be to hunt in forbidden woods!"

"But surely none is forbidden the King's stepson?"

"The King's stepson is not the King, alas!"

"Indeed no. And methinks that the King remembers that, though his stepson may appear to have forgotten it."

It was reproof, for he was too bold, and she would have him

know that it was unwise to be so. But she was excited and exhilarated; she was susceptible to his handsome charm. Life had been dull these last four months and there was nothing Jane loved so much as gaiety. And now the King was home, but he was a different man from that Edward who had left England four months ago. She had looked forward to a passionate reunion; she was deeply shocked to realise that she could no longer feel passion for the King. That was why she was faintly alarmed by the bold glances of this attractive young man.

She sought now to change the subject. "What think you, my lord Marquis, of this French affair?"

Dorset smiled. He thought very well of it indeed. He was one of those who were richer for the venture. "The people want glory," he said. "They want to hear names like Crécy and Agincourt again. They are bewildered now, but, never fear, Edward will subdue them. What a King! He has but to smile, to lure money from their pockets."

"The people will surely be glad to see their men safe home."

"Rest assured they will, and give not a thought to the money they paid to the King. Edward can melt the heart of a nation as easily as he melts the reluctance of his women."

"The war in France has changed him. He looks ten years older than he did."

"Too much good living in Paris. And then . . . his fever. It pulls a man down when he begins to climb up his thirties, and Edward has always partaken too freely of the good things of life."

The dance was over, another had begun. To her dismay Jane found herself unable to refuse the partnership of Hastings.

The face of Hastings was haggard, his eyes in their deep sockets were mournful. He still watched Jane with brooding desire; she wondered now why she had ever been afraid of him. She told herself she hated him still, but she found that even her dismay was partly feigned, for the man's devotion was truly flattering, and it was stimulating to have the men home again. She needed gaiety; she needed to exchange bright words with Dorset, cruel ones with Hastings . . . for the King had come home a different man from the lover who had gone away.

She saw that Hastings was angry now, and that was because he had been watching her with Dorset.

"Well, Jane," he said, "this is the happiest moment of four long months."

"You did not enjoy your stay in France?"

"You know I could not when a stretch of water separated us two."

"I'll warrant you found much to amuse you."

"I thought of you continually."

"Enough of such talk, for I like it not."

"Mayhap you like it better from Dorset?"

She flushed. "You are insolent, my lord."

"I would warn you that Dorset is the biggest rake at court."

She was angry now. She had been foolish. She had let him see that she was attracted by Dorset. "Since when, sir," she said, "did you resign the title to him?"

"Since I became so enamoured of you that none other could please me."

Jane laughed. "Deceive yourself not. 'Twas cruel age not faithfulness that forced you to give way to Dorset."

Hastings was angry as only she could make him angry. "One day you will be sorry for this."

"So you still continue to plot against me?"

"I plot only for your happiness."

"That has been very clear to see, right from the moment you planned my abduction."

"Will you never forget a youthful folly?"

"Never! If I ever have a chance to repay you, rest assured I will."

"You are so kind to others, so cruel to me. Why?"

"Because I hate you. Because I have always hated you."

"It is a relief to know you are not indifferent. One day you will come to me, and on that day you will have become a wise woman."

"You may not be the biggest rake at court, but you certainly are the biggest coxcomb."

"I must be proud, Jane, because I am the man you will one day love. The King grows old, and you grow out of love with him."

"How dare you!"

"You give yourself away, Jane. Will you never learn to be wise? Dorset has nothing but a beautiful body . . . and misery to offer you. I grow old, but I can love you deeply and tenderly. Jane, forget me not."

"I shall never forget you . . . never forget my hatred of you."

"You should not have danced with Dorset for so long. The King's eyes were on you."

"I see they are on me and Hastings," she retorted. "I will take your hint and see that I do not dance over long with you."

She sat long beside Edward and together they watched the dancers.

"I saw you dance with Dorset. Have a care, Jane." His fat hand, with the rings embedded in it, patted hers. "That young stripling hath a reputation as evil as . . ."

"As evil as your own," laughed Jane. "Nay, my lord, there is none at this court to be compared with that of its King."

He laughed, but he was quickly sobered. "But, Jane, 'tis a handsome fellow, that young stepson of mine."

"You have brought jealousy back from France as well as a fever. There is none in this court to compare with yourself. Ask any, and you will be told that is so."

"There will always be those to tell a King what he wishes to hear."

"When I pass the lad I will avert my eyes, if that is Your Grace's pleasure."

"It is our pleasure," he said seriously. "Nay, our command."

* * * * *

The two little Princes were playing together in Jane's apartment. They often came, for Jane encouraged them; she had longed for children of her own, and since none had come to her it seemed natural that she should give her attention to Edward's sons. The Princes were lonely children. The Queen was fond of them, but she had little time to spare for them. Elizabeth Woodville would always be Queen first, mother second. So to Jane they came.

They were shouting at her now. "Come on, Jane. You're not the warder now, you know. You are the King of France. All you have to do is to sit on your throne and look wicked. Oh, Richard, look at Jane looking wicked!"

Richard rolled on the floor in his amusement at Jane's impersonation of the French King.

Sitting on her stool, looking sly and crafty as the French King, Jane's thoughts ran on uneasily. She was out of love with the father of these children. Strange that she should be the one to be tired first. He must never know it, of course. He seemed so old nowadays. At this moment he was in his room in the castle—for they were at Windsor—poring over his charts and crucible, for now he was obsessed by the thought of changing base metal into gold. And Jane, although she was twenty-six, was young still.

She must not complain, for life had been good to her. She was rich now in her own right. Edward had given her a small but delightful house with beautiful gardens which ran down to the river; it was a charming place, luxurious enough for the entertaining of a King. But her friends told her she was a fool. She could have been the richest woman in the country, for Edward would give her all she asked. Ironical it was that now she had ceased to love him he seemed to love her more.

"The treaty is signed," said Edward shrilly. "We're back in England now."

"Let's play prisoners," said Richard. "I like that better than French treaties. That happened long ago."

"Not so long," said Edward. "Two years."

"But that *is* a long time ago, and there are always prisoners."

"Richard, you shall be prisoner," said Edward; "and Jane,

you will have to challenge us as we come through the Traitor's Gate."

"Holy Mother," cried Jane, "can you not play a more cheerful game?"

"Be ready," insisted Richard.

"I will. Now. In the King's name!"

Her thoughts had gone back to the King. It was two years since he had returned from France, and as each week passed he grew less like the man she had loved. He was very fat, diseased and often violent; it was true that that inimitable charm was still with him, but the change was tragic. She had lost Edward, not to another woman as she had always feared she would, but to age and disease. Edward had grown old, and Jane had stayed young. She tried not to see too much of Dorset.

Everything was changing about her. Kate had left her; she had married Cook Belper and lived with him in his quarters at the Tower of London. Anne of Gloucester had left the South and was living with Richard in her old home at Middleham Castle.

The boys were looking at her expectantly.

"In the King's name I challenge you!"

"A dangerous rascal," said Edward. "It will be the torture chambers for him."

They were both pleased with Jane's shudder; it was so realistic.

"Let me see the warrant," said Jane severely.

"Here it is; and I would have your acknowledgment of the prisoner."

"Take care how you ascend the steps," said Jane. "They are very slippery, and many a prisoner has fallen and broken his bones."

"Ha," said Edward, "they'll be broken fast enough on the rack, never fear."

"Speak not of such matters," said Jane in earnest.

"Bah!" said Edward, while Richard squealed with delight. "Thou art over-squeamish, man."

"You may rack me to death and you'll not draw my secrets from me," cried Richard proudly; and at that moment there was a tap on the door, and, being bidden to enter, Thomas Grey, Marquis of Dorset came in.

"Thomas!" shrieked Edward in delight, while Richard ran to his half-brother and began climbing up his legs.

Dorset smiled at Jane over the children's heads. "What ruffians are these?" he cried. "I declare these crude manners cannot belong to the future King of England and His Grace the Duke of York."

"You must forgive them, my lord," said Jane. "They have so recently played a pair of blackguards that they need a little pause before they remember their rank."

Jane saw the adoration in the boys' eyes as they gazed up into the handsome face of their half-brother; she herself was uneasy as she always was in this man's presence. He reminded her so vividly of long ago days; he made her feel as she had felt in the shop in Lombard Street when her lover had come courting her. But the courtship of Dorset was a secret thing. She knew he was an ambitious man and could not forget that she was the King's mistress; he would remember too the sudden violent rages of the King; he had no wish to cause them. Always, it seemed, he waited for a sign from Jane. She gave none. At least, she had given none so far. He had now come to this apartment not to see the Princes but to see her. Standing there, he regarded her with his slow smile, whose meaning, except that there was a good mixing of desire in it, she did not completely understand. She guessed his intentions; his reputation was known to all, so how could she be ignorant of it? He was not the type of man any wise woman would have chosen for a lover; but when was Jane ever wise? His attraction was of a peculiar nature, for while he fascinated he repelled; but he excited madly; and Jane longed for excitement.

She said now: "I had not noticed the lateness of the hour. I must retire."

His smile was almost sardonic. "Is it not a strange thing,"

he said in mock sadness, "that when Dorset comes in Jane Shore must go out? Why must it be, I wonder?"

"The King will be expecting me."

"The King is closeted with my grandmother," said Dorset. "They consult the stars. The King does not miss you. But the King's sons and the King's stepson would miss you sorely if you went away."

"You shall stay, Jane," said Edward imperiously, for Edward, in his preparation for kingship, was often imperious.

Richard supported his brother. "You must stay for my execution, Jane. You have to be my mother watching with the crowd. Jane cries beautifully, Thomas."

"Cry or laugh, I'll warrant she does either . . . beautifully." Dorset took Jane's hand and as she would have withdrawn it he seized that of young Richard. "I like not this game of execution!" he said. "I know a better. It is a court banquet, and at the table all the old and sick are nodding, for they have eaten too much and drunk too freely. The minstrels have come into the gallery and all the young and beautiful have risen to dance. You are the young, brothers, and Jane is the beautiful. Come." He began to sing as he seized Jane. The children stood by watching breathlessly for a moment or two, then they joined the dance.

"Be not afraid," said Dorset.

"Afraid? Why should I be?"

"Methought you feared the wicked Marquis."

"Are you wicked then?"

"As wicked as you are beautiful. I ought to warn you, Jane, that when I set my heart on something I usually get it."

"What does Thomas say?" called Edward.

"Nothing of importance," retorted Jane. "He but repeats the idle chatter of the court."

*   *   *   *   *

The King had half an hour to spare before he went into conference with his French ambassador, so he went to Jane's apartment. He was very worried, and as usual the cause of his worry was his brother George. He had just left the Queen, and there was no tongue that clacked quite so fast as the Queen's when there was something she wanted. She never upbraided him; but she went on and on until she got what she wanted. And now what she asked was the imprisonment of George. She was right doubtless, but Edward was a family man, and he shrank from the task. From imprisonment to death could be a very short step. Edward had no wish to fall into that temptation.

He stretched himself out wearily and looked at Jane; he smiled because she never failed to delight his eyes nor his ears. It was a good day when he had gone to the goldsmith's place. He never regretted it.

Jane came to the couch and stretched herself out beside him. "It is George again, is it not?"

"It is always George."

Jane nodded. She knew that since his wife's death George had been trying to bring about an advantageous marriage for himself, and that his choice had fallen on Mary of Burgundy. George could never be allowed to have Burgundy, for his first plan would be to lead an army against England and try to win the throne for himself. Edward had refused to allow the match, and foolishly, at the Queen's request, had tried to persuade Mary to marry Lord Rivers, the Queen's brother. This was absurd, of course, for Rivers would never be considered as a suitable parti; but Edward, under the Queen's influence, had given way. George was furious that he should be slighted while the low-born brother of the Queen was promised what he himself desired. George was out to make fresh trouble.

"There will be no peace for me while he lives," said Edward slowly.

Jane looked at him in alarm. "You do not plan . . ."

"Does he not deserve anything that I might plan for him? Do you not know that had he been able he would have despatched *me* long ere this?"

"Yes . . . I believe he would." Jane laid a hand on his arm.

"But, Edward, I beg of you, do nothing which you would regret all your life."

"Regret!" Edward made an impatient movement. "Why should I regret . . . whatever I might do?"

Jane watched him uneasily. Anger made of him an old man; the veins at his temples stood out like knotted string. She felt a great tenderness towards him.

"You promised your father to look after him, and it was a sacred promise which you will never forget. Whatever he does to you—and I do not deny that he has deserved the worst you could do to him—you must forgive him, because he is your brother, and your father made you promise to look after him."

"Yes," he said slowly, "I promised. But how weary I am of the miserable affair! I would to God that brother of mine would catch a pox and die. Sit at my feet. I like to touch your hair. It looks as it ever did, as if it were sprinkled with powdered gold." She sat at his feet and his fat sparkling fingers fondled her hair. "You heard doubtless," he went on, "that George caused two of his servants to be hanged at Warwick. He trumped up a charge against them of poisoning his wife and child. I cannot allow him to usurp my power thus. He presumes too much."

"I fear the drink destroys his mind."

"Drink and his ridiculous opinion of himself will destroy his body, should he go on in this way. Were he any other he would have gone to the block long ere this. He turns his drunken bloodshot eyes towards the throne, Jane. I must act soon against him. The Queen . . ." He stopped and smiled wearily. "There is nothing that will please her but to see his head on London Bridge."

Now Jane understood. The Queen was urging him to get rid of Clarence. Elizabeth would not care how, as long as it was done. Edward was plagued by the Queen. He wished to remove his brother, but he was superstitious, and he could not forget a promise he had made to a dying father. So he came to Jane— tender-hearted, sentimental, unambitious Jane. She would plead for her worst enemy, because she was a soft-hearted little fool.

Jane could be relied upon to beg Edward to have no hand in murder.

And that was what Edward wanted. Pleasing his women had become a habit.

Now she said: "Try reasoning with him, Edward. Try to make him understand you wish him no ill."

"You talk like a fool, Jane. While I would reason with him he would set a dagger at my throat."

"Yet would you be haunted all your life if aught happened to him through your orders."

He sighed. "Well you know me, Jane. But there is a new turn to this affair of my brother Clarence. A servant of his, a certain Thomas Burdett, has become involved in a charge which has been brought against him and two others."

"What charge?"

"They have worked for my death and that of my sons by magic and necromancy."

"And this man . . . is a servant of George's?"

"Who," said Edward flushing purple, "doubtless arranged this matter. This man has talked of my early death and that of my sons. Of a certainty this is George's doing. And you ask me to forgive him! I tell you, you are a fool, Jane."

"And what will happen to this servant of his?"

"He has already been found guilty and hanged. And even then George would not let well alone. After I had left for Windsor he rode hot-foot to Westminster, and there in the council chamber, before the councillors, had a declaration of the innocence of this man read aloud . . . a man, mark you, who had perished at my command. The Queen is right. There'll be no peace until George's head rolls on the straw at Tower Green. And Jane, you would have me lenient! Always it has been your habit to come to me and beg forgiveness for this man, mercy for that."

Jane rose and, going to him, put an arm about him. He feigned to ignore the caress but he liked it.

"Mercy brings friends, not enemies," she said.

"And softness leads to disaster." He turned her face up to

his. "You are very lovely, Jane, and I fear I give way to you overmuch."

She hid her face in his jewel-encrusted jacket. She did not want him to see the pity in her eyes. She understood him too well. He did not want trouble; he wanted only to indulge his love of luxury; he wanted to see his coffers filling up; he wanted to enjoy his mistresses; he wanted wealth, and peace that he might enjoy it. He had had strife enough in his youth. She longed now more than ever to recapture the passionate love she had once had for him.

He kissed her and remembered it was time he went to the audience chamber. Relations with France were friendly; Louis was paying regularly to keep the peace, but to-day the French ambassador had evil tidings. He had heard that the Duke of Clarence was involved in a plot to raise an army on the Continent that he might march against his brother.

Edward did not trust the French, and the motives of wily Louis were so twisted that it was not easy to unravel them. He thanked the ambassador and decided to set fresh spies in his brother's home at Warwick Castle. These spies soon had news for him. They brought an incredible story, but then everything that George did was incredible. In the dungeons, below Warwick Castle, George kept a boy—probably a bastard of his or even Edward's—who was remarkably like George's own son. This boy was being trained to act and speak exactly in the same manner as George's son, so that George might send his own boy to the Continent to lead the army to England, while none would be aware that he had gone. It was a crazy plan conceived doubtless in a drunken dream. It was preposterous, but typical of George. And there was danger in it.

Edward commanded George to come immediately to Westminster, and when the two brothers stood face to face, Edward accused George of treason.

The result of that interview was that George found himself committed to the Tower of London.

*   *   *   *   *

Richard, the little Duke of York, was feeling bewildered, for though he was but five years old it was his wedding day.

There was a great fuss about this matter. He had been told what he must do, and his mother had talked to him for a very long time yesterday. He was a little afraid of his mother.

"You must remember that you are the son of the King," she had said. "You must remember that, when you are married to Anne to-morrow."

"Yes, gracious mother," he had said; and he had knelt when she talked to him, for although she was his mother he must never forget that she was also the Queen.

"Every eye will be upon you to-morrow, Richard. You must remember that, when you walk into St. Stephen's Chapel. You must remember that Anne is your bride."

He was a little afraid of Anne. She was two years older than he was and seemed very grown up. He felt that it was all very well to be married when you were seven, but when you were five it was a very different matter.

His brother Edward had been nonchalant enough.

"Why must I marry before you?" Richard had asked.

"I shall marry a princess, naturally, for I am to be the King. *You* are just my brother. *My* marriage will be a very grand affair."

"I wish I were seven," sighed Richard, for he was sure he would not in the least mind being married if he were but seven.

But now his mother said something startling to him. She bid him stand, and laying her hand on his shoulder looked solemnly into his eyes. "Richard, you must never forget that one day *you* may be King of England." He stared at her. "It is not impossible, my son. Your brother Edward is the elder, but if aught should happen to him, then the burden of kingship would fall upon this head."

She kissed him and bid him depart and not forget all she had told him of the importance of the morrow.

If aught should happen to Edward! The words made him shiver. There was so much in the world that he did not understand. A short time ago he had not known of marriage, and now he was to be married. His father—his big father who rumbled when he laughed and had the purplest face Richard had ever seen—poked him in the ribs and laughed at him. "So you are to have a wife, eh? Well, I'll tell you a secret. See that you always get your own way with her." His father laughed loudly at that, so Richard laughed too, for although he did not know what his father meant he supposed it was very funny.

He had repeated what he had to do, and very soon his nurse would come to dress him. His ceremonial garments were laid out waiting for him. He looked at them, touched the soft scarlet velvet and ran his finger over the cloth of gold. It was to be an important day, his nurse had told him, and he was to be the most important person of the day. "You must not forget that you are the Duke of York, the son of the King." How many times had that been said to him? He must not forget. . . . He must not forget. . . . He was not a little boy merely; he was the Duke of York, the son of the King.

Suddenly his face puckered. It was all very well for them to say there was nothing to worry about, and all he had to do was walk beside Anne and repeat the words the priest told him. But suppose there was something about marriage they hadn't mentioned! Life was full of so many surprises, and there was much he had yet to learn.

He ran to the door, and he did not stop running until he reached Jane's apartments.

Jane was sitting on a stool at her mirror and two women stood beside her; one was dressing her lovely hair while the other did something to her gown. She did not look round when he entered, but one of the women cried: "Why, 'tis the little bridegroom!"

Jane swung round then. "Richard!" she cried, and he ran to her, scrambling up on to her lap, his wide frightened eyes studying her face. She did not ask questions. She seemed to understand, as she always did understand, exactly what was troubling him. She put her arms round him and held him tightly as though he were merely a little boy—any little boy. It was undignified, but he didn't care. He wanted to be undignified; he wanted to forget what they were always insisting he should remember.

"Why," said Jane suddenly, "it is going to be great fun this day, Richard. I hear they have decorated the chapel in most magnificent fashion—and all for you. Beautiful carpets are hanging on the walls. You will walk under a canopy which, I dare swear, will be the colour of gold. Oh, this will be a day to remember."

"Jane," he said, in a whisper that only she might hear, "I do not want to get married."

"But you will," she whispered back. "You will like it. Anne is excited. She will love getting married."

"But she is nearly seven, and seven is different. Edward is seven."

"But you will be seven soon."

"Why, yes." He brightened. "So I shall." He buried his head against Jane's soft breasts. "Jane, what does it mean? What shall I have to do?"

"You will walk to the altar and Anne will be there, and you will say what they tell you to say. And afterwards there will be a wonderful feast at the palace and everyone will drink your health—yours and Anne's—and you shall eat as much as you wish."

"Yes," he said, admitting with a nod that all that was very exciting. "But what—after, Jane?"

"After? Oh, after that you will go back to your lessons and you will do all the things you do now. It will be just as though——"

"Just as though I am not married?"

"Just like that."

His relief was apparent in the deep breath he took. "But then," he demanded, "why do they want me to be married?"

"Well, when you are fourteen you will go and live with Anne —or Anne will come and live with you. Anne will come to Baynard's Castle if that is where you are living, and there you will have a lot of children and be happy for ever after. You will like that, Richard."

"How old did you say?"

"Fourteen."

"It is years and years away."

The women wiped their eyes, and Jane laughed and said his nurses would be missing him, for it was time he dressed, so she carried him to the door and kissed him tenderly. "There is nothing to fear, dear Richard," she whispered. "Shall I come back to your room with you?"

He wished he need not go, for he was deeply in love with Jane. He wished he could stay, resting his head on her soft bosom, talking about when he would be fourteen; but of course he must remember that he was the Duke of York.

"Thank you, Jane," he said. "I will go alone."

He was not frightened after that, and when his mother held his hand and led him up to the altar of St. Stephen's Chapel he was almost happy. His mother pressed his hand reassuringly. She was very pleased about his wedding because, so his brother had told him, Anne was the richest little girl in England, and as heiress to the Duke of Norfolk she was considered worthy to marry into the royal family.

Richard listened to the service; he repeated what he must. He heard Anne whisper her responses as she stood beside him, her little chest naked, her long hair flowing over her shoulders, her rich skirt trailing the ground so that there was so much more of velvet and cloth of gold than there was of Anne Mowbray. He wanted to tell her not to be frightened, for after this all would be just as it had been before.

In this little chapel, with its magnificent decorations all in honour of his wedding, were the highest people in the land. First his father, looking bigger and more sparkling than ever; then his mother, smiling and gracious because she was so pleased. Uncle Richard and Aunt Anne had come down from the North to be present at his wedding. Uncle Richard was pale and stern-looking; and Aunt Anne was pale also and looked very ill. Their little son Edward was with them. Poor little cousin, he looked very tired. Richard wondered when he would have a marriage.

His other uncle was not there. Richard wondered why, and at the same time he was glad. He did not like Uncle George any more than he liked Uncle Richard. They both frightened him in their different ways; they were not a bit like Richard's father, who, although he was King, was really very kind. Still, it did seem strange that Uncle George and Cousin Edward and Cousin Margaret were not at the wedding.

There was little time for these reflections, for they were leaving the chapel now, and he heard the shouts of the people who had come to see him and Anne. Uncle Richard was scattering gold coins among the people. There was great rejoicing throughout the land, his mother had told him, for there was nothing the people liked so much as a royal wedding.

And, once the ceremony was over and the celebrations began, Richard was happy. All the guests drank his health—his and Anne's—while they stood together, hand in hand.

"Do you like being married, Anne?" he whispered.

She said she did; but he knew she rather despised her bridegroom because he was younger than she was. She would have preferred Edward. He forgot that, though, as he watched the jousting and sat down to the banquet just as though he were grown up. Then he felt there was a good deal to be said for getting married.

On and on went the laughter and the music so that it seemed to Richard it would never end. It was the longest day of his life, he thought; and then suddenly it faded away. His head sunk on to his jewel-trimmed jacket, and at the height of the festivity which was to celebrate his wedding the little bridegroom fell asleep.

*   *   *   *   *

The court was in residence at the royal palace of the Tower of London, and for days there had been banquets, jousting and pageantry, for the King wished to entertain his brother Richard before the latter's return to his duties in the North.

There was little the King liked better than pageantry and to know himself the centre of his gay court, more dazzling than any member of it. And at this time he needed distraction, for he could not forget that while he fêted one brother the other was a prisoner in the Bowyer Tower. The eyes of his father continued to haunt him. Surely, he told himself, if his father had foreseen what George would try to do he would have understood the predicament in which his eldest son, the rightful King, now found himself.

He could not enjoy the feasting nor the jousting; he could take no delight in the performance of the wild beasts from his menagerie. All about him people were applauding, crying out appreciation of some particularly daring feat of his bearward; but the King did not see the performing bears nor the artful tricks of the monkeys; he could think of nothing but his treacherous brother and the promise he had made to his father. Sitting there, staring moodily before him, he decided this could not continue. He would release George, since that was the only way to ease his conscience. If George made more trouble doubtless he would be able to deal with him, for George was, praise the saints, the most stupid man in England.

When the display was over, Edward hastily distributed a few purses of gold to those responsible for its arrangement and made his way alone to the Bowyer Tower. At his approach the warders sprang to attention, but Edward waved his hand and said: "I would be conducted to the apartments of the Duke of Clarence."

He was led up a spiral staircase, along corridors, and right to the top of the Tower, which had been deemed the safest place for one who might prove a slippery prisoner. The door was unlocked and the warder stood aside for the King to enter. "I will have the key," said Edward. "You will receive it later."

He took it and went in, locking the door behind him. George started up when he saw him. George's eyes were bloodshot and he had been drinking even more heavily than usual.

"Now, George," said Edward, in a conciliatory voice, "this is a sorry state of affairs."

George laughed; when he was with his brother his jealousy and hatred of him stifled every other emotion, even ambition. If he had had a dagger he would have attempted to kill him there and then. Edward knew this and had come well armed.

"Sorry indeed," snarled George, "when out of his jealousy one brother must trump up a charge against another."

"Let us have none of this folly," said Edward sternly. "You know full well that any less soft than myself would have had you despatched long ere this. But for the promise I made to our father I myself would not have endured your insults and your treachery as long as I have. You should have died with your traitor-accomplice Warwick. But you are my brother—and for this reason I have forgiven you."

"Forgiven me! So that I may suffer the indignity of confinement in this place with low rascals to guard me!"

"You have been treated with great mercy, and you know it."

George, inflamed by wine and jealousy, threw himself on to his bed and pummelled his pillow. He was working himself up into a mad rage. "You stand there," he shouted, "you—good King Edward! Everything is as you will have it. Was it not always the same? Our mother—our father—all of them bowing down and worshipping you. The handsome one—the eldest son —the King. Every man ready to follow you to death. Every woman begging the favour of sharing your bed. Edward the magnificent."

"Be silent, you fool," said Edward.

"I will not be silent. You are a cheat. You are a liar. You practise black magic. It was sorcery that gave you the throne, and through sorcery you keep it. The Queen is a witch. Jane Shore is a witch. And you——"

"Pray calm yourself, or I shall go away."

"The Queen is a witch—a witch and a harlot." George was losing all control now. "A harlot—just as Jane Shore is a harlot. Burn them all, I say. But save the biggest faggots and the brightest flames for the Woodville harlot. She is no Queen."

"What are you saying, you knave?"

"Only this, brother. The Queen is your harlot just as Jane Shore is. The Queen is no wife to you."

"Enough of this folly, for you tempt me sorely."

"It is not for you to say 'enough.' What of Eleanor Butler, eh? She was your wife—aye, and alive when you went through a ceremony of marriage with Elizabeth Woodville."

"You are drunk, George."

"Drunk—drunk—drunk on Malmsey. And you are drunk with power—too drunk to see what goes on around you. Good Bishop Stillington can bear me witness. King Edward has not long to live—and then God save King George!"

Edward said calmly: "This story is yet another of your foolish fabrications. I advise you not to speak of it further, if you value your life. I had come to speak to you in friendly fashion, but I see I must put that off until I find you influenced more by good sense and less by good Malmsey."

George had slipped back on to his bed, murmuring insults against the Queen. Edward went out and locked the door. He made his way out of the tower, called a warder and gave him the keys. He asked that the Constable of the Tower be conducted to him without a moment's delay. When the man came to him, Edward said: "My lord Stillington, Bishop of Bath and Wells, is to be arrested immediately. Place him in solitary confinement in the most inaccessible part of the Tower."

The Constable hastened to do the King's bidding.

*　　*　　*　　*　　*

Edward was furious with a fury born of fear. Out of the past a ghost had risen up to threaten him. He scarcely remembered what Eleanor Butler looked like, for it was years since he had known her. She had died, he had heard, in a nunnery; and that must have been ten years ago. How had George come to learn of that incident from his past life? Stillington knew. Who else? Some of Eleanor's family. But they would not dare do anything about it. Edward was sweating under his heavy garments in spite of the January cold.

George could only have recently acquired the information. The story had been smuggled in to him. By whom? Stillington? Well, Stillington was under lock and key, and he would not know freedom again until he learned not to speak of matters touching his betters. But what of George? George was never to be trusted; as long as he breathed he would think treason, and act treason if he had a chance. The throne was now unsafe for Edward's sons. And who would have thought that Eleanor, mouldering in her grave, could have brought him to this! She had been a widow—just as Elizabeth had. He had a fondness for widows, mayhap. Shrewsbury's daughter—and her husband had been a son of Lord Butler of Sudely. It had been one of those passionate affairs in which he had indulged so lightly during his youth. Eleanor had been as determined to get a promise of marriage from him as Elizabeth had been. "Your mistress I cannot be." How many times had he heard that? And in every case he had managed to get round it, to make vague promises which he had no intention of keeping. Elizabeth Woodville had been too clever and too attractive for him to resist. Eleanor, it seemed, had been clever also, for while Elizabeth shared his throne, Eleanor returned from the grave to assert her rights.

It was no use pretending to himself that this was not a serious matter that had come to the knowledge of his greatest enemy. It was true, every word of it. He cast his mind back to a young and ardent man, an unwise man where his desires were concerned. "Why, then, I will marry you," he said. Then he had not been the King, merely the Earl of March with the promise of kingship; and he had desired Eleanor Butler so urgently that he had made his rash promise and been fool enough to make his vows before Stillington. That had been her family's work, but when he had later, as all-powerful monarch, refused to recognise the marriage, they had been wise enough to keep silent on the matter. There had been a child who had died, and Eleanor had, most obligingly, disappeared into a nunnery. When he had heard of her death, some years after his marriage with Elizabeth, he had dismissed the matter as done with.

And now here it was—and because it deeply concerned Elizabeth, he went to her and told her what George had said. He had never seen Elizabeth so frightened. She felt her throne shake under her. Her dignity, her power, and the future of her children were in danger. She did what he had rarely seen her do : she lost her calm.

"It is a lie," she cried.

"It is the truth," said Edward.

"How could you have been such a fool as to promise her marriage—to go through a form of marriage? You must have been mad."

Angry lights appeared in the King's eyes. "No more so than when I acted similarly with you."

"This marriage cannot be legal."

"According to the law it is."

"And that means . . ."

Alarmed as he was, he could not resist baiting her. In some small measure it made up for all her coldness to him. "It means," he said, "that it might be difficult to prove that you and I are married, in which case the people would declare you no longer Queen."

Her eyes looked black in her drawn face as she clenched and unclenched her hands. "It is false." Suddenly she turned to him and flung her arms about him. "Edward, our children! Little Edward and Richard. This must not be!"

No, of course it must not be. He was too old to get more children by a new wife. He had too many illegitimate sons already; he did not wish to add Edward and Richard to the tally. This thing had to be fought; Eleanor was dead; let her story die with her.

"George must die—at once," said Elizabeth, and she was cold and calm once more. As he was silent, she cried : "Will you let him live now to destroy your children's future?"

"He is a prisoner. No harm can come while he is a prisoner."

"Prisoners escape."

"He shall not."

"Have you forgotten he is in the Tower on a charge of treason? Why—oh, why . . ."

"Because it is not easy to kill one's brother."

"Kill! Kill! You talk as though you were asked to wield the axe yourself."

"Whoever wielded the axe, it would be at my command that he was struck down."

"Edward, you are a fool!" She had lost control again, so great was her fear. "First you get involved with a woman. How could you be so soft?"

He turned on her, his eyes blazing: "You should know, madam. She tried the same tricks as you did, and—as with you —they worked."

She shrank from him, but quickly regained her poise. "Edward, I implore you to think of our children. George must die, and with him Stillington—or let his tongue be cut out and his hands cut off that he may not speak or write this thing."

"Your ambition is great," said Edward coldly. "Have a care. It would be well to remember that it is for me to say what shall and what shall not be done."

He left her then, remembering with relief that his brother Richard was in the palace. He sent for him, and when he was sure they were alone he told him everything that had happened.

Richard looked grave. "You say Stillington is already a prisoner. And who knows about this but Stillington and George?"

"None of import, or we should have learned something sooner. Richard, what am I to do with this brother of ours?"

Richard bit his lip. He walked to the window and looked out, though he did not see the lawns and the grey walls of the Cradle Tower. He was thinking that to Edward, egoistical in the extreme, this was but a personal problem; it astounded Richard that Edward did not realise its significance to him—the very man in whom he was confiding. George was in the Tower on a charge of treason, Edward had no legitimate son living, and as for Edward himself, that corpulence, that heavy breathing, those recurring fits of fever—all these things could mean but one thing: Edward could not live much longer. Was he blind? Did he not see what a dazzling prospect he had opened up for his brother Richard? What Edward was saying was this : "You, Richard, in a few short years—or mayhap months—will be the rightful King of England."

To wear the crown, to hold the reins firmly in one's own hands, to dedicate oneself body and soul to the country one loved better than anything else on earth, better than wife or child or even one's own life !

Richard sought to control himself. He must hide his emotion. He must listen to what Edward had to say. He must advise.

"Is there no reasoning with him?"

"Reason with George? As well talk to a tiger. If this story be bruited abroad . . ."

"Ah," said Richard, his eyes gleaming, "then the people will not have young Edward on the throne after you."

"It was not a true marriage," said Edward quickly. "I made a few promises. There was no church solemnisation."

"Nay, but such vows are considered binding nevertheless."

Edward was in despair. "Dickon, what can I do? I see only one way out of this. Is he not in the Tower on a charge of treason? Death is the reward of traitors."

"And justly so."

"I have suffered much sleeplessness over George. The sensible way is to rid myself of this false brother." Edward looked round sharply. "What was that?"

"Only the wind stirring the hangings."

"I promised our father," said Edward, and he continued to look over his shoulder. It seemed to both men then that their father's spirit was in the room. Neither could meet his brother's eye, for each was afraid the other would see his guilty looks. George dead and I would be safe; my children would be safe, thought Edward. George dead—and the way to the throne is cleared for me, thought Richard.

Richard spoke first. "You have told the Queen?"

Edward nodded.

Richard's lips curled. "She trembles for her children?"

"She does, brother."

Holy Mother! thought Richard. Even now he does not see.

He thinks his secret safe with *me*. Had he, carelessly possessing these things, forgotten that there was no sight more beautiful than a glittering crown, and that power was the most cherished gift earth had to offer. Yet—there was honour.

Did the hangings stir? wondered Richard; and he remembered clearly his father's noble face. How simple it would be to say to Edward, "Destroy George." That was what Edward wanted him to say.

Never had the Duke of Gloucester experienced such mixed feelings. Never had his love for his brother been so great and never before had he so despised him as a fool. Never had he been so elated, never so depressed. And all the time he had the uncanny feeling that his father was in the room watching them.

It was a great struggle, but his sense of honour overcame ambition.

" 'Twould be murder," he said at length. "If you kill George because you fear he will speak against you, then you betray the trust our father fixed upon you."

Edward laid a hand on his brother's shoulder. "You are right, Dickon. I thank the Virgin you were here when I most needed your counsel."

Richard hurried away, and no sooner was Edward alone than he was again beset by doubts. It seemed to him that he heard the laughter of women—women whose names he had forgotten, women who, in that vast crowd, were now merely a remembered laugh, a voice, a flash of a smile, a shudder of ecstasy. Now they mocked him. He had had his way with so many; he had been the conqueror, they the vanquished. Now it seemed they banded together to mock him, to whisper : "But were we the defeated, Edward, or were you?"

He could not endure to be alone, so he went to Jane, and to her blurted out the whole story. "The Queen says there is one way out and one only," he finished.

"But you could not do it, Edward. You must not do it."

He smiled with relief, and holding her against him kissed her with great gentleness. "You are my good angel, Jane. I cannot do it. Richard agrees with me. He advised me not to do it."

"He advised you not to do it," said Jane slowly. "Yet if you did—then he would be heir to the throne."

Edward's face was purple suddenly. "Richard, heir to the throne! What nonsense you talk! Have I not two sons?"

"But if your marriage to their mother was no true marriage . . ."

He put her from him and she saw the veins stand out on his temples. "It shall not be said!" he thundered. "It shall never be known. I tell you this affair with Eleanor Butler was nothing—nothing." He strode to the window, then he swung round to face her, and she saw that his eyes had grown fierce. She felt suddenly tender towards him, remembering the greatness of a love that was past. He was begging her to help him, to agree that George must die. But she must be true to herself; she must be as she had always been, bold and reckless, but truthful. She went to him and looked up into his angry eyes.

"Edward, nothing is gained by turning from the truth. Whether your marriage with the Queen is legal is not what we have to talk about. The urgent problem is whether you shall have George executed because he has learned your secret. If you kill him because of this, you will have murdered one who was put in your care."

"You are too bold, Jane."

"If I had not been I should never have left my husband and come to you."

"There's truth in that." He smiled suddenly and charmingly. "And if you were not bold you would not speak truth to me when others lie. Tell me, Jane, why should I stop at this? Are my hands so clean? I have killed before."

"This man is your brother, Edward."

"I would to God I could forget it," said Edward bitterly.

*   *   *   *

There was no rest for the King. He could not sleep, he could not eat. There were voices in his ear all the time. "Kill him!

Kill him! It is the only safe way." And then: "My son, look after your brothers. I leave them in your care."

He felt he had lived through ten years in two days. Every time a messenger came to him he was startled. What now? he would wonder. Has it leaked out, then?

The Queen's eyes appealed to him. They cursed him for a weak fool. "Kill! Kill! Kill!" said the Queen's eyes.

Never had sons seemed so fair, so promising; never before had he known how he loved them. Their mother's eyes followed them yearningly. "And what sort of a father are you, my lord," she asked bitterly, "thus to expose your sons to treachery?"

If he could but forget the solemn vow he had made! If he could feel young again, young, bold and careless of death! He *was* young, but his body had enjoyed too many experiences not to have aged beyond his years. He was grossly fat and the tertian fever he had caught in France had never left him. He had enjoyed too much rich food, too much good wine, too many strange women. Now he asked for peace and comfort and it was denied him. There came a time when a man must make his peace with God; his sins should be committed in the flush of youth; age was the time for repenting old sins, not for the committing of new ones.

I could not do it, he would tell himself; and then he would see the Queen's eyes, dark with misery, hear her lips murmur: "It is so easy. Kill, kill, kill!"

*   *   *   *   *

Would this night never pass? wondered Jane. She had never before known Edward so disturbed. He lay beside her in the elaborate bed, but he did not sleep. His face had lost its rich red-purple colour; it looked a dark and smudgy brown in the light of the candles. He had insisted on lighting them. This night he could not bear the dark.

"Edward," she whispered, "you must try to sleep."

"It is no use, Jane. There is no rest for me this night."

She smoothed his hair back from his forehead. "It is because you have as yet made no decision about George. Edward, decide now . . . that you will do what is right. Decide, and let matters run their course."

"Jane," he said, catching her hand and holding it firmly, "you do not understand. You cannot understand."

"I can and I do."

The candles flickered, and it seemed to the King that the room was more full of shadows than was usual. "How dark it is!" he said. "It is the darkest night I ever knew."

"Shall I light more candles?"

"No, stay here with me. Stay close, Jane."

They were silent for a while. Then his arms tightened about her. "Jane," he whispered. "Saw you something?"

"Where?" she asked.

"There by the door. Methought . . ."

"'Tis nothing but the hangings."

"Methought I saw a figure standing there."

" 'Twas but the wind stirring the hangings."

" 'Tis a gusty night, Jane, a dark and gusty night."

Again there was silence, then he said: "Jane, you do not sleep either."

"It has deserted us both this night."

"I am glad, for I would talk with you. You know what those two boys mean to me. They are my sons. I have made great plans for them."

"It is natural that you should, Edward, but . . ."

He interrupted her sharply. "Why do you say 'But'? What means that 'But'?"

"If your son has no right to the crown it would be better if some other wore it."

He laughed suddenly. "You consider not what you say. With my brother George on the throne none would be safe. England herself would be in danger. Better if I broke the vow I made my father. . . ." She noticed that he was staring at the hangings by the door. "I say," he said in a louder voice, "better if I broke my vow to my father than that George should sit upon the throne."

She knew now what was in his mind; she guessed now what he had done. She lay beside him, shuddering.

"Try to sleep, Edward," she whispered. "In the morning can you think on these things."

But there was no sleep for either of them. They lay still, feigning sleep, both conscious that just beyond their window the grey walls of the Bowyer Tower rose up to the February night sky.

*   *   *   *   *

A butt of Malmsey. George hiccoughed and surveyed it with satisfaction. Sent in by Edward. Edward was trying to propitiate him. And no wonder! To think that in George's hands lay the power to crush his greatest enemy; for his enemy, he had always insisted, was not his brother, but his brother's wife. What joy to see her pride humbled! She, who had made others kneel before her, should kneel until she fainted with fatigue. As for her precious little bastards . . . well, no matter. That could wait until Edward was dead and George upon the throne.

The Malmsey was good. It had ever been his favourite wine. What pleasant dreams it could conjure up even in a prison cell. How long could Edward last? Edward was over-fat, rotten with disease. A different Edward now from the brother of George's childhood. "The King is dead," he muttered. "Long live the King! Edward is dead. Long live King George!"

He drank to King George. The son of George, Duke of Clarence, not Edward's son, would one day be Edward the Fifth of England.

He drank more wine. He grew very drowsy and he did not see two men come into his cell. They were clad in dark and inconspicuous garments, and as they looked at the drunken man they talked in whispers and they avoided looking into each other's faces.

The solitary lantern which stood on a ledge in the wall threw a feeble light round the room. On the bed the Duke snored and groaned in his sleep. His face looked yellow in the lantern light; his rich coat was sodden with wine.

The two men came silently to the bed and looked down at him. Then one seized his feet, the other his head, but as they would have lifted him George opened his eyes. "What's this?" he asked sleepily.

Both men immediately took their hands off him. One said: "Your Grace, a thousand pardons. We did not mean to disturb you."

"We thought your Grace asked for another drink," said the other.

"Drink? Bring me a drink . . . here now. . . ."

The man who had been holding his feet came to the head of the bed. He bent over and whispered: "Alas, Your Grace, the Malmsey is in the butt. We can assist your Grace to it."

George was very drunk, but the mention of Malmsey revived him a little. He nodded, closed his eyes and began to snore.

The men whispered together.

"He is very far gone in drink."

"That is good. I counted on it. Try again."

The man bent so that his mouth came down to the Duke's ear. "Your Grace, we will assist you to the wine."

George protested only mildly as the men lifted him from the bed. He was not even surprised when he found himself looking into the butt of wine. He bent over it. It was nectar; it was an opiate that brought beautiful dreams. He could taste the wine now. There was nothing but wine. He could not breathe; he was slowly choking. He could not raise his head, for two strong men were holding it down that he might take his fill of his favourite wine.

He gasped and struggled, but what were the feeble struggles of a drunken man against two intent on murder!

It was not long before George, Duke of Clarence, ceased to struggle. Then did his murderers lift him and tip him into the butt so that his head and shoulders were deep in the wine.

THE TOWER OF LONDON (PART II)

ONCE again the plague stalked the City of London. Through the riverside alleys it came, striking down men and women and children; it left them groaning on the roadside, calling for help which none dared give. From the narrow streets with their refuse-laden gutters stinking in the hot air, it spread to the main thoroughfares. The polluted Fleet, alive with flies that fed on the filth thrown into it by the butchers and tanners, carried it onwards, until the entire City lay groaning under the death-dealing invader which saw fit to invade its streets every few years.

The court had moved to Windsor, and into the great castle there had seemed to creep a tension which did not diminish with the passing weeks. The King's attacks of fever had become more frequent and people were asking each other, "How long will he last?"

Jane's feelings towards the man she had loved so passionately were peculiarly mingled. It was saddening to see him who had been so magnificent, surpassing all others, grown so fat that he could scarcely move with ease. Edward had been Nature's darling; he had come into the world equipped with every quality and opportunity which should have made him great. But what a bad fairy it was who at his christening had given him that deep sensuous love of pleasure, that self-indulgence which was to grow to such magnitude that it had strangled every virtue. To see him now, aged beyond his years, pitiably trying to regain that virility he had squandered, was heartbreaking. The handsome irresistible man had become the repulsive roué.

The great change in him had come with the death of his brother George, who, it was said, had been drowned in a butt of Malmsey, but Jane, who had lain awake with the King on the night of George's death, could not believe that it had been an accident. She knew that every time the Duke was mentioned the King was shaken, and his bloodshot eyes looked beyond the company as though he thought he might see something which was invisible to others. Jane believed that Edward had ordered the murder of his brother.

"I will always love you," she had cried passionately to the handsome merchant in Mary Blague's house; she had believed it, and in a measure there was truth in that cry of hers. The man she had loved was a different man from the Edward of to-day. The charming witty philanderer had become the murderer of his brother, prematurely old while Jane was young.

Wandering in the Great Park among the noble oaks and the wide-spreading branches of the beech trees, Jane fought a battle with herself. She would walk the great avenue and survey one of the finest panoramas in Europe; she would climb the tower of the third Edward and look across the green and pleasant countryside which was cut in two by the gleaming river; and she would try to suppress the wild and raging passion that was in her for the man who was bewitching her as once the King had done.

She thought a good deal about Hastings too. She enjoyed her meetings with him, enjoyed reviling him, so great was her hatred of him. She did not know that she thought more of him than she had ever done before, and that when she was not occupied with thoughts of Dorset, Hastings filled her mind.

One gusty March day as she was walking in the Home Park, Dorset saw her from a window of the castle and hastened out to her. She saw him coming and leaned against the trunk of an ancient oak to steady herself, for the sight of him never failed to disturb her.

He seized her hands and kissed them. "Why, Jane," he said, "you must be a witch, for I declare you look more beautiful in a March wind than you do at a court banquet."

She was frail, she knew, and life with Edward had taught

her to need the frequent excitement of physical love. Dorset in his handsome garments reminded her poignantly of Edward when she had first known him. He smiled at her, sensing the effect he had upon her. It was no novelty to him. He charmed with his very brutality, with his evil reputation. "Dorset is a brute," women said, "an attractive, irresistible brute." It was his virile masculinity that attracted, not his character.

"Why do you keep me waiting, Jane?" he said.

She pretended not to understand. "When have I kept you waiting?"

"You know my meaning. You know for what." He thought it was fear of the King, and not loyalty, that made her hold back. "Who is your lover now? Do not say Edward. How does he spend his time? He looks into the future; he seeks the philosopher's stone. Oh, Jane, the present would be good enough for me, if you would share it; and I know more pleasant things to look for than a non-existent philosopher's stone. Jane, you were not meant to be neglected thus."

He seized her roughly, and was amused to find her trembling. He laughed at her feeble struggles. "You know you do not want to escape. Be truthful."

"*You* to tell me to be truthful! Do you, who so sadly lack the virtues, look for them in others?"

He put his handsome face close to hers. "I do not need to be anything but truthful, Jane. It is true that I have no virtues. What of that? Vice is so much more attractive than virtue."

"More fashionable, you mean." There was evil in him, she knew, and she was fighting hard to suppress the longing he aroused in her. Part of her wanted to escape, but part wanted to stay with him. "I will be truthful with you," she said with a touch of her old spirit. "There are many at court who find it difficult to refuse you, but do not make the mistake of thinking that because some do, all must."

She saw the flush under his skin. His eyes gleamed at her. "Mayhap not all," he said, "but methinks Jane Shore is among them that do."

Jane, pressing her hands against him, held him off. "Then think again, Thomas."

But he was forcing her back against the tree, kissing her mouth.

"Not yet," she pleaded. "Thomas . . . not yet."

"Holy Mother, have I not sought you long enough?"

"If the waiting grows wearisome," she responded tartly, "then, my lord, you should seek elsewhere."

He raised his eyebrows, mocking her. "You would send me to others then?"

She beat against his chest. He was a big man; Jane was a small woman. "You haven't a chance, Jane," he said, and his laughter was quiet and mocking.

"You have the laughter of a demon," she told him.

"That is what I am. A satyr to waylay you in the forest, to make you a bed among the bracken. Once you have tasted the joys I know of, you will never have the will to say Nay to me."

"I could not deceive the King," she said faintly.

"Can you then so rely on *his* fidelity? He grows old. He would not know that you, as you put it, deceived him."

"But *I* should know, and it would make uneasy knowledge."

" 'Twould be forgotten in the joys that I should show you. You may well look alarmed. Do you think I do not know you long for me? I will beckon and you will come. And if not . . ."

"If not?"

"What I cannot have by asking I will take by force."

"You *are* a demon, Thomas Grey."

His eyes were laughing. "Mayhap you are right, and you will sell your soul to me when I take your body. In this forest demons are abroad. We will go to Herne the Hunter's blasted oak, and there I will make you a bed of bracken."

"You will not. I wish to return to the castle now."

"And if I do not choose that you should return to the castle?"

"You find it amusing to tease me, but I do not share your amusement. Pray stand aside."

She was afraid, for he had laid the palms of his hands against the trunk of the tree and she was imprisoned; but in her, mingling with her fear, there was a longing that he might take her by force, that she might satisfy her senses and say, " 'Twas no fault of mine. I had no choice."

He seemed to read her thoughts for he laughed and said: "You are wise, Jane. When submission is inevitable, 'twould be foolish not to relax and enjoy."

She felt her anger rising to meet her passion. "You are mistaken in me. . . ."

"I think not, Jane," he said. "I think not. . . ."

They both heard the shout; they both turned their heads and saw Hastings. Jane could not understand her emotions. She was filled with a wild unreasoning joy because Hastings had found her with Dorset thus. She was glad that he could see the wild disorder of her dress, and the red patches on her throat and chest where Dorset had roughly kissed her. Hastings glowered angrily, while Dorset smiled insolently at him, though his hand had come to rest on the hilt of his sword.

"I heard your call for help," said Hastings, "and so did hurry to rescue you from this man."

"I gave no call," said Jane maliciously. She knew that he was jealous of Dorset's youth. Dorset was thirty, Hastings fifty-three. Dorset had won honours effortlessly through his mother; Hastings was a clever statesman, a brilliant soldier, and he had fought beside the King. Hastings had desired Jane for many years and his desire for her obsessed him. He could not bear that Dorset, notoriously light and cruel in his love affairs, should succeed where he should fail.

"My Lord Hastings," said Dorset, "can you not see that we do not require your company?"

"I heard Jane's protests," insisted Hastings.

"I assure you, my lord," said Jane quickly, " I can defend myself should the need arise."

"That may be, but to my mind you need protection from this man."

Dorset swaggered towards him, drawing his sword. "I would know the meaning of such words."

Hastings' sword was out. "Methinks you do know, Marquis."

Dorset was young and lithe; he had parried the blow and they stood, swords crossed, glaring into each other's eyes. Jane forced a way between them. "Put away your swords at once," she cried. "My Lord Hastings, you have no need to fear for me. I can take care of my own affairs. I beg of you both, if you would please me, to put away your swords." They did so, but with reluctance. "I am going back to the castle," said Jane; and she turned and walked from them. Dorset and Hastings, silently hating each other, each vowing that before long Jane should become his mistress, walked on either side of her towards the castle.

*   *   *   *   *

The King opened his eyes. Dark shapes were in his room. This was the end, he knew. He was old and tired, and death was beckoning. News had been brought to him that the King of France was deceiving him; the Dauphin, promised to Edward's daughter, was to marry the heiress of Burgundy. The shock had been too much. The King had fallen into one of his violent rages. He had been carried unconscious to his bed.

He was sure that he would not rise from it again and there was much to be done. He must make the future secure for his little son; he must make his peace with God, for he feared he had lived a sinful life.

He saw Jane at his bedside and he remembered her as she had been when he first saw her in the goldsmith's house. He remembered that he had deliberately gone to that house with the intention of taking her from her husband. Then it had seemed an amusing adventure; in the face of death he knew he had done an evil thing.

"Jane," he said. "Jane . . . I took you from . . ."

She knew what troubled him; he felt her tears upon his hands. "We were so happy," she whispered. "I would not have had it different."

He thought of all the light women who had amused him temporarily and lured him from her side. He tried to tell her that he was wishing he could go back to the beginning of their union.

The Queen came to him. He must not let her influence him now. There was his son to consider, for very soon the thirteen-year-old boy would be King. He declared his son to be under the protection of his brother Richard. "Into his care I deliver my son, the Prince." The Queen was displeased. Was she not his mother? "No, no, Bessy," he murmured. Didn't he know her family? They were bloated with the power which he, at Elizabeth's request, had bestowed upon them. No. Young Edward must be in firm good hands, and there was only one pair of hands he trusted for this duty.

He asked that Dorset and Hastings might be brought to him. Edward could not see them clearly, but he knew that the tall glittering figure was his handsome stepson, and the more soberly clad, shorter, older man was his friend and counsellor, Hastings.

"William," he said; and Hastings knelt by the bed and kissed the fat hand that was now clammy and turning cold. "I—I have sent for you two—because there is enmity between you."

The dying Edward knew that Jane was involved in that enmity; but it was not Jane only; they were natural enemies. Dorset was one of the main pillars of the Woodville party, and Hastings had never liked the Queen's family. If there was trouble after his death, Hastings would be with Richard, Dorset against him.

But there must be no trouble, for what could a boy of thirteen do against such cunning warriors as these? There must be friendship among the nobles if there was to be peace for little Edward.

"I beg of you—with my dying breath—I beg of you—be

friends. Let me see you shake hands across my bed. William, my old friend; Thomas, my son—I command you. Peace between you two."

Jane watched the two men, saw them shake hands as Edward bid them. She saw genuine grief in the eyes of Hastings, but the face of Dorset was inscrutable.

Edward was satisfied. He lay back, watching the shadowy shapes about the room. Everything was fading. His lips moved. "Jane—Jane—we have been happy. No, George . . . Father—Father . . . I did not want to do it, Father. Forgive me. I did it for my sons. It was the only way. Bessy was right. . . . It was the only way."

Then he forgot Bessy, forgot George, forgot Jane. He had sunk into unconsciousness.

*   *   *   *   *

The dead King lay in state, his once beautiful body covered only from the navel to the knees, for all to see, so that none might doubt that Edward the Fourth was indeed no more. Mourning for its most loved King hung over the City. There was much to recall of him—the charm, the gaiety, the gracious beauty. In the streets the sentimental recalled him in the glory of his youth; the more practical turned their eyes towards the palace and wondered what mischief the King's death would set afoot.

In her apartments Jane sat numbed, thinking back over the past. Dorset saw her wandering through the park. She would be easy game now, he reckoned; but let her wait. She was sentimentally mourning the man she had ceased to love long ago, and she would, as yet, make an inadequate mistress. Moreover, his head was full of plans which were of greater importance than dalliance with Jane Shore. So he did not seek out Jane, but went to his mother's apartments. Elizabeth welcomed her son warmly; they shared each other's interests and there was no need for her to choose her words carefully.

"Think not," she said, "that I shall allow Gloucester to rule this land. The King is but a child, but *I* am his mother."

"Mother," he reminded her, "we are fortunately placed, the King being at Ludlow, in our hands, while Gloucester is in the North."

"And you, my dearest son, as Constable of the Tower are in a happy position. Was I not right to get you so placed? Should the occasion arise we could hold all London against any who might assail the City."

"Aye, Mother, and who rules London rules England. Gloucester has not a chance."

"He is a crafty man, Thomas, as fine a soldier as his brother was."

"Never fear, everything must be settled before he reaches the South."

"He has powerful friends in London."

"Hastings for one." Dorset smiled slyly. "I would not care to have Hastings against us. He is an enemy of mine for more reasons than one. I never thought to wish him my friend. But were he with us, and not against us, I should say certain success was ours."

"Could we not win him to our side?"

"Bribe Hastings! You do not know the man, gracious mother. He is a strange man—not one man but two. Debauchee in his youth—and mayhap still is. To women he will lie and scheme to rob them of their honour. That is one Hastings. But the statesman, the soldier—he sets honour high. Methinks you could offer him the crown in return for treachery to Gloucester and he'd refuse it."

"We should certainly not do that," said Elizabeth grimly. "But to my mind all men have their price."

Dorset laughed suddenly, for he had caught sight of Jane in the grounds. "Even Hastings has his price perchance," he mused. And then: "There goes Jane Shore. She mourns the King more deeply than does Your Grace."

"Poor Jane! She has lost all."

Dorset smiled at his mother. Edward had been merely a

source of power to her, and she could not understand that he could be anything more to Jane.

"Mother," he said, "if we need Hastings we shall win him to our side."

"You think we could achieve that, Thomas?"

"There would be ways, I doubt not."

They talked for a long time of what they planned to do; and as they talked the citizens of London filed slowly past the dead body of the most handsome King who had ever sat upon the throne of England.

*   *   *   *   *

Dorset did not let many weeks pass before he sought out Jane. He had marked the hungry looks of Hastings. Dorset's eyes were sly. It was stimulating to link passion with ambition. He dressed himself with the utmost elegance in his doublet, which was trimmed with cloth of gold and cut short to show his beautifully moulded legs; he wore a ruby at his throat and another in his cap, and he sprinkled himself with the musk with which Leppus supplied him regularly. He was a fine fellow, he assured himself; what other man would be setting out to seduce the most beautiful woman in the court and be thinking of— Lord Hastings? The beauty of Jane and the power of Hastings. He thought of little else. Hastings was a power in London, for the City was faithful to the strangest people. Why had it taken Hastings to its heart? He did not know.

Boldly he went to Jane's apartments. It was a simple matter to overcome her resistance. Weakly she pleaded, as he had expected, that the King was so recently dead.

"Fear not the dead, Jane," he had said, slipping her gown from her shoulders and laying his burning lips against her skin. "Holy Mother, there is more to fear from those alive than those who moulder in their graves." Throwing himself down beside her he had laughed in his triumph. "This is the end of your reluctance, Jane. We shall change rôles, you and I. You shall be the suppliant. You shall not say, 'Not yet.' No, Jane, not that. You shall say, 'Now—for I cannot live without you.'"

That was the beginning. Loving Dorset was like slipping into a quicksand, and Jane slipped fast. Her purely physical need of him dragged her down; she would be submerged very soon, powerless, his completely.

She felt at times ashamed, degraded. This was passion without love—a burning flame that scorched her spirit, no gentle warmth. He would lie beside her and talk casually of his affairs with others with a frankness that hurt and shocked her. He meant to shame her; he meant to degrade her. She tried to break away. She had the house which Edward had given her; she would leave the court. And then he would come to her and she would sink deeper and deeper into the quicksand.

Hastings was furious. People were laughing at him. It was said that for years he had waited like a hungry dog for the King's titbit; and now Dorset had pounced on it before he had had time to seize it.

"You are a fool," he told Jane when he waylaid her. "Dorset is the very devil with women. To think that you should join that sorry crowd!"

"I do not need your pity. Keep it for others," she said angrily.

"You will need it ere long. Think not that when he has done with you, you can come creeping to me. I would never take one of Dorset's cast-off mistresses."

"I'll not tolerate your insolence," she cried, and hurried from him that he might not see her tears.

Jane moved to the palace of the Tower. Dorset had his duties there and he would have her near him. She told herself and him that she would not go, for good sense said, "Retire from court life. Regain that dignity which was yours while Edward lived." But passion overruled good sense.

It was pleasant to have Kate near her again. Kate longed for confidences, but she did not get them. There was no one to whom Jane could talk of the terrible fascination of the Marquis. So Kate talked instead about the happenings at the Tower.

"Messengers come and go the whole day through," she told Jane. "What they are about, Heaven may know, but I can only guess. Why, 'tis as though we are preparing for a siege. There's more soldiers about the courtyards every day, and now they've fixed a cannon on Tower Hill. The arms are being brought out from the armouries."

Kate was right; and the whole of London was uneasy; but Jane could think of little but her lover.

*   *   *   *   *

A hooded figure stepped into the boat and asked to be rowed across the river. The boatman was eager to obey instructions, for in these days of uncertainty, when those who had been great yesterday were no longer great, a poor boatman could never be sure what influence a patron might have. This was a lady with a soft and gentle voice; she showed little of her face, but enough for him to see that it was of great beauty. He wondered what her business across the river could be. She looked sad and was silent, and he did not like to see one of her sort making her way to Southwark. She paid him well and thanked him graciously, and he watched her make her way along the waterfront until she was lost to his sight.

Jane was going to see Dorset. She felt guilty and ashamed, yet exalted. She could scarcely wait to feel her lover's arms about her, and she had to remind herself over and over again that she must go cautiously, and that even now there might be someone following her, someone who would discover her lover's hiding place, and betray him and Jane with him. For Dorset was in hiding. His plot and that of his family had failed. Richard of Gloucester, riding South, had been warned in time by the Duke of Buckingham, and now the little King was in the charge of his Uncle Richard, as his father had intended he should be; and Lord Rivers, his uncle, and Richard Grey, his half-brother, were the prisoners of Gloucester. London, largely due to the intervention of Hastings, had received Gloucester and the little King with a warm welcome, and the Queen had

had to fly to Sanctuary with her family. As for Dorset, he could only hide until he or his friends could gather strength and men to fight.

Running, and glancing over her shoulder to make sure she was not being followed, Jane came to a short and narrow street. She stopped before the largest of the houses and hastily knocked at the door, which was opened after a few moments, just an inch or so, and a man with hollow eyes and an oddly twisted mouth looked out at her.

"Oh, Danok," said Jane, "let me in quickly."

Danok undid the heavy chain which prevented him from opening the door for more than an inch or two, and Jane stepped quickly into the house. The door was promptly shut behind her and the chain fixed in its place.

She was shivering, partly from relief at having reached the house unobserved, partly with the horror the place never failed to inspire in her. It was an evil house, and its quietness was more horrible because occasionally it was broken by strange noises—the soft padding of feet, the low rumble of voices, the faint moaning of some young creature in distress, and some-times the agonised shriek that might come from a woman in labour. Jane felt this house to be full of all human evils—of lust and avarice, of misery, pain and death. She hated coming here, yet come she must, for Dorset commanded her.

A door opened and a woman glided towards her. She was dressed in dove grey, and about her neck, on a heavy chain, hung a silver cross.

"Would you be so good as to step in here before you are conducted to his lordship?" asked Madam quietly.

Jane nodded, and followed her into the room she indicated.

"Your ladyship must be very careful on your journey here." The woman let her heavy lids fall over her eyes. "I thought I should warn you. His lordship was one of our most frequent guests . . . in the days of his prosperity. It might be that his enemies would expect him to be with us. It is true that, in the ordinary course of events, it is the gentlemen who come here to visit ladies . . . but there are some who might suspect such an illustrious lady as yourself. . . ." Madam smiled as Jane flushed hotly. She shrugged her shoulders and went on : "We have the reputation of being most accommodating to our gentlemen. Nothing, many realize, is considered beyond our power to provide for them."

Jane's anger flared up suddenly. "And as," she said caustically, "refuge in time of trouble is as expensive as pleasure in time of peace, there are some who would suspect *you* of helping his lordship at this time?"

"You get my meaning exactly. Some little matter came to light last evening. One of my ladies was asked by a visitor some very unusual questions about the company of this house."

"Should that appear so very distressing and uncalled for?"

"Indeed, yes, when I tell you the questions concerned his lordship. And I took the precaution of looking into the inquiring gentleman's background. He was of the household of His Grace, the Duke of Gloucester. That is why I suggest you show even greater care than usual."

"Never fear, I shall be careful. And now may I be conducted to his lordship?"

Madam went to the door and clapped her hands. A bold-looking girl of about sixteen, whose face was already marked with debauchery, came in answer to the summons. "This is Kitty," said Madam. "She waits on his lordship, and I hear he is very pleased with all she can do for him."

Kitty led the way down two flights of stone stairs, through a dark passage which was flanked on either side by walls in which were several doors, all shut. Moisture trickled down the walls and the stone floor was slippery. Dorset was so situated that he could, at the first signs of danger, slip out of the house through a back way which might not be suspected of belonging to this house.

Kitty knocked at the door before which she had paused. Dorset's voice said : "Who's there?"

" 'Tis Kitty, my lord," said the girl. "With a lady to see you."

Dorset unlocked the door. "Jane!" he cried. And to Kitty: "Be off with you. And if I find you listening at the door I'll have you whipped." He shut the door and stood leaning against it. "That will settle the slut. She knows I mean that. Now, Jane, what news?"

The first thing he thought of was news. There were plenty in this house to amuse him, but only Jane could bring him news from his friends outside; none but Jane could take messages from him to the Queen.

She said: "There is little news. Gloucester is at Baynard's Castle, and the King is to leave the house of the Bishop of London for the palace of the Tower."

He kissed her then, but calmly. "What news of my mother?"

"She stays in Sanctuary with young Richard and her daughters."

"She should not have fled there. It was a confession of guilt. She could have been more useful elsewhere."

Jane tried to soothe him, to turn his thoughts from his ill-fortune to herself. She said: "Gloucester does not want trouble. He is glad that the affair has been settled without bloodshed. I think that when he is assured that your family is prepared to accept him as Protector of England and guardian of the King, he will forgive you."

"Forgive us? It is not for him to forgive. Think you we shall ever accept him as guardian of the King? You talk like a fool, Jane."

"Better to talk like a fool than to act like one!"

"Now, Jane," he said soothingly, for he did not forget how useful she could be to him, "you did not come here to quarrel, I'll swear."

"I did not. Oh, how I hate this place!"

"Yet you come to see me."

"I cannot stay away."

"Sweet Jane. You are mine . . . absolutely and unconditionally."

"It would seem so, Thomas. Were you to retire from court, I am convinced Gloucester would be your friend."

"What! Should I seek friendship with that ill-favoured pig, that traitor. . . ."

"He is not a traitor. Edward left his son in his care, and he has come to London to perform his duties."

Dorset's face was purple with fury. "So you are on the side of Gloucester. You are for your friend Hastings. Holy Christ! Have you become his mistress then?"

It was Jane's turn to grow hot and angry. "I hate the man, and well you know it."

"But he does not hate you; and would not Hastings, the friend of Gloucester, make a better protector than Dorset in hiding?"

"I do not seek protectors. Nor have I ever."

"Did you never put yourself under the protection of the King?"

"I left my husband for Edward because I loved him."

He took her hands. "Forgive me, Jane. I am overwrought. Here I am in this place, bribing whores and a procuress to keep me hidden."

She softened at once. "I understand what you have suffered."

"There is so much to bear. But for that traitor Buckingham this would not have befallen us. Buckingham and Hastings . . . together they proved our undoing."

Jane found herself defending her old enemy. "Hastings did what he thought right. He was loyal to Edward, and he will be loyal to Gloucester and the King. Come, rest a little. Let me pour some wine for you." She went to the table and poured out some wine.

"Jane," he said soberly, "you run great risk in coming here, particularly as you go about the court and bring me news. There would be short shrift for you were you caught. Why do you do it? Why do you not find a more agreeable lover? The great Hastings is panting for you. Yet, you wrap a cloak about you and come to this place. If you were caught, even Hastings might not be able to save you. Why do you do it, Jane?" She stood over him with the wine and he drew her down beside him. "I'll tell you why. You come because you cannot help yourself. You'd follow me to hell, Jane, an I beckoned. You'd follow me to damnation." He stroked her hair. "You cannot resist me. Well, you are very fair and you are very loving, and I love you truly. And while we love, what should we care for what happens outside these four walls! That is the glory of love such as ours. You can forget all else in me . . . and I in you. That is the very essence of its appeal for you and for me. I'll warrant Gloucester never found a woman to love his miserable deformed body as you love mine."

Once more he was battling down her resistance. She could not escape his fascination.

Later, when he lay quietly beside her, he began to talk of Hastings once more.

"Often as I lie here thinking of my ill-fortune I remember this, Jane: Had Hastings been with us, and not against us, there might have been a different story to tell. What odd favourites London chooses! The old City took Edward to its heart for his charm and his beauty, and because he was a fine fellow who liked to seduce its citizens' wives. And when he grew fat and lazy and demanded his benevolences, London still loved him. So with Hastings. Hastings followed his royal master's habits and London loves Hastings. London listened to Hastings, Jane, when she ought to have listened to me."

"What good can all this bitterness bring you?"

"Why does Hastings support Gloucester, think you?"

"Because he considers it his duty so to do."

"You have a high opinion of the man you pretend to despise."

"I should not have thought you cared so much for me,

Thomas," she said sadly, "as to be so jealous on my account."

He covered her face with kisses, but she sensed a lack of warmth in them. "Ah," he whispered. "He is an upright, honourable man, but the most upright and the most honourable can be seduced from their duty."

"What do you mean?" asked Jane.

But Dorset did not answer. He laughed wildly, caressing her, kissing her; and then he began his love-making all over again.

*   *   *   *   *

Later, when Jane looked back on that period of her life, it seemed to her that her passion for Dorset was a madness that possessed her and blinded her to everything but the need to satisfy it.

One day when she went to the house in Southwark she found him in a passion of fury.

"Shut the door," he commanded, as soon as she entered; he took her by the shoulders, but there was nothing lover-like in the gesture.

"You have news, Thomas?" she asked, startled.

"News of treachery and betrayal. Holy Mother! We have to act now and act quickly."

"What is this news?"

"It is a lie. It is an evil fabrication of that hog Gloucester. What news, say you? Just this, Jane. He has forced Bishop Stillington to tell the wildest, wickedest lie before the Council that was ever told."

"Bishop Stillington?" said Jane, her memory stirring.

"He says my stepfather was never truly married to my mother. Edward, he says, was precontracted to a woman who bore him a child and died in a convent, but who was living when he married my mother."

"Yes," said Jane slowly, "I remember."

He seized her by the arm and shook her. "*You* remember! What nonsense is this? What do you remember? It happened long before you came to court."

"But Thomas, it is true. Stillington was in the Tower for talking of it. It was . . . about the time that the Duke of Clarence was . . . found dead. I shared Edward's confidences. It is true that he was married before he married your mother."

Dorset lifted his hand as though to strike her. "If you ever say that again," he said, "I . . . I'll kill you."

She looked at him; her eyes were cold. He cared nothing for her; he cared only for ambition. He smiled suddenly, seeing in her eyes that which he knew he must dispel.

"Forgive me, Jane. Forgive me, sweetheart. It is this fresh disaster. Do you not see that if this is bruited abroad it is the end of us?"

"The end of the Woodvilles," she said coldly.

"Then of *us*, Jane, for you are one of us. You and I have been too close for aught else, my dear."

She was softening towards him already. "Clarence discovered this," she said. "He taunted his brother, the King, with it."

"Who else knew beside yourself?"

"The Queen and Gloucester. Edward said the secret was with those whom he could trust."

"Those whom he could trust! That pig and viper Gloucester. And Stillington knows. My father was a fool to let him go free."

"He was ever one to shelve unpleasant matters. Stillington promised secrecy, so he freed him."

"On payment of a handsome fine, I'll warrant. My stepfather could be trapped into folly with the utmost ease. In his youth it was women; and as he grew older, gold."

Jane turned to him appealingly. "Look at the truth, Thomas. Your mother was not truly married to the King, and the Princes are not truly Princes. Therefore is Richard of Gloucester King of England."

"Be silent! I'll not have it said."

"It is the truth."

"So you are against us also? Whom can one trust?"

"I am not against you. How could I be when I love you? But Richard is true King of England."

"Where is your loyalty, Jane? To me . . . to Edward? You owe something to Edward if not to me. He trusted you, Jane. Are you going to turn against him? It was his wish that young Edward should sit on the throne. Richard of Gloucester is a traitor, for did he not know his brother trusted him and so believed him to be the last man to turn against the little King, that he left the boy in his charge?"

Watching Jane, Dorset saw her troubled eyes. What a fool Jane was! She was too emotional, too generous, too good-hearted. She had come into the world with great gifts—beauty and charm; but she was soft and foolish, too careless of herself. She would come to an evil end one day when her beauty had faded and with it her charm; she would find herself destitute in a careless world.

She wanted to believe Dorset was right. She was thinking of Edward, and how easy it was to think—when it was what she wanted to think—that Gloucester was a traitor, inasmuch as he had promised to care for his brother's son and as soon as his brother was dead set about trying to put himself on the throne.

"Jane," said Dorset, "you will help Edward's boy?"

Help young Edward, whom she loved as though he were her own child? Indeed she would. No matter what was right and what was wrong. Love was more important in Jane's eyes than right. For the sake of Edward the King for whom she had abandoned her virtue, for the sake of Edward his son, and for the sake of Dorset, who bound her to him with the bonds of physical desire, she would help.

"You love those children, do you not, Jane?" went on Dorset. "Not only Edward, but little Richard too. What will become of those poor innocent children if Gloucester takes the throne? They would have their supporters. There would always be those to doubt Stillington and Gloucester. There would be some who would try to put little Edward back upon the throne. And Gloucester? Have you ever looked into those fish's eyes of his? What would Gloucester do, think you, to two innocent boys who stood in his way?"

Jane's eyes were wide with horror. "But what can I do, Thomas? Richard is truly King of England. Oh . . . but I cannot bear to think what might befall little Edward."

His face was alight with enthusiasm, and he was very handsome thus. Enamoured of that beautiful face, Jane found it easy to believe in his sincerity.

"This marriage was but a promise. Shall those innocent children suffer for that? Shall all England suffer? Jane, you can help. You must."

"How?"

"You could rally people to our cause. There is one who, doubtless, could be persuaded to do aught you asked him."

She stared at him in horror, for Hastings was never far from her thoughts. "I could do nothing of that nature, Thomas," she said quickly.

"Why not? Hastings loved Edward. He loves Edward's son."

"He is Gloucester's friend, and you know that well."

"He is more eager to be your friend than Gloucester's."

"I understand you not." Jane was trembling, and although her eyes flashed, her face was very pale.

"A word from you, Jane, and Hastings would listen. You could talk to him."

"And what should I say?"

"With soft words you could bring Hastings to our side."

"I could not do that, Thomas."

He could have struck her, but he kept his control. He had dominated her before; he would do so again. "Does it mean nothing to you to see me brought low?"

"It breaks my heart to see you thus."

"You have a proud look for one who suffers from a broken heart. You condemn me to death; for let me tell you that will be my portion when Richard is on the throne, unless I can

escape to France. You condemn the little Princes to the same
evil fate. And yet would you but give a word and a smile to a
man who would do anything you asked of him, you could
save us."

"You think Hastings would desert Gloucester for you—because I asked him?" She wished she could subdue her excitement; she wished she could stop thinking of Hastings as her
lover. Afterwards she would say to him, "There! You would
have betrayed *me* once. Now I have betrayed *you*."

"You could bring him over—if you were his friend."

"His *friend*! What do you mean by that?"

He did not answer, and she turned fiercely on him. "How
dare you suggest this! What have you ever cared for me? Be
his friend, you say. His friend! I hate you!"

"You are behaving like a child, Jane." Dorset's lips were
coldly prim. "And, by the Virgin, you mistake me. I said, 'Be
his friend'; and I meant 'Be his friend.' You say you hate me.
By God, you shall retract that statement in a very short time."
He took her by the shoulders. "I declare you relish him. You
are a shameless harlot. You are weary of me. You long for
Hastings."

Jane beat her fists against his chest in such anger as she had
never known in the whole of her life. "I hate you," she said,
half sobbing. "I think I've always hated you."

"How like you, Jane! You say you hate me when you love
me. But you say you hate Hastings also. Can it be that you do
not know the difference between love and hate?" She had grown
quiet, and he drew her to him and touched her hair with gentle
fingers as he talked. "Am I not the most jealous of men? Would
I not rather suffer the torment of obscurity and certain death
than that you should do—that which it came into your mind to
do?" She stirred, but he would not release her. "But you could
speak with him; you could even promise him—for what are
promises when one is desperate? You could tell him that between themselves Stillington and Gloucester have concocted
this story of a marriage. I'll warrant loyal Hastings would be

truly loyal and ready to fight for his little King—should you ask him."

"But they did not concoct this story, Thomas."

"Very well. Let Gloucester continue with his evil purpose. What do I care? I cannot live my life in this place. I shall try to escape and doubtless be caught. I shall be thrust into the Tower and tortured, and when to torture me further would be to kill me, they will lead me out to Tower Green, and you will be there, Jane, looking on, to see my head, streaming blood, roll in the straw. You will shed a tear and be sorry then that you did nothing to save the head you once loved, for love me you did, Jane."

"I still love you," said Jane.

"No. You love me not. I know it now. Misfortunes, I have learned, come not singly." He kissed her and drew her on to the couch. He wanted to be sure he had lost none of his power over her. "Jane, I have asked too much. You must not come here again. It is too dangerous."

He bent his handsome head to kiss her throat, gently at first, then deliberately he let his kisses grow more passionate. Her eyes were half closed and she was returning his kisses. The moment was approaching for them both when there was nothing but their fleeting need of each other.

"Jane, sweetheart," he said, "you will bring Hastings to our side?"

She said then that she would do anything he asked of her. She would talk to Hastings and see what it was possible to do.

"Bless you, Jane," said Dorset. "I knew you loved me truly. I knew you'd not fail me."

*   *   *   *

Jane was dressing herself with great care, and rarely had she looked so beautiful. She was wearing her favourite blue and her lovely hair was flowing about her shoulders. She was excited glad that she had decided to bring about the betrayal of Hastings. She had changed, she supposed, since she had come to court. She, the kind-hearted, the most easy-going woman in

London, was planning revenge and finding the thought of it sweet. How delicious to play a trick on him, as he had tried to trick her all those years ago!

I am wicked, she thought. I am as bad as the preachers at Paul's Cross say I am.

This morning, as if by accident, she had met him as he made his way to Baynard's Castle, whither he was bound for conference with Gloucester. He had bowed, and his face had lit with pleasure at the sight of her.

She had said to him: "Good day to you, my lord." And she had spoken in a more gracious voice than she had ever used towards him before.

"Good day to you, Jane," he had answered. And then: "You look distraught. Is anything wrong?" A tender line played about his mouth; a look of yearning was in his eyes; he longed to help her.

"I have much on my mind, my lord. I am a foolish woman, and there is none with whom I can discuss my troubles."

It was a direct invitation and he had seized upon it. "Could I be of any help?"

She had been filled with exultation at the eagerness of him. She was no longer important, and yet he was as anxious to please her as anyone ever had been. He did not taunt her with her fall from power. Doubtless there was some good in Hastings; but she was not going to let herself be deceived. She would not forget the past; she would not let her hatred soften.

"It would mean a waste of your time, my lord."

"A waste of my time!" She caught the warmth of his eyes as they rested on her; the longing of years had been in that glance, brightened by such hope as she had never seen there before.

"When, Jane?" he had asked.

"You mean, my lord, that you can spare the time to talk to me?"

"Would you come and sup with me to-day? That would give me the greatest pleasure."

"You are good to me. I feel that in view of everything . . ."

"Nay, Jane, forget what went before. That is what we have to do. Forget the past. Shall I see you at four of the clock?"

She had faltered, her sense of shame making her recoil.

"Please, Jane," he had insisted. "It will give me the greatest possible pleasure."

He had had to hurry off then, for he could not keep Gloucester waiting.

Jane had then gone to her house near the river, where, since Dorset had been in hiding, she had lived. The encounter with Hastings had disturbed her deeply. What have I become? she asked herself again and again. She was like an animal that altered its skin to resemble the environment in which it lived. Beside the might of Edward the King she had been serenely comfortable, never dabbling in affairs of state, begging favours for those in trouble; gentle, kindly, witty Jane Shore. But now, through her love for the scheming Dorset, she herself was deep in intrigue. Where was the gentle, forgiving Jane Shore in this woman who now found such pleasure in contemplating revenge for a long-ago injury that had come to nothing? Was it revenge she sought? But what else should she want of Hastings?

She must be wily, cautious and brave. Spies watched her, the spies of Gloucester, the most important—some said the most ruthless—man in England. Danger was stimulating, and so she tingled with excitement as she prepared herself to visit Lord Hastings.

She reached his apartments in good time. One of his attendants, in the brilliant Hastings livery, ushered her ceremoniously in; and immediately she was surrounded by bowing men and women who had evidently been told to expect a person of great importance to their master. She saw then a man she knew to be a certain Catesby, a friend of Hastings. He recognised Jane, bowed to her and went out of the house. Jane wondered then how long it would be before the court was whispering that Jane Shore and Hastings were on terms of intimacy.

Hastings himself had now appeared and was coming forward

to greet her; immaculately dressed, he looked very distinguished. The years had softened his face, and the tenderness in his smile made him pleasant to look upon. He was very pale, and Jane saw a nerve twitching in his cheek.

"Jane, it was good of you to come."

"Nay, my lord, it was good of you to receive me."

He waved a hand to dismiss his attendants, and they were alone. He said: "Could you not call me William, since we are to be friends?"

She laughed. "Friends! After how many years is it—William?"

"Many weary years. Too many to count." He led her into a small but elegantly furnished room. "But they have dealt kindly with you, Jane," he added.

"And not unkindly with you."

"It is gracious of you to say so; but let us go to the table and I will have supper served immediately."

She sat down and he went to the bell rope. Menservants came hurrying in to serve the meal. Everything was of the most luxurious. It was as though he said, "See. I can entertain you even as did the King."

She could see that he could not stop comparing himself with the late King; she could see that his hopes were high and that he considered this *tête-à-tête* supper to be an introduction to that relationship he had always desired should exist between them.

Peacocks, feather-decorated, were brought in by silent-footed men and maids; there were quails and roast pheasants, ducks and chine of beef. He had been most careful in selecting the choicest of his wines. It was as though he, the epicure, spread his talents before her.

As they ate he talked lightly, and it was not until after they had had their fill, and the serving men and maids were dismissed, that he, leaning his elbows on the table and watching her earnestly, asked if she were not lonely, living as she did.

"Living as I do? How do you know how I live?"

"I draw conclusions. Tell me, there is no . . ."

"Protector?" She laughed lightly. "Nay, though England has one, I have not."

"I am glad of that, Jane. I had hoped . . ."

She steered him away from the subject. "My lord—William —these are troublous times."

He shrugged his shoulders. "The Protector is a strong man; and England, like you, Jane, has need of a strong man."

"But England has a King, has she not?"

"A litle boy. Jane, there is much I would say to you and have been trying to say to you ever since you came, but it is not easy. You know my feelings for you. Right from the beginning . . ."

"Oh, William, how that takes me back! Right from the beginning! It reminds me of the time when I was a little girl and my father took me to see a procession."

"I rode in that procession."

"You looked at me—and that was the beginning of everything."

"You would not have supped with me thus unless you had meant to be my friend, Jane?"

"I am your friend, William."

"You know it is more than friendship that I need from you."

"Then let us speak frankly, William."

"That is what I would wish." He had risen and came over to fill her glass. He rested his hand on her bare shoulder; it was feverish and its touch was a caress. She lifted the hand from her shoulder and put it from her.

"Yes," she said, "let us talk."

He pulled a stool up close to hers and leaned his elbows on the table, watching her face. "This night," he said, "is the happiest of my life since Edward brought you to the court. You must believe me, Jane, for I have never ceased to reproach myself for what I did. Jane, will you forgive me?"

She touched his hand lightly, and he seized hers and held it. "If you ask forgiveness of me," she said, "then must I ask it of you. I have been spiteful to you—for years I have taunted you. So please do not let us speak of forgiveness."

"You were wont to hurt me with your tongue," he said, "but I did not forget that you had other powerful weapons which you did not use against me. Some would have ruined my career. Edward's ear was yours, was it not? People used to say that more court was paid to you, in Edward's time, than to any other in the land. You could have had me sent from court—banished—ruined. Oh, Jane, you are not only the fairest, but the sweetest of women."

Her eyes filled with sudden tears. "Nay," she said swiftly; and she was at once miserable and ashamed.

"But yes," he insisted. "There is not a soul in London who would not agree with me. You are the dearest of women, and I love you."

She could not look at him. "There is much to say," she stammered. "Remember, William, it is I who came here to talk to you."

"You came here to tell me of your loneliness, Jane. I am lonely also. Why should not you and I give each other the comfort we need?" He laughed suddenly. "That is an ill way of expressing what we could give each other. Comfort! Is Heaven to be spoken of in terms of comfort? Let us forget the past, Jane."

"We were different people in those days, William."

Yes, she thought, we were very different. I would never have come here to him for this purpose in those days. I had some sense of honour then, some dignity. But I have changed, even as he has; but he has changed for the better; I for the worse. Dorset has changed me, brutalised me; a woman cannot allow herself to be used as he used me without such treatment leaving its mark upon her.

He went on talking, making excuses for that Hastings who, in his reckless adventuring days, had sought to abduct her, and had laid wicked plans for so doing. He covered his face with his hands. "And so did I lose you, Jane, for many years. My cruelty was to blame, my vindictiveness towards the goldsmith. How often have I tortured myself with the reflection that it

was I who gave you to Edward! I—who willingly and most
stupidly gave away that which I longed to possess and cherish."

"It is done with and forgotten," she said gently. "We are no
longer young and foolish."

"And being no longer young and foolish, let us grasp at that
which offers delight to us both."

"Such matters cannot be hastened. I did not come here to
talk of myself. There is something else, and I wish to ask your
advice. I am distracted. Please, William, help me in this matter,
and then—mayhap we can think of—ourselves."

She saw the hope leap into his eyes. Had she said, "Help me
in this and I will be your mistress"? Had she said it as crudely
as that? What had happened to her to make her tremble at the
thought of this man's embrace?

"Tell me what troubles you, sweetheart," said Hastings.

"It is the little King, William. He is nothing more than a
little prisoner in the Tower."

"No, no, Jane. He is no prisoner. He is lodged in the state
apartments, awaiting his coronation."

"While his mother, his young brother and his sisters are kept
in Sanctuary?"

"Kept in Sanctuary? They stay there, remember, of their
own accord."

"Because they fear to come out."

Hastings shrugged his shoulders. "The Queen was guilty of
a planned rebellion. That much was made clear by her hasty
retirement into Sanctuary as soon as she knew the plan was
foiled."

"A plan for rebellion?" Jane's cheeks burned. The wine was
exciting her; it was more potent than she had guessed, and she
suspected Hastings of knowing this. She thought of the sleeping draught which he had induced Kate to give her. She must
remember that, for it hardened her against him. "Rebellion
against whom? Against the King? Or his uncle? There is a
difference, you must know."

"No, Jane, there is no difference. I pray you, sweetheart, if you will talk of these matters keep your voice low. There are spies everywhere. And, remember, you were once on most friendly terms with one of the chief members of the Queen's family." She flushed, and he hurried on : "Forgive me, Jane. That is over and done with, is it not?"

"Do not speak of it again."

"Nor will I. But remember this, my dear one : you would not be suspected unless you talked with indiscretion. His Grace of Gloucester is most friendly disposed towards you. We have talked of you."

"You have talked of *me*?"

"With the utmost friendliness on both sides. He forgets not what you once did for him and the Duchess. There is much I have never forgotten—nor ever will."

"You do well to warn me. I speak without caution. But I will repeat, William my friend, that to side with the little King is not to side with the Duke."

"What have you heard, Jane?"

"That he conspires with Stillington to take the crown from Edward's son."

Hastings was astounded. "How knew you this, Jane?"

"Such news travels fast. Soon all London will be talking of it."

"I did not know that it had leaked out."

"I have heard that Stillington proclaimed it at the Council. William, what has happened to Edward's friends, those who swore loyalty to him? They swore to protect his son. Edward never thought his own and trusted brother would turn against the boy."

"You are hot in defence of the boy, Jane."

"Because I love him. He and his brother were often with me. I longed for children—and they *were* my children. Do you believe this story Stillington has brought to the Council?"

"I know not what to believe. But if it can be proved, then Richard of Gloucester is rightly Richard the Third of England, as the son of Clarence, through his father's treason, has been attainted."

"Richard swore allegiance to his brother's son, did he not?"

"He did, but if this can be proved, it is not Richard who owes allegiance to young Edward, but Edward to Richard."

Hastings is right, she thought. But what of little Edward, whom she loved as if he were her own child? What of Dorset? But during this meeting with the man whom, she must constantly remind herself, she hated as she had never hated anyone before, Dorset was becoming more and more remote. When she did think of him she saw the cruelty of his mouth, and she compared it with the gentleness of Hastings' smile. She had longed for gentleness; she had always wanted love with passion. She knew suddenly that she was doing now what she had longed to do for some time—that was, escape from Dorset. She was bewildered, not knowing what she wanted, to love or to hate, to tease or to surrender. These foolish men, she thought, with feminine logic. A pox on their quarrels! What does it matter who is King—Edward or Richard? Why cannot we all be kind and loving to each other?

Hastings was saying: "There is good evidence that Stillington speaks truth."

"But would it not be easy for Gloucester to concoct such a story?"

"If he were of such mind, doubtless it would."

"And do you believe him to be of such mind?"

"I believe him to be a man of honour."

"Honour? What is honour? That which is evil to some men could seem good to others. Gloucester swore to his brother to protect the boy, and did he not know of this matter before his brother's death? My lord, might it not be that Gloucester seeks to take the crown from that innocent boy's head and wear it himself?" She laid a hand on his shoulder and noted with pleasure that by a touch she could drive all thought of Gloucester from his mind. "William, you promised loyalty to Edward. Your loyalty has been that quality which I most admired in you. If you desert the King now, how can I go on believing in your honesty?"

Hastings seized her suddenly and swung her off her feet.

Her face was on a level with his. "What do you mean, Jane? Tell me truly. What do you mean?"

"You promised loyalty to Edward," she said. "If you desert his son I could never trust you."

"These are matters in which you should not become involved."

"Then put me down, my lord, and I will go."

He shook his head. "You are not going, Jane. You will stay here with me. You will stay for ever."

"No," she said; but she knew she was going to stay, and she knew she wanted to stay. "How could I, when you are preparing to betray Edward's son—the little boy I love!"

He pressed his mouth against hers. "What have such matters to do with us? God in Heaven, how I have wanted you! How I have dreamed—and at last you are come to me."

She thought: I have dreamed too. Nightmares. Did I really want him all the time?

"You must hate me, William," she said slowly, "for what I have said to you. Gloucester is your friend and you love him well. You will be faithful to him, unto death—more faithful than you would be to me."

She heard his voice, slurred with passion, yet soft with tenderness. "Hate? Sometimes I have thought I hated you, but that was only because I loved you. You are right when you say that Gloucester is my friend; but what are friends set side by side with lovers? What could Gloucester ever be to me beside Jane Shore? My Jane, my own—whom I have yearned for and dreamed of these many years. But now you are come to me, and now you shall stay. You shall never leave me again."

"I do not know," she said weakly. "I cannot say . . ."

"You are a madness in me," he told her, "a madness that has been chained to my heels for many long years. This was meant to be, Jane. I have always known it. I loved Edward well until he brought you to court and showed so clearly that he meant to keep you there; then I longed for his death. Such was my love for you."

"It was not true love," she insisted. "If it had been I might have loved you when you came to me in Cheapside. It was because you played false that I have hated you ever since."

"You would have loved me then, had I acted differently all those years ago?"

"We promised we would not speak of the past. I trust you now. I have drunk of your wine, though in view of what once happened I might so easily have been afraid."

"Everything that happens now between us must be with your most willing agreement. I am not such a fool as I once was."

"Then I think I should go home."

"I beg of you to stay. I have not said all I wish to. You came to me because you were distressed on behalf of the King. What did you hope that I would do about this matter?"

"I hoped that you might see the boy—comfort him. I hoped that you might bring your powers to work for him and not against him."

"I had hoped you came because you were lonely and sought my company."

"Mayhap there was something of that in it."

"Stay with me, Jane."

"I cannot think clearly. Let me go now—and another time . . ."

"You slipped away from me before, and I cannot let you do so again. You no longer hate me. You never did hate me. Confess it, Jane. You never did."

"It was not hatred then. I do not know what it was—but it had the look of hatred."

"When I kiss you," he said, "you tremble. Jane—you need me."

She did need him. She was lonely and she wanted to be loved, not cruelly but tenderly. She must escape from Dorset, and Hastings would show her the way. She needed the devotion of Hastings to heal those wounds she had received through Dorset's brutal treatment.

She lifted her face to Hastings. If this is hatred, she thought, it is peculiarly stimulating, exciting—and deeply satisfying.

Hastings smiled, and his smile was one of triumph.

*   *   *   *   *

Was she acting a part—the part of Hastings' mistress? How easy, how delightful it was to play! How pleasant to run to him when he returned to her, to beg him to take care when he went out, to return his kisses!

One day, she thought, I shall laugh scornfully at him. I shall say, "Now, my lord, this is how you would have made me suffer. I wonder how many of your victims have felt as you do now!"

Yet she would weep real tears when he went to one of those council meetings. She would start with terror when she heard a commotion at the door. For they were more than lovers now; they were conspirators. How easy it was when he lay beside her, indolent after satisfied passion; shorn of his power like Samson of his locks, how simple to win his loyalty for little Edward! How easy to let him believe that between them Stillington and Gloucester had concocted this story of Eleanor Butler! Hastings was deeply in love. What did he care for Gloucester? He cared only for Jane Shore. He was completely happy; he had attained that goal for which, over many years, he had strived.

The excitement of her relationship with Hastings soon made Jane impatient of politics. Her thoughts were concentrated on Hastings the lover; Hastings the statesman, now head of the new secret party, was remote. She did not realise the immensity of this matter for which she was largely responsible. Hastings was winning more important personages to his side; they came secretly to his house and were shut in with him for hours at a time; Jane did not think of what they might be planning; she was only angry that they took him from her side.

He would talk to Jane of what he had done, this day and that, until she would stop her ears and refuse to listen. Then he would laugh and kiss her, and tell her he was glad she kept aloof from these quarrels; he would forget everything then, but themselves; and they would enjoy their love together.

She had finished with Dorset now, for not since her early days with Edward had she known such happiness.

Hastings said: "Sometimes I fear I have dreamed all this, and that I shall awaken and find you not beside me. For in truth, Jane, this happiness you have brought me makes my days pass as though I dream."

He was right. It was like a dream. An odd, exciting, fascinating dream of hate—or love.

*   *   *   *   *

There was one man who watched the lovers with calculating eyes. He was a man named Catesby; of great ambitions, he had been a close friend of Hastings and enjoyed his confidences. He had come a long way, largely owing to the help of Hastings, but he looked ahead to greater achievement. He knew, as Hastings' friend and confidant, that the noble had recently changed sides. This was folly, reasoned Catesby, and Hastings was surely bewitched. How could Hastings succeed when his opponent was the cleverest, subtlest man in England? Catesby had decided on which side he was going to be. He had to choose, and he chose Gloucester.

Not that he told Hastings this. Why should he? It was simple to go to Hastings' meetings, to listen to his plans. The Protector had already noticed him and commended him. How much more warmly would the great man commend him if he disclosed the Hastings plot to him.

Hastings was a fool—a love-sick fool. He seemed hardly aware of the danger he was in. If ever Catesby had seen a man being led to disaster, that man was Hastings; beckoned on, he was, by beautiful Jane Shore. What a fool he was to let a woman lead him to oppose the mighty Gloucester, for Gloucester would have no mercy; he cared nothing for his friends; he only cared for England.

One would desert one's patron for the future King of England if one were wise, and Catesby was wise. It was hardly a week after Jane's first visit to Hastings that Catesby strolled along to Crosby Hall and begged an audience with the Protector, stressing that it was of the utmost importance that the interview be granted. He was conducted to Richard at once.

Richard had changed in the last weeks. He was paler than ever; his eyes were alert and he seemed almost furtive in his watchfulness.

He was deeply shocked as he listened to Catesby's story. His cold eyes kindled into such heat of anger that Catesby seemed to shrivel before it.

"You dare accuse—*Hastings*—of treachery!"

"My lord, Your Grace, I know it to be so. Hastings has taken me into his confidence. He has been bewitched by Jane Shore, who, Your Grace knows, was mistress to Dorset. She is with him night and day. She is a witch, Your Grace, and witches can seduce strong men from duty. He will go whither she beckons, and she beckons him to treachery."

Richard was full of anxiety. He had looked on Hastings as his most reliable friend.

"This must be false," he said sadly.

"I would it were, Your Grace. I had loved Hastings. It is the woman who has bewitched him."

"Good men are not bewitched, Catesby, nor lured from honour. How can I know you speak the truth?"

Richard closed his eyes. The heat was oppressive to-day. He felt tired and sick. Whom could he trust if Hastings failed him? He could never trust any again. He would have trusted Hastings with his life.

"There are many of his household who could be questioned, Your Grace."

"You are right, Catesby."

"I trust I pleased Your Grace in coming."

"You did the only possible thing, Catesby. When traitors are abroad 'tis the duty of every right-thinking man to expose them. Go now, and speak of this to none. I trust you, Catesby."

"Your trust is not misplaced, my lord Duke."

"You may leave this to me. I will attend to it."

He watched Catesby depart. His face puckered suddenly. Not Hastings! Not his old and trusted friend! Hastings had been Edward's friend—one of his ablest statesmen, one of his most admired friends. Richard had thought he had inherited that friendship. But if Catesby had spoken the truth Hastings was at this very moment plotting against him.

Anger surged up and drowned his sorrow. Hastings should regret this day. There was no time to lose. He must test the truth of this story, and if it proved to be true, he would know how to act.

*   *   *   *   *

In the privacy of their chamber Jane helped Hastings prepare himself for the meeting of the Council. Now she must help him into his coat; now she must fetch his shoes, and flick imaginary dust from his garments, for the joy of touching him.

She knew the truth now. She loved Hastings. She wanted to explain to him her wanton wickedness, how she had meant to lure him to love her, and then turn from him and laugh at him, as he would have laughed at her all those years ago.

It was no use trying to explain. There was no time for explanations; there was only time for happiness. They had wasted so much time, he said. They must waste no more. Every moment must be a joy to her as it was to him, for his heart's desire had come to him, and what more of life could any man or woman ask?

Sometimes he was afraid of so much happiness; then Jane would laugh at him. Jane was ready to snatch at all the happiness about her, as her due. She showed him how to do the same.

And now, as she fluttered round him, they would pause and smile in this delightful intimacy, laughing now and then, not at anything in particular, but just because they were happy.

"Jane," he said reluctantly, "I must hurry, or I shall be late."

"You'll not be late. Your barge is waiting at the steps."

"It will not do to keep Gloucester waiting."

"Oh—he is easy-tempered enough."

"Easy-tempered when things go well, but he does not care to be kept waiting."

"But, my lord, you are so clever; most graciously would you excuse your lateness."

"What should I say? 'My lord Duke, I beg your pardon for my lateness. But Your Grace himself would have been late had he to bid farewell to the loveliest lady in the world.'"

They laughed, with the quick delight of happy people.

"Make me not your excuse, sir," laughed Jane. She was sober suddenly. She put her arms about him and scanned his face. "William, sometimes I grow uneasy."

"Uneasy? Why, bless you, Jane, there's naught to fear." He kissed her tenderly. "I'll be back shortly. You will see. Watch for the barge. I'll come straight back to you."

"But you go to the Tower, and I never liked the place. There is an overpowering melancholy about it. I remember little Edward's saying that young children were built into those walls years ago. I am foolish, I know, but I wish this meeting was not at the Tower."

"You must not be uneasy, sweetheart. I swear I'll be back soon. 'Tis nothing—a meeting fixed weeks back."

She looked at him solemnly. "Before you changed sides?"

He laughed. "Listen, Jane! We are right. We plan no treason. We fight for the rights of Edward the Fifth. Only traitors need fear the Tower."

"Only traitors? Many an innocent man has passed through the Traitor's Gate, William!"

"'Tis unlike you to be morbid, and I'll not have it." He lifted her and kissed her. "Come, kiss me, Jane. I'll be back with you by midday."

She kissed him and went down with him to the barge.

"Turn and wave to me, William," she said. "Do not forget."

"Forget you, sweetheart? 'Tis something I could never manage, as you well know."

He was gone. She watched the boatmen row him down the river . . . down towards the Tower. Hastings waved his hand. She continued to stand on the bank watching. In the distance she could see the fortress that seemed to brood like a great sentinel over the City. She shivered and wondered if Anne Neville was watching Richard set out for the Council in the Tower.

Hastings sat back in the boat, thinking of Jane, impatiently longing for the time when he could return to her. Strange, this fever in his veins. Love had soured his life for many years and at last had sweetened it. He could see the flower gardens along the river banks. The roses were beautiful, for it was the month of roses. He smiled at the yellow flowers of the St. John's wort that grew in such profusion, tangling itself about the frailer stems and strangling the life out of them. The grass was more green this year; the trees were more beautiful and abundant in their foliage. Never before had he realized how very beautiful was this City. Perhaps, though, it had never been so beautiful as it was now. Perhaps this year, which he would always remember as the first of his union with Jane, was indeed a glorious year, not only for him but for all London.

He thought of the years stretching out before him; they were to be the happiest of his life, for Jane had brought him such deep peace and pleasure as he had never thought to enjoy. Tender devotion, tempered with passion and the weight of experience to give deep understanding to one another—that was what they had come to. He had built up a pretty story about himself and Jane. It was a delightful romance of sadness and misunderstanding. They had loved right from the beginning; but he had not known it then. Young and hot-blooded, he had imagined that what he felt for her was the same as he had felt for others; and he had disappointed her so that she had turned to Edward. That was easy to understand. Glittering Edward had been the most powerful man in the country, charming and irresistible. And all the time it was Hastings whom she had truly loved. A pleasant thought. But now the great grey towers were throwing their reflection on the sunlit waters; the boat shot rapidly along, and then the boatman was tying it to the ring, and Hastings was swinging out of the boat, mounting the damp and slippery steps, and walking swiftly to the council chamber.

He glanced towards the palace to see if there was any sign of the little King. There was none. He met Lord Stanley and Bishop Morton, and they went in together.

It was cold inside those thick walls after the warmth of the sun. In the big room the men seated themselves at the council table and waited. The Duke of Gloucester was late. Hastings drummed his fingers on the table. Where was the Protector? It rarely happened that he was late; it was a nuisance. His lateness would prolong the Council and it might be that Hastings would not be with Jane at midday as he had promised.

He was lost in a sensuous dream. He was not in this gloomy chamber, but in his own comfortable quarters. He saw his bedroom, made delightful now with the evidence of Jane's presence about it. Jane was sitting on a stool, combing her hair as it glinted like real gold in the sunshine.

The councillors had risen, for the Protector had entered the room. Richard was smiling, though he looked pale, and there were deep shadows under his eyes, which suggested sleeplessness. Hastings was sorry suddenly for the Protector, pitying his frail body; there was something inherently unlovable about Richard of Gloucester. Hastings laughed at himself—Hastings, the crafty statesman, thinking of love at a council meeting called by the Protector, the man he himself was plotting to overthrow!

In the presence of the Protector he felt unsure. It had always been so. Unlovable, cold and distant, Richard might be, but he inspired respect. There was a certain icy nobility about him. If he was accepting the Stillington story, thought Hastings, it must be because he believed it to be true.

Richard was exchanging pleasantries with Morton now, complimenting the Bishop on the fine strawberries he had seen growing at Ely House when he was last in Holborn. The

Bishop must send him some, for he was fond of strawberries. Sly old Morton, who hated Gloucester as a mouse hates a cat, was obsequiously bowing and promising the best of his strawberries. He declared he would immediately despatch a servant to gather them for the Duke.

"My lords," said Richard, "would you excuse me for a while? Continue with your deliberations. There are matters which require my attention in this place. I pray you therefore proceed. I will be with you ere long."

He went out. Strange, thought Hastings; he scarce looked my way.

It was almost an hour before Richard returned. His face was grey, his hands trembling, and from the working of his mouth and the glitter of his eyes it would seem that this trembling was an indication of anger.

He strode across to his seat in the council chamber. There was silence, awed and tense. He sat down, and still the silence lasted. He seemed to be struggling within himself to find words.

Suddenly he stood up and, in tones most unlike those it was his custom to employ, he began to shout.

"My relationship to his Grace the King," he cried, "is close. It was I whom my brother entrusted with the administration of this country."

The Council, puzzled, could only murmur its agreement. A silence of some seconds prevailed, then Richard cried: "And what punishment, think you, my noble lords, should those deserve who seek to bring about my destruction?"

Nobody spoke, but Hastings felt an icy coldness grip his body.

"Answer me!" cried Richard, banging on the table.

But none dared answer. Some looked to Hastings, for he was the Protector's oldest friend. If any dared speak, then must it be Hastings.

He stood up and faced the Protector. "My lord, surely they deserve to be punished as traitors, whoever they be."

"Whoever they be," said Richard; and he laughed suddenly

and bitterly. "Then shall I tell you who these traitors be! I shall tell you who they be who plot against me. There is my brother's widow. And for another . . . she who was his mistress. You know which I mean . . . Jane Shore. Both of these have worked together to destroy me."

At the mention of Jane's name Hastings had turned pale. He knew that every member of the Council was watching him, for there was not a man there who did not know the relationship he himself bore towards Jane, nor that he had come straight from her that morning.

"Your Grace," began Hastings; but now Richard had turned on him, now he was coming to the great moment towards which he had been working.

"Well, my Lord Hastings?" he asked; and his voice seemed suddenly shot with malice and contempt.

"If they have done such things, Your Grace, and if it can indeed be proved against them," began Hastings.

Richard silenced him. "And do you answer me with your 'ifs' and 'ands'?" he shouted. "I tell thee, traitor, that they have done it." Every man round the table caught his breath as the word 'traitor' fell from Richard's lips; every eye was now on Hastings. "And I," continued Richard, very slowly so that not one word was to be lost, "I swear by St. Paul that thou hast joined them in this villainy."

Richard was indeed sick at heart, for he had known for certain from the moment he had mentioned Jane Shore's name, that Hastings was a guilty man. Hastings . . . whom he had thought to be his friend. He looked at the man standing before him, bold and defiant. And I thought he loved me, thought Richard, even as he loved Edward my brother. What is it that Edward had and I have not? Edward was a light liver, a man who did not always keep a sacred promise; yet men loved Edward, as they never love me.

There came to him an inclination to say : "Hastings, go your way. I cannot see the death of one who, though he may have changed, was once my friend." But that was fools' talk. A man would indeed be asking for failure if he allowed a traitor to live. He must lash himself to fresh fury. He must see this man, not as one he had loved, but as the traitor he was; and there was one state and one place in which traitors should be —and that was headless on Tower Green.

He turned from Hastings.

"I swear I'll not dine before your head is brought to me, traitor!" he said; and as he did so he struck on the table with his fists which was a sign for the guards, waiting outside, to enter.

"Treason! Treason!" cried the guards, rushing into the council chamber.

"You know your duty," said Richard. "Every one of these men is to be placed under arrest." With scorn he watched the members of the Council. He saw Stanley resist arrest, and watched the blood streaming from his mouth as a consequence. The guards did their duty. And, as Richard watched, it was of Hastings he thought. Hastings he had almost loved; and he had believed Jane Shore to be his friend. Morton he had never liked nor trusted. But that Hastings should betray him! False friends were more to be feared than lifelong enemies. He would deal with Hastings expeditiously. There should be no softness for Hastings

"Ha, traitor!" he said, looking straight into Hastings' face. "You are under arrest, and by the Virgin, I'll not dine this day till your head and body have parted company!"

The guards had heard. They hurried the members of the Council to cells awaiting them. Their arrest was precautionary. It remained to be seen whether they were all guilty. But Hastings had had Richard's trust. There should be no leniency for Hastings. They faced each other. Two stalwart warders gripped the arms of Hastings; another held his halberd at Hastings' chest. They awaited the Duke's commands, for had he not said, regarding this man, that he would not dine until his execution, and was not his Grace of Gloucester ever a man to keep his word?

"Let him be taken to the Green at once," said Richard.

"At once!" cried Hastings aghast. "I have never heard the

like of this. Am I to have no trial? No chance of proving my innocence?"

"You are already proved guilty, my lord," said Richard.

"Is this a new law the Protector would impose on England?" asked Hastings haughtily.

"It has ever been the law of England that those who plot against its government shall die the traitor's death."

"Without being proved guilty?"

"I have proved you guilty, my lord. Your perfidy is well known to me . . . and that of your mistress."

"I implore Your Grace that, whatever you do to me, you will spare Jane."

"I do not take revenge on foolish women. She shall be punished but . . . My lord, I refuse to discuss this matter with you." He shouted to the guards, "Take him away! Take him to the Green!"

"You cannot mean this," said Hastings. "There was never execution such as you propose since England promised a fair and honest trial to all. The block must be prepared and . . ."

"Doubtless," said Richard grimly, "a piece of wood which will serve as a block may be found."

"You would deny me a priest then?"

Richard hesitated.

"Take him to the Green," he ordered. "See that a priest is sent for. Let him make his peace with God. And hurry . . . for I have made a vow I will not eat while Hastings lives."

*   *   *   *   *

Jane was uneasy—restless. She longed for the return of Hastings. When he returned she decided she would tell him everything; she would try to explain the madness Dorset had wrought in her. She wanted Hastings to know that he had rescued her from enslavement.

She went into the garden and back and forth to the river's edge; she could not keep her eyes from wandering towards those grim grey towers.

But at length she could not bear to stay there longer, watching and waiting for his return. She went into the house and tried to occupy herself with reading, but her thoughts wandered out to the garden, to the river, to the Tower; and on the page before her she saw the river glittering in the sunshine, the fields of red sorrel and white moon daisies stretching out beyond the City, and brooding over the scene, the Tower of London.

And because she could not shake off her fear, she tried to pray. She was disturbed at her prayers by an attendant, knocking urgently on her door. She bid the woman enter.

"There is someone below who begs to see you, Madam," she was told.

"Who is it?"

"A woman, Madam. She says that the matter is urgent. She is very distressed."

"Then bring her to me quickly," said Jane.

Kate came running in. She was breathless and there were tears on her cheeks.

"Kate, Kate, what is wrong? You have come from the Tower. . . . Is it . . . my lord?"

Kate nodded.

"What, Kate . . . oh what?"

"If you would see him before he dies, there is not a moment to lose," said Kate.

The room seemed to sway. She could not be hearing aright. Before he . . . died? But only this morning he had been in this room . . . so much alive . . . so much in love with her and with life.

"Perhaps even now," said Kate, "it is too late. But he was promised a priest."

"Kate, Kate, what are you saying?"

Kate was weeping bitterly. "I heard it was to be, just before he was arrested. Come, my little love, or you will never see him alive."

She let Kate lead her from the house, down across the soft

grass to where Kate's boat was waiting. How slowly they moved towards the cruel fortress!

"I heard it from the guards," said Kate. "It was at the council meeting. My Lord Gloucester was in a fury. He had discovered a plot, 'twas said."

Jane stared unseeingly at the lovely banks, at the flowering shrubs and the fruit trees that marched down to the sun-dappled water. After this, she thought, I shall hate all summer days.

She knew she had betrayed Hastings. Her revenge was complete. He had given her to Edward and now she had given him to Death.

They left the boat; they ran along the path between those oppressive grey towers; past the Beauchamp, past the White Tower. . . . She saw the church on the Green through her tears; and then the Green itself, with that little group of men.

"Stand away there!" called a voice; but she did not heed it. Her running footsteps carried her on; her streaming eyes sought those of Hastings. She saw the colour rush into his face, which previously had been grey as the weather-washed walls of the towers.

"Jane!"

"William, my dearest!" She flung herself at him.

"You should not have come," he said.

"I had to come. There is so much to say. I must confess it all. I love you, William. What will my life be without you?"

"You have made my last days happy ones, Jane," he said.

She shook her head. "William . . . I came to you . . . I came to you . . ." The words would not come, but she fancied he understood.

"Nothing matters now, Jane. Forgive all I tried to do to you."

"There is nothing—nothing. It was I . . . I did not come—to you in love. But now that is changed. I love you, and I have brought you to this. . . . Oh, God in Heaven, could we but go back a few short days! It is I, who love you, who am taking your life."

Hastings put her from him. "You must go from here. Go now, Jane. Go quickly. Stop for nothing. Hide yourself—and stay in hiding. In a little while it will be safe for you to come forth. But now—you are in danger."

"It matters not."

A guard stepped forward and touched Hastings' shoulder. "My lord . . ." he began.

Jane, shuddering, turned her eyes back to the Green, where a piece of wood, hurriedly taken from the chapel, where repairs were in progress, had been laid on the grass to do service as a block.

Hastings nodded. His eyes seemed to look beyond the walls of the Tower, beyond the river, into eternity. Already he had taken on the look of a man who has left the world behind him.

Somewhere on the river Jane could hear the splashing of oars. The ravens came close and croaked hideously.

"Goodbye," said Hastings. "Remember this. You made my last days the happiest of my life. Go now. You must not see the end." He appealed to Kate. "Take her away—quickly. And look after her."

"I will, my lord," sobbed Kate.

They took him to that rough piece of wood, for there must be no delay. The Protector was an impatient man, and he must not be kept from his dinner.

Kate was pulling Jane away from the tragic Green. Hastings shrugged his shoulders. This was the end; the end of ambition, the end of love. He had had fifty-three years of adventure and a whole week of love.

He scorned to have his eyes bandaged. He stood erect taking in the scene. One last look at the sparkling river; one last look at the grey towers. Goodbye, London! Goodbye, Jane! Goodbye to love and life!

Calmly he laid his head on the rough wood. Swiftly and silently the axe descended. His head rolled on the straw; there was a short and horrible stillness everywhere before the ravens resumed their croaking.

LUDGATE

THE procession wended its way slowly through the streets of London. Measured was the tread of the pious churchmen; they walked, chanting, the palms of their hands pressed together, their eyes turned heavenwards. There was one among them, white-robed and scornful of face, who carried the great cross, holding it high as he walked, and chanting with the rest. And before him, her feet bare, and with nothing to cover her except a plain kirtle of rough worsted which fell from her waist to her feet, walked a woman. Her beautiful golden hair spread itself about her shoulders to cover her nakedness, and she carried a lighted taper in her hand. This was no common harlot of the streets; it was Jane Shore, King's favourite, judged guilty of harlotry by the Lord Bishop of London, who had sentenced her to do penance that she might make amends for the sinful life she had led.

The cobbles were hurting her feet; already they were sore and bleeding; the sun was hot upon her naked skin that gleamed white as milk, through the yellow of her hair. Merchants and apprentices, housewives and prostitutes, rich men and beggars had lined the streets to see the greatest show for years. Jane Shore, rich and powerful—to whom in the days of King Edward more court had been paid than to any noble in the land—was brought as low as the commonest harlot from the stews of Southwark.

But Jane did not feel the contempt of the churchmen; she did not hear the tittering murmurs of the crowd; she scarcely felt this shame, for there was no room in her heart for anything but bitter remorse. What mattered it that she must parade thus, half-naked, through the streets of London? What mattered it that she was branded Harlot? What mattered anything? for

Hastings was dead, and she had sent him to his death. "Oh, God," she murmured as she stumbled on, "would that I had died with him!"

It was hot, and the stench from the Fleet stream was polluting the air more evilly than usual on this Sunday morning. Many pairs of eyes watched the beautiful woman, eyes that scorned and eyes that pitied; and many that followed the unconscious grace of her looked longingly and lecherously upon her, even as they called her "harlot." But only vaguely did Jane hear the mutter of their voices; she was not aware of the scorn and lust, the indignation and the pity; or of the quirking lips that professed their horror that such shame could befall a woman, and showed so plainly that it delighted them to behold such shame. Jane's downcast eyes did not see her cut and bleeding feet; she saw nothing but the eyes of Hastings as he had looked his last on London's river.

Her eyes were hard and bright, and the crowd marvelled at her dignity.

"See how proudly she walks! Has she no shame, then?"

"Shame? Shame on them that would shame her, I'd say."

"And I. And I. When I was a-starving in the plague year it was Jane Shore who saved the lives of me and my fatherless little ones."

"Aye, a good woman, for all her harlot's ways. Our good King Edward loved her. God rest his soul."

The procession had halted, for it had reached the cathedral. The pious ones had grown more pious, the scornful more scornful.

Jane was lifted temporarily out of the misery which thoughts of Hastings must bring her, for she realised that the moment had come when she must enter the cathedral and offer her lighted taper to the images of the saints.

She could say to herself, "I am sinful. I sent the man I loved to his death, and I no longer care to live." What a mockery was this! These men about her with their chants and their prayers and their secret lusts—for there were few who were guiltless—would now see her do penance; they would enjoy her shame while pretending to deplore it. They, who had paid court to her while the King lived, who had dared show nothing but respect, now drew their robes closer about their bodies as though fearing contamination. "Purge this woman of her sins," they prayed. And they thought: "Thank God I have the good sense to keep my secrets."

How she and Edward would have laughed at these men, could they have seen into the future! What would Edward have said, had he seen his fat bishops who had done such honour to his favourite mistress, now condemning her for having loved him too well? But Edward was dead; Hastings was dead; and Jane envied them.

The heat in the cathedral was stifling, and the faces of the images looked back blankly at her. She threw back her hair and caught the glistening eyes of sweating priests upon her, and, flushing, quickly covered herself with her veil of hair.

A penance, she knew, was a lucky escape, for she might have been sentenced to death. Swift death would have been sweet. She thought lovingly of the clean cut of the axe. One last moment to look over the sparkling river, to sense the sweet beauty of a summer's morning with that clarity which she knew had come to Hastings. The grey towers, the blue sky, the warm sun—and then a quick stroke, a firm cut—and one stepped from all that was familiar into the unknown. She had longed for it. But Richard of Gloucester had decided to be magnanimous. He had washed his hands, reserved his judgment, and handed her over to the Bishop of London. And so the Bishop had, most righteously deploring that immorality to which he had turned a blind eye during Edward's lifetime, sentenced her to this penance. Disgrace instead of death. The familiar streets instead of the unknown. A crowd of sightseers instead of her Maker.

The respite was short. Now she must leave the cathedral and face the crowds once more. Now she must go to Paul's Cross and there make public confession of her sins, as the Bishop had said she should. She must be a warning to those women who might fall into temptation, as she had fallen. She was to be an object of ridicule and shame to the poor of London who, as a result of the many services she had been able to render them when the affection of the King had been hers, had come to see a virtue in her sin, and had condoned—nay, admired her—in her evil life.

She heard the hush that went through the watching crowds as she came out into the sunshine, and she longed again for death. She folded her hands across her breasts and made her way to the cross.

In the crowd someone murmured a curse on the Protector for subjecting good and beautiful Jane Shore to such public indignity. The bishop had sentenced her, it was said. Well, bishops did what their masters told them, and the Protector was to blame.

There was one person standing on the edge of the crowd who was watching with great interest. Mary Blague, as fashionably dressed as ever, had aged, her skin had grown more wrinkled, her eyes more sly. How she had hated Jane Shore! Loved by Edward. Loved by Dorset. Loved by Hastings. Who would be her next lover?

She turned to the man beside her; his lips were slack, his eyes glazed as he kept them on Jane Shore.

" 'Tis a pity, sir," said Mary, "to see a woman brought so low."

His face hardened, his eyes grew cruel and his lips tight. "So should all harlots confess their shame," he said in anger.

"You speak truth," said Mary; and inwardly she laughed and thought, Look your fill. She is not for you.

There were few in London that morning who were not thinking of Jane Shore. In Baynard's Castle the Duchess of Gloucester wept for her. Even the Protector could not get her out of his thoughts. He had been lenient with her. He wished the people to cast aside the glorified pictures they had made of her in their ignorant impious minds. They must see her now, evil and lewd, with the lighted taper in her hands; they must see that she was no better than any slut from Southwark. He must destroy her influence with the people. She had earned death, for she was as treacherous as Hastings; but his wife had pleaded for her, had bid him remember what Jane had done for them; nor did he feel real anger towards her. But she must suffer, as all must, who worked against Richard of Gloucester.

His good friend Catesby came in to report to him.

"Your Grace, the woman has done her penance. I never saw such a crowd in all my life."

"What think the people now of their goddess?"

Catesby was silent.

"Answer me!" said Richard.

"Methinks, my lord, that though some were glad to see her shame, there were many to pity her."

"Pity! They should congratulate her on her good fortune."

He knew in his heart that this was another example of the love and respect which these charming people managed to win from others. Jane Shore, the harlot, was loved; and people were sad to see her disgrace. Richard of Gloucester, who sought nothing but his country's good, was not liked at all. He glanced shrewdly at Catesby. The man had not said there were murmurings in the crowd against himself; but were there? He suspected that if he pressed Catesby he might discover the truth. But why should he? He knew without asking.

* * * * *

Jane was free. She had been tried by the bishop; she had listened to his diatribe on her wickedness; and she had done her penance and might go now and mend her ways.

A concealing cloak wrapped about her, she came out of the bishop's palace into the streets, those streets which had formed the backcloth of the stage on which she had played so many parts. She could never pass Lombard Street without remembering her life with Will; and in Cheapside she must recall her father's household. It was in Bishopsgate that she had first seen Hastings; and now she could turn her eyes towards the fortress and think of days spent in the palace there when Edward was her lover, and that other day just behind her when Hastings was taken out to the Green to die.

The rain was beginning to fall and a mist was floating up the river. She hurried on. She was tired of the streets which held so many memories. She must remember that now she had to start a new life; and as she did not know what sort of life it was going to be, she must get away from the streets and think about it.

She went towards that house which Edward had given her some years before his death. Edward had filled it with treasures when he had given it to her. The richest plate was hers; the hangings on the bed itself were worth a fortune; but now the place looked dark and gloomy. She knocked at the door, but no one came to answer it, and turning the handle she found that the door was open. She went in slowly, wonderingly. The hall had been stripped of everything it had contained.

She called to her maids. "Janet! Bess! Anne! Where are you all?" Her voice echoed through the house in a hollow fashion.

She ran across the hall and pushed open the door of her favourite parlour. All the rich hangings had been removed, the carpets had been taken from the floors.

"Janet!" she called again, and listened to the echo of her voice through an empty house.

Understanding came to her. Her servants had gone; her goods had been taken from her. Mayhap the house itself no longer belonged to her. It would have passed with its rich contents to the Crown, for had she not been guilty of treason to the Lord Protector? She went slowly to the staircase and sat down on the bottom stair. She covered her face with her hands and laughed. She who had been so rich in love and worldly goods was now unloved and penniless. She was crying now, hysterically, telling herself that she would stay in this empty house until she died.

She was not sure how long she sat there, but dusk had begun to creep into the house when she was suddenly aware of a movement outside. Someone was standing on the other side of the door which she had left ajar. Jane stared at the door. It moved, half an inch at first, then it was pushed open. A woman stood there looking at Jane; and as Jane stared at her she shut the door behind her as she came into the hall.

"Good evening to you, Jane Shore." The voice was expressionless, and in this light Jane could not see the woman's face, but she fancied she had heard the voice before, and though she could not say to whom it belonged yet a great uneasiness came to her.

"Good evening. I think I know your voice. Who are you?"

"Of a surety you know me, Jane. I am an old friend."

Jane struggled to her feet, and as she did so her cape fell open, betraying the fact that she wore nothing but the kirtle in which she had done her penance.

"So they took your clothes as well," said the woman.

"They have taken everything—everything I had."

"Then right glad I am that I came." The woman came closer and opened her cape. Jane looked into her face, and at that moment ceased to think of death and was filled with an urgent desire to protect herself against the evil she had come to associate with this woman.

"Mary Blague!" she cried.

"None other." As Jane moved away from her Mary extended a hand and caught her arm.

"Please leave me," said Jane quickly. "I . . . I can fend for myself. I have friends in London."

"And here is one who has come to you, guessing that here she would find you."

"It was good of you, but . . . I have those to whom I can go."

"I was in the crowd," said Mary.

"It seemed all London was there."

"I came here to offer you help."

"It is good of you . . . but I cannot accept your help."

"Come, Jane. You are half faint with lack of food and exposure. You grow hysterical. You remember against me that it was I who, in my house, arranged that you should meet the King. But he asked it, Jane, and who was I to refuse him?

You are sick and ill and you have not eaten for days. Let bygones be bygones. It is true I acted wrongly with regard to you and the King. It is true, as you know, that I own a house of ill-fame in Southwark. Oh, Jane Shore, have you not yet learned of the terrible things that can happen to a woman who is alone and friendless? If she has money . . . that is another matter. Come, Jane. I am human. I wronged you once. Give me a chance to repay that wrong."

Jane was swaying. Mary Blague's talk of food made her feel dizzy. She had scarcely eaten since the day they had executed Hastings. She felt light-headed, and had to keep reminding herself that the penance was over; she was here in a house which had once belonged to her, and Mary Blague was standing before her, offering assistance.

Mary had an arm about her; Mary's small eyes seemed half-closed. "Come, Jane, you are dizzy. Come home with me. Oh, do not shrink from me. Of course I do not mean to Southwark. I mean to the house where I make my lace. Oh, there was a time when your eyes would dance at the thought of coming there. What the years do to us!"

"I cannot go with you," said Jane.

"Oh yes, my dear, you must; for believe me it is the wisest plan. With me you can rest awhile. You are sick and ill, and have need of rest. But come with me you must, for, look, I am here, waiting to succour you."

"I do not care what becomes of me."

"Your sadness is too close to you, my dear. It is ever thus when tragedy stands close. But remember it is behind you now. You have passed it, and every day will carry you farther from it."

Jane turned from the woman to the emptiness of the house. What did it matter where she went or what became of her? But she could not go with Mary Blague—not that evil woman. Her thoughts turned fleetingly to Kate. But dared she go to Kate? She must not forget that she was under suspicion and by the grace and mercy of the Lord Protector had been given a reprieve from death. What might happen to Kate if she were suspected of treason through her friendship with Jane Shore! She must not go to Kate.

The woman was speaking soothing words. "Come, dear Jane. Know you not how it has been on my conscience all these years that I helped ruin your marriage with Will? Give me a chance to expiate my sin."

"I know when Edward commanded you to do what you did it was not in your power to refuse."

"Then you'll not hold it against me, Jane?" pleaded Mary. "You will be my friend?"

Friend? That was impossible. Yet her very dislike of the woman was helping her to forget that tragic morning on Tower Green. She was wavering, Mary saw, and she smiled triumphantly.

"Come, Jane, come. Hot food, clothes, rest, friendship. I offer them to you, my dear."

And so did Jane allow herself to be led out of the bare cold house to that in which she had first known the passionate love of Edward the King.

*   *   *   *   *

Nothing was too much trouble for Mary Blague if it contributed to the comfort of her guest. Jane must have the best of everything; good food, excellent wine, and a wardrobe worthy of her.

"Never forget, my dear," said Mary more than once, "the King loved you. It is something of which a woman should always be proud."

Listlessly Jane accepted this hospitality. It was characteristic of her that she should suppress her doubts even in the face of what she knew of this woman. Jane could never learn any lesson from life. It was so easy to forget the horrors she had glimpsed in that house where she had visited Dorset; it was so easy to forget what Anne Neville had whispered to her in those days when they had been friends. Mary Blague had given her food and shelter, comfort also; and surely no human being was wholly bad.

Mary waited. The silly little fool, thought Mary. How easily duped she is! No wonder Dorset decided to use her. No wonder she is in her present position. Good fortune was heaped into her lap, and for her uncontrollable lusts she threw it all away. She is stupid and deserves her lot; which, considering her idiocy, will be very good indeed. And what a treasure she will be to me, for from far and wide will come the richest in the land to enjoy the intimate friendship of the beautiful and notorious Jane Shore!

But Mary was a business woman and did not intend to keep Jane in idleness for many more weeks. She came in one day, professing deep distress and went straight to her guest.

"My dear," she declared, 'I have to-day seen that which grieves me greatly. Pour out a little wine for me, please do." Mary sipped her wine and turned her sly eyes on Jane. "It was outside your house . . . the house that was once your house."

"Yes?" said Jane.

"There was a crowd."

"Looking for me?"

"Alas, I fear so."

"They had come . . . to arrest me?"

"The idea does not seem to disturb you!" said Mary tartly.

"It does not. I do not think I greatly care."

"You talk like a fool. Life has much to offer you. You are beautiful. You had wit once. Do not tell me that you have forgotten how to amuse and charm the great. Do not forget that many still will long to talk with and . . . admire Jane Shore, who was the King's favourite for as long as his life lasted. You are most richly endowed, my friend."

"They were Gloucester's men you saw this morning?"

"Indeed they were not. They were merchants to whom you owe money. They sought payment."

Jane turned pale. "I had forgotten. I must owe a great sum."

"You do. And it is money you will have to find somehow, or you will go to Ludgate Jail."

"What curse has come upon me?" cried Jane. "My wealth has been taken from me . . . everything I possessed. They might at least have paid my creditors before they robbed me of my possessions. Oh, Mary, tell me what I should do now."

"You must remain hidden until you can pay your creditors."

"But how shall I ever be able to pay them? These debts were incurred when I had no notion that I might not be able to settle them. I still had much until . . ."

"Until you played traitor to the Protector and so incurred his displeasure."

"I have none but myself to blame," said Jane, looking back on those fantastic months of her servitude to Dorset. But for that folly she and Hastings might have been happy together now.

"No," said Mary briskly, "you have none but yourself to blame. Yet I will help you. There *is* a way in which you can remain hidden for as long as you wish. I will look after you. I will protect you as carefully as ever did your lovers. And while you remain hidden you can earn money, you can pay your creditors; you can pay me for the comforts I have showered upon you. My dear, you look startled. What do you imagine it has cost me to furnish you with the fine clothes you now wear?"

"Oh," said Jane faintly. "I'm afraid I did not think. . . ."

"Mayhap it is not your way to think overmuch. Have there not always been others to think for you? First your father, then Will Shore, the King, Dorset, Hastings . . . and now . . . Mary Blague."

Jane stood up, realising suddenly what Mary Blague had planned for her. "So . . ." she began.

But Mary had also risen. "The answer to your problems, Jane Shore, is my house across the water." She laid a hand on Jane's shoulder, but Jane brushed it aside so angrily that Mary staggered back.

"I will leave your house at once."

"Indeed, and why? I can assure you my house in Southwark is the most luxurious of its kind. You were glad enough to come to it once to visit Dorset. I offer you a more dignified position. It shall not be you who come to visit your lovers, but they who come to visit you."

"Be silent!" cried Jane.

"You forget, do you not, that you are not now the King's mistress. Edward is mouldering in his grave. God knows what has happened to Dorset. And rest assured he has long tired of you. Hastings is buried. And you do naught but flout one who has some hope to offer you."

"I would never for a moment consider accepting your offer."

They faced each other in silence for a moment, then Mary said: "Be sensible. You have nothing between you and starvation. What will you do? Beg in the streets? You'll not be allowed to. As a fine lady you incurred debts which the miserable creature you have become cannot hope to pay from what she will get by begging. The very clothes you are wearing do not belong to you. At least, shall we say, my dear, they have yet to be paid for?"

Jane was furious—more with herself than with Mary Blague. How could she have been such a fool? She undid the girdle about her waist and let it fall to the floor. She slipped the dress off her shoulders while Mary went into shrieks of mocking laughter.

"Very fine! And so you would scorn the shelter I offer you . . . you who have walked the streets as a harlot with a lighted taper in your hand? You will go forth into the streets clad only in a cloak and kirtle! Very noble!"

Jane took Mary by the shoulders and shook her until she was gasping for breath. "Be silent, you wicked woman, or I will kill you."

"So you would practise murder as well as harlotry. Well, perhaps you are well versed in the art. They say the King ever took your advice, and there were some mysterious doings in the Tower of London."

Jane's hands dropped to her sides. The woman seemed to be urging her to more acts of wanton folly.

"I shall leave this house at once," she said.

"You will not forget that you are deeply in my debt. I have

a little bill for you. It is rather high. You see, I thought that nothing but the best was good enough for Jane Shore."

"You are the most evil thing that ever touched my life."

"You did not think that when I so skilfully managed your affair with the King. Then it was, 'Good Mary Blague.' '*Dear* Mary Blague.' You are a fool. If you were not, you would jump at my offer. You would say, 'Bless Mary Blague,' as you did once before."

"I shall never say that. I will find some way of living . . . of paying my debts."

"But you have never worked . . . except to please your lovers. You are fair enough still, I grant you; but these last weeks of your life have scarce added to your charm. Be reasonable."

"There is no point in talking further. I shall leave your house at once."

"You shall not take those garments with you. They are not paid for, remember."

"I shall take nothing but what I brought."

"And there again you are wrong, my headstrong girl, for you shall take another debt with you. But you'll come back to me ere long."

"I never shall."

Jane ran up to the room which Mary had said she might use during her stay in this house; she threw off the garments with which Mary had provided her; she put on her kirtle and wrapped her cloak about her. Mary was waiting for her on the stairs.

"Do you think you can go like this?" she demanded. She caught Jane's arm, but Jane twisted herself free. "Where will you go?" blustered Mary.

"You cannot imagine I would tell you that?"

"I demand payment of my bill."

"You shall be paid in time."

Speculation shot up in Mary's eyes. "You know where Dorset is, do you not?"

Jane smiled. Let her think that she knew that. Let her think that Jane Shore was not completely alone and helpless.

"You will be steeped further in treachery towards the Duke of Gloucester," cried Mary. "Do you think a man like Dorset will ever succeed against the Protector?"

She sought to detain Jane, but Jane threw her off.

"I never want to see your sly face again," said Jane; and she ran downstairs and out of the house.

Janet, Mary's maid, stood gaping after Jane.

"After her . . . quickly," cried Mary. "Don't dare come back until you have found out where she has gone."

Jane, running swiftly through the streets, had one thought, and that was to get to Kate. Kate would know where to hide her; there were more hiding places in the Tower than anywhere else in England. As long as her disgrace did not reflect on Kate there was nothing to fear. From Kate she would get food, clothes, temporary shelter and friendship.

Janet watched her turn in at the Tower gate and then went back to her mistress, and told her what she had seen.

Mary smiled grimly, reminding herself that it was better to be Mary Blague, rich brothel-keeper, than beautiful Jane Shore fallen on evil times.

*   *   *   *   *

Jane felt temporarily at peace in the room over the kitchens. It was a small room, thick-walled, and its narrow windows, deep set in the thick stone, did not let in much light. Kate had brought her some clothes, and Belper had plied her with as much food as she could eat in a week. They were glad and proud to have her. She tried to warn them of possible danger, but they would not listen. They would keep her coming a secret, they said, although there was not a man or woman in the Tower who would give her hiding place away.

Kate was excited, and delighted that it was to her that Jane had come.

"Why, bless you," she said, "I know the underground passages of this Tower as I know the palm of my hand. I was very good friends with one of the jailors, and he showed me

. . . well, perhaps a little more than he should have showed me. But that was all to the good. I could put you in a place where none would think to look for you."

"Kate, you're a comfort."

"We always stuck together, mistress, and that's a pleasant thing to do. A pity you didn't come straight to me instead of getting into the hands of that creature."

"It was a pity, Kate, but don't let's think of that now. I am here, and only my friends know it. I cannot see what is to become of me, for I cannot stay here for ever. And I have nothing . . . nothing at all."

"Shame and pity!" cried Kate. "What His dear Grace the King would say I don't care to think." Kate crossed herself and looked up at the ceiling of this room, which was so like a cell. "To make *you* parade the streets in such fashion. . . ."

"It is over and done with," said Jane, "so let us not speak of that. Times change and we change with them. I, who was so beloved, am now almost alone; but I have you, Kate, and I do not forget it. I have you and kind Belper, and doubtless many a good friend could I but find them. Perhaps life will be gay for me again. Dry your eyes, Kate."

Kate was ready enough to dry her eyes. "Ah, yes," she said. "for you are so beautiful. There will be one near as handsome as His Grace was. I swear it; I know it." She was pensive suddenly. "This is like old times. I could almost believe we were together in Cheapside or Lombard Street or the palace. I have been thinking where I will hide you. There is a chamber of fair comfort between the White Tower and the Beauchamp. We shall furnish it with as much comfort as we can manage, and hide you there. You'll not be afraid?"

"I do not think so. I used to fear the dead, but so many I have loved are among them. Edward? Hastings? They would do naught but help me. I do not believe my father would wish me any harm. And Will? Ofttimes I wonder what became of Will."

"Doubtless he found himself another wife."

"I hope so. And with her, happiness. Kate, do you ever see the little King?"

"Hardly ever."

"Yet he is still here, in the Tower, is he not?"

"Yes, he is still here. But I hear they have brought his little brother to him to bear him company."

"Little Richard! How glad I am! He will enjoy having Richard with him."

"So now both the little Princes are in the Tower. Oh, I know one is the King and one the Duke of York, but people speak of them as the little Princes."

"How I should love to see them!"

Kate's eyes sparkled. "Mayhap we could arrange the matter."

"Do you know where they are lodged?"

Kate shook her head. "But I could discover. I am rather friendly with one of the attendants."

They began to laugh together as they had in the old days. They would find a way of communicating with the boys. With excitement, the colour was returning to life.

But as they sat in that room, planning, they heard a shout from below which was followed by the tramping of many feet. Kate, turning pale, ran to the window and looked out. The face she turned to Jane was sufficient to show what she had seen.

"They have come for me?" asked Jane.

Kate nodded. "Oh, Holy Mother of God!" she whispered. "They are here . . . and it is too late to hide you."

*   *   *   *   *

Jane had never known that there was such misery in London, until she entered Ludgate Jail. During her first days there she scarcely noticed the passing of time. She lay on the stone floor, overwhelmed by the terrible plight in which she found herself. The foul smell of decaying flesh floating in through the narrow barred windows from the nearby fly-haunted, disease-ridden Fleet, made her retch, until after a few days it ceased to disturb

her. She turned in disgust from the filthy walls down which
trickled the accumulated slime of ages. She was appalled by
the men and women who shared the great common hall in
which they ate and slept and passed their miserable days and
nights. They were like hideous effigies of real people—unkempt, terribly gaunt, some ferocious, some meek; many,
suffering from horrible diseases, lay dying on the cold stones.
Through the apertures the flies came in thick black streams
and with them the wasps that were bred in the filthy refuse
on the banks of the Fleet. And mingling with the terrible
smell that came through the windows was another as hideous,
that of diseased, unclean humanity.

Most of the inmates of Ludgate prison had little hope of
regaining their freedom. Many were in for debts which their
captivity gave them little hope of paying off. Jane's offence,
she heard, was more than debt; she was accused of conspiring,
by sorcery, against the life of the Protector.

The weather was hot; the loathsome wasps and flies buzzed
continually; children, some of whom had been born in the
place, wailed in their misery; others ran about and fought each
other for the crusts of bread which some poor prisoner had
been too sick to eat.

It was difficult for Jane to understand at first the very depth
of this degradation to which she had sunk. She had never in
her wildest imaginings conjured up such a horrible invention.
Often she had passed the prison near the gate. Then it had
seemed just an ancient edifice, a rather charming addition to
the landscape, rising as it did beside the wall of the City and
the old gate. When she had been a child she had often begged
to be allowed to fill one of the baskets which the poor prisoners
lowered down as they called their piteous pleading cries
through the barred windows, but her father had never allowed
this. In the jail, he had said, were lepers and people suffering
from plague. One should keep well away.

Now she could smile at the memory of that admonition,
smile with great bitterness. Now, *she* was one of those who
must be avoided. She had never known that such brutality and

indifference to suffering could exist. The jailors had been respectful to her on arrival. She was well dressed—in Kate's clothes—for a prisoner; she had a gentle, cultured voice. A lady, thought the jailors. Here is a chance of making money.

So was the whole iniquitous business of bribery laid before her. Her food, it was explained, would be bread and water, and not over much of that, unless she liked to pay. Why, then, a roast duck? A thick wedge of succulent beef? Good wine? Nothing was too much trouble for a jailor to bring to a prisoner who paid him well. There were many in Ludgate who lived like the quality. A good table. Their own quarters. Lady friends to visit the gentlemen, and gentlemen to visit the ladies. A nice little gambling game to pass the time. Nothing was too much trouble. But a jailor had to live, just as luxuries had to be paid for.

Jane said quite simply that she had nothing at all. Then did they shrug expressive shoulders. No money? Then she must go back to the common hall. So back she went to listen to the growling, quarrelling human voices, to the miserable groans and the obscene jests; she watched the weary old prostitute, who had wine sent in to her every day, lying on the floor in a state of maudlin drunkenness; she listened to the crazy parson, who had never been able to get over the disgrace of being sent to Ludgate, preaching, as he did continually to the crowd of people who sometimes roused themselves from their indifference to jeer at him; she saw an old thief instructing a new thief how to pick pockets; she saw an emaciated mother feed her newly born baby; she saw an old man die while a man and woman cast aside their rags and attempted to satisfy their lust; she listened to the continual cry of beggars. And she could not realise that this had become her world, in which she must live out the remainder of the days left to her.

*   *   *   *   *

"Pity the poor prisoner! My lords and ladies . . . free men and women . . . pity the poor prisoner!"

Try as she might, Jane could not shut out the tired and hopeless voice. If only the woman would stop. Listening to her, Jane forgot her indifference to life in her anger against those who could pass by, ignoring that poor plea. What hope, she thought grimly, that any passing Ludgate Jail will give a thought to a poor prisoner, let alone the requested alms?

Anger and pity welled up in Jane. She could hear the drop of the basket; now it would be dangling outside the walls, and some passer by might look up at a hopeless face that would seem like that of a caged animal, shudder and turn quickly away. The woman who held the basket was old; her hair hung about her head like verminous, writhing grey snakes; she was a sad sight with her twisted mouth and sunken red-rimmed eyes.

The huge black flies cruised about gaily in the stifling air. They were the only gay things in Ludgate Jail. Odd, therefore, that they should give only additional annoyance and irritation.

"Pity the poor prisoner. . . ."

Beside Jane, on a bed of dirty straw lay a woman whom Jane had noticed before because there was a look of respectability about her. Jane had seen her shudder at some of the sights which it was necessary for them to witness, and try again and again to preserve some decency. Jane had tried to be friendly, but the woman would have none of her. She knew who Jane was, as did most of them, for it was impossible to be oblivious of such bright beauty even in this dim hall. People would stare at her, round-eyed; some jeered and made their obscene remarks, but many were over-awed, for Jane's habit of giving help to the poor was known throughout the London jails. This woman had a daughter, Bet, who could not have been more than eleven years old, and in spite of dirt and lice, inadequate food and such environment, she was not an unattractive creature. She was often missing from her mother's side, and to see the poor woman's frantic search for her moved Jane deeply. She was terrified that some evil would befall the girl, as indeed it might.

Now the girl was by her mother's side, and they both watched the beggar at the grating. Glancing at them, Jane

saw their faces grow suddenly alert. The reason was obvious.
Someone outside had put something in the dangling basket.
The woman at the window looked furtively over her shoulder;
saliva dripped from her toothless mouth; her red-rimmed eyes
gleamed. That was all, but it was sufficient to show many who
watched her what had happened.

"Holy Virgin help her," prayed Jane.

Wheezing with excitement, the poor old woman was hauling
up the basket which was evidently heavy. There was silence
except for the buzzing of the wasps and flies. Now the basket
was up, and immediately there was a sudden stealthy movement towards the old woman. Jane turned away. She had seen
many horrible things in the few days she had been here, but
this she could not bear to look at.

She heard the scuffle, the snorting rage, the wild shrieks,
the wail of frustrated anger, followed by a sudden silence; and
turning, she saw the crowd of starving people who had been
fighting for the contents of the basket, huddled together and
staring at it, for it lay on the floor, its contents scattered.

Jane shared the horror of all those who looked, for the basket
had contained nothing but three large stones. Someone in the
world of freedom had thought it a fine joke to put those stones
in the beggar's basket, and let her haul it up.

The silence was broken by the old woman who, squatting
on her knees, began to wail. The mad parson, seeing a crowd
gathered together, began to cry : "Repent ye, for the Kingdom
of Heaven is at hand."

Someone turned on him and kicked him violently. He
yelped. "Blessed are ye when men shall revile you. . . . Repent!
Repent! Ye have need of repentance."

Life had returned to normal.

Jane saw now that the woman who had interested her had
been hurt in the fight and was near to fainting. Bet was missing, and the woman sat propped up against the slimy wall,
blood mingling with the dirt on her tattered sleeve.

Jane went over to her and said in that musical voice which
had charmed so many : "You are ill. You must let me help."

The woman did not answer, but she smiled faintly when Jane tore a strip from her petticoat.

"We will wash the wound," said Jane, and took her into the yard. The air did the woman good, and Jane kept up a stream of conversation as she bathed the wound. "Fortunate we are to have this water. Twenty years ago, had we been here, it would have been denied us. I remember my father telling me that some lady paid a lot of money to have fresh water in this prison . . . fresh water for the prisoners, and without payment. Doubtless many would tell us we should be grateful."

The woman was not listening, but as she felt better the anxiety came back into her eyes.

"Did you see my girl?" she asked.

"No. I missed her after the fight."

"I fear for her. This place . . ."

Jane nodded.

"She is young," said the woman in a burst of confidence. "She is comely. People notice. The gamblers give her scraps . . . for waiting on them. I am afraid. . . ."

"I understand."

They were silent; but the frightened mother was glad to confide her fears in someone and Jane was glad to have found a friend.

They went back to the hall. Bet was there. She came and sat down beside them.

Evening fell. They heard the drunken singing of the prostitutes who came by night to those who could afford to pay for them.

"Is it nothing to you," called the mad parson, "all ye that pass by?"

The old beggar woman sat dismally at the grating until the daylight faded.

"Pity the poor prisoner! My lords and ladies . . . pity the poor prisoner!"

*   *   *   *   *

Each summer's day spent in the fetid atmosphere of the jail was like ten.

"You have friends outside," said the jailors. "Money's what you want. Money will buy everything you can desire. Why, there's people as come in here for a rest. It can be as comfortable as that."

Jane shook her head. She had a good friend outside. Kate had paid money that she might have a word with her; and Jane had seen the horror leap into Kate's eyes when they met. She could not stop herself from staring at Jane. She had brought rye cakes and bread and meat pies from Belper's kitchens; but Jane could not ask Kate for money. Kate would come again, she assured Jane; and she was as good as her word; Jane need not fear starvation while she had Kate and Belper outside, ready to serve her.

Every other day Kate came, and Jane would hide the food she brought; then she would take it into the yard where Bet and her mother and some of the poor sick children would share it with her. Jane's was the smallest share, and while she ate it she would think constantly of the poor creatures in the hall to whom she could not offer a part of what Kate brought.

Kate's visits were the only brightness to lighten these days. To Kate, Jane would talk of Bet. Could Kate find a place for the girl? She might hear of someone who needed a kitchen girl, for Bet would be able to leave since she was in jail through no fault of her own, but because her mother had got into debt when her father died, and there was nowhere else the girl might go. But people were not anxious to take a girl from Ludgate Jail. And now the mother was doubly worried, for there had come to the prison a terrifying creature of evil habits and possessed of much money. He was known throughout the jail as Highway Ned, because he had grown rich by robbing travellers on the highway. He had taken the best quarters in the prison since he was a man of means, and it was said that he had got himself arrested for debt that he might hide for awhile from some confederates whom he had cheated and who had sworn to have his life. Ludgate had often proved a refuge for such men, since it could provide a safety that would have been difficult to find outside.

Ned had his friends in every day to visit him; thieves and prostitutes gambled and sang bawdy songs in his quarters; and there was nothing that was too much trouble to be done for Highway Ned. His coming had made a difference to the entire community. Several of the women sought to attract his attention, without success. Why should he look at the poor starved creatures when he could have his pick from outside? Hot food came to him regularly every day. Some of the prisoners loitered in the quadrangle merely to smell it as it was brought in. Jane had never seen Highway Ned, but she disliked all she heard of him, and her indignation on behalf of the prisoners was intensified.

Three days after the arrival of Ned, Bet caught his eye. He called her to him, asked who she was and gave her a savoury meat pie. She ate it, and ran to her mother to tell what had happened. Sick with apprehension, Bet's mother confided in Jane. "Highway Ned would never give something for nothing, now would he?" said the woman.

It was heartbreaking to watch her; she would rise up from her sleep and grope for the girl. Every time she heard Highway Ned and his friends carousing in his quarters she would shake as if with the ague. Jane knew she must do something to help her.

On several occasions she had seen a man pass through the quadrangle. He was middle-aged, soberly but very well dressed. He had dignity and was obviously some person in an important position. Jane had seen that, as he walked through the prison, sniffing his nosegay, he scarcely glanced at the prisoners. This she construed as meaning he had a kind heart and did not care to look upon so much misery; and if he were kind as well as important, might he not be prevailed upon to do something for Bet? Jane decided that the very next time she saw him she would speak to him. She did not have to wait long.

She hurried towards him and stood before him. "Good day to you, sir."

Her hair had lost much of its sheen; she was pallid and had lost her plumpness, but her smile was still dazzling.

He stammered an acknowledgement of her greeting. "You will let me speak to you, will you not?" begged Jane. "I wish to ask your help. Oh, do not be alarmed; it is not for alms that I wish to beg."

"I . . . I am not a rich man," he said.

She smiled. "There are many here who would consider you wealthy as a king. Perhaps I was wrong to ask you. Would you be so good as to tell me to whom I speak?"

He hesitated, gave a quick look at her, and surrendered to her charm. "I am the King's solicitor."

She smiled. "Oh . . . tell me, please, how is the little King?"

"The *little* King?"

"Edward. Little Edward."

He shook his head. "You are shut away from events, Madam. I speak of King Richard."

"But . . . what of Edward?"

"He stays in the Tower with his young brother. His Grace the King has behaved with wondrous kindness to his brother's bastards. But . . . may I ask who *you* are, Madam?"

"My name is Jane Shore," she said.

She fancied she saw horror creep into his eyes. He stammered uneasily: "I see. Good day to you." And he left her.

He will never come near me again, she thought.

*   *   *   *   *

Thomas Lynom, the King's solicitor, came out of Ludgate Prison and walked through the City's gates. He was thoughtful, and even as he crossed the Fleet Bridge he forgot to bury his face in his nosegay. He sauntered along Fleet Street and stared unseeingly at the clumps of trees which dotted the Strand; he looked past the gardens and orchards to Fickets Croft and the meadows beyond. The little brooks were sparkling in the sunshine, and the view which stretched out beyond Temple Bar was fair indeed, but he did not see it, for he was in a deeply thoughtful mood. What a strange encounter that had been! What startling eyes the woman had! They had glowed like lamps in her emaciated face. He could not forget the charming line of that face; and her long hair, unkempt though it was, was the most beautiful he had ever seen.

A beggar . . . nothing more. "I would ask your help," she had said. And then: "It is not for alms I wish to beg." But did not they all say that? Was it not the beggar's plaint? Oh, it is not for myself, but for a sick child, an aged mother, a crippled father . . . anyone . . . anything, but not for myself.

But she had a beautiful face . . . a *good* face. Yet how could it be good since it belonged to Jane Shore? When she had spoken, though, she had made him believe her; he had found her beauty and her charm engaging. And then he had understood; she was Jane Shore—a prisoner, a harlot who had walked the streets barefoot, a taper in her hand. He would have none of her. If he saw her again during his visits to the prison—and he must make an occasional visit there in the course of his duty—he would turn away.

" 'I would ask your help,' " he said aloud. "Indeed you would, Madam. 'It is not for alms I beg.' Indeed not, Mistress Shore. I know your sort. I'll have none of you."

But he continued to think of her, while he assured himself he would have none of her. His master would be displeased if he befriended the woman and it got to the royal ears, for Jane Shore had proved herself an enemy to King Richard; and Thomas Lynom valued the patronage of the reigning monarch too much to disturb the favour he enjoyed.

He would not give the woman another thought.

He went his way until he came to the small but pleasant house which was his most proud possession. He had done well for himself. He had followed his father's profession, but how far had he outstripped his father! His father had been a solicitor; Thomas Lynom was the King's solicitor. He was a quiet man, a man who had worked hard and whose life had been uneventful; he had not sought adventure and adventure had not come to him. What should he want with the woman?

What happened to the adventurous? Sometimes they won a crown as Richard had done; sometimes they lost their heads, as Hastings had done. But a humble man, such as a King's solicitor, could be dragged to Tyburn and hanged by the neck; or he might have his ears nailed to the pillory, his tongue cut out; he might find himself in Ludgate Jail. Adventure, he was sure, was best left alone.

But what had adventure to do with a Ludgate prisoner? Nothing at all. Just because the woman had a dazzling smile, just because there was beauty in her eyes, he must not forget that she was an enemy of the King. He would do well to keep clear of Jane Shore.

His housekeeper bustled towards him. She was a comely enough creature, round as a tub and purple-rosy as a plum. She kept the serving men and maids in right good order, and she ran his house to perfection.

Now he could smell his dinner and it made his mouth water. Chine of beef. A pie with savoury meats. Good wine and plenty, to wash them down. It was ready and waiting. He sat down to enjoy it and his needs were anticipated as they always were. The rushes on the floor were clean and sweet. He would have perfect order, as much cleanliness as possible in his house, for visiting prisons in the name of his royal master had given him a taste for such things. He had them; he had everything he wished.

He drank a good draught of elderberry wine and smacked his lips appreciatively. He cut himself a wedge of beef, good and succulent, done to a turn. But after the first mouthfuls his thoughts strayed from his table. He wondered what Jane Shore would say to such a meal. He pictured her, sitting opposite him, leaning her elbows on the table and smiling at him.

"I want to ask your help. Oh, it is not alms I want. . . ."

"I wonder," he said aloud.

But his appetite was gone; it was replaced by a desire to know what it was she had wished to ask him.

     *   *   *   *   *

The next day Jane saw Thomas Lynom in the quadrangle. She smiled at him and he flushed a little, for her smile was more dazzling than he remembered it. He felt ashamed of the good breakfast he had had; then he shook himself free of such folly. It was prisoners who should feel ashamed before honest men.

"Good day to you," said Jane. "There is a sharpness in the air. It was not here yesterday."

"That is true," he said, and moved closer to her, while the good sound commonsense he had inherited from his father bid him take care. But her smile was so pleasant, and there could be no harm in exchanging a word or two with her.

He said: "You wished to ask me something when I encountered you yesternoon."

"Yes." Her smile had grown warmer. The sun brought out some of the colour of her hair; her lovely eyes had softened. Ludgate had only dimmed her beauty; it could not obscure it completely. "It is a girl here. A poor young girl. She is but eleven years old."

He raised his eyebrows and looked away from her to where a part of the prison building loomed up beside the City gate. "A girl of eleven. I do not know what I can do about that."

"She has done no harm. Nor has her poor mother who is here because she is in debt."

"She has lived beyond her means," he said sternly.

"Yes, but . . ."

"Then, Madam, she has deserved what has befallen her." His own household accounts were always neatly balanced. He had ambitions; he had been tempted to live beyond his means, but he had seen the folly of such a course, and he despised those who did not see with his own clear vision.

"But it is so hard when one is poor," she said.

"That is no excuse."

"But how do we know the temptations! How can we judge until we know all?"

"Madam," he said, "I do not see what it can be that you wish to ask of me."

"I will tell you. You are a man of means, of influence. I see that."

He was more gratified than such a simple remark should have made him. "Well, I would not say . . ."

"Oh, but I would." She laughed and he thought, So must she have laughed for King Edward. "You *are* a man of influence, I know, sir. And you have sought me out that you might help me."

"I can promise nothing. Why, I do not even know. . . ."

"Then I will hasten to tell you. This poor child should not stay in this place. She is young, and the air is infected not only with hideous disease, but with cruelty and wickedness. It is not right that children should grow up in such an atmosphere."

"I agree with that, but what can I do?"

She moved closer to him. "Mayhap you could find . . . some work for her to do . . . outside. There is no reason why *she* should stay here. She is free enough to go."

"Work?"

"Doubtless one of your friends . . . or mayhap you yourself need a good serving maid. She is a strong girl. She would do well, I am sure, could we but get her away from this foul place."

"Madam, I could not consider the matter. Dost think my friends would want a girl from such a place as this?"

"She has done nothing wrong."

"There are too many honest girls looking for a living."

"I see."

"Good day to you, Madam."

He looked into her face and saw that there were tears in her eyes, and the tears unnerved him. He did not understand her. He had thought she must be a brazen woman; one did not expect a woman, who had left her husband to become the mistress of the King, to shed easy tears over a fate which must necessarily befall many. He wanted to think of her as brazen and unscrupulous; and he could only be interested in her.

He strode away, but before he had reached the end of the

quadrangle he was turning back to her. Jane smiled through her tears.

"It is a hopeless case," he said gruffly. "But I might see what can be done about it."

"Thank you," said Jane. "I thought you would. You have the look of a good man."

He went on his way. He had the look, she had said, of a good man. He kept repeating that to himself as he went towards his home.

*   *   *   *   *

Of course he had no intention of doing anything about the matter. How could he ask one of his friends to take in a girl from Ludgate? The idea was absurd, and he would dismiss it from his mind. He did not think he would have occasion to visit the prison for some time to come. Therefore would he put Jane Shore from his mind.

But as he entered his beautifully ordered house he found himself wondering whether he could take in another kitchen maid. His housekeeper was a good, sound, just and honest woman; she would be the right kind to look after a high-spirited girl who had already come into touch with evil things. But what was he thinking? He would have no jail-birds in his house.

He had work to do, and this afternoon he had an audience with the King. He worked hard all the morning before he set out for the palace; and in the King's presence it was impossible to think of aught else but his royal commands, for the pale, slender young man with the unhappy eyes had an undeniable presence.

But when he left the King and came home again he was still wondering whether there might not be a place in his household for the girl.

He called his housekeeper to him. She came, her plum-coloured face creased in respect, her capable hands spread over her stomach.

"Mistress Browner, there is something I wish you to do for me. You are a most excellent and capable woman, and that is why I am asking your help in this matter."

She was flatteringly eager to serve such a good master. He realised afresh how far he had come and how foolish it would be to mix himself in some unsavoury matter. But what unsavoury matter was this? Let Mistress Browner take the girl into her kitchen. Then he need never see the woman Jane Shore again.

So he told the housekeeper about the girl. She pursed her lips. Did her master realise the wickedness that grew in jail-birds?

He found himself repeating Jane's words. "But how can we judge, Mistress Browner, unless we know everything?"

"She comes of bad stock, master."

"She has done no wrong. It is true her parent is getting her just deserts, but the child . . . for she is little more . . . has done nothing. No, Mistress Browner, we must not judge. You can use an extra girl in the kitchen. Oblige me by taking this child. The example of a woman such as yourself, a woman of sound good sense and much virtue, I am sure will be the making of her."

It was done. He was very eager to go and tell Jane Shore what he had arranged.

*   *   *   *   *

After he had taken Jane's protégée into his household, Thomas Lynom did not, as he had intended, curtail his visits to the prison. He began to call every day.

There were other matters that disturbed him now. He could not sleep at night for thinking of Jane in that wretched place. He could not enjoy his food for thinking of Jane's living on bread and water.

He made a habit of taking in a basket of good things for her to eat. She was grateful, and he was delighted until he discovered from the mother of young Bet that she shared everything she received with her fellow-prisoners. She was a strange woman. Of course he had heard tales of her when King Edward was living. The poor of London had always looked upon her as a sort of saint, which had seemed to him ridiculous

in view of the life she was living. Now, he began to understand.

He paid for special quarters for her, for he could not bear to
think of her sleeping in that filthy hall with those wild creatures
all about her. She accepted his help with a natural grace. He
learned that she shared the quarters, which he had provided,
with sick children whom she fed and looked after.

He began to dread and yet to long for his visits to the prison.
He knew those dreadful creatures whispered together about
him and Jane; that was shocking and horrible to a man such
as he was. Sometimes he swore he would never go back, but he
always did.

He would dream of Ludgate Jail. The cries of the prisoners
would penetrate his dreams; he would hear the coarse singing
of the prostitutes and the mad shouts of the crazy parson;
sometimes he dreamed of Jane.

As for Jane herself, she was growing fond of him; she said
so in her natural easy way.

"It is so good of you to come, Thomas. Your visits enliven
my days. How dreary they would be without your coming!"

She longed to hear news of what was happening outside the
jail, and he stored up all the information he could get, that he
might have something of interest to tell her.

A few weeks after the beginning of their friendship he
asked her to walk with him in the quadrangle. The air was
fresh and there was a faint drizzle falling, but neither of them
minded that.

He said quietly: "We live in terrible times, Jane."

"What has happened?" she asked eagerly.

"There is trouble brewing in this country. The King has
many enemies . . . they are everywhere . . . all over the
country; and there is trouble brewing on the other side of the
Channel."

"You mean . . . with the French?"

"Worse than that. With the Earl of Richmond, Henry
Tudor, who, it is whispered, prepares himself to attack the
King and to wrest the crown from his head."

"He will never succeed . . . against Richard."

"He never will," said Lynom, wondering what would happen to the King's solicitor if the King fled into exile, or, worse still, lost his head. "But that is not all I have to tell you."

"You have worse news?"

"News which will disturb you greatly, I fear. I regret that I should be the one to bring it to you, but you have asked me to tell you all that happens."

"You do right to bring me news. I starve for news. But pray tell me quickly."

"It is but a rumour. Mayhap there is no truth in it." He hesitated, then rushed on. "It is . . . the little Princes in the Tower. They . . . it is said . . . they are no more. They have been . . ."

He looked about him and it was Jane who said the word. "Murdered?"

"So it is whispered."

"But who . . . ? The . . . King! Oh, I cannot believe it of him. He would not do such a thing. They are his little nephews and he loved them. I swear he did."

She thought of little Richard at his wedding to Anne Mowbray. "Early wed, early dead," said the old proverb. But how could she think of that bright little boy . . . dead! She broke down and began to weep bitterly. Lynom was beside her, his arm about her, comforting her. "Jane, Jane! Sweet Jane, you must not weep. 'Tis but a rumour. Doubtless there is little truth in it."

"How could such rumours grow out of nothing? Something is there . . . I know it. Oh, Edward . . . dear Richard . . . I would I could have kept you beside me." She lifted her face to the man who stood beside her. "I loved them. They were as my own. All their childhood I was there. We played together. I might have been their mother."

He winced. He did not like her references to her life of sin. There were so many times when he must remind himself that she was a sinful woman. But how he tried to forget it!

He could not comfort her; he could only repeat: "It is but a rumour which runs round the town."

She said: "Kate will know. I can find out from Kate. It cannot be true. Why should the King kill his brother's children?"

"Speak not so loudly. If any should hear . . ."

"Thomas," she insisted, "why should he? Tell me that. He has the crown. He has taken that; why should he want their lives as well?"

"The crown is his by rights, for there is proof that the Princes are bastards."

"That is true, and why, therefore, I ask you, should it be necessary to take their lives?"

"Ask me not. I know not the ways of kings."

"I do not believe it," cried Jane passionately. "I will not believe it."

"I was wrong to bring you such news."

"Nay, you were right. I pray you will always bring me news. Think not to spare me, for I would not wish to live in ignorance."

He would have kissed her hands, but she held him off. Jane, in tears, was irresistible, and even while he regretted that she restrained him, he knew he should feel relief lest he be betrayed into saying something which might prove fatal to his future.

She said: "Leave me now. I can think of little else but this. And I long for you to come and tell me that it is not true."

She stayed in her room, weeping bitterly, and when at length she emerged her eyes were red-rimmed and dark with misery.

"Bad news from outside?" she was asked; she nodded, for she could not speak.

She must comfort herself by assuring herself that it was but a rumour. Why should Richard murder the Princes when they had been proved illegitimate, and did not stand in his way? There was no reason why he should.

She awaited Kate's coming; and what relief Kate brought!

" 'Tis a lying rumour," declared Kate. "The Princes still live. I have seen them this very day."

"Thank God! Praise the Virgin!" cried Jane.

Everyone marvelled at her gaiety; and afterwards she looked back on that day as one of the happiest of her life.

*   *   *   *   *

Lynom was in love and everyone knew it but Lynom. His housekeeper knew it, though she was far from guessing who might be the object of his passion. Quite a number of the prisoners knew it, but they were not in the same ignorance. It was a mighty joke to consider the King's most dignified solicitor in love with Jane Shore. Jane knew it; she thought a good deal about the man; she was fully aware that there had been many occasions when he had been on the point of declaring his passion and devotion. Jane could not help thinking of all he could do for her. There was a possibility that he might even obtain her release; he could certainly pay her debts; and was he not favoured by the King? The thought of freedom was very sweet, but with it came the bitter memory of Hastings. I could never love Thomas Lynom, thought Jane. How foolish was it to be unable to love a man who could promise so much! But then, had she not always been foolish? It was her folly that had brought her greatest happiness and her greatest sorrow. Yet sometimes she thought, I would give anything in the world to be able to leave this place.

The jailors were full of respect for her now that she had become the cherished friend of one of the most important men who ever visited the prison. And how much more would he do for her? Yet, he reminded her of Will Shore. I had no mind for Will, she thought. I would have no mind for Thomas. And when he would seek to declare his feeling for her she would divert him from the purpose.

As for Thomas, he thought of little else but Jane. He had taken to picturing her in his house, giving orders to Mistress Browner and entertaining his friends. There would be a certain amount of scandal, of course, for Jane Shore was notorious, but he would have to endure that! Yet how could he marry Jane Shore? The idea was preposterous. She was a prisoner—the King's prisoner, and he would have to get the King's consent, and what would His Grace have to say if his quiet and trusted solicitor suddenly explained that he wished to marry Jane Shore? Thomas had gone over this again and again.

One October day, going to the room it had been his privilege to provide for her, he found her gay and radiant. Her happiness restored some of that great beauty which had been hers before she came to the prison, and he was struck afresh by her grace and charm.

"Thomas," she cried, and held out her hands, for she was more friendly and demonstrative than any woman he had ever known, "I have heard from Kate that the Princes live."

He knew that she was the most kindhearted of women; he caught her emotion.

"I rejoice with you, Jane." And then suddenly, she being close to him, he put his arms about her and gently kissed her forehead. "Jane," he said, "you know my feelings?"

"Why yes, Thomas." He was taken off his guard; he had not expected her to admit that.

He stammered: "Why, I love you, Jane. I want . . . if possible . . . that you should be my wife."

His wife! She had not thought of that. Was she not still the wife of Will Shore?

She said gently, "But, Thomas, I am already a wife."

His legal mind had already considered this problem. "How many years is it since you left the goldsmith?" he asked.

She told him.

"And where is he now?"

"I do not know. It may be that he has left the country."

"It may be that he is dead. Indeed—and I trust you will forgive my referring to this painful matter—the penance you were forced to do might well be considered in the nature of a divorce. We will verify these matters, and believe me, Jane, I have no doubt that we shall succeed in settling them to our satisfaction."

Jane felt he was carrying her along too far. She liked Thomas. He was the kindest of men. But marriage! She shook her head.

"Jane, I beg of you. Think what marriage with me will mean."

She did think. What did the future hold for her? She seemed to see Mary Blague's cruel eyes leering at her. She saw again the people thronging the City's streets to see her do penance.

She felt the importance of this decision. She was offered a comfortable life, a chance to go back to what she had left all those years ago; only instead of a goldsmith she would have a solicitor for a husband. She would know kindness and eventually obscurity . . . and with it Thomas. And, if she did not accept, what would become of her? Even if she should come out of this foul prison, whither should she go? She was alone and penniless. She had a few friends, but how could she throw herself on their mercy? How could she keep herself? And here was Thomas offering so much. But she did not love him, any more than she had loved Will Shore.

"Jane," he was murmuring, "I will arrange it. You must leave this to me. Never fear . . . I will arrange it."

He would have put his arms about her, kissed her, but she held him off, for in the dim light he reminded her so much of Will. She had not loved Will, and she had betrayed him. What if she, not loving Thomas, betrayed him also?

"No," she cried. "Not yet. Not yet, Thomas. I must have time to think."

*　　*　　*　　*　　*

After he had gone she laughed at herself. You are a fool, Jane Shore, she told herself. This is a chance that will never come to you again.

But I do not love him.

Love! What did love bring you? Great happiness with Edward; but Edward died, nor was he faithful to you. And what misery did you suffer on those occasions—particularly in the beginning—when you discovered his infidelity. Dorset? That was not love; that was lust and torment. Hastings? Brief as a summer's day, and on a summer's day it ended in such tragedy that pray you'll never meet again. That much for love!

And Thomas Lynom? He is a man of some position, but not too much. A hard-working and conscientious man, a man who will love you and rescue you from the terrible plight into which you have fallen, care for you, make you happy in your middle and old age. You are a fool to hesitate for a moment.

But remember Will.

Then you were hot-blooded, and there was Edward to come courting you. Edward is dead and you are no longer young. You are a poor, penniless prisoner in Ludgate from where you will never emerge without the help of some powerful person such as Thomas who loves you.

But to marry Thomas seemed in some small measure like going to Mary Blague. That she had scorned; she had never faltered in her determination to turn her back on that way of life.

But it was not the same. She would be a good wife to Thomas and he loved her. A good wife to the solicitor as she had been to the goldsmith?

To be free again, to walk the streets, to stroll out to Fickets Croft on a summer's evening, to walk along the river bank, to glance towards the grey towers of London's fortress and to remember so much that was gay and happy and so much that was best forgotten!

Thomas came next day, eager as a young man in love, awaiting her answer.

"Thomas Lynom," she said gravely, "you are a man of some years and good sense. Why do you do this thing?"

"Because I love you," he said.

She was moved. It was so good to be loved again. She would marry him. She would be true to him. Here was a chance to be the good wife she had not been to poor Will.

"Jane, you will marry me?"

"I do not think that is possible."

Thomas Lynom in love was a giant in achievement. "You will see, Jane. I have the ear of His Grace the King and I fancy he is not displeased with me."

"But he is displeased with me, Thomas."

"Not in any great seriousness. I will sue for his mercy, and then, Jane . . ."

She felt the fire of his love warming her. He was picturing her, the grime of the prison washed from her, sitting at his table, discreetly jewelled, becomingly gowned; and the picture made him very happy.

"Jane," he said, "you will?"

"If it be possible . . . then mayhap I will."

It was only after he had gone that her elation left her. Freedom she sought, but would she be free? In a charming, well-ordered house, she might be a prisoner just as she was in Ludgate Jail. Such a prisoner had she been in Lombard Street . . . until she had flown.

"It must not be," she said; and her indecision began again.

*   *   *   *   *

The King was astounded when he heard from Lynom that the man wished to marry Jane Shore.

"You are bewitched, man," he cried; and he meant it. He had persuaded himself that Jane, in company with Elizabeth Woodville, had tried to work her black magic upon him. That had been necessary to ease his conscience. He had wanted to destroy Jane's popularity with the people; he had hoped her penance would have done that; but her beauty and charm, together with the dignified way in which she had undergone the ordeal had, if anything, aroused the sympathy rather than the scorn of the people. Therefore had he felt it necessary to keep her out of sight until she was forgotten. This he had done, and now she was attempting to seduce Thomas Lynom, an honest and sober solicitor.

He saw the firm set of the man's jaw. He liked Lynom; he trusted him; and Richard longed to keep his friends. Moreover, Anne talked often of Jane and was disturbed that he had been the one to send her to Ludgate. If good came to Jane, Anne would be pleased; perhaps, after all, Jane was just a foolish woman, to be watched because of the effect she could have on men of importance.

He laid a hand on Lynom's shoulder. "You are acting like

a fool, good Thomas," he said. "But if a man will act thus . .
and is set on marriage . . . we would not wish to stand in his
way."

Lynom knelt and kissed the hand extended to him.

"Your Grace is good to me."

Richard laughed grimly. "Ah, my friend, it may be that in
a short while you will not think so. It may be that then you
will wish I had said you nay."

"Your Grace is bountiful, and it is my greatest ambition to
serve you well."

Richard was pleased with these expressions of devotion. "I
doubt that not," he said. "But, good Thomas, I would have
you wait awhile. Because I know you for my friend I would
first make certain of the good conduct of this woman. I shall
write to my Lord Chancellor of Lincoln on this matter.
Mayhap he will speak to you, and if, after that, you are still of
the same mind . . . and if the matter may stand the law of
Holy Church . . . well, then, it is your matter, my friend;
and I wash my hands of it."

"And if I should pay her debts, Your Grace . . . ?"

Richard waved his hand. "Then she would have our free
pardon. But I pray you, be not hasty. Wait until this matter
has the sanction of the Church, and until Lincoln has spoken
with you."

Lynom was dismissed.

There should be no delay, he assured himself. He was aglow
with plans for his rosy future. Mistress Browner should indulge
in a great cleaning of his house. He was longing for the
moment when he would take Jane home. How delightful it
would seem after Ludgate Jail! But he must not forget that
she had lived in palaces.

But something was happening which was to delay matters.

The King had a few friends whom he thought he could
trust, and the chief of these was the Duke of Buckingham.
There was one thing Richard had forgotten, and this was that
in Buckingham was a strain of royal blood, which worked

like a fever in his veins. He could not forget it. Who would have thought, he asked himself continually, that Richard of Gloucester would come to the throne? A dead man here, a bastard there, and one whose hopes had seemed small could grasp the crown. Buckingham was several moves from the throne, and there was one, alive and ambitious, itching to grasp it. This man, it would be said, had a claim prior to Buckingham's. Well, Buckingham could wait. The man he was thinking of was Henry Tudor, Earl of Richmond, now in exile in Brittany.

Buckingham was a weak man. He recognised the strength of Richard, and thoughts of treason would never have come into his head if Richard had not made the great mistake of putting Bishop Morton in his care.

Morton, Bishop of Ely, had been a member of the Council, and had been arrested at the time of the execution of Hastings. Richard had been lenient with the Bishop, for he liked to stand well with the Church; he had, instead of sending Morton to the Tower, put him in the charge of the Duke of Buckingham, in whose castle at Brecknock he would be treated more as a guest than a prisoner. It was simple for wily Morton to sum up the character of Buckingham, whom he considered vain as a peacock, as ready to crow as a bantam, and as eager to chatter as a monkey. The Duke was malleable material in the hands of the clever Bishop.

Morton knew the whereabouts of Dorset; he knew how to get into touch with Henry Tudor. But these men, including the Bishop, were prisoners or outcasts. They needed help from someone who could give it unsuspected. And who should that be but the man whom Richard in his folly had delivered up to the Bishop!

How easy it was to sow the seed of discontent!

"My lord Duke, you have the look of a King. It surprises me not, for you are of royal descent, are you not?"

The Duke strutted about his room, seeing himself as the King of England. Why not? Did the Bishop know he was descended from Edward III?

"Indeed, an I did not, I could see it in Your Grace's face."

The Duke became a frequent visitor to the Bishop's apartments. How easy it was for Morton to drop the words of criticism of the King!

"I am not one to labour against what God hath pulled down. You, my lord Duke, are an honourable man. The fate of our country means much to you. But what do I say? I am a foolish old man. Forgive me. It is my wish to retire from politics and devote myself to God and my books. Even so, to see our beloved country groaning under—under a . . . But my tongue runs on."

"Have no fear," said the Duke, "that what you might say would go beyond these walls."

They had done with subterfuge.

"The King is a usurper. He has taken the crown from its rightful place and put it on his own head," said Morton.

It was well to vilify Richard, but such was not without its complications, for if Richard was the usurper, then was not young Edward the true King? And if he died, or disappeared, there was still his young brother Richard who must succeed him.

The two little boys were undoubtedly a nuisance. They crept into the best-laid plans. For how, thought Buckingham, could I sit upon the throne whilst those two lived? For though they might be proved illegitimate, are not my claims based on what took place on the wrong side of the blanket? And unless we declare them the true heirs to the throne, how can we accuse Richard of usurping it, since he has but taken that which is his by right?

Morton's thoughts worked on similar lines. If Henry Tudor were to come to the throne, how could he enjoy the people's approval while the Princes lived? Richard must be proved a knave, and he could only be thus designated if the Princes were the true heirs; and if they were, then would the people say: "Let young Edward have his coronation at once." No, the Princes must be proved legitimate and at the same time they must not be allowed to stop Henry Tudor's passage to the throne. Therefore they must be removed. They must be declared the rightful heirs and—removed.

It was an uneasy matter to speak of, even for a clever Bishop who feels he has a vain and silly Duke in his power.

"The Princes . . ." began the Duke, and averted his eyes.

The Bishop stared at the ornate ceiling of his luxurious prison. "They are young," he said. "They can scarce know the meaning of life. It will be necessary to remove them when . . ."

". . . when the usurper Richard has been removed," said the Duke, who was more blunt of speech than the Bishop.

"Let us remember the deaths of men who have crossed him. Hastings comes to mind. One more crime laid upon him . . ."

The Duke nodded. "But, my lord Bishop, how could this matter be laid at Richard's door? What motive could he have for murder? With the aid of Stillington he has proved the Princes illegitimate. Whether they live or die the throne is still his."

"If this story of Stillington's was proved to be false, a motive for the murder would be supplied, would it not?"

"But will the people believe it?"

"We must make them believe it. We will see that posterity believes it. I assure you it is not an impossibility. Have you forgotten that I am writing a history of these times? The Princes must die . . . but not yet. Richard must go first and they must follow him. But if we will have the people believing that Richard was responsible for their removal, why then, *before* Richard's death, the rumour must go forth that the Princes are dead. And then, when there is no longer a King Richard, must the deed be done."

"My lord Bishop, I like it not."

"My lord Duke, your scruples do you credit. Two innocent children, you say. But remember England. For England I would die this night; and so would you." The Bishop brought his face close to that of the Duke. "And so must they."

* * * * *

The prostitutes brought the news into Ludgate Jail and the

rumour spread. There was trouble outside, and terror stalked the streets of London. Few dared go out after dark. Thieves and murderers had grown overbold. During the day people hurried along with downcast eyes, hardly daring to speak to one another for fear they should be tricked into expressing an opinion and find themselves accused of treason.

There was tension inside the prison. If there was fighting and it spread to London, the prison gates might be flung open, and the prisoners of to-day might be the free men of to-morrow.

There was many a fight in the jail during those days of suspense. The prisoners were taking sides.

"I am for the rebellion. A Dorset! A Buckingham! A Tudor!"

"Take that, you traitorous cur! I am for the King. King Richard—and England."

The mad parson screeched excitedly until he was hoarse. "A house divided against itself. . . . Oh, God, have mercy on these miserable sinners."

Jane shared the excitement and the tension. So Dorset was alive and involved in this rebellion. She thought of him dispassionately and wondered who was his mistress now. Did he ever give a thought to poor Jane Shore? She hoped he did not. The Dorset episode was one she would always remember with shame, and she did not wish to be remembered by him.

And, thinking of Dorset, she began to see how impossible it was that she could ever marry Thomas Lynom. Always when she was alone she felt thus. It was when he came to her full of plans, looking into the future with a serenity which could not fail to move her, that she wavered and let herself take a part in these plans. Sometimes she thought she would rather stay in this place for ever than marry a man she did not love. But would she? She would never grow hardened to the miseries of others; her heart was too soft, her imagination too keen. And yet what would it be like when the winter came? "I must marry Thomas," she would murmur, and so was her mind continually changing.

Then again she would remember the frustration, the humiliation of her life with Will Shore. To marry Thomas would be like completing an ugly circle. "I cannot do it," she said.

She was relieved that the matter must necessarily be shelved for the moment.

One day, when Thomas came to see her, pleasure was written on his face and in his manner.

"The rebellion is over," he said. "The King has victoriously quelled his enemies. Love live King Richard!"

There was cheering now through the prison. "Long live King Richard!" Those who had itched to take up arms against the King either slunk away or shouted louder than the rest: "Long live the rightful King!"

"And Dorset?" asked Jane of Lynom.

"Has fled. Doubtless to France. And with him Morton and others. Buckingham is dead. He lost his head, as he well deserved. God was on our side."

The mad parson took up the story. "If ever we wanted proof, God has given it to us. He has shown us the right. Down with all traitors! Down with mock marriages! Down with these bastard slips! God has shown us."

The mad parson went about all that day marvelling at the power of God.

Later Lynom brought in more news. Henry Tudor, he had learned, had turned back to France before landing, because he had heard of the defeat of his friends. After the captured Buckingham's head was severed, Richard rode in triumph to Exeter, acclaimed wherever he went.

"Once more," said Lynom, "has the King saved the throne for himself and England from civil war. God save him!"

* * * * *

In the little room which he had acquired for her in the jail, Jane faced Thomas Lynom.

"I cannot do it, Thomas," she said. "It is not in me to do it. I should wrong myself and you if I did."

His face twitched with emotion. "You cannot mean it, Jane. This is pardon for you—and a new life."

"Thomas, my dear, try to understand me. Long ago I married the goldsmith. He was a good man and he loved me truly. My father wanted the marriage; I did not; but I yielded. You know that I wronged my husband, that I left him for the King. He left Lombard Street soon after that and I do not know what became of him. But I know this : it was wrong to make such a marriage. Nor will I do so again."

"You will live on here in this foul place? Do you not see— this is a way out?"

"I cannot do it, Thomas."

"You do not mean it."

"Alas, I do. I would I could give you the love you deserve. I loved others who loved me not as you do. I fear I am a foolish woman, but somehow I know that this marriage could never bring happiness to either of us."

"To me it would. And you too, Jane."

"It must not be. Go away from here, Thomas. Forget you ever knew me. Find some woman more worthy."

"But, Jane, in marriage is your freedom."

"There is no price that can be paid for love, Thomas. I have loved—sinfully—but always it *was* love. And as I see it, there was more sin in my life with Will Shore than with any other; for the others I loved, and Will I did not love. I was married to him for a secure future, and that is why you would have me marry you. I cannot do it. And you must consider what this would mean to you, Thomas. People know of me."

"I care not for that."

"I was a wanton. So said my father; so said the Bishop. But I never sold myself. It was my father who sold me to Will Shore. Please, Thomas, leave me now. I have made up my mind because I see this thing clearly."

He left her then because he could see it was useless to try to persuade her.

She went out into the courtyard. The prostitutes from outside were just coming in. On her straw in a corner a sick woman lay dying. The mad parson was preaching to an imaginary congregation. Somebody began to sob wildly; it was a newcomer. The miserable life went on.

Jane sank down in despair. She had shut herself in with misery. Thomas, good man, respectable citizen, had offered her escape and she had refused it. She had none but herself to blame.

Oh, Jane Shore, she thought, what a fool you are! What a fool you always have been!

*   *   *   *   *

Out of the gates of Ludgate Jail walked Jane Shore. In her pocket was a purse that was full of coins. She was a free woman. Thomas had paid her debts and sent her this purse; and the King had given her his pardon.

She was a free woman; and her freedom was a gift, something she had not had to buy.

Thomas had written to her: "Your debts are paid. Here is some money to help you along. And if you should ever change your mind I shall be waiting."

The fresh air after Ludgate air was breathtakingly strong.

She walked along by the river, wondering what she should do.

How beautiful was the City with the sparkling sunshine on it! It would soon be November and the mists would hang over the spires and rise up from the water. November. And in June she had thought she had found happiness.

How deceitful was life—promising much and offering no fulfilment of her promises!

A new life was waiting for her. She must not stand here all day staring at the river. She must get on. But whither should she go?

EAST CHEAP

THE little room over the Bansters' shop, which was now Jane's, was mean and almost bare of furnishings. It contained little beside a table and a stool; and every night Jane made herself a bed of straw in that room. There were no hangings to disguise the ugly walls; the one window was without glass, but it had a shutter, which either excluded all light or exposed the room to the weather. The rushes on the floor were none too sweet, but the room seemed luxurious after Ludgate Jail; and, living thus, Jane reckoned that the money which Thomas Lynom had given her would last for a year or more.

The Bansters had been good to her. They would insist on feeding her and would take only the smallest rent for the room, which they had given up to her while the whole family were crowded into the room behind the cook-shop.

When Jane considered the kindness of her friends her self-pity would evaporate. There were times when she would remember Edward in all his splendid manhood or the fleeting beauty of her week with Hastings; and then she would bitterly lament her ill fortune. But she was by nature ebullient, and when she thought of the horrors of the jail from which she had been so recently freed, she would rejoice at the good fortune which had brought her friends like Thomas Lynom, Kate and Belper and the Bansters.

On a day soon after her release she sat at her window looking down at the crowds thronging through the flesh market of East Cheap, and her thoughts must necessarily go back to that day when she and Will had set out to see the King.

Have done with the past, she scolded herself. Remember this is the beginning of the year 1484, and the year that has gone has been the most tragic of your life.

To-day King Richard and Queen Anne would ride through the streets of London, showing themselves to the people after the quelling of the Buckingham rebellion. Jane was going out, but not to see them. She would make her way to the Tower, and her visits to the Tower were what she lived for these days.

What a comfort it was to make her way through the great gate and turn her steps towards the Belper kitchens! She was never challenged. The guards and warders knew and respected her. They knew she but came to visit her friend Kate Belper, and Kate, like Jane, was well liked throughout the Tower.

It seemed to Jane, in her love for Edward's two boys, that they grew daily more like their father. They were always delighted to see her. It was dull, they said, living as they did. Of course, they were not prisoners as poor Jane had been in Ludgate; their surroundings were luxurious indeed; they were the nephews of the King even if they were bastards, for no one could deny that Edward the Fourth was their father; but their lodgings in the Garden Tower were dull indeed, and the small conspiracy which the coming of Jane must necessarily mean was very welcome. They were boys still—thirteen and eleven years old.

Jane looked at her face in the old mirror as she put on her cape. It was true that the mirror was mottled with age, but the Jane who looked back at her was sadly different from that Jane of a year ago. Her skin was yellowish; she doubted whether she would ever regain the healthy delicate colouring which had been one of her greatest charms. She did not need a mirror to show her that her long hair, luxuriant as ever, had lost that look of powdered gold. Kate's clothes hung loosely on her, for she was very thin. Was it really necessary to hide herself beneath the hood? Would any recognise her as the once dazzling Jane Shore?

She shrugged her shoulders. She had left her youth behind her in Ludgate Jail. What mattered that? Most of those whom she had loved were dead, and the Princes did not notice that her beauty was fading. To them she was Jane whom they had loved dearly when they were very little boys, the two most important little boys in the land.

Jane started to descend the spiral staircase. The wood was broken and it was necessary to tread warily. A strange contrast this to Windsor Castle and the Palace of Westminster, which but a short year ago she had considered her homes.

Mistress Banster met her at the bottom of the stairs.

"The streets are filling."

"They'll not be going my way," said Jane. "I shall slip through Candlewick to Tower Street. The procession will not pass that way."

"Be in before dusk," advised Mistress Banster. "There'll be roystering in the streets this night, I'll swear. We're boarding up the front of the shop. We don't want rogues and vagabonds breaking in. A good journey to you. And don't forget: be home by duskfall."

"I will, never fear."

Out in the streets Jane caught the excitement. She pushed her way through the crowds. The air of East Cheap was filled with the smell of meat and the cries of the butchers. The cook-shops were doing good trade. People stood about eating and drinking. Beggars whined and showed armless and legless bodies, declaring they were old soldiers. Jane dropped many a coin she could ill spare into an open hand.

She was thinking as she went on along East Cheap of the extraordinary twists of fortune. Here she had found Anne Neville all but starved to death in Mother Clack's cook-shop. Mother Clack had left East Cheap now and Anne Neville was Queen of England. Jane paused. She would take the opportunity of seeing Anne again. The little Princes would like to hear something of the procession and would be disappointed if she had nothing to tell them.

She retraced her steps. In a very short time the cavalcade would be passing through the Poultry and into Cheapside on its way to Ludgate, when it would go along Fleet Street and on to Westminster. Jane could hear the trumpets now. The church bells were ringing out. The royal pair could not be far off.

Jane took her stand close to the old Cross and waited. From here she could see the walls of her father's house. There was another mercer living there now and she was saddened recalling her father. Thank the Virgin he was not alive now to see her brought so low!

First came the heralds, the knights and the squires. She recognised Catesby, and near him rode Sir Richard Ratcliffe and Lord Lovel with the Duke of Norfolk—all the strongest adherents of the King. They had passed, and a special cheer went up, for here was the King, ablaze with jewels; the King was on horseback, and the Queen in her litter was equally dazzling.

The royal pair passed, the cheering died down and the people talked together.

"How sick looks the little Queen! And so pretty, poor lady."

"It is well that she has already borne the King a son."

"I dare swear she is not long for this world, poor soul."

Poor little Queen! thought Jane; and was assured of her own strength. She could take care of herself. She had been bred in these colourful streets with their yelling townsfolk, and she knew she would never be entirely unhappy while she was free to roam them.

She hurried eastwards, turning into Tower Street. As she approached the Tower one of the warders called to her merrily, and she stopped to exchange a word with him. Then she went through the postern gate and down the stairs to the kitchens, where Kate was waiting for her.

"I had expected you earlier," said Kate as they embraced.

Jane explained that she had stopped to see the procession. Kate herself would have liked to see it, but she did not complain that she had stayed behind that she might conduct Jane to the Princes.

"You'll have a bite to eat before we go?" asked Kate; but Jane was eager to be gone and said so.

Kate wrapped her cloak about her and they came out into the

grounds and made their way towards the Garden Tower. Jane
was always afraid at such times that there would be someone to
bar their way and to tell them that these visits must be stopped.
It was pleasant to reflect that almost everybody was busy merry-
making on this day. Besides, the Princes were not so carefully
guarded as they had been in those days when people still called
young Edward, King. Richard was firmly on the throne now;
but doubtless he still considered it wise to be in full knowledge
of the whereabouts of his nephews.

They entered the Garden Tower. It was cold, and the bells
of St. Peter Ad Vincula that were pealing to welcome the procession seemed to take on a mournful note.

Jane shivered, and Kate said slowly: " 'Tis always cold
inside these towers—winter and summer alike."

There were guards outside the Princes' apartments. Kate
grinned at them saucily, and they returned the grin.

"Visitors for the young gentlemen," said one to another; and
when Jane smiled at them they bowed and stood aside.

Jane and Kate went into a small antechamber and knocked
on a door.

"Enter," said a boy's voice, which Jane recognised with
emotion as being young Edward's.

The two boys were seated at a table by the window, poring
over a book. They did not look up for a second or two, thinking it was but an attendant with more logs for the fire which
burned in the great fireplace. But when Jane called them by
their names they leaped up and ran to her. Richard flung himself at her; Edward was more dignified. Richard was still a
child, but Edward had—though very briefly—tasted the honours
of kingship.

"My dearest ones!" cried Jane. "How fare you to-day?"

"We are weary of this place," said Edward. "But your coming has brightened it. Your hands are cold, Jane. Come—you
too, Kate. Come to the fire and warm yourselves."

Jane went with them to the fire, where Edward sat at her
feet and Richard leaned against her. They plied her with ques-

tions and she told them how she had just seen the procession. And, as she talked, she looked about the apartment which had been the little Princes' home for so long, and she wondered when the King would see fit to let them leave it.

The walls were hung with rich cloth and the big room was furnished in a manner suited to the apartments of the sons of Edward the Fourth; but there was a gloom about the place that depressed Jane. From where she sat she could look out on the Green, and she wished that it was not to this room that she must come to see her beloved boys, for never did she look through that window but she must remember seeing Hastings stand there with the faraway look already in his eyes. She preferred the southern end of the room, which was fitted as a bed-chamber. The bed was beautiful and its curtains richly woven; it was a big bed for two little boys to sleep in. She wondered if they were afraid as they lay by night in that great gloomy chamber, and whether they drew the curtains close so that they might not see the window in that inner partition which faced the bed. Young Richard had been a fanciful child. She was glad, though, that the two boys were together.

"Jane!" Edward seized her hands and looked earnestly into her face. "Do you think my uncle is ever going to let us leave this place?"

"Assuredly I do. But you must know that he has been very busy of late. He will remember soon that you are here, and then he will send for you to go to court."

"Mayhap I shall join my wife," said Richard, "for I am a married man, you know."

The two little boys laughed. "It is odd indeed," said Edward, "that Richard should have a wife while I have none. They thought to make a very grand marriage for me—and now it may be that I shall never marry."

"You will, my little lord," said Kate. "I see it in your face." She took his palm and looked at it while the boys watched her face gravely. "A long life and a merry one!" cried Kate. "I have visited a wise woman in Shoreditch, and that is what she promised me. Rest assured if Kate is to have these things, how much longer and merrier shall be the life of Princes."

They all laughed. That was how it was when Kate and Jane visited them. Laughter ran high; and so did hope. It was impossible to be with these two and not believe that some day, soon, everything would come right.

"What of our mother?" asked Edward gravely. "We never see her now, nor our sisters."

Richard's lips quivered. He was only eleven and he longed for his mother. Elizabeth Woodville had been more tender to her boys than to any of her children.

"I do not believe my mother wished me to come here," said Richard. "She would rather we were both with her and our sisters in Westminster Sanctuary."

"Oh, Jane, how long must our mother stay in Sanctuary?"

"Not long now, you will see. Why, now that your uncle has put down the rebellion he will be able to give thought to your family. Doubtless in a few short weeks you two will be riding in processions."

They laughed at that. They saw themselves on white horses, richly clad; they pictured reunion with their family.

"Jane," said Edward suddenly, "what would have happened to us if the rebellion had not failed?"

Jane and Kate exchanged warning glances, for they had seen hope leap up in the little boys' eyes. The two women thought— just as the boys did—that if the rebellion had been successful, little Edward would have mounted the throne.

"You will not speak," said Edward. "But I know."

"Yes," said Richard. "Edward knows."

"It is not wise to speak of it," said Jane. "You never know who listens."

They were silent for a while; then Richard, who forgot these matters more easily than did his brother, said : "Edward, let us show Jane our little room. The one we discovered the other day."

"Yes," said Edward; and the two boys jumped up.

"We found it a week back," said Richard. "It was hidden by the hangings—this door was." He went to the east side of the room, drew back the curtains and disclosed an old door.

"At first it did not seem to open," said Edward.

'We spent hours trying to make it," added Richard. "I do not think it has been opened for years and years. Look. There. It hardly seems like a door at all."

The four of them stood close together looking down at a dingy staircase that wound out of sight.

"Whither does it lead?" asked Kate.

"To a small vaulted chamber," said Edward. "We were disappointed. It just leads to the chamber and stops."

"Yet it is fine to have our own little room," said Richard. "Our secret room."

"Well," said Kate, "I hope your little Graces will deign to show it to us."

"Come, follow us," said Edward; and he led the way.

They descended the short staircase to a small chamber about which there was a smell of age and dust.

Outside, the bells of St. Peter Ad Vincula stopped momentarily, and when they started again it seemed to Jane that there was a melancholy foreboding in their pealing.

*   *   *   *   *

Elizabeth Woodville was not the person to remain tranquilly in Sanctuary. It was not a year since the death of Edward, and yet she had become almost as insignificant as the widow she had been when Edward had first met her in Whittlebury Forest. She did not intend to stand by and wait for ever. She had made plans, and her children were at the centre of these, though not of course the two little boys in the Tower, for Richard was firmly on the throne and it would take a successful war to dislodge him. And who would fight for two fatherless boys?

She believed, though, that there was one man who might take the throne from Richard, and that was Henry Tudor, who was now on the other side of the Channel awaiting his opportunity.

One day in early March she sat with her daughters as they stitched at their embroidery. The five girls were talking together, as they often did, of the old happy days when their lives had seemed so full of promise and their father the King had arranged such grand marriages for them. Listening to them, Elizabeth Woodville's eyes rested on her eldest daughter, that other Elizabeth, who, she hoped, would, through her mother's cleverness, restore her family's fortunes.

"What hope have we of ever marrying?" Cecily was saying. "We shall stay here for ever."

But Elizabeth was looking at her mother and had caught a glint of something in her eyes. "Mother," she cried, "you know something. Oh, pray tell us, gracious Mother."

Elizabeth Woodville nodded and plied her needle thoughtfully. "As I see it, my children, our troubles are beginning to end."

"Our troubles ending! Our cruel uncle is stronger than ever." That was Elizabeth—an ambitious girl, her mother's own daughter, she longed to make a match worthy of her, and she could not forget that she had been promised the Dauphin of France.

"Kings and Queens are never safe, my children. Why, even a man such as your father had his troubles. Why, your little brother, King Edward the Fifth, was born in this place, and I was kept alive and tended by poor citizens of London who believed in your father's cause."

"I know," said Elizabeth the younger. "But I never thought we should come to this—now. And in those days none could keep my father from the throne for long. But now he is dead, and I—who was to have been Queen of France—am betrothed to a poor exile."

Elizabeth Woodville smiled slyly. "Never fear. Your father was once, as you call it, a poor exile. Poor exiles, daughter, can become kings."

"You think Henry Tudor will ever be King of England?" Elizabeth laughed scornfully. "There is a rebellion and he does not even land. He lies off Plymouth and scuttles back to France."

"Often there is wisdom in flight." Elizabeth smiled at her daughter. "Listen, foolish girl. I gave my consent to your betrothal to Henry Tudor, did I not? What have we to lose? Nothing. And what to gain? One day, depend upon it, Henry Tudor will come to England, and when he does there will be those to rise against your uncle. Henry Tudor has sworn to marry you. Could you hope that he would do that were he already on the throne? Remember your false uncle has set all England calling you bastards."

"Gracious Mother, mayhap you are right."

"There is no knowing what will happen, and I feel good things in the air. I have felt much lightness in my heart ever since I was approached to make this contract with the Tudor."

There was a sudden knocking on the door, and when Elizabeth gave permission for whoever was there to enter, a messenger came in carrying a scroll in his hand. This he handed to Elizabeth the ex-Queen, saying that his royal master awaited her reply when she could conveniently give it. With great dignity Elizabeth accepted the scroll, and when the messenger had withdrawn proceeded with all eagerness to read it. When she had done so she tapped her eldest daughter with it, and said with some severity : "Daughter, you were a short while ago wondering at the wisdom of my conduct."

"Oh no, gracious Mother, I am assured that whatever you did was right and proper for us all."

"It is well that you have as much good sense. Now, children, listen to me. I gave my consent when our friends across the water wished your eldest sister to be formally promised to Henry Tudor. That was at Christmas time in Rennes when, as you know, the young man took the oath that if ever he came to the throne of England he would marry Elizabeth of York. This matter has now come to your uncle's ears, and, as you can imagine, he likes it not. And here is evidence of it. In this paper is a statement that if we leave this Sanctuary and put ourselves in the care of the King, we shall suffer no hurt and husbands shall be found for you all. For me there is an allowance. Now what think you, children, of your mother's strategy? Your uncle does not like it that I should have betrothed my eldest daughter to Henry Tudor. He offers us a bribe—doubtless to stop the match. Never fear, we shall rise again. Look, dear daughters, look at the signature on this document. Even you, Bridget, can read that, can you not?"

"Ricardus Rex," read Bridget in her high piping voice.

Elizabeth Woodville burst into laughter. "Let him call himself King if it pleases him." She laid a hand affectionately on the shoulder of her eldest daughter. "Mayhap it will not be for long, eh, daughter?"

*   *   *   *   *

That year slipped away quickly for Jane. The money Thomas Lynom had given her was gradually disappearing, but Jane had never been concerned about money. All her life there had been someone to provide for her; in her heart she believed there always would be, for even when she was desperately poor and alone in Ludgate Jail, Thomas Lynom had come to succour her.

She was beginning to recover from the weakness which the events of the last year had put upon her. She was growing healthy again, adapting herself to the life which was hers. Her thoughts of the two men she had loved were less frequent and painful now, and she no longer wished for a lover, for she had left her passionate youth behind her, and her affections were now in the possession of the two little boys in the Tower. How pleasant it had been to be able to tell them that the King had already made a move in their favour, since their mother and sisters now had apartments in Westminster Palace! She was sure, she said, that it would not be long before the little boys joined their mother and sisters. But the weeks passed into months and the Princes continued to be lodged in the Tower.

She had heard with great sorrow of the death of the King's

only son. Poor Anne Neville would be heartbroken, she knew; and in the streets they were saying that the Queen was too sick to bear the King another child.

Elizabeth Woodville's emotions on that matter were quite different from Jane's, for no sooner had she been installed at the palace than she sought to improve her position. She began to feel that in affiancing her daughter to Henry Tudor she had not been so clever. What had Henry Tudor but ambition!

At the palace, living close to the King, it was possible to realise the power of the man. He was no Edward, who had surely been every handsome inch a king, but he had power and presence, and many feared to have the cold eyes of Richard turned on them in anger. Unlike his brother though he was, King Richard bore the stamp and mould of Plantagenet.

Elizabeth slyly watched her daughter, for the girl was old enough to have hoped for much from life. She still yearned to be Queen of France, but how much more gratifying to be Queen of England!

"My dear," said Elizabeth Woodville one day, as they looked through the window of their obscure apartments out to the grounds of Westminster Palace where the King walked in earnest conversation with his friend Lord Lovel, "your uncle is a man of some attractiveness, I think."

"Attractiveness? He is too short of stature, and I admire a man more of my father's girth."

"There is a look of your father in his brother, I declare."

"You may see it, gracious Mother. I do not."

"You would an you looked for it. Methinks, daughter, that the King hath a fondness for you."

"For me?"

"Why should he not? You are comely enough. Holy Mother, there is much a woman can do for herself and her family."

At last the daughter understood. "But he is my uncle!"

Elizabeth Woodville shrugged her shoulders, sweeping away difficulties as eagerly now as in the old days when she had wanted something from Edward which it had not been easy to obtain. "Uncles . . . nieces . . . what of that? In certain circumstances His Holiness the Pope can be most obliging."

"You have forgotten my aunt."

"Anne Neville is half dead already and it is the King's duty to get sons. . . ."

Elizabeth Woodville smiled. She had seen the hope leap up in her daughter's eyes. The girl was now looking at the King with a new interest.

* * * * *

Christmas came and Jane spent it with the Belpers in the kitchens of the Tower. Belper had surpassed himself, and his table was loaded with the choicest foods. He entertained warders, jailors and soldiers, and even the sworn tormentors and the executioners crept in.

Jane set the table laughing as she had done in the banqueting halls of palaces. These people were glad to have her in their midst, and she was glad to be there. In the morning she had visited the Princes, who were now assured that their captivity would soon be over. Everything was coming right, Jane felt; but when the talk turned to the King and his Queen she was saddened.

"The King," said merry Belper, "may be a king, but a king is a man for all that he is a king." Everyone laughed as they always did at Belper's remarks. "Why, bless us all," he went on, "the Queen is nothing but a sick invalid, they say; and a man may be a king . . ."

Someone ventured: "They say the King has cast his eyes upon the Lady Elizabeth."

"I do not believe it," said Jane. "She is his niece."

"A niece is a girl for all she is a niece," pointed out Belper, chuckling as he stood up to carve the boar's head.

"It is a rumour . . . an evil rumour," said Jane. "Why, I remember well a rumour that the Princes were dead . . . murdered. But was there any truth in that?"

"Nay. 'Tis odd how rumour starts."

"The poor Queen is sick and ailing," said Kate. "She has lost her son and there is no heir to the throne. So rumour will supply the King with a new Queen. . . ."

Belper pointed his knife at Kate. " 'Twill take more than rumour to give the King an heir!"

Everyone laughed and Belper had to lay aside his knife to wipe his tears of mirth. Jane laughed with them, but her thoughts were mixed, for she had known intimately these people who were just names in Belper's kitchen. What did it mean? How far would the ambitions of Richard take him? And what did that cunning woman, Elizabeth Woodville, plan for her daughter?

Richard was strange and cold; and none knew him well. But Jane remembered his face when she had taken him to East Cheap and he had seen Anne, ragged and dirty; then had he, the exquisitely clad dandy, held out his arms to her, and into that pale face of his had come a glow of love.

"I do not believe he contemplates marriage with his niece," said Jane. "Why, if you could have seen him with his Queen, and how he loved her . . . you would not believe these rumours."

They were silent as they always were—silent with respect—when Jane Shore gave her accounts of life at court. There was nothing they liked better than to listen to a tale of great ones; and who was better equipped to tell than Jane Shore?

So now she told them of poor Anne Neville whose fortune had tempted that Duke of Clarence who had died so mysteriously in the Bowyer Tower. And they listened to how the Duke hid the girl, and how she escaped to the squalor of an East Cheap cook-shop, until she was found and became the Queen of England.

"And Richard came to her," said Jane, "and dearly he loved her. I know it, for I was there to witness it. Nay, listen not to evil rumours." She lifted her glass and cried: "Long live the Queen!"

"Long live the Queen!" echoed those around the table.

*   *   *   *   *

All along East Cheap people stood in little groups. Jane had drawn back the shutters of her room to look down on them, and friends and acquaintances called up to her as they passed.

"There is something of the devil in this," called an old market woman; and Jane nodded as she looked along the fast darkening street. It certainly seemed that the devil was at work up there in the sky. What did it mean? Was it the end of the world? There was an uncanny feeling in the cold March air.

Mistress Banster called up for Jane to come down.

" 'Tis the end of the world. 'Tis Judgment Day. Come down, and let us all stand together against the forces of evil."

Jane took her cloak and wrapped it round her. Charlie was with his mother, and several people were standing inside the shop, some covering their eyes, some praying, and every now and then peering up furtively through the window to the sky.

" 'Tis getting mighty dark," said Mistress Banster.

An old beggar woman, who had come in to shelter with them, whispered: "And methinks when the sun disappears we shall never see it again."

"It is the wickedness of us," said another. "We have brought this on ourselves."

"The wickedness of *some*," said Mistress Banster significantly.

The March wind penetrated the shop and the air grew colder as the darkness increased.

"Day into night," said the beggar-woman. "God has turned day into night to show His displeasure. An evil omen, this. I had it from a friend in Shoredith that there was bad times a-coming."

"Mayhap it is a sign of good times," said Jane.

"Good? What good could there be in the sun's hiding its face?"

"When it emerges from the darkness it will be like good coming out of evil. If it is a sign . . ."

"Who said it will come out? I never knew the like. 'Tis the devil up there."

"Take another look, Charlie," said his mother.

" 'Tis too bright to look, Mother. Wherever I look I see the sun . . . though my eyes be shut."

"Devil's work."

"Ah," said the beggar-woman. "Mayhap when the rightful king sits on the throne times will change."

"Be careful what you say," whispered Jane. "You know not who may overhear you."

"Bah! What matters it? You will see this darkness is but a beginning. Terrible things will happen. I feel it in my bones, lady, and my bones don't lie. Where's the two little boys, eh? The two little Princes? The rightful King and his little brother? Strangled, some say . . . and their innocent bodies dropped in the river!"

"That's a lie!" said Jane. "I saw them but lately. Only last week I saw them."

The old woman shook her head, refusing to allow such a firmly rooted belief to be dislodged.

" 'Tis the truth I speak," insisted Jane. "I tell you I saw them but a week ago. They were well and happy, awaiting re-union with their mother and sisters."

As they were speaking the sky had grown darker. An old woman had taken her beads in her hand and began to mumble her prayers. Others followed her example. A darkness like that of night was over the earth. Looking through the glazed window of the cookshop, Jane saw faint pinheads of golden light springing up on the black background of sky. Greatly daring, she turned her eyes towards the sun. A great terrifying black shadow all but obscured it.

Outside in the street a woman screamed and lay fainting on the cobbles. Others knelt down, covering their faces, waiting for a terrible vengeance.

"This is the end!" screamed the beggar-woman. "This is the Judgment Day."

Minutes passed and the darkness grew deeper, and then someone whispered: "It is growing lighter. I swear it." And looking through the window Jane saw the sun emerging from that dark shadow. Out in the street the crowds had noticed too.

"The Virgin be praised!" shouted a man. "It is over and

done with. The vengeance of the Lord has been turned from us.''

In the cook-shop everyone began to talk at once.

"The sun has been given back to us."

"This is another chance."

"We have not lost the sun."

"Praise to Christ! Praise the Holy Mother!"

People stood about long after the eclipse of the sun was over. They marvelled and speculated as to its meaning. That it was a display of divine omnipotence was admitted by all. It was a warning, most agreed.

And before the day was ended the bells of London were tolling dismally. From St. Clement Danes within the Temple to St. Clement's in East Cheap, they gave out their mournful tidings. The news was whispered from mouth to mouth as it spread through the City.

"The Queen is dead."

"God have mercy on us, she must have died at the very moment when the Almighty in His wrath hid the sun's face from us."

People were asking strange questions.

"Why should God show His displeasure by covering up the sun's face at the very hour when the Queen was dying?"

"How did the Queen die?"

"The Queen could have no sons, and they say the King is enamoured of his niece the Lady Elizabeth."

The old rumour regarding the Princes was revived, and, although there were many who declared the Princes still lived, people shrugged their shoulders. Why were the boys kept in the Tower? Why did God hide the sun's face on the day the Queen died?

These were questions which swept like a murmuring wind through the City's streets.

*   *   *   *   *

The saddest man in England was its King. He was really alone now. There were one or two men about him whom he thought he could trust, and in whom he must believe, yet how could he help it if suspicions leapt into his mind? He never had a whole night's rest. Dreams troubled him. In them he would see Hastings' guilty eyes looking at him across the council chamber; and perhaps those eyes would become blurred and would seem to change to those of Lovel . . . or Ratcliffe . . . or Norfolk. No, these men were true friends. Yet had he said at one time, Hastings is my friend. If only Anne had been strong! If only she had not died but had borne him many sons! If only he had Edward's personality and charm! But Anne was dead, and there were some of his subjects who suspected him of killing her. There was no happiness for England's King.

Thoughts of a marriage with the daughter of Elizabeth Woodville, like the whispering of evil spirits, were in his mind.

"I must have a son, Anne," he murmured. "Understand this. I must have a son." She would understand; she always had.

He had been glad when Catesby and Ratcliffe had opposed the marriage on the grounds that it would not please the people. The matter had been laid before his counsellors. If he did not marry Elizabeth himself, might she not consider her engagement to Henry Tudor binding? What if she escaped to Brittany and married his enemy? Would that not strengthen the Tudor rogue's chances? Would not more be ready to flock to his banners if he should effect a landing in England, once he was married to the daughter of Edward the Fourth, a lady whom many still believed to be a legitimate Princess?

"Let the girl be removed," advised Catesby; and she had been removed to Sheriff Hutton Castle—the ambitious Princess who had hoped to marry her uncle! That was a good move and should do much to stop the pernicious rumour that the Queen had met her death by poison.

There was discontent everywhere. Enemies were all about the King. Dorset was in France waiting to spring, and the King must prepare for war. It was almost two years since he had taken the crown and there had scarcely been a happy moment in the whole of that time.

In London the people murmured against him, for he was taxing them heavily in his preparation for war. A silly rhyme was stuck on the door of St. Paul's Cathedral, which was a direct insult to the King and his councillors.

> "The cat, the rat, and Lovel our dog,
> Ruleth all England under a hog."

No one could fail to understand its meaning. The cat was Catesby; the rat, Ratcliffe; the dog was Frances Lovel's badge; and the boar was Richard's own cognisance.

Hating violence, Richard had nevertheless been forced to resort to it. Weakness was folly, and he would never be accused of that. The writer of the lines was found and subjected to the horrible death accorded all traitors. Crowds gathered to see him suffer on Tower Hill.

The King's popularity was at its lowest when news reached him that Henry Tudor had landed at Milford Haven.

* * * * *

It was hot August at Bosworth Field. In the shadow of Ambeame Hill was the traitor Tudor's army encamped. Opposite them, eager for the fight, the archers and billmen of the King made ready.

Richard was exultant. He had dreaded this so long, and now that it was upon him he had at least rid himself of the suspense. He was a great statesman, but perhaps a greater soldier. He had come successfully through many campaigns. Here was his chance to settle the Tudor for ever, for Henry Tudor himself was there in that opposite camp; and that was a matter for rejoicing, since so elusive had the fellow so far proved, that although his supporters had been routed many times, he had ever managed to escape his deserts.

There was a fear that haunted Richard now. Of his own will, of his own bravery, of his ability to look death unflinchingly in the face he was sure; but as he looked at those men who stood beside him and professed their friendship for him, he must wonder, Can I trust them? Will they be true? Norfolk, Catesby,

Lovel, Ratcliffe—these, my friends, will they follow the example of Buckingham and Hastings? Lord Stanley was on the flank of Richard's army—and Lady Stanley was the mother of Henry Tudor! Could Stanley be trusted?

Agonies of doubt beset the King as the sun rose to a brilliance that made the armour plate and basinets shine like silver. Pikes and swords gleamed in the light of day. The battle was about to begin.

The King, small and slender though he was, looked mighty on his grey horse. His steel suit was polished to a shining brilliance and any deformity was lost in the magnificent way he sat his horse. His courage made of him a giant, and men remembered his successes on the fields of battle. Over his head flew the red-embroidered banner of England; and Parker, his standard bearer, held it bravely, a smile curving his fine young lips. How could brave Richard fear the cringing Tudor, the crafty schemer who had no military prowess and who, it was said, was not over-eager for the fight?

Richard addressed his men. The moment was at hand. With eager fingers the archers were bending their bows, the soldiers were buckling their helms. Soon the trumpets and kettle drums would give the signal for the battle cry. "For England! For Richard! Death to the Welsh traitor!"

A fair hot day, and the most courageous leader in England was a King who had never lost heart on the field of battle. His eyes gleamed in his pale face beneath the basinet. But in his mind, as he scanned the ranks of waiting men, there was the haunting doubt. Treason. Could he trust Northumberland? Could he trust Stanley?

His horse was rearing with impatience. Now—to the fight.

Soon he was too much occupied to notice the aloofness of Northumberland's men, who, under their treacherous master, were standing by, waiting to see how the battle went before allying themselves with Henry Tudor. As for the traitor Stanley, he had changed sides before the battle began; and so the King's army had an enemy beside it, in its very lines, where it was thought to have a friend.

The confusion wrought by this was terrible, for soldiers beneath the red and white banner of England were fighting each other, not knowing who was friend and who enemy.

Richard was now aware that what he had feared most had come to pass. There was treason in the very heart of his army, and men, fearful of Tudor revenge, were deserting him now.

Ratcliffe was slain, fighting beside the King. There went one true friend. Lovel, Norfolk and Catesby, too, stood firm beside him. His spirits rose. Praise the saints, I have some true friends, then!

"The day is not yet lost, Francis."

Francis Lovel laughed, his eyes gleaming. Thank God for Lovel, true friend and loyal subject.

Lost! Indeed it was not lost. Nor should it be if courage could prevail over cowardice, true men over traitors. The smile that passed between these two friends brought new hope with it. Richard knew now that it was victory or death.

Norfolk was down, mortally wounded. Surrey, Norfolk's son, was taken prisoner. Lovel was fighting on. The King shouted, rallying his men, and the men took up the battle cry.

"A Richard! A Richard! England and Richard! Death to the Welshman!"

And the King, swinging his bloody battle-axe, hacked his way onward through his enemies.

His men were falling all about him, and he, good soldier that he was, sensed their lack of faith in victory. They had been betrayed and many were deserting the King and going over to the enemy before it was too late. The day was all but lost, but super-human courage might save it yet.

The King had such courage; and there had occurred to him a daring plan. It was the only way in which to win this battle. Could he but slay the traitor Tudor he had won the day, for what was an army without a leader, and would not those who had deserted the red and white banner for the green and white as readily turn back to the King as they had an hour before turned to the Tudor? And somewhere, not far off, was this man whose death or capture alone could save the day for Richard.

"Fix my crown upon my head!" cried the King. "For by Him that shaped both sea and land, King of England this day will I die!"

His courage was a flame which lit that of those around him. There were not many left, but those that remained would follow him to death if need be. The King was godlike in his glittering armour. The sun's rays caught the circlet of gold about his helm. There was no fear in him. He was staking his crown, his life, on this.

Parker held the standard above the King's head as Richard, his axe in his mailed fist, rode forward, straight towards that spot where, surrounded by a few supporters, Henry Tudor cowered in terror.

Richard laughed with desperate relief. The day was not lost. Once Henry Tudor lay dead, all those who supported him would turn back to Richard. Stanley and Northumberland should go the way of all traitors.

As for the Welshman, Richard could laugh—the crafty Welshman, cunning as a monkey, was timid as a mouse before the roar of the English lion.

This was not merely the foolhardy bravery of a desperate man; it was high strategy. The routing of the Welshman's army was impossible—but man to man, courage against cowardice must prevail. The English line of kings should not be thrust aside by a cunning Welshman.

He was almost upon the Tudor now—but what a bloody way he had come! He must hack his way through flesh and bone, and even as he cleared his path others rose up to defend the Welshman. Richard had split the head of the Tudor standard bearer and the red dragon worked in white and green silk went down into the blood and dust. But brave Parker held the standard of England aloft over the head of his fighting King; even though Parker had lost both his legs he could still sit, a fixed smile on his bloodless face, holding high the flag of England.

England's King was superhuman. None could fight as he fought. Henry Tudor was slipping behind his supporters, his little eyes wide with terror; but always there was some brave man to leap forward and defend him and then to fall to Richard's axe.

But Stanley, the traitor, hearing what was happening, and knowing what his fate would be if the King won the day—knowing, too, that if it was a matter of single combat, Henry Tudor would not put up any fight at all—came galloping to the spot with three thousand men behind him.

The battle was over. One by one the true knights of England fell beside their King. Richard fought to the end. He would never surrender. His standard bearer had gone down now, but the King still sat his horse, mortally wounded, brave and bleeding from too many wounds. No surrender! No surrender! And victory would have been his but for the treachery he had dreaded ever since he had worn the crown.

They were surrounding him now, and he could see nothing for the blood in his eyes; but he went on fighting.

"Treason!" he cried. "Treason!"

He slipped from his horse, and only then did his crown roll from his head.

"Treason!" he murmured; and so bravely died the last English King.

*   *   *   *   *

The woman who walked down Tower Street towards the Tower of London was subdued in manner; and people, passing her, recognised her and wondered why she, who was always so ready to laugh and chat, was now preoccupied. She was beautiful yet, although she had never recovered from the ravages of Ludgate Jail. To-day the serenity of her eyes had disappeared.

She walked across London Bridge and, looking down on the grey waters, she was thinking of all the colourful personalities she had known and who now were no more. She herself lived on, but what a different Jane Shore was this thin little woman in cheap worsted from that glorious jewelled creature who had graced the court of King Edward!

She was thinking now of Richard, that cold, pale man, whom

neither she nor any—not even Edward—had really understood. She had heard men talk, with tears in their eyes, of Richard's glorious last hour. She pictured him, the circlet of gold flashing on his basinet, going into battle, hacking his way towards the cowardly Henry Tudor; weak from his wounds, his horse jaded, but his courage burning brightly, a glorious example to all who beheld him. And then—defeat, through the treachery of those who called themselves his friends. It saddened her to think of the man in death, his body dirty and bloodstained, lying on the battlefield, where his enemies found it; they had stripped him of his armour and flung him naked across a sweating horse in the vain hope that they might dishonour him who, but a short time before, had ridden in glistening steel to shame the shivering man whom they now called King of England.

What would this mean to the citizens of London? wondered Jane. How could one know what a new dynasty would bring? Who were these Tudors? Henry Tudor, it was said, had shown poor prowess on the field of battle. How would the English like a Welshman and a coward on their throne?

But, to humble folk, what did it matter who sat on the throne? There was still poverty, and taxation meant little to those who had not the wealth to make taxation worth while.

Yet what was it going to mean to those two boys in the Tower? That was what worried Jane. That was what had set the furrows on her brow.

Henry Tudor had already ridden into London. And what a disappointment awaited the assembling crowds, for the man came in a closed carriage! A victorious King should come in splendour, like a hero, magnificent in scarlet and gold. London wanted another Edward, but it had got something very different in Henry Tudor. Was this the beginning of a new age?

As she reached the Tower, Jane noticed that the grass on Tower Hill was dry and brown. How soon would that grass be stained with blood? Defeat in civil war must mean many an execution, for these were savage times. Jane shivered, for Henry Tudor's claim to the throne lay by way of illegitimacy, so how

could he take it from little Edward? How was he going to
reconcile with justice his seizure of the throne while those two
little boys lived? He was going to marry their sister, and
already she was on her way to London from Sheriff Hutton;
but how could he marry an illegitimate girl? And if Edward's
daughter was not illegitimate, neither were his sons. And if
those two little boys were the legitimate sons of Edward, how
could Henry Tudor mount the throne?

Jane's head ached with the problem; she had had no sleep
because of it. Horrible fears beset her, for the ambitions of men
were unbounded and there was no foul deed they would not do
to win a crown. Love of money? Love of women? What were
these things compared with love of power?

There was excitement in the kitchens. There would be grand
doings, prophesied Belper. Had Jane heard that the new King
was to be united to the Princess Elizabeth? This would mean
great doings at the Tower Palace, for the new Queen, in accordance with royal tradition, would come to the Tower of London.

Kate, in private, turned up her nose at the new monarch.
"Call him a King! Holy Virgin, an old-young man who shuts
himself up in a closed carriage! Knows he not that his subjects
would have a look at him? Doubtless he knows he is not worth
looking at. There are those among us who remember great
King Edward in his prime."

"Silence, wife!" said Belper. "There'll be many heads to
grace London Bridge ere long, but I'd not have yours one of
them."

Then were both Kate and Jane sad with their memories of
other days, until Jane said: "Kate, I would you could take me
to the Princes. What think they of this change?"

"All mad with excitement, I'll tell you. They think this is
going to alter things for them. The little boys have no grief for
their uncle. That's how it is in royal families. . . ."

"Let us go to them." As they left the kitchens, Jane said:
"Kate, I have a horrible fear that we shall soon not be allowed
to mount the stairs to the Garden Tower unmolested."

20

"Why, whatever has come over you? It would seem you have seen a ghost. You haven't, have you?"

"No, no. My thoughts but run on. I am mistaken. Who would stop our visits? What harm can we do?"

"No one will stop our visits, lovey. I'll see to that. Jemmy, the chief warder, is a special friend of mine. He'd not stop us."

"But he would have his orders," said Jane, and her teeth began to chatter.

"Why, you're cold."

"It is this place. I never did greatly care for it. There is little sunshine in it and too much gloom and shadow."

Jemmy was on guard. He gave Kate a smacking kiss on either cheek and bowed to Jane.

"All's well then?" said Kate.

"All's well," said Jemmy.

The Princes were glad to see their visitors. They were changed. It seemed to Jane that new life had come to them, for their eyes sparkled and they laughed more loudly and frequently.

"It will not be long now," said Edward.

"We shall ride in the procession," added Richard. "We have been playing at processions."

"It was a silly game," said Edward, "but it helped to pass the time. Soon we shall leave this place and shall not have need of so many light pastimes. There will be important things to do."

"When our sister is the Queen!" cried Richard. "Odd, is it not? We thought Edward would be the King, and now it is Elizabeth who is to be a queen."

"There is no knowing what will happen to any of us!" said Jane.

"Jane," said Edward earnestly, "when we are out of this place . . . when we have what is due to us . . . then shall you come and live with us."

"Yes," agreed Richard. "We have talked of it often, but it did not seem worth while to mention it to you before. Now it is different. Soon we shall be free. We shall not be prisoners in the Tower. We shall have a place at court and much influence, for, after all, we shall be brothers of the Queen. Then shall you come and live with us. You, too, good Kate."

"Well, I have a husband," said Kate.

"If he were to die, you shall come."

"Let us not talk of death now that everything is becoming bright," said Jane quickly. "Tell me, have you heard any more news?"

"None but that our sister is soon to marry the new King."

"Ah, yes," said Richard, "and Jemmy has said that he has heard it whispered that he is to go away, he and his men . . . And that we are to have other attendants . . . men of greater importance such as are due to our new rank."

"Your new rank . . ." began Jane, suddenly turning cold.

"Of a certainty," said Edward. "Now that the King is to marry our sister, we shall be brothers of the Queen, and until a lodging at court can be found for us, we are to have new guards. That is what Jemmy said. Why, Jane, what ails you?"

"Nothing," said Jane.

"You seem to be staring oddly. You see nothing, do you?"

"There is nothing to see. I wish the bell would not toll so dismally."

"We have grown accustomed to it," Edward said. "Have we not, Richard?"

Richard nodded. "It tolls so often."

It seemed to Jane that the entire chamber was full of the dismal note. She shivered for, as it echoed through the room, it sounded to her like a passing-bell.

*　　　*　　　*　　　*　　　*

Never, it seemed to the two Princes, had a day passed so quickly. It was full of excitement. It was the day after Jane's visit, and they were awakened as usual by the sunlight streaming on to their bed through the window in the alcove which was just opposite it.

Richard said : "We forgot to draw the curtains last night."

Edward nodded. Why should they draw the curtains? Simply

because Richard had had an unpleasant feeling that someone
. . . the departed spirit of one of the many who had suffered
in this place . . . might look through the window at them.
Edward had not been without fears, but being older than
Richard he had not voiced them.

But last night they had forgotten to draw the curtains. It
was because they had been too excited, too excited for fear.
They knew that they were not to spend many more weeks in
this room which they had come to regard as a prison. Glorious
events awaited them, for their sister was to be the bride of the
new King. The glittering power which they had been brought
up to believe would one day be theirs was lost to them, but
that did not matter now. The only important thing was escape
. . . escape from the Garden Tower, not to be watched, to be
allowed out for more than a short while each day to exercise
their limbs, to be the free brothers of the Queen.

Small wonder that they had forgotten to fear the shadowy
ghosts of the Tower. They laughed now, pleased that they had
forgotten. They would never draw the curtains of their bed
again. What folly it was to fear the dead! Ah, soon they would
leave the Garden Tower for ever.

Their food was brought to them by a new attendant, a black-
browed, dark-haired man with deep throaty laughter and a
manner which might, to some, have seemed over-hearty, but
to the two boys seemed merry indeed.

"Good morrow to you, gentlemen," he cried. "I'm your new
attendant. Will Slater by name. Called Black on account of the
colour of me. Black Will, my lords, at your service."

Black Will laid beef, beer and bread on the table.

"Got from the kitchen of Master Belper, my lords. Eat
hearty; and if your appetites should not be satisfied, nor your
thirst content, then will Black Will down to Belper to re-
plenish your platters and your tankards."

The boys exchanged smiles. Life was changing.

After breakfast came Sir James Tyrell to see them. Tall and
handsome, he bowed low before them. Did they guess why
he had come? he wanted to know.

Edward answered. "Yes, it would seem to me that you come, sir, because those who heretofore had charge of our needs are now considered too lowly, for our sister will shortly sit upon the throne, and thus should we, her brothers, be treated with the respect now due to us."

"That is so, my lord Prince. I am sent here by His Grace King Henry the Seventh to do honour to you, and to assure myself that you are receiving treatment in accordance with your rank. Now would I show ʒou those whom I have ordained shall serve you . . . until a better lodging may be found for you. There is one John Green, a good and honest man. John, come hither and honour your gracious masters."

John Green came forward. A short man with thick hands and feet, he bowed low and his light eyes beneath their sandy lashes looked full at the velvet-clad figures before him.

"Rise, John," said Edward, who never forgot the dignity that had become second nature to him.

"I thank Your Grace," said the man. "I vow that I will serve you faithfully."

"There is one other I would bring to your notice, my dear lords," said Tyrell. "He is a man I have selected on account of his trustworthy nature—in short, my own groom, John Dighton. Go, Green, and bring Dighton that the Princes may know him."

Green went out and Tyrell looked about the room. " 'Tis a comfortable lodging your Graces have here in the Tower."

"We are weary of it," said Richard.

"Say you so?" Tyrell turned to the boys and smiled. "Methinks 'twill not be long ere you change it for a better."

"Pray tell us when we shall leave," begged Richard.

"That I cannot say." Tyrell had gone to the window in the alcove and looked out; he stared down at the path which ran alongside the apartment. Then he swung round and smiled at them. "Rest assured, the matter shall be dealt with as speedily as I can arrange it."

"Then we shall indeed be indebted to you," said Edward.

"Ah, here is Dighton," said Tyrell as Dighton, tall and spare and wearing the clothes of a groom, entered, and bowed awkwardly before the Princes.

"At your service, fair sirs," he muttered.

"Dighton will clean your apartments and do anything you ask of him."

"That is well indeed," said Edward.

"Dighton, you may go now," said Tyrell. When he had gone, Tyrell added : "It is the King's wish that you shall have every attention worthy of your rank. If there is anything you desire . . ."

"There is nothing we desire," said Edward.

"But doubtless we shall think of something," said Richard.

"Then I shall see you to-morrow, my lords."

"Mayhap to-morrow you will bring us news of when we may be permitted to leave this place," said Richard.

"Who knows, my lord!" said Tyrell, and he smiled wanly. "Methinks, fair sirs, that you will not much longer sleep in yonder bed."

"That is the best news we have heard for a long time," said Edward.

"Since the death of our father the King," began Richard, but Edward signed to him to be silent. Tyrell saw the sign and was unexpectedly touched, so that he was seized with a great desire to be out of the chamber.

"Your lordships will forgive me if I hasten away. I have much to attend to. I shall call to-morrow to see if your wishes have been carried out. You may trust my servants to do what is expected of them."

He bowed and kissed a hand of each Prince before he went out.

Richard was so excited, he began to dance a merry jig.

"Ere long, brother," he cried, "you and I will ride through the streets of London."

"On grey horses," said Edward.

"At the wedding of our sister. . . ."

"To the King of England!"

They began to prance round the room as though they rode

their horses, seeing—instead of the thick walls, the alcove and the great embrasures—the cheering people, the London streets.

Edward stopped suddenly and looked out of the window.

"What ails you?" asked Richard, stopping also.

"I was but thinking."

"Thinking what?"

"That when you have thought to be a King, it is not such a merry thing to find you are but the brother of a Queen."

"That is certainly a far-from-merry thought," agreed Richard. "But is it not a good thing, when you have been a prisoner, to know that soon you will be free?"

That was certainly a pleasant thought, and soon both boys were prancing round the chamber on imaginary steeds.

*　　　*　　　*　　　*　　　*

All through the afternoon they heard the strange noises. A banging, a tapping, and then a sound as though a great slab of stone had been dropped. They could not understand it.

"Some repairs in progress," said Edward. "I think I know. They are doing them before our sister's triumphant entry into the Tower."

"Everything must be in order for that," said Richard happily.

They sat at their books, but it was impossible to concentrate. The banging and the tapping went on.

"It sounds close," said Richard, and he went to the door and opened it. "It may well be coming from our chamber . . . our little one we found."

"Nonsense! Who would wish to repair that? No one ever goes there."

"Except us. Let us go and see for ourselves."

Edward was not very interested, for his thoughts were far away in the future, but he rose and followed Richard down the narrow staircase.

"I am sure the noises come from behind that door," said Edward, but he found that the door was locked.

"It was not locked before," said Richard.

They knocked on the door and the banging and tapping

ceased. Edward knocked again, but the silence persisted, although on the other side of the door they heard the sound of very heavy breathing.

"Who is there?" cried Edward; and there was no answer.

Richard began to tremble, for he had always been a little afraid of that chamber with its smell of dust and age, and he would never go to it unaccompanied by his brother. Edward was bolder.

"Open this door, I say."

There was still no answer and Edward banged on it with his fists. "Do you hear me? I demand that you should open this door."

A voice answered then. "An you wish, my masters." The door opened and Dighton stood before them. There was dust on his eyebrows and it clung to his cap; the air was so full of dust that the boys began to cough and splutter.

"What means this?" asked Edward, and he would have forced his way into the room, but Dighton put out a hand, very respectfully, to stop him.

"My lord, go not in there. It is most unsafe."

"Unsafe?"

"Yes, my lord. My master, Sir James Tyrell, has examined this chamber. He sent me to work on it at once. You must not go in there, my lords. It would be most unwise."

"I see," said Edward. "Come, Richard."

They returned to their apartments.

"How did Dighton get into the chamber?" wondered Richard. "He did not go through the door we used, and down the stairs."

"Doubtless there is another way in."

"We did not see it."

"When the repairs are done we shall be able to find the other entrance. That is, if we are still here."

"How concerned Sir James seems for us," said Richard. "Already he notices the unsafeness of the chamber."

"Ah! Once we were of small importance, now it is a different matter."

Richard shivered. "Edward, how terrible if we had been in that unsafe chamber . . . and something had fallen on us. We might have been buried there."

"It is well," said Edward, "that there are now those to be concerned for us."

All through the afternoon the sounds could be heard.

*   *   *   *   *

The boys lay in bed. They had not drawn the curtains about their bed, for why should they be afraid of evil spirits? All the same, they could not sleep on a night that had followed such a day. They had got to know Black Will rather well, they believed. He was amusing, and he had told them of his adventures in the wars.

"I liked not Dighton, though," said Richard.

"That was because we found him in our room. He looked so queer with the dust on his face."

"I liked him not," insisted Richard.

"Well, we need see little of him. We could ask Sir James to have him removed. We need not have attendants whom we do not like. Remember we are brothers of the Queen."

"Mayhap to-morrow I will ask him. Though the man would be hurt, and he has done naught of which we could complain."

"And Tyrell would be angry with him as he has failed to please us."

"Edward, Tyrell has a cruel face. Let us not tell him that we like not Dighton."

"We will not. So you thought the man had a cruel face?"

"At first I thought there was much kindness in him. It was afterwards—when he turned from the window, I think—there was a wolfish look upon his face."

"Nay. He looked like a man, not a wolf. Still, there are men one does not like, even as there are wolves."

They laughed together; then Richard said: "What shall we wear at our sister's coronation?"

"Cloth of gold and ermine."

"We shall ride grey horses."

"Magnificent horses."

"Shall we ride ahead of the King and Queen?"

"Mayhap."

"Edward, what manner of man is this new King, I wonder?"

"I wonder also, Richard."

"I hope he will not prove stern like Uncle Richard."

"I doubt there was ever man so stern."

"He is related to us doubtless."

"Doubtless."

"Then, Edward, if he be related to us, why is it that you, who are our father's eldest son, are not the King?"

"You know they call us bastards."

"Then is Elizabeth, our sister, also a bastard?"

"We are all bastards. So said Uncle Richard, did he not?"

"The new King does not mind that our sister is a bastard——" Richard stopped abruptly. "Edward! Did you see? Did you see that, Edward?"

"See what?"

"There—I saw it. It was a face that did look in at us through the window."

"A face? I see no face."

Richard was shivering. "It has gone. It was there but a second. I was talking—and I fancied a movement there. I looked up. It was there but a second."

"You have always feared to see a face there."

"This night I did see a face."

Edward said : "I will go and see."

"I will come with you."

The two boys got out of bed, Edward disbelieving, Richard white and trembling, certain that he had seen a face. He kept behind Edward as they approached the window. Edward looked out on to the path that ran just beneath it.

"There is none there, Richard."

"I swear I saw a face."

"What sort of face?"

"I know not. It was there—and gone. The cap was drawn down over it. But I know it was evil."

Edward soothed his brother, but he did not really believe

Richard had seen a face. It was so easy to imagine faces in this chamber. One thought of others who had occupied it, and grisly pictures rose in the imagination. Richard was over-excited, for Richard was easily over-excited.

As they lay in bed Richard kept close to his brother.

"Edward, do not go to sleep first."

"No. I will wait for you."

"Edward, who was it, do you think, who looked in upon us?"

"It was a fancy, Richard."

"Was it? I hope it was. It seemed so evil."

"We will not speak of it. Let us talk of the coronation."

"Oh yes."

"And afterwards, Richard, we shall have fine apartments at court. Elizabeth will see to that."

"We shall see our mother. It seems so long since we last saw her."

Richard was forgetting his fright. They both shut their eyes and continued to talk of the splendours that awaited them. It was not long before they slept.

And as they lay there sleeping a face appeared at the window. It remained there for several seconds; then it disappeared, and cautious footsteps might have been heard going swiftly along the path outside the window.

*   *   *   *   *

The footsteps continued along the path. They stopped at a door which led to the Garden Tower. The man who had looked through the window was joined by another, who whispered: "Well?"

"Jesus Christ! I thought they would never sleep."

"Then all is ready?"

"All is ready. Dighton waits below."

"Come then."

Green and Will Slater crept up the staircase, and at the Princes' chamber they paused.

"Quietly now. I should not like it if they were to waken."

"Bah! Afraid, Will?"

"Afraid! Me—who's cut the guts out of many a man!"

"And yet . . ."

"Come! Let the deed be done."

The door was opened very softly. The two men, in stockinged feet, crept across the floor. There was nothing for them to fear. The walls of the room were thick and a few screams would not be heard; and yet they were consumed with an anxiety not to awaken the boys.

They stood by the bed, looking down on the youthful figures. The younger was gripping his brother's garment and his face was hidden in the pillow as though he wished to cover his eyes. Edward lay sleeping on his back, and his lips were curved as though his dream was pleasant.

Green nudged Slater. Why did the man wait? The moment had come and the sooner the deed was done the better. Green went to one side of the bed and Slater to the other. Why did they hesitate? Perhaps because it was easier to cut out the guts of a man in battle than to murder two sleeping boys.

Green's eyes met those of Slater, and both were determined not to show the other his softness. Slater took the cushion he had brought with him and pressed it over Richard's face. The little boy gasped—struggled—then struggled no more.

Edward lingered only a second or so after his brother.

It was done, and there was ghostly silence in the gloomy chamber. Almost shamefully, and stumbling in their eagerness to finish their evil task, each man took one of the boys and slung him over his shoulder. They carried them down to the grave in the little chamber, which Dighton had been preparing for them all that afternoon.

*   *   *   *   *

At the spot where East Cheap joins Candlewick Street a little old beggar-woman sat, day in, day out, summer and winter alike. Her hair was long and grey; there was hardly any flesh on her bones, and so small and wizened was she that she looked like a shrivelled doll. Her face was brown and wrinkled; but there were some to take pity on her and throw alms to her that she might just keep alive.

She was such an old woman—surely one of the oldest in London. All those she had known in her youth were dead. It was said of her: "She once knew great splendour. She declares she is none other than Jane Shore, and they say that she was the favourite mistress of Edward the Fourth." But it was scarcely possible to believe that this old woman was beautiful Jane who had charmed a King.

Jane knew they doubted her. What mattered it? She would shrug her thin shoulders and smile sadly. There was nothing for her to do but sit and beg as she dreamed of the past and waited for death.

All those she had loved were dead. Kate had died of the sweating sickness which had ravaged the City soon after the disappearance of the Princes. Even the memory of the Princes scarcely moved Jane now, for it had happened so long ago. Jane guessed what had been the fate of the boys. They had been murdered at the order of King Henry the Seventh, for they had stood in his way and they had to die. She had heard that Sir James Tyrell had gone to France with a big pension from his royal master, and later when he foolishly returned to England he was imprisoned in the Tower and executed suddenly without a trial—a dangerous man because he held a dangerous secret. Elizabeth Woodville had been banished to a nunnery. Was that because she demanded to know what had happened to her boys? It was possible to understand these matters if one had lived near the throne and could piece together the small events to make the picture complete.

She had seen so much in her life; and she had lived so long that her mind was full of pictures. She had seen the coronation of Edward's eldest daughter and the risings of Lambert Simnel and Perkin Warbeck; she had glimpsed Will Shore on his way to Tyburn, where he had been executed for clipping gold coin. She had heard the whispering of the people. " 'Tis Will Shore, the goldsmith. 'Tis said that years ago he was the husband of Jane Shore."

But the years passed over her and she forgot that day which was made sad by remorse.

Bishop Morton, now a Cardinal, was writing the history of the last years. She saw him now and then walking through the City with his protégé, Thomas More. Not only did the Cardinal write history, but he sent forth false stories of what had happened in the past. People believed him, for was he not a great Cardinal? The young man with the noble countenance, whose name was Thomas More, believed him. Why should he not? He had not the experiences of the old beggar woman on the corner of East Cheap.

Nothing was too ridiculous for the Cardinal to say of brave Richard. How simple it was to accuse him of poisoning his wife, and of the murders of Henry the Sixth and the Duke of Clarence! He was even accused of murdering the little Princes, for this was simply a matter of altering the date of their disappearance to that time when Buckingham and Morton put forth their rumour. But who would listen to an old beggar woman when all the Cardinal's lies were endorsed and applauded by a grateful King! The old dynasty must be discredited to bolster up the new. The silly tale that Richard had been two years in his mother's womb was circulated; it was said that she had suffered hellish pains in his delivery and that he had come into the world feet first, with all his teeth, and a head of hair that reached to his shoulders. Rumour turned the slight deformity into a crooked back, so that to all those who had never seen him Richard came to be known as Crookback. It was said that he was a monster, hideously formed, and that his left arm was withered; and such rumours, spread by a lying Cardinal and a cowardly King, came in time to be accepted.

The years slipped by. Jane saw the coming of the Spanish Princess, Katharine of Aragon, and her marriage with Prince Arthur. She saw the funeral of Arthur and marriage of Katharine to his brother Henry.

She saw the coming of the new King—big, ruddy, golden of

hair and of beard—with such a look of his maternal grand-father that Jane felt young at the sight of him.

More years passed and still the old beggar-woman continued to sit on her corner.

One day, when she was so old that she had ceased to count her years, she saw a lovely girl ride through the streets of London, and she heard the people say: "The King is deep in love with her. So much so that they say he will rid himself of his Queen to marry her."

And, crouching on the pavement, Jane felt herself slipping away from this Tudor-governed land. She thought it was years ago, when the House of York was triumphant and that the lovely laughing girl who passed through the streets was Jane Shore, not Anne Boleyn.

*   *   *   *   *

"Poor old woman!" said those who carried her body away. "She's been begging here for as long as we can remember. 'Tis a happy release, for the lot of a beggar is a hard one. And doubly hard, it would seem to her, for if she spoke truth she was once the wife of a goldsmith. From goldsmith's wife—to beggar-woman! What terrible things can happen to us in this cruel world!"

THE END